Y0-BDB-899

CAMELOT

Also by Caryl Rivers

INDECENT BEHAVIOR

INTIMATE ENEMIES

GIRLS FOREVER BRAVE AND TRUE

VIRGINS

CAMELOT

Caryl Rivers

Z
ZOLAND BOOKS
Cambridge, Massachusetts

First edition published in 1998 by
Zoland Books, Inc.
384 Huron Avenue
Cambridge, Massachusetts 02138

PUBLISHER'S NOTE
This book is a work of fiction. Names, characters, places, and incidents are either the product of the author's imagination or are used fictitiously. Any resemblance to actual events or persons, living or dead, is entirely coincidental.

FIRST EDITION

Book design by Boskydell Studio
Printed in the United States of America

05 04 03 02 01 00 99 98 8 7 6 5 4 3 2 1

This book is printed on acid-free paper, and its binding materials have been chosen for strength and durability.

Library of Congress Cataloging-in-Publication Data

Rivers, Caryl.
Camelot / Caryl Rivers.—1st. ed.
p. cm.
ISBN 0-944072-96-8 (acid-free paper)
I. Title.
PS3568. I8315C3 1998
813'.54—dc2198 98-20796
CIP

To

STEVE, CONNIE, AND LAUREN

and

ALYSSA AND OGIE,

with all my love.

And thanks to ALAN,

For all his support and encouragement.

The life and times of John F. Kennedy have been chronicled by a number of historians and journalists, whose work has been very helpful in the writing of this book. They include Doris Kearns Goodwin, *The Fitzgeralds and the Kennedys;* Nigel Hamilton, *J.F.K.: Reckless Youth;* Peter Collier and David Horowitz, *The Kennedys: An American Drama;* Theodore Sorensen, *Kennedy;* and Arthur Schlesinger, *A Thousand Days.* For the events of November 22, I relied on the account of William Manchester in *The Death of a President.* For many of the actual events described, the March on Washington, JFK and Martin Luther King press conferences, the visit of the astronauts to the White House and other events, I relied on my own firsthand observations and notes.

CAMELOT

He opened one of the glass doors that led from his office to the garden. It was dusk, the hour, in Washington, when the starlings began their raspy chirp from the ledges of government buildings, when the deepening twilight unearthed the ghosts of the city's past. By day the buildings and monuments belonged to the civil servants and the busloads of tourists, but in the moments that formed the edge between daylight and dark, the past slid from its moorings for a brief instant. If he listened carefully, he could hear the footsteps of Cordell Hull clacking down the Gothic corridors of the Old Lady of Pennsylvania Avenue, the ugly building next door that had once housed all of State, War and Navy. He could hear the steady pacing of Abraham Lincoln on the polished floors of this very house, as Lincoln grieved for his son and tried to imagine a way to keep his bloodied nation from tearing apart. For an instant, he could see Jefferson walking up the avenue (which was only a dusty thoroughfare in a city not yet built when he first came to this house). Jefferson was saying, again, that slavery would ring like a firebell in the night through the years to come.

By day, Washington was a dull town, where the wheels of bureaucracy ground steadily, monotonously on. At night, silence and muggers took over. Only at dusk, for a few minutes, the ghosts of history danced, and it was a magic place. Or perhaps that had just been in the overheated imagination of a sickly boy who read romantic stories and found the past a far better place to be.

He stepped out onto the grass and looked to his right, half-expecting the shadow — like the city's ghosts — to be there, a specter in his peripheral vision, sliding away so quickly he did not really know if he saw it at all. For many years, nearly as long as he could remember, it had been there, dark, silent and certain. He had grown used to death being there. It had made him not mordant but casual. He often asked his friends what they thought was the best way to die, prodded them, when they were skittish, to continue. Death was not a chill companion; its touch was damp and warm.

He had felt it when he was swimming in the dark waters of the Pacific, after they shot his boat out from under him. When he was given the last rites of the Catholic Church after a back operation, the shadow was all around him, warm, deep and dark, the world a small point of light in the distance. He came back to the light, and to the world. His father thought the passage had made him invulnerable. His father had said to his friend, when the son was walking to the ocean's edge, "God, Dave, did you see the legs on him? He's got the legs of a fighter or a swimming champion. I know nothing can hurt him now, because I've stood by his deathbed three times, and each time I said good-bye to him, and each time he came back even stronger."

He looked to his left. The shadow was not there. He was Irish enough to know that it would never move too far away, but he was also Irish enough to believe in luck. There was no moment he could name when he knew, it did not happen suddenly. But slowly, surely, he was beginning to believe it could belong to him.

He took several steps out into the garden and looked around. The future shimmered in the deep blue-pink haze, the shade of a lilac, that hung lightly over the city. It was not the place he had imagined would hold his destiny. When had his father's dream become his own, exactly? No matter. Now, it was. He had been a boy longer than most men, well into his adult life, son of a father who at times seemed to grow so large he blotted out the sky. Now it was the son who cast the longer shadow. Inexplicably — it seemed to him at times a miracle — he had become one of the heroes in the books he had read as a thin, tired schoolboy with dark circles under his eyes. He was tall and strong and golden, and he would do battle with giants. It was nineteen hundred and sixty-three, and he was, at last, lucky.

His name was John Fitzgerald Kennedy.

HER HEELS began to sink in the newly warm, moist earth of the Rose Garden. She had worn her prettiest, highest heels; a mistake. They were like lance points against the earth. She felt herself sinking, as if into quicksand. They would have to get a crane to pull her out, so deeply embedded were those stiletto heels. It would be mortifying. She would see it on national television — the crane was huge, and it was lifting her up, up, up, high into the air and out across Pennsylvania Avenue, and people were pointing and laughing.

She saw a familiar face. "Look, it's Sandor Vanocur," she whispered to the young man standing beside her.

"He's around a lot," Jay Broderick said. He was standing with his hand on his hip, his Nikon draped casually around his neck, as if it were nothing at all, being at the White House, waiting for President Kennedy to emerge. She envied his nonchalance. Each time she stole a sideways glance at the Secret Service men, with their hard, flat faces and watchful eyes, the muscles in her stomach quivered. It would not have surprised her in the least if one of them came over to her, took her firmly by the arm and led her away, saying, "We know you. You are Mary Elizabeth Springer, you are only the treasurer of the Class of 1956 at Belvedere High School, and you have no right to be here. Come with us."

And they would take her away, to some dark, secret chamber in the bowels of the White House, where J. Edgar Hoover would beat her with a rubber hose. President Kennedy would walk by and say, "Edgar, aren't you being a little rough?" and J. Edgar would reply, "You never read *I Was a Communist for the FBI?* They are everywhere. Even in Belvedere High School." The president would nod sadly and say to her, "Sorry, kid, I tried."

She shifted her weight, pulled one of her heels from the earth. Her apprehension turned to dismay. The dirt clung to the suede as if it had been coated with glue. Surely they were ruined, and they were brand new and cost her fourteen dollars. Thrift was bred into her bones; for an instant, she even forgot to be terrified.

Another face swam into view. It was pale and creased, but the eyes seemed young and alert. The man wore a striped dress shirt with what seemed to be an unusually high collar, which gave him an aspect that was distinctly not contemporary. He could, she thought, have been a gentleman from the nineteenth century.

"Eddie Folliard from *The Washington Post,*" Jay told her, and she said, "Oh," letting her breath out a little. She had seen his byline often in the crisp, bold Bodoni type of the *Post.* Names in those bylines seemed like the names of gods. Occasionally, she would try to imagine her name in that Bodoni type, but she felt both guilty and a little apprehensive as she did it. Such hubris might bring down punishment from His Terrible Swift Sword. When she was a child, she'd had nightmares about that sword after the Reverend Mr. Swiggins's Sunday sermons. It was a metaphor of which he was fond. The sword was huge and sharp and glittered in the air, and it cut down sinners in a single bloody stroke. After such dreams, she straightened her room and did not lie for a week.

She turned and saw, standing next to her, a youngish man with a bemused look on his face. He was so familiar that at first she wondered if someone else from Belvedere could possibly be there. But then she realized it was David Brinkley, wearing the same expression he wore on *The Huntley-Brinkley Report* each evening, one that said the world was certainly an odd and interesting place. That was how it was with television people. They weren't like movie stars, remote and glorious. You saw them so often in your living room that it was easy to mistake them for the grocer or the man who sold you shoes.

"Hurry up and wait, it's always like this around here," Jay complained. He seemed so much older and sophisticated here — in a way that he did not back at the paper — that she stepped closer to him, to move into the circle of his nonchalance.

"Hi, Jay, how's it hanging?" A reed-thin man, whom she judged to be in his early thirties, moved next to Jay.

"Jeez, I could use a sale. What's AP buying these days? I got zilch the last stuff I sent."

"The new guy likes tits. But respectable, no nipples. No bodies, unless it's mob guys or coloreds."

"I got one. Mob guy, twenty-seven bullet holes, had a sex change, grew up in Harlem."

"Bullet holes in the tits?"

"Nope. Got her in the crotch."

"Crop it at the waist and you're golden," the thin man said and walked away. Mary fairly hissed at Jay: "We're in the Rose Garden at the White House!"

Jay chuckled. "Photographers would crap on the Taj Mahal. We're not civilized."

Just then the door to the Oval Office opened and out walked John Kennedy — followed, a few steps behind, by John Glenn and Alan Shepard. Her jaw dropped, unattractively. She hauled it up again. Her first time at the White House and she got the president and two astronauts. What a stroke of luck.

The members of the press corps surged forward and crowded around. Kennedy's lips parted in the beginning of a mischievous grin. He liked surprises.

"A couple of servicemen dropped by. They're not Navy, but we fed them anyway," he said.

"What did you give them?" asked Reuters. Reuters, for some reason, had a thing for menus.

"C rations on the Eisenhower china," Kennedy said. "Military all the way."

The two astronauts grinned, and the reporters pounced; it was more than they had expected. The announced guests were a bunch of kids from Iowa who were giving the president a 4-H award, and a diplomat from Cameroon. The president stood like a proud papa displaying precocious children as the astronauts fielded questions.

Mary moved, carefully, so as not to attract attention, to the edge of the throng and found a spot where, if she wanted to, she could have reached out and touched the president. As she did so, an errant shaft of sunlight caught the president's head, glinting from his brownish auburn hair. All Mary could think of was the haloed Christ praying in a beam of light in the garden of Gethsemane — a favorite piece of art of the Reverend Mr. Swiggins. She stood absolutely still, looking at him. He was, she realized, larger than his pictures made him seem, full in the shoulders and chest, the lines in his thickening neck quite visible, but his face tanned and young. He seemed so remarkable, standing in the beam of sunlight, that all she could do was stare. He must have somehow felt the intensity of her gaze because he turned his head to look at her, and for a moment those bright blue eyes looked directly into hers. Startled, she looked away. But then, since the other reporters seemed busy with the astronauts, she spoke. Afterwards she wondered how on earth she had ever gotten the nerve.

"Mr. President, can we really beat the Russians to the moon?"

He looked at her again, those blue eyes seeming to appraise her, and suddenly she was terrified once more, thinking that he must be about to say "What are *you* doing here? Somebody remove this person, it's all a mistake, her being here."

But he didn't. She looked so absurdly young, and green, that he smiled and said, "Yes, it's the new ocean, and these are the men who will sail it."

She scribbled furiously in her notepad, making sure to get every word just exactly right, and UPI stepped in front of her and asked a technical question about the Russian lead in space. Then, very quickly it seemed, the president said he had to get the astronauts back home before taps, and they were gone, and the shaft of sunlight fell on the steps where they had been.

"We'd better get back," Jay said. "I got something at four."

With the rest of the reporters, they walked back through the corridor that led to the large foyer to which the small press cubbyholes were connected. She tried to walk as nonchalantly as the other reporters, not gaping at the pictures on the walls. She and Jay strolled out the door and down the driveway, past the guard booth, out onto Pennsylvania Avenue, where Jay had found an illegal parking spot a block away. He ripped the ticket off the windshield and tossed it into the backseat of his battered 1955 Chevy. Mary climbed in and was able to maintain the aura of cool detachment until the Chevy hit 15th Street. Then she began to bounce up and down in the seat.

"He talked to me! Me! The President of the United States talked to me! Oh, my *God*!"

Jay looked at her and laughed. "See. I told you that nagging Charlie for a White House pass was a good idea."

"Yeah, well, it wasn't easy. I had to cut my thumb and let the blood drop on his desk while I swore I'd only go there on my days off or before working hours."

"I got off easy. I promised him my firstborn."

"Oh, Jay, it was so exciting. The astronauts! I almost wet my pants when the three of them came through the door. Is it always this exciting?"

He shook his head. "Mostly it's boring. You just sit around the press room waiting for a photo op and you get two minutes with the prez and some ambassador from Lower Slobovia and you sit some more and you get a lid and that's it, no more news."

"Jay, I've got an exclusive quote. I don't think anyone else was listening." She told him what Kennedy had said.

"With my pictures, that's a center spread for sure."

"President Kennedy told the *Belvedere Blade* —"

He interrupted her, "Told Mary Springer and Jay Broderick from the *Belvedere Blade.*"

"Oh yeah, right. I took a lot of notes, I can do color about how the astronauts looked, and the Rose Garden. And the literate conversation about tits and coloreds."

He laughed again. "That you'd better leave out."

She smiled and thought, all of a sudden, about Mary Jane Jelke, the most stuck-up girl in Belvedere High, sipping her coffee, the bile rising in her throat when she read about Mary Springer chatting with the president. The nasty taste would climb all the way up her throat to her (once perfect, now fatty) cheeks and she would choke on it. Maybe she would gasp and die, her dirty bleached blond hair spreading out across the words *By Mary Springer.* Vengeance was indeed a dish best served cold.

She liked the taste of it. She smiled. Why settle for a tiny bite? She thought about the three girls she had envied most in high school.

Barbara Brownlee. She was the majorette for the Belvedere High School band, and she strutted down Main Street wearing skintight white short-shorts and a halter top with spangles, bewitching the crowd by wiggling her cute little butt at them while she threw her baton high into the air. She usually caught it. Once she missed, in the Fourth of July parade, and knocked one of the Worthy Matrons of the Eastern Star who was marching just ahead of the band momentarily senseless. The matron lay sprawled in the street, with her white parade dress hiked up over her rolled-up stockings and bulging thighs. Barbara didn't usually miss. But that day, the town fathers were relieved that they had nixed the flame batons that Barbara liked to use. The Worthy Matron might have been immolated right there on Main Street, perhaps upsetting the children as they munched on their hot dogs.

Mary practiced to be Barbara, secretly, in her bedroom, with the baton she had bought from Kresge's, wearing her underpants and a bra, trying to wiggle her ass the way Barbara did. She smashed two mirrors and a lamp before she realized that her hand-eye coordination left something to be desired. She tried wiggling her behind — which was cute and curvy — but it never seemed to come out right. She looked as if she were having a seizure, which, she concluded, was not very bewitching. If she led the parade, she'd wipe out a whole battalion of Worthy Matrons and get carried off by the paramedics to boot.

Mary Jane Jelke, she of the pretty cheeks. She was, by Belvedere standards, rich, since her father owned several convenience stores. Mary Jane had her own convertible and an air of insolent disdain that comes from small-town money and the best clothes in school — in her case real angora sweaters, fourteen-karat gold pins to wear on her collars and a real alligator bag and shoes. Mary bought an angora sweater and turned out to be allergic to bunnies, bunny fur being the main ingredient of angora, and broke out in huge red hives. When she tried insolent disdain, the school nurse stopped her and asked if she were feeling unwell.

Becky Bellingrath. She was a tall, thin girl with smoky blond hair who described herself as a beatnik. She always carried a copy of *On the Road* by Jack Kerouac, and she wore black turtlenecks and long black skirts and a black beret. She said she planned to die before she was thirty, and she wrote poems about sex and death, which she read aloud in English class, much to the befuddlement of Mr. Wattles, who was hard of hearing anyway. She would stand up and recite, in a deep, throaty voice:

In my grave I rot
My thighs turn to worm-riddled mush
My lover's semen long dried
Upon them
The memory of his sex
Upon my lips, long dead,
My lips a pulp
Of dirt and slime.

Mr. Wattles would smile and say, "That's very nice, Becky. Now, we will read 'Hiawatha.'"

All the other girls regarded Becky with awe, and it was rumored that not only had she lost her virginity but she had Done It with a Negro jazz drummer. Officially, every girl in Belvedere High was a Virgin — those who weren't didn't talk about it. Even Barbara Brownlee, who spent more time in the backseats of cars than anyone, swore up and down that while the necking was hot and heavy, she was saving her pearl of great price for the man she would marry.

In Mary's fantasy, somehow — it was not clear how such disparate personalities would get together — Barbara and Mary Jane and Becky had signed up for one of the public White House tours. Barbara was a chubby mother of four, her once bewitching hips stretching out a spandex size 16 girdle, her middle bulging under a cheap wool dress. Mary Jane, with her now-squirrelly cheeks, had come upon hard times when her father's stores went bankrupt. Now she was wearing hand-me-downs from the Goodwill bin in Silver Spring, and her look of insolent disdain had long since faded to a dull-eyed glare. Becky Bellingrath had been knocked up by her Negro lover, had an illegal abortion and was now a drug addict. She still wore black, which did not go at all with her greenish skin tones. Anyway, one day the tour that included the three of them just happened to pass by the Rose Garden, where Mary, chic in a linen suit, matching pumps and perfect hairdo, was chatting with John F. Kennedy about his policy on Cuba. All of a sudden, Barbara shrieked, "Oh, my God, it's Mary Elizabeth Springer, and she's talking to the president!"

And Mary, her perfect hair not even ruffled by the faintest of breezes, turned and gave them a dismissive wave.

"Who are they?" President Kennedy asked.

"Oh, they're nobody," she said. "Nobody at all."

"God," she said to Jay, "just think about what it would be like, on the White House beat full-time. You'd get to travel with the president, all over the world, you'd meet generals and prime ministers and kings. No more Rotary lunches."

"No more Rainbow Girls."

"No more Worthy Matrons of the Eastern Star."

"No more store owners cutting fucking ribbons when the new supermarket opens."

"We've been in the Emerald City, and they're sending us back to Kansas." She sighed.

He chuckled. "Keep your ruby slippers packed, we'll be back. Listen, I'd better call in, the desk may have something for me." He stopped in front of a Peoples' Drug in Silver Spring, and Mary waited while he used the phone. When he got back in the car he said, "I think we got a fatal. Plane crash. Can you handle it?"

"Oh, Christ, of course I can handle it."

"Sorry, you're new on Cityside."

"I can fucking handle it, OK," she said.

"All right, let's go."

Journal: Donald A. Johnson

Today, I begin this Journal, in the Year of Our Lord 1963, in the presidency of John Fitzgerald Kennedy, in what I believe will one day be called the era of Martin Luther King. I am 24 years old, male, Negro, Catholic, a graduate of the George Washington University, a resident (sometimes) of Washington, D.C. I am six feet tall, weigh 180 pounds and bat and throw right-handed. So much for stats.

I am going to put it on paper, now, what I have said only in whispers to myself, aloud only to my father in an act of bravado, never to myself because it sounded so — what? Absurd? Pompous? Because I was scared shitless to say it?

I am going to be a writer.

My father thinks that this is a phase, that it will pass, like my wanting to be the Lone Ranger when I was six. Writing is not a trade by which a Negro man can earn a living, except perhaps if he is fortunate enough to get a job with *Ebony,* he said. I told him I didn't want to be a journalist, that I wanted to be an essayist or novelist, like James Baldwin or Richard Wright. He looked at me with that sadder, wiser expression he puts on when he wants to get the upper hand in an argument. I call it his *De Lawd* expression, but not to his face. He told me that writing was not a fitting profession for a man anyway, even a white man. I brought up Hemingway, and he snorted.

"Man runs around all the time shooting things," he said. "Runs around in Africa, shooting lions. Damn fool thing to do."

And thus was Ernest Hemingway dismissed from the company of serious men by Thomas Jefferson Johnson, M.D., literary critic and practitioner of internal medicine.

"I'll be like Frank Yerby," I said, straight-faced.

He took the bait. One thing about my father, he always does. His face knotted up into a scowl. I smiled again. My grandma Johnson had stacks of trashy novels by Frank Yerby in her bedroom, much to my father's disgust, with titles like *The Saracen Blade* and *Goodbye My Fancy.*

"He's a Negro, you know," I said, "and he makes *piles* of money."

"Damned trash," my father muttered. "I can't see why in the world she reads that stuff."

I could. I certainly could. More bosoms were bared in the oeuvre of Frank Yerby than in all the harems of Arabia. Milk white ones, usually. The fact that Frank Yerby was a Negro was not widely known among his legions of fans. Even his picture on the book jacket wasn't a giveaway. He looked vaguely like Cesar Romero, the movie actor. He was what my grandma Johnson used to call high yellow (my father hated that phrase, thought it common), light enough to pass.

Sometimes a bosom was "dusky" in Yerby's books, but that was as dark as it got, sort of Mediterranean. I used to laugh, thinking of all the crackers reading those books, sweating over those imagined white bosoms, never knowing the imaginer was a lot duskier than they thought. That would make them pee in their pants.

Someone was always ripping bodices in Yerby's books. I never knew there was a word like *bodice* until I read his books. People I know did not go around saying, "Wow, did you see the bodice on that chick?" But in past centuries women all wore bodices, pieces of cloth that seemed to be made specifically for tearing off. You could practically hear the racket as the stuff came shredding apart in virile male hands. The ladies seemed to like it, a lot. Grandma would read for hours, her foot tapping. Sometimes the foot would tap a little faster, and I figured another bodice just bit the dust.

I used to steal her books when she wasn't looking, because I figured I wasn't supposed to read this stuff. Frank Yerby wasn't any Hemingway, though. Can you imagine Hemingway writing dialogue like "Ah ha, proud wench, you will come crawling to me in the end!" But he was very good at metaphors about torn bodices: flowers bursting into bloom, or ripe pomegranates. It was instructive for me at the time, because the only female chest I'd actually seen belonged to my sister, Darlene, who was seven then and flat as a board. Dusky, but no melons or rosebuds in sight, just a couple of brown bumps that were not at all like pomegranates — whatever *they* were.

Grandma knew I took her books, but she never chastised me for it. She never chastised me for anything, come to think of it. My father's mother had lived with us as far back as I can remember. It's funny, but it was my grandma who immediately swung into action when my sister or I got sick. My father never looked at us until we were at death's door, typical of doctors and their own kids. My grandmother had her own limited but effective methods. Witch hazel was her therapy for most things, especially fevers. She'd strip us down to our underpants and sponge us all over with witch hazel and cool water, until our fevered bodies started getting goose bumps and we were in danger of getting Pee-new-monia, as Darlene used to call it. Then she'd march us to the kitchen for a bowl of Campbell's chicken with rice soup, another healing substance Grandma swore by. It wasn't very exotic — grandmothers are supposed to toil for hours over homemade brews. Not mine. She just opened a can, dumped the gooey jell into a saucepan, added water and that was that. Witch hazel and Campbell's soup from a can. They cured most things.

But the very best part of being sick was when Grandma would read to us. Children's stories, when we were little, but soon she graduated to sterner stuff: Jack London's *Call of the Wild* and books by Edgar Rice Burroughs, *Tarzan* and *The Land That Time Forgot*.

She never in her life had been north of Baltimore, or farther west than Belvedere, Maryland, where my uncle has his church, but she loved stories of the Alaskan wilderness, of a campfire flame glowing orange in the eyes of wolves. The way she read the stories, in that deep voice of hers, when she described the howl of wolves in the starry Alaskan night, I shivered with delight and felt the cold against my skin and heard the mournful cry hurled to the moon. At that moment, I believe, I actually *became* a wolf.

Grandma was just as much at home in the Jurassic as she was on the Alaskan tundra. I saw pterodactyls tearing at human flesh and mammoths thudding once more upon the earth in *The Land That Time Forgot*. Grandma had no truck with literary realism. Give her orange-eyed wolves and flesh-tearing birds, and of course, heaving bosoms.

Frank Yerby might have dreamed up Tarzan, but in his book, Lord Greystoke would have spent most of his time feeling up Jane. Edgar Rice Burroughs, more Victorian by temperament, drew a genteel veil over Jane and Tarzan's private life, much, I am sure, to Grandma Johnson's dismay. She liked to see it all hang out, in a manner of speaking.

Frank Yerby might have ruined me as a writer, with all that ripe imagery, if it hadn't been for Thomas Walsh, S.J., of St. Aloysius Gonzaga High School. He smacked my hands with a ruler whenever I used too many adjectives.

"Simplify, young man, simplify," he'd say. "Prose should be as pure as a martyr's soul." If Frank Yerby had been in Father Walsh's class, ole Frank would have had both hands in casts. Father Walsh had absolutely no truck with fruit-imagery — nor with bosoms, I imagine.

He never seemed to notice that I wasn't white like all the other kids in the class. I mean, he *really* wasn't aware of it, so intent was he on whacking out all my adjectives. He was the first person who told me I could write. Very matter-of-factly he said to me one day, "Young man, when one has a gift, it is a sin not to nurture it." He never called any of us by name. I wonder if he knew them. I could hardly believe my ears, and I said, "Me, Father? A gift?" And he said, "You have a dangling participle in your third paragraph." And that was that.

But I couldn't stop grinning all the way home from school, even when my lips felt stretched and sore. I had a *gift.* I felt this swelling inside my chest, as if somebody inside me was blowing up a balloon. And I knew that my life had changed forever. But I never had the courage to say it out loud. Now, I do.

I, Donald A. (for Abednego) Johnson, have a gift.

But that presents a problem. I have been working in the South with the Student Nonviolent Coordinating Committee on a voter registration project. I first came south on one of the Freedom Rides, probably the way Hemingway went to the Spanish Civil War, because he believed in the cause and that's where the action was. I saw for myself how much work has to be done here, important work. I applied for a fellowship in the creative writing program at Georgetown University as a long shot, never expecting I'd get it. I did, to my astonishment. But I wonder, should I take it? There's so much happening now, I think I ought to stay in the South. But I have this feeling that if I don't strike out now, really try to be a writer, I'll never do it at all. I used to wonder if Father Walsh was the only person who'd say I had talent; maybe it was easy to be good in high school, where the competition isn't great. But I was selected from among five hundred applicants for this fellowship; it pays full tuition and a stipend, and the possibility of going on to get a master's at the university. My friends here are telling me to go; they say if I get homesick, they'll give a rednecked sheriff a bus trip north, and he can lecture in my class on the Bubba factor in southern literature.

I don't know. It's something I'll have to think about.

As Jay put his foot down on the accelerator, the sullen mood he'd worked up earlier that morning was barely a memory. Belvedere, Maryland, was enough to make him sullen. He was twenty-seven and slightly desperate, and he could not forgive Belvedere for not being Burma or the Sahara or the subcontinent of India. At least it was only forty-seven miles away from the White House, and that was something. Belvedere was a city waiting for its future, anxiously, as a commuter waits for a bus. Early in the century Belvedere had the best manufacturer of lawn mowers in the East, precision blades, cast to last a lifetime, with sounds that were gentle swishes, a joy to the ear as the mowers sailed across American lawns from Syracuse to Toledo. The stately white homes on Main Street were built on a mountain of new-mown grass. But the coming of the power mower doomed the company and the city that had grown up around it. The postwar prosperity that engulfed the nation simply passed over many small urban pockets like Belvedere, as the Angel of Death passed over the houses of the Israelites. But Belvedere waited. Washington, to the east, and Baltimore, to the north, were growing like giant amoebas, part of the galloping megalopolis that the East Coast was becoming, and Belvedere could not fail to be engulfed. The new storefronts, with their smiling expanses of plate glass, were badges of hope. They hung on old buildings, false as dentures, waiting for prosperity to arrive.

This geography was the reason for the reemergence of the *Belvedere Blade,* financed by chicken money from the Eastern Shore. It was young, feisty and the equal of the Triangle Shirtwaist Factory in its munificence of pay. Its young staffers saw it as a way station on the way to the *Post,* the *Times* — and, for the most ambitious among them, the Pulitzer Prize. Their newspaper office was a converted warehouse, and a portrait of John Fitzgerald Kennedy, ripped from the pages of *Life,* held a place of pride on one of its walls. He was *their* president — the others had been old men — the first to be born in the twentieth century, and he had stood eyeball to eyeball with the Soviets, and the other guy blinked. They were young, their country was young and so was their president, who said to them, "Ask not what your country can do for you — ask what you can do for your country." They were not old enough yet to be cynical, or to believe there was anything Americans could not do. It was 1963, and everything was possible.

It was under that portrait, that very morning, that Jay had been busy at a task he deemed worthy of his talents. He had come in, on his own time, to examine the photo essays he had been preparing. The paper was put out by a new process called photo-offset, and pictures came out crisp and clear, not faded and murky like they did in most newspapers, and the *Blade* used many photographs. A project he especially liked was on Belvedere, in the manner of the Ben Shahn Depression photographs. *Images of Belvedere* captured the bleak eyes of the old men who hung around the railroad station and the shacks in Niggertown and the vacant, sagging second stories of the buildings that wore the flashy new storefronts. He gave the pictures to Milt Beerman, the city editor. Milt looked at them and said, "Christ, Jay, this makes Belvedere look like the Black Hole of Calcutta."

"In Calcutta they talk about the Black Hole of Belvedere."

"Can't you work in a couple of happy pictures? Charlie wants happy pictures. How about children frolicking in a schoolyard?"

"How about children rolling a Spanish-American War veteran?"

"I like the spread, but it's unbalanced. A couple of happy pictures, or it's no go."

"OK, OK, I'll get pictures so happy they'll make you want to vomit."

He walked back to the desk and resumed work on another of his favorites, *Life at the White House.* He had pictures of astronauts and film stars and Kennedy relatives, and of course the President, and Jacqueline, who appeared on occasion to champion a special cause, often in the arts. He spread a series of photographs of her out across his desk. He thought her exquisite, with her wide, dark eyes and dark hair, and her whispery, girlish voice. He suspected her primness concealed a deep well of sensuality. The fashion, these days, was for blond goddesses with enormous breasts, but he agreed with the functionalists that less is more. He liked to imagine that deep well in her that had not been tapped, fully. Yes, her husband was movie star handsome, but he was away a lot, and there were those rumors that floated around in the press corps. He thought how lovely it would be if, one day, as he followed her on a photo tour of the newly redone White House (he'd be with *Life,* of course), her eyes met his over an eighteenth-century Hepplewhite chest, and she reached out with her white-gloved hand and took his, and she led him upstairs to a small but beautifully appointed room. Her breasts would be small and elegant, white as marble, and he would make ardent love to her on a green silk-covered settee under a portrait of Alexander Hamilton. She would moan, delicately (this was a respectful, high-class First Lady fantasy, no whooping or thrashing or semen stains on the green silk). She might give him a delicate, passionate nip or two with her small white teeth. That would be nice. Afterwards, she would touch his face gently with her white gloves — she never took them off, and that drove him mad with passion — and murmur, "I never knew it could be like this." And then they would continue the tour, under the eyes of Secret Service agents and visiting diplomats, she displaying her gratitude with only a slight pressure of her gloved hand on his arm as she pointed out a cabinet from the early Federal period.

Or he might be sailing on the world-class yacht of a patron of the arts, leaning against the rail, looking out at the calm ocean, and suddenly he would be aware of someone beside him. He would turn, and there she would be — her husband was off someplace talking to Khrushchev about nuclear war — and in her gentle whisper she would say, "I so admired your photographs, in *Life,* of the great cathedrals."

And he would smile, and they would talk of Chartres and Notre Dame, and her hand would rest lightly on his as they spoke of the great rose window, and how magnificent it had looked in his photos. Their eyes would meet, and she would put her small white-gloved hand in his, and they would go down the stairs to the state-room paneled in rare Brazilian wood, with a single perfect Matisse hanging over the bed. She would ever so delicately slip out of the white silk gown she was wearing, and when they were both naked she would take his chin in both her gloved hands, and look deeply into his eyes. Gently, gently, her gloved fingers would travel down his well-muscled body (when he was a rich photographer, he would work out), down, down, murmuring in French all the while. And then, when she came to a strategic place, she would sigh and whisper, *"C'est admirable!"* He would kiss her marble breasts, and they would make passionate but tasteful love — the little nips of course — under the Matisse, and she would say that he was an artist, but not only with his camera. Back on deck, the wind would play gently with her hair, and she would rest her hand ever so gently on his arm as they talked some more about cathedrals.

He picked up another picture of her, at a musicale at the White House. That gave him another idea. Lincoln Center, and he would be looking out at the lights of the city and she would be there, whispering, "Your photographs of the Great Masters. What feeling!" He had a whole bagful of elegant settings for her, always properly tasteful. He was not, after all, a slob. She was not meant for sweaty grappling or crotchless panties and peekaboo bras from Frederick's of Hollywood. He was certain that she wore only delicate silk panties with lace edges, and that she would drop dead on the spot from the sheer bad taste of no-crotch panties or black polyester garter belts.

Milt Beerman looked up and called out to him. "Did you do the Puppy of the Week yet, Jay?"

The spell was broken. He was not in Lincoln Center or the White House, her gloved white hands on his quivering body, but in Belvedere, Maryland, being asked about a task that demeaned his talent. He groaned.

"Oh, Christ, the fucking puppy."

"I got to have the puppy on Wednesday. You always forget the goddamn puppy."

"Can't we use the extra I did last week? The one with the schlong?"

"Let me see it."

Jay passed him the print.

"My God, that's obscene, that animal is bigger than I am."

"They call it the ladies' special down at the animal shelter."

"Airbrush out the schlong and we'll use it."

"Airbrush it? It's only a dog!"

"We are a family newspaper. We do not use dog schlongs."

Jay rolled his eyes upwards, "What am I *doing* here, what? *Life,* come and take me away from all this!" It was difficult to maintain his fantasy as the puppy's prick disappeared under the careful application of the airbrush. He could hardly imagine her coming up to him, elegant in her Chanel suit, and whispering, "The dog with the enormous penis — truly a work of art. I shall hang it in the East Room."

Going to the White House leavened his mood, of course. Astronauts could get him to *Life* a lot faster than oversized puppy genitals. And he had to admit that showing off a bit for a female colleague wasn't bad for his ego either.

He looked over at her now. She was sitting forward in her seat, her hand on the dash. She had eyes, he noticed, very much like Jacqueline's, wide set and with heavy lashes.

"How long have you been on Cityside, anyhow?" he asked.

"Seven months."

"Covered any fatals?"

She shook her head.

"Scared?"

She looked at him, then looked away. "I can handle it."

"That wasn't what I asked." He said it gently, and she caught the note of understanding in his voice. She leaned back against the seat and sighed.

"Yeah, I'm scared. I'm scared a lot in this job. It's still pretty new, a lot of it."

"This is easy. A lot of guys glamorize it, make it seem tough. The cops or the fireman have all the information you need. Then you throw in some color stuff. That's it. I've even written these things, and I can't write for shit."

The land stretched out now, green and forested on either side. Jay increased the pressure of his foot, and the car lurched ahead. His palms were moist, and he could feel the wheel growing slippery under his hands. He wiped first one, then the other, on the edge of his seat. He felt the excitement rising in his throat. Something unexpected and perhaps awful had happened and they were rushing towards it. He looked at the young woman sitting beside him. Her hand gripped the dashboard, and her breathing was fast and shallow. He pressed even harder on the accelerator, and the car fairly flew along the highway. "Hang on," he said, and he laughed, and she laughed too, a high, nervous laugh that spoke not of humor but of exhilaration.

"We could waste a lot of time looking for this thing," he said. "There are a lot of roads that go back in the woods."

"There's a little store and gas station up ahead."

Jay spotted the store and pulled into it. "We're from the *Blade*," he said to the man who ambled out. "We're looking for the plane that went down."

"I heard it. Sounded like the engine cut out. One of the county fire trucks went by a few minutes ago. Took the dirt road up ahead."

Jay gunned the engine, and the Chevy was back on the road. They found the dirt road, which was narrow and rutted from the spring rains. Jay drove slowly, impatient but afraid of getting bogged down in the mud. Finally he spotted the rear end of the fire engine, blocking the road. There was a green Ford parked behind it. Jay frowned when he saw the car.

"Oh fuck. Phillips."

He pulled the car up behind the Ford. As he climbed out, a man wearing a hunting jacket with two cameras slung across his chest like bandoliers emerged from the bush.

"Hi, kid," he said. "I was hoping you wouldn't get here."

He was a heavyset man, unshaven as usual. "I got some great stuff. One with the guy's eyes hanging out of the sockets. The *Enquirer* will use that kind of stuff."

He looked at Mary, who had climbed out of the car and was digging into her pocket looking for a notebook. Phillips grinned at Jay and made little kissing noises with his mouth, sotto voce. "Getting some of *that,* kid? Nice pussy."

Jay ignored him. "Which way?"

Phillips pointed to a narrow path, and Jay motioned to Mary to follow him.

"Who's that?"

"Phillips. He's a freelance. A death specialist. He gets to all the fatals before everybody else."

"Nice."

"He's got a police radio in his car. Not that he needs it. He's a vulture. He can smell it in the air when somebody is going to die."

They walked in silence, brushing away the branches that overhung the path. That old turd, Phillips. The sight of him had spoiled the excitement. Phillips was the nightmare phantasm of his own future, what he might become if *Life* didn't get him. He saw himself, old and unshaven, driving from fatal to fatal, keeping gory photos from accident scenes in his file cabinet so he could take them out at times to show to ugly, sodden women so he could bang them.

"Death makes broads horny," Philips had confided to him.

He shivered. Another lousy accident scene, that was all it was. The deaths he photographed were senseless and stupid, there was no drama to them. Some kid smashed into a tree going seventy, crumpled and ugly and mottled with blood; the woman drowned in the boating accident, brown water dribbling out of her mouth. Not like Capa's picture of the Spanish soldier, head thrown back, at the moment of the bullet's impact. He no longer wanted to see what was ahead. Jesus H. Christ, would he have to spend the rest of his life schlepping around taking pictures of corpses?

He walked along, smelling the damp earth and the molding vegetation. At the edge of a small ravine he saw a policeman, his slicker buttoned against the chill. The man looked at Mary.

"I wouldn't go down there, Miss."

"I'm from the *Blade.* I'm a reporter." There was an edge to her voice, the same tone she had used when she said, "I can handle it."

The trooper shrugged. "It's not pretty."

"It never is," she said, her voice flat and world-weary.

They climbed down the edge of the ravine, and Jay stopped to let Mary come very close to him. "It's never pretty?" he said.

She grinned. "Barbara Stanwyck. I forget the movie. How was it?"

"Could have fooled me."

As they neared the bottom of the ravine, they could see the wreck through the trees. It was a single-engined, blue-and-white Cessna. Only the tail section was intact; the front of the plane was folded up against a tree like an accordion. On the ground near the plane lay the body of a man, and firemen were hacking at the wreck with axes, trying to get a second body out.

Jay moved to the bottom of the ravine, next to the body that lay face up on the ground. Someone, perhaps wishing for a hint of dignity, had draped a large white handkerchief across the face, through which the blood had seeped. Jay raised his camera, then lowered it, thinking of Phillips and his file cabinet. When the body had been removed from the wreck, the man's pants had snagged on a piece of metal, and a section of the pants were torn away. The brand name on the waistband of his shorts, Jockey, was clearly visible. His stomach, covered with thick black hair, bulged above the waistband.

Jay stared at the blue, distended letters. Make a statement out of that, Cartier-Bresson. Find a moment of truth in flab and elastic, Capa. He looked up to the tops of the trees, where the sky above was pure and clean, and then he looked down again at the corpse.

"Want to see what you are, buddy? Take a look. This is what you are."

Corpses always talked to him; the woman who drowned, bloated with water, her eyes vacant; the kid in the MG, his head dangling out of the car. "Want to see what you are?"

"Shut up," he said to the corpse.

"What?" said the fireman next to him.

"Nothing," Jay said. "Hey, cover him up, will you?"

Then he noticed that Mary had moved beside him. She was looking down at the body. Her pretty pink shoes were soaked and caked with mud, and her pink dress under the khaki raincoat made her seem impossibly vulnerable and out of place. He watched her pale face; it remained impassive. She might have been looking at a pile of leaves. But he noticed that one small vein, above her eye, twitched and then was still. She watched as the firemen covered the body, then walked over to talk to the fire chief.

Jay turned to the wreck and saw the firemen were removing the second body. It was a bloody mess, and Jay turned away, no longer wanting to see it. When they finished, he turned to the wreckage and began to shoot. Wedged in the hashed and bloodied metal of the cockpit was a wicker luncheon hamper, and in the hamper were three sandwiches folded into pink napkins, neatly, the way a woman would fold them. The pink-wrapped sandwiches brought the pity into his throat, and he gagged on it. The bodies hadn't done it, but the pink sandwiches had.

He walked back to the center of the clearing, where the second body had been laid out next to the first. A fireman standing next to him reached into his slicker and pulled out a sandwich.

"Shit, peanut butter. I picked up the wrong one."

He looked at Jay. "You like peanut butter?"

Jay shook his head, and the man turned to Mary. "How about you?"

"No, thank you."

"What the hell." He shrugged, and he walked over to the chief, munching on the sandwich.

"Oh barf," Mary whispered to Jay. "He's *eating.*"

"A true gourmet," he said.

There was a crashing noise in the brush, and two firemen walked into the clearing, carrying two shiny, rectangular green bags. They unfolded the bags, and with the help of the other men slid the bodies into the bags and fastened the metal catches at the tops. Jay followed them, shooting, as they loaded the bags onto stretchers and started to move up the slope. Mary fell into step beside Jay.

"You got enough?" he asked her.

She nodded. "Yes, I've got it."

They walked behind the men with the stretchers, an impromptu procession. There was no sound except the heavy breathing of the firemen and their boots in the mud.

"Joe," said the man at the head of the stretcher, "you bowling tonight?"

"Dunno. My back's been botherin' me. This shit won't help."

"We didn't have enough guys against Frederick last week."

"Well, maybe I will."

Jay turned to Mary. "Idents?"

"De Lucca and Wilder. Out of a private airport in Richmond."

On the way back to the paper, they were both subdued as they drove past stretches of woods and farmland. He was acutely conscious of her body beside his, of her breathing and a warm human smell that was at once sweet and musky. He wanted to touch her. He didn't know why. Maybe just because she was alive.

"Well," he said, "that's it. Now you know."

"It wasn't what I expected."

"How so?"

"I didn't have any trouble looking at them. I was afraid I was going to feel like throwing up, but I didn't. It was the bags. Bags are for — groceries."

"Yeah, it's crummy. Not like the movies. No violins."

"One minute those guys were alive, and the next minute they were in a . . . a goddamn bag. I had this feeling we ought to be doing something."

"Like what?"

"I don't know. But I was taking notes and the cops were doing their thing, and the firemen were talking about bowling — and here these two guys were, dead. It was all so routine. Is it always this way."

"More or less."

"Do you get used to it?"

"The guys around it all the time, I guess they do. At National Airport once, I saw a guy walking around with a box full of pieces of people. Just pieces. Christ, I had nightmares for months, but this guy, he was just walking around, putting stuff in his box. *Hey, an elbow. . . .* "

She sighed and was silent for a minute. "It ought to be important. I mean, you only get to do it once."

"That's an interesting way of putting it. I don't want to do it at all."

"But we have to, don't we? I mean, this morning, there was Kennedy and the astronauts and it was like they were going to live forever and so were we, but, but"— she paused and her brow furrowed. "I feel like this curtain was pulled back, and I just saw death straight on. There's no curtain anymore. It looked back at me." She laughed nervously. "I guess it's just a 'first fatal' thing. But, my God, the bags. The bags. Does it scare you, Jay?"

He looked at her. Her eyes were an even brown, intense as two points of light. He was tempted, for a minute, to lie to her, to enlist the grim reaper as a partner in deception. He wanted to be older, wiser, to impress her. He wanted to be a man who could stare death down. But those brown eyes would not accept a lie.

He exhaled and told the truth.

"Scares the shit out of me."

He walked along the beachfront, feeling the coolness of the salt-laden air on his face and the still warm sand between his toes. He had been with his father. It was unsettling. The old man could not speak, or walk; he was imprisoned in a body that no longer worked. Even that iron will could not make it work. He shivered. Better if they had let him slip away, when they had the chance. The man who had been so huge, who had been able to bluff or buy or bully his way into whatever he wanted, should not have been brought so low.

He looked out at the sea, which had always called to him, mysterious, restless, unforgiving. He thought of Tennyson's "Ulysses," one of his favorites.

> *Death closes all; but something ere the end,*
> *Some work of noble note, may yet be done.*
> *Not unbecoming men that strove with Gods.*

That should be left him, that one more noble thing.

He had never imagined his father could be powerless, because he had always been able to do everything, fix everything. There were threads of love and fear, gratitude and resentment between them. As the second son, he had been shielded from the driving glare of his father's ambition by his older brother's perfection, allowed, to some degree, to think, to read, to explore, to fail, free from those relentless dreams.

If he had been given to introspection, and he was not — in a family where children jostled for position like racehorses at the rail, too much self-examination was regarded with suspicion — he might have been candid about the facts of his own creation. It was in part his father's doing. The father's ambition was born of an ache so great and deep that only a son's uncontested triumph could assuage it. One night, the father had waited, alone in his room at Harvard, a popular young man, friendly with everyone, confident that the knock on the door would come, and he would be told of his selection to the most prestigious eating club in the Yard. All around him he heard the footsteps and the laughter and the sound of celebration. He waited, as the minutes ticked into hours. Joseph P. Kennedy, American, with none of the muck of Wexford on his shoes, waited for the knock on the door that would never come.

The older son was sent hurtling into the world, a missile that would at last, finally, heal the wound, but he died in a reckless bid for heroism, frozen forever in first place in his father's heart.

"I'm shadow boxing in a match the shadow is always going to sin," the second son told a friend. But he picked up the fallen standard, dutifully, and walked into adulthood shaped by his father's dreams and his own formidable will. It was, after all, particularly American for men and women to invent themselves. They inherited a land hacked out of the wilderness, where there were no edges and no rules. A young man from the tenements of New York had become the Western outlaw Billy the Kid, and another sickly young man turned himself into a Rough Rider, and the son of an East Boston barkeep became the ambassador to the Court of St. James's.

He learned from his father. He learned to use money brutally, to create a juggernaut of cash and influence that rolled over men his seniors in age and experience. He learned to use women like limousines, as he had seen his father use them. He liked power. He liked being president. His saving grace was that he still believed those stories that he had read so many years ago beside this restless sea, of knights and wizards and dragons and noble quests. For the father, getting there was all. The son wanted, with Tennyson, "To strive, to seek, to find, and not to yield."

But he was a Tory at heart, naturally cautious, seeking compromise, possibility, the surer thing. His natural caution warred with the hidden romantic inside him. In the corridors of power, the careful man often trod lightly. In his words, the dreamer came alive. Which was he, really? Perhaps even he did not know. But a generation heard the words, and their lives were forever changed. They believed they could move the sun and stars.

He walked to the edge of the jetty at the end of the green swath of lawn and stared, again, at the sea. He was his own man, at last. He had been a passable congressman, an indifferent senator, but at last he was growing into the job he was meant for. He was smart and he could listen and he could learn. He was growing surer and bolder with every passing day. Greatness hung, like the evening mist over the sea, almost within his grasp.

All he had to do was reach out and take it.

"JAY, LOOK AT THIS for a minute. I think the stiff's heading the wrong way."

Jay walked over to a lighted table where a young man was pasting up the centerfold section of the next morning's *Blade.* Jay scanned the page; the mistake was obvious. In one photo of the crash scene, the stretchers were being carried to the right of the page, in another picture, the opposite way.

Jay pried the picture from its moorings. "Tell the guys in the darkroom to flip it. Nice catch, Andy."

Mary Springer walked into the room and looked at the table.

"Ready?"

"Except for one picture, yeah."

"When's the Kennedy spread going?"

"Tomorrow. Charlie said it'll hold for a day."

She leaned over to look at the page, reading carefully. Other reporters did a quick once-over, then signed their initials; Mary always read every word. Sometimes she ran her fingers along the columns, as if there was pleasure in the feel of the words. A strand of dark hair fell across her cheek, and she brushed it away, impatiently. It intruded on her work. The lack of vanity in the gesture intrigued Jay. He scanned her face, liking the way the lights from the table accentuated her cheekbones and the strong, tight line of her jaw. It was not really a beautiful face, less a pretty one. He would photograph her someplace with rocks and surf. The strength in that jaw would be absurd in a garden.

She leaned forward to see better, and he noticed the curve of her breasts under the cotton dress she was wearing. He had always thought of her as thin — a false impression, because of her height and small bones. He thought, idly, that she was one of those women who would look better naked than with clothes on. He leaned over the table, enjoying being close to her. "Good story."

"Thanks. I think I got it. This makes it"— she paused to consider — "better."

"Better?"

"Serious. Like it should have been. The pictures and the words make it — serious. Does that make sense?"

Her intensity was almost physical; he thought he could hear the air around her hiss with it. He wondered if she would just burn up with it one day. She let out her breath, and her shoulders drooped with fatigue. "I guess it's just the 'first fatal' syndrome, huh?"

"You'll get over it."

"I don't know if I want to. It should be new and terrible every time. If it isn't, you've missed something. I wish I could see everything new and fresh."

"Even that?"

"Even that."

"You'd go crazy. You have to block things out, to survive."

"*You* don't. Not when you're shooting. I've watched you. You're open. Exposed. Like I was today."

He looked at her, a little awed. How the hell did she know that? Some photographers used the camera as a wall, they felt safe behind it. With him, things blazed and burned through the camera lens. It was a hole the world could leak through. He was trying to think of something to say about that when she laughed and shook her head.

"Jay, I'm sorry, I'm all wound up. I'm going to go home and go to bed. I think I sound a little crazy tonight. See you tomorrow."

Jay walked to his desk, picked up his Nikon and started towards the door. Mrs. Fitts, the receptionist, said good night to him with the usual veiled invitation. Mrs. Fitts had the hots for him. She liked to jiggle her size 99's at him as he went by, and he always tried to manage a leer. It was the least he could do. She always gave him his messages on time with the numbers right. If Mrs. Fitts liked you, you got a panoramic view and the right numbers; if she didn't, you saw buttons and at least three wrong digits.

As he walked out to the car, he thought of Mary saying, "I'm going to go home and go to bed," and the sentence sprang a sudden, erotic image on him. He was lying, naked, on a bed, and she was naked too, lying between his thighs, her lips on his, and he could feel the pressure of her body along his entire length. Her shoulders were pale, with a sprinkling of freckles across them, and her breasts were full with small, elegant nipples that he could feel against his chest. The image was so sudden and so unexpected that he found himself trembling. At the same time, he felt an overwhelming protective urge towards her. In his mind, he saw her standing by the wreck, wearing her pink dress and her khaki raincoat, her pretty pink shoes sodden with mud, so terrifyingly vulnerable that he was afraid the sky might fall in on her. He had never thought about her that way before. He had hardly thought of her at all. She was just the girl at the next desk, married to some local, who could say *fuck* and make it sound charming.

What the hell was going on? Probably something to do with pulling aside the curtain, as she called it, seeing death so clear, the fog of everyday living just blown off by death. But what was happening below his belt was familiar enough.

Say the rosary, son, and take cold showers. He chuckled. It was jerk-off time again. He had so many variations on that particular art, he thought, that he could be on the Ted Mack *Amateur Hour.* He'd be more interesting than the guy who played "Yankee Doodle" on his head with spoons.

There was always Norma. He decided to drive by her house. The lights in her apartment were out. *Damn.* Norma was chubby, and her blond hair had dark roots, which annoyed him in the same way as somebody scraping his fingers down a blackboard. But she was energetic at least. The first time he took her out, she invited him up to her apartment and started taking her clothes off right away. He was a bit shocked; he'd heard there were women like that, but all the girls he knew took some coaxing and necking first.

Norma liked crotchless panties. Purple ones, with ribbons on them, the sort that would have made Jacqueline shriek with dismay. Once, while she was showering, he saw them on the bed, looking like some peculiar insect that was feasting on the bedclothes, engorged and reddish purple. Norma was a Frederick's of Hollywood kind of girl. He imagined her wandering into the French boutique from which Jacqueline ordered her underthings, rummaging through the little silk panties and lace camisoles and saying, "Jeez, don't you have anything here with a split in the crotch and holes in them for the boobs?"

He didn't like himself much for hanging out with Norma. He didn't love her, he wasn't sure if he even liked her. He just used her for crotchless-panty sex. That seemed to be all right with her; she made no claims on him, didn't seem to need him for anything but a quick fuck. It should have been ideal.

He was suddenly, unaccountably depressed by the thought of Norma, her dark roots and the purple panties and the debased coin of their relationship. The shabbiness of his life surrounded him, oppressive as humidity. Now, the White House only made it worse. It was as if he lived at the edge of a garden where everything was beautiful and exciting, and they let him in once in a while to look around, but he could never stay. He was too old, he had started too late, nothing more was ever going to happen to him. The old feeling returned, like teeth nibbling inside his gut; it was either melancholy or an ulcer, he was not sure. He would spend his life waiting for something wonderful to happen, like his father did, and it never would. He remembered that his father had finally stopped singing, wonderful aching ballads of love and death and the Easter Uprising. There was one he had always liked as a kid. *Her hair hung down in ringlets; they called her the queen of the land.*

As his father sang, he liked to picture the woman in the song, on a dark, windblown moor, her hair wild in the wind. He saw Norma on a moor, the wind whipping through the Clairol No. 25 blond, scattering the dandruff in her dark roots. *Jesus, Mary and Joseph.*

He turned the car away from Norma's apartment and thought again about Mary in her pink dress. He could picture her on a hill-side, dark hair blowing. The erotic images returned; he saw her on a bed, her hair spread out across the pillow like a fan. Her hair would taste salty against his lips. There was an inexplicable sense of promise in those images.

He shook his head. That was crazy. His ideal woman (Jacqueline didn't count, she wasn't really available) had hair like cornsilk. She looked, in fact, like the woman in the Breck ad — and she drifted around his Manhattan penthouse like a wraith. He had never been in a Manhattan penthouse, but it was very clear in his mind's eye, the Chrysler Building framed slightly off center in one of the windows and lots of cold steel, modern furniture and white walls. His photographs would hang, just so, on the pristine walls. The Lady in Black — that's what he called her — would drift about the rooms and run her fingers across the pictures and murmur, "How beautiful." If *she* was a little fuzzy in his mind, the frames weren't; they were either of high-tensile white metal, the screws hidden on the undersides so as not to interfere with the play of the shapes or the explosions of color, or of slender high-grade aluminum that barely kissed the edges of the prints. The Lady in Black did two things; she murmured "How beautiful," and she took her clothes off. She had milk white skin, no zits or warts, and she too moaned delicately when she fucked; she didn't bellow like Norma. She didn't have dandruff. She never had bad breath, and she never was crabby before her period. She never had periods. She was perfect and she was waiting for him, somewhere. Not in fucking Belvedere, Maryland.

The Lady in Black didn't have white gloves, but that was a nice touch, so he added it. She could take him in her white-gloved hand and caress him, and with her finely tuned artistic sense, she would once again murmur, "How beautiful." He wasn't immense, but he wasn't puny either, and he was, he thought, nicely formed. His penis didn't stick out at a weird angle or bend in a strange way.

Jacqueline, an artiste, would have thought it certainly as nice as the curved leg of a Hepplewhite, and the Lady in Black would agree. He saw them, slim and chic, lunching together, sipping white wine and chatting agreeably about his penis.

He sighed. He had moved up in the world, in his fantasies at least. For one thing, Father Hannigan never appeared in them anymore, to chastise him, as he used to do. In the old days, Jacqueline would have given him only the first delicious nip when Father Hannigan would have stormed in, cast her one of his famous stony glances, and made her put her Oleg Cassini dress back on. He'd have scolded, A nice Catholic girl, too, now, Missy, you stop this and say the rosary, and she would have grabbed the dress and scampered off. Father Hannigan would have called the Lady in Black, who was vaguely Protestant, a common whore, and she would have stalked off in a huff, taking her white gloves with her. Norma would have unhinged Father Hannigan completely. He'd have taken one look at her, in the purple panties and the bra with the nipples peeking through, and he would have fallen to his knees, waving the cross at her, crying out, "Get thee behind me, Satan!"

Norma would have grinned and said, "Hey, kinky! Let's do it!"

He tried to think about the Lady in Black, but her face, never too clear to begin with, just melted away, dripping like wax, and it was Mary's face that replaced it. Some unexplored cavern of his mind was in charge now, and it was useless to resist it. He lay astride her on the bed, her breasts gentle against him, and he was kissing her mouth, a kiss at once passionate and infinitely tender. Her mouth was warm and soft, and he kissed it deeply, never wanting to stop, feeling that his entire body and soul was flowing out of himself and into her. He felt again a sense of calm, as if the phantom kiss had the power to heal him.

He shook his head. Things were rattling around tonight. It had been a long time since he had been out on a fatal. He had forgotten the power of death's face to unhinge him.

He pulled the car up in front of the Victorian house he shared with two reporters from the *Blade.* One of them, Sam Bernstein, was sitting on the sofa doing the *New York Times* crossword puzzle.

"What's a three-letter word for the ruler of a kingdom of fools?" he asked.

"JFK."

"Levity at this hour? Jesus."

"For Chrissake, Sam, why don't you give up on that goddamn thing? You spend more time on the fucking *Times* puzzle than anyone I ever saw."

"It's my talisman."

"Your what?"

"The day I can do the entire *Times* crossword puzzle, that's the day I die. I'm safe till then."

"If you quit doing it you'll never finish."

"That's cheating."

"Columbia J School rotted your brain. I got a better one. The nine first Fridays."

"What's that?"

"You go to Mass and communion the first Friday of every month, and you die in the state of grace."

"So?"

"Straight up, you heathen. Right to the harp section. You can steal, murder one, sleep with goats, but you go direct to heaven."

"That's absurd."

"You're jealous because you're Jewish and you only get to the porch."

"I don't want to hear this."

"Jews aren't baptized, so they don't go to heaven proper. There's this little porch tacked on, for the Jews who lead good lives. God's Irish, so I figure he doesn't want people around who don't drink and who are smarter than He is."

"They didn't actually teach you this stuff."

"I swear to God they did. Did you know that just before the end of the world, all the Jews will be converted?"

"Oy."

"So if you ever wake up with this wild urge to go to Mass, it's all over. Trumpet time."

"I should have voted for Nixon."

"Nah, it's time we had a Catholic president. The thumbscrews give the Oval Office a little class. Hey, where's Roger?"

"Out with Giggles."

"Oh fuck. How did I get stuck in the room next to Roger? His love life comes right through the walls."

"I miss the folk singer."

"Not me. One more night of humpedy-hump followed by 'We Shall Overcome' and I would have personally burned a cross on Roger's bed."

Sam laughed. "Roger was covering the state NAACP convention yesterday. Nice story, except he called it the National Association for the Prevention of Colored People."

"Roger's a great writer, but he's sort of fuzzy on details. What do you hear from the *Post*?"

"Al Friendly likes my stuff, they say they got me in mind. Christ, sometimes I think I'll be stuck in Belvedere the rest of my life."

"You know where we should be. In Ala-fucking-bama," Jay said.

"Right. Getting knocked down by fire hoses."

"Hit with billy clubs by southern sheriffs."

"Bitten by police dogs."

"Shot at by white trash."

"God, that would be great! We're missing it all, Jay. History is passing us by!"

"Shit, yeah."

"Want to go down to the Sahara Room? Drown our sorrows."

"I'm beat. I think I'll hit the sack."

"Pretty gory?"

"Not really. Just . . . depressing."

He climbed the stairs slowly. Things were still rattling around. No use putting it off. He was going to think about his father tonight. His own life seemed tangled with his father's, a coil that circled around on itself so that it was impossible to tell where one strand ended and the other began. He had tried, and failed, to give himself absolution.

Bless me Father, I have sinned.
Yes?
I didn't love my father enough, and he died.
Not loving enough isn't a sin.
Yes, it's the worst one.
You were angry at him for getting sick.
It wasn't fair. I needed him and he got sick.
So you punished him by not loving him.
And he died. I made him die.
You think you have the power of life and death?
No. Yes. I don't know.
You were only fifteen.
If I had loved him, he wouldn't have died.
You were fifteen. ***Ego te absolvo.***
No, you can't.
I absolve you. Accept it.
You can't.

He remembered.

His fingers spread across the belly of the ball, strong, thin hands, long from joint to joint. His father's hands. He moved back, looked. He was Johnny Lujack. The crowd sucked in its breath; he threw. A wondrous arc, hanging in the blue, suspended in time and space, and the crowd went "Ahhhhhhhhhh —"

"Jay, those damn kids messed up the catchers' mitts. I tell 'em every time, don't mess with the displays. Juvenile delinquents."

Johnny Lujack was quick frozen. Jay counted the mitts. "There's only seven. There were eight when I counted them last time."

"It was the nigger kids, you bet. I'm going to get a nice store in Silver Spring, that's where the good people are. Washington has gone to hell. Niggers and riffraff."

Jay nodded. He was not expected to answer. He owed his presence at AA Blitz Sporting Goods to the fact that Mr. Blitz was his mother's cousin. He was family, he came cheap and he didn't steal.

"I been meaning to ask, Jay, how's your dad?"

"He's been in bed for a couple of days, but he'll be up soon."

"Tell your father I was asking for him. I see some of the drivers down at Haps. They ask for him too. A gentleman, your father. Not like some. Jay, are you going to the game? You can leave early if you are."

"I'm not going."

"I thought you liked basketball."

"I like to play it. I don't like to watch it."

"I'm ordering the trophies for the team, ten dollars each. Nothing but the best for St. Anthony's. That nigger kid is good. How come these nigger kids get so tall?"

Jay started arranging the mitts. The one good thing about AA Blitz was that he could slide his hand across wood and leather and be Lujack or Cousy or DiMaggio. At the game, he was no one. He would watch the players, the gym lights glinting on their bare shoulders, and the envy would inflate inside him until he thought he would simply float to the top of the gym, hanging there like a huge balloon. His father had been All-City, and so Jay had the game in his genes. The coach had asked him, more than once, to come out. But Jay was stuck with AA Blitz in the afternoon. His father was out of the cab more days than he was in it now, and he got nothing for the days he did not drive. It was only his father's lousy kidneys that stood between Jay and a blue-and-crimson All-Star jacket. Scouts from Maryland and Notre Dame would be in the stands to watch him. He would pick Notre Dame. You could Lose Your Faith at those other places. Sister Mary Catherine always said it that way, in Capital Letters, and Jay had visions of himself Losing It and then rooting about in garbage cans to get it back, finding it someplace between the orange peels and the old newspapers.

"Hey, Jay, you ready?"

Vincent J. Sheehan presented his shining face across the catchers' mitts. Vinnie always looked scrubbed. The nuns loved him. He could get away with murder.

"Nah, Vinnie, I'm not going."

Disbelief darkened Vinnie's face.

"Not goin! You said you were. I came all the way over here!"

"I never said for sure."

"You said, Jay."

"Not for sure."

"Yeah you did. If we beat Gonzaga, we got the Catholic League title." He jabbed Jay with his elbow. "Maybe after, we can get some action."

"I dunno."

Vinnie was always talking about "action," but of course he would have run in terror from the prospect of the real thing. By sophomore year, some of the more advanced boys had actually felt female flesh, or at least the outside of a fuzzy sweater at places where it bulged. Jay and Vinnie went to movies and still traded baseball cards. They were not advanced.

"Claire Ryan is having a party at her house after the game."

"Oh, Ryan," Jay said, dismissively.

"What's wrong with Ryan? She's built."

"She hangs around with Phil Mazzarato and those guys from the team. I bet she'll just ask seniors."

"So what? We'll crash. Seniors. Big deal."

He was standing in a corner of Claire Ryan's house, leaning against the wall, smoking a cigarette. He looked virile and mysterious.

He had spent a considerable amount of time practicing smoking. He tried Bogart — cool, disdainful puffs. Gable was brisk, in command, the cigarette an afterthought. Alan Ladd was more romantic, a stream of smoke floating through his lips as he eyed some dame who was falling in love with him. Jay often coughed when he inhaled, something Alan Ladd didn't do much. He'd have to work on that.

Claire Ryan came up to him, her hair falling in small ringlets against her white throat.

"Why are you standing here alone?"

"I like to be alone."

"How strange you are. I never met a man like you."

"Let's go."

"Where?"

"Away from here."

"I can't go." Her eyes met his. "But I must go with you."

In actual fact, he had said eleven words to Claire Ryan in his whole life. "Do we have pages 12 to 14 in algebra to do?"

"Yes," she said.

Someday he was going to grow up and move to a place where they talked like they did in the movies. Nobody in his neighborhood talked like that. *"I must go with you, my love."* Mainly they said, "Marie, I want a fucking beer," and "What do I look like, your damn maid?" In New York they probably talked the other way.

In a large bed in a white room, she lay naked beside him. "Jay, I can't help myself. Be gentle with me, Jay."

Picturing Claire naked was a mortal sin, you'd burn in hell for that. The real Claire in the flesh might be worth it, but for a minute's imagining it wasn't. So he put one of the naked women he had seen in *National Geographic* beside him in bed. That was probably only a venial sin, because he didn't know her, she was colored and she had on a grass skirt and carried a spear. She looked a little weird in his bed under the Notre Dame pennant, especially with the spear, but at least it wasn't a mortal sin.

"I haven't got all day, Jay, you coming or not?"

"OK, Vinnie, I'll fucking go. I got to stop at home first, to tell my folks."

The rose-colored chair in the living room had been empty for four days. It was a relief not to have to go by that chair and see his father staring out the window. Jay would grip his books and hurry past, guilt trailing him across the hall runner. His father would be OK. People didn't die from kidneys. All they did was store up piss.

"Hey, Jay, you know where Ryan lives?"

"Yeah."

"We ought to know, in case we want to crash."

"Sure we want to crash. You said you wanted to."

"Well, sure I want to. Crash."

"It was your idea."

"Yeah, I'll do it. I will."

"You always chicken out, Vinnie. Big talk, no action."

"Not me, man. I won't chicken out."

"Yeah you will."

"I wonder if Ryan does it with Mazzarato."

Jay frowned. Carnal speculation was OK for most girls, but not for Claire Ryan. He was certain she was pure. A temple of the Holy Ghost. The thought of Claire *Doing It* with Phil Mazzarato, who had brows that joined in the center of his forehead and who was covered with so much hair he looked like a gorilla — or so Jay thought when he glanced sideways at him in the locker room — made Jay feel queasy. The colored lady with the spear was more Phil's type. Gorillas wouldn't faze her, she living in the jungle and all.

"What's the matter, Jay, you got a thing for Ryan?"

"I don't give a shit for Ryan or any of 'em."

"Sure, we know, Jay."

"Don't be a shithead, Vinnie."

"We know."

"Vinnie, you are a real pain in the ass."

They walked up to the red brick rowhouse where Jay's family occupied the first two floors. The door was ajar. That was strange. Jay's mother was afraid of burglars and always kept the door bolted. Jay pushed the door open and walked in. Mrs. Calloway from the third floor was in the living room. His brother's wife, Irene, a pale, tired-looking young woman, sat on the couch holding her baby. No one said a word.

Jay started to run up the stairs, his feet pounding on the faded daisies on the runner. His momentum carried him into the hall and through the open door of his parents' room. The people in the room turned to stare at him. His mother was there, and his older brother, Frank, and Father Clevinger, the assistant from the parish. His father was lying in bed, very still. His eyes were closed, his face was pale, and his false teeth were not in. His mouth looked all dry and puckered without his teeth, and his breath made a whooshing sound as it came in and out.

Frank grabbed Jay by the arm and pulled him into the hall.

"Don't you know better than to come busting in here like it was a fire? Don't you have any sense, Jay?"

"Frank, he's not going to — he's going to be OK, isn't he?"

"Keep your voice down! We're saying the Rosary!"

"Why didn't you call me? I was at the store."

"He's been like this for hours. There's nothing you could have done."

"She called you. Why didn't she call me?"

"Stop behaving like a child. Mom has enough sorrow now. Don't you go adding to it." Frank always talked that way, as if he had read a book that had sentences in it that grown-ups were supposed to say. Jay thought he was a pain in the butt.

"Why didn't you put his teeth in, Frank?"

His brother looked disgusted and turned and walked back into the bedroom. Jay followed him and went down to kneel at the end of the bed, as the rhythmic chant of the Rosary hummed along. He joined in. He hated the Rosary because he could only get through three Hail Marys when his mind would start to drift off, sometimes, horror of horrors, to the lady with the spear. Surely it was a mortal sin to be saying "Hail Mary" at the same time you were thinking of the big brown bazungas of a lady from *National Geographic.*

"Glory be to the Father, the Son, and the Holy Ghost."

Jay looked at his father's face, pale as the bellies of the fish his mother cooked on Fridays. Now, his father's breath had begun to come out in little puffs through his lips. It sounded like he was breathing the letter *P.*

Jay stared, unbelieving. This wasn't happening. People didn't die when they were forty-eight years old. Any minute all this weird stuff would stop and his father would put on a clean shirt and go downstairs to supper; he always wore a clean shirt to supper.

"Now and at the hour of our death. Amen," his mother said. She was a small, thin woman who always seemed drained of energy. He thought he remembered a time when she had been wiry and laughing, but he was not sure if he had simply imagined it. His father was tired all the time, too, but under the weariness was an anger that curled the long hands into a fist that clenched and unclenched.

Jay was afraid of his father's anger, not that it would be used against him, but that it could be there at all. Jay looked at his father's hands, and a memory flashed into his mind. He thought he remembered the back of a green car as it sped away from where he lay in the street. He was bruised, nothing more, but his father held him at the edge of the street, and Jay felt he would crack in the desperate embrace of those hands.

"World without end. Amen."

They did not talk much. Words were a chore to both of them. In the past few months there were times when Jay had felt his father's eyes on him. In a flicker of a second he met his father's eyes, and they were filled with an anguish that terrified him. What was there in the world that could hurt a man so strong? He did not want to know, so he grabbed up his books and called out, "Bye, Pop," as he hurried out the door.

The prayers flowed on, and Jay's knees began to hurt where they pressed against the floor. He tried to concentrate on the words, seeing each one in his mind, but it didn't work. It never did.

He walked into the living room of the Ryan house. The music stopped. Everyone turned to stare. Phil Mazzarato, his one long eyebrow furrowed, glared at him.

"You don't belong here."

Jay gave him a cold look, part Brando, part Bogart, then ignored him. He walked over to Claire Ryan, to lead her to the floor where the couples were dancing. Phil Mazzarato grabbed his shoulder. Jay shook the hand away, contemptuously, like Monty Clift had done to John Ireland in Red River. *Phil Mazzarato swung. Jay blocked the blow and sent Mazzarato to the floor with one punch, like John Wayne did in* The Quiet Man. *The rest of the seniors jumped him. He knocked two of them down before they got him, but there were too many, even for him. He lay on the floor in a (small) pool of blood, and Claire screamed and ran to him. She lifted his bruised head, gently, like Natalie Wood did to Tab Hunter in (what was the name of that movie?). She did not care that his blood was staining her black velvet dress.*

"Cowards!" She sobbed. "He has more courage than any of you." Later, when they had gone, he recovered and she lay in bed beside him and there she was again, the naked lady with the spear . . .

"World without end. Amen."

Claire and the lady with the spear vanished, and the green pyramid of his father's foot beneath the blanket rebuked him silently. Remorse rattled through him. "Oh, God, I'm sorry. Please, God, I'm sorry."

"May perpetual light shine upon him and upon the souls of all the faithful departed. Amen."

Jay had heard that prayer as long as he could remember. He always thought of a huge railroad station, bigger even than Union Station, where the souls of all the faithful departed were standing around, holding suitcases. Waiting. His father would be there soon. He looked at his father and thought, *I love you,* and tried to project the thought inside his father's head. It would not go in.

"Jay, go and get Father Clevinger a glass of water," Frank ordered.

Jay walked down the hall to the bedroom. He picked up a clean glass and filled it with water, and then he saw, sitting on the back of the tank, the glass with his father's teeth in it. He had seen them only a few times before; his father had hardly ever let anyone see him without his teeth since the gum disease had cost him his natural ones years ago. The few times he had seen them, they'd seemed to Jay to be a separate creature. He would not have been surprised if they had hopped out of the glass, clattered over to the rim of the sink and started chatting with him. They were repulsive and interesting at the same time.

It occurred to him that there was still something he could do for his father. He picked up the glass with the fizzy cleaning stuff in it. The teeth seemed to smile at him. He put the glass down. He would never have the nerve to do it, just like he would never have crashed Claire Ryan's party.

He picked up the glass again, hesitated, then plunged his fingers into the liquid and gently pulled he teeth out of the glass. They were cool and wet, like he imagined a snake would feel.

Then he picked up a washcloth, spread it on his palm, and put the teeth in the center of the washcloth. He walked carefully into the hall, where he nearly ran into Frank coming towards the bathroom.

"Jay, I asked you —" He stopped, looking at the teeth, resting like crown jewels on the washcloth. "What in the name of God are you doing?"

"He ought to have them in. It's not right that he doesn't."

"Are you out of your mind?"

"He doesn't like people to see him without them in."

"He's dying, you stupid little jerk. Don't you know that!"

"You're the jerk, Frank."

Frank made a grab for the teeth, and Jay pulled them away. The teeth slid off the washcloth and bounced when they hit the carpet, coming to rest in the center of a faded yellow daisy. They grinned up at them.

There was a sound from the bedroom; his mother's voice, half a choke, half a cry. Jay picked up the teeth and ran to the bedroom behind Frank. His mother was bending over the bed, her face against her father's hand. There were no more *P*'s coming from his father's throat.

"Lord, receive the soul of thy servant, Frank Broderick. May perpetual light shine upon him and upon the souls of all the faithful departed. Amen."

Jay walked out of the room, into the hall and down the stairs, past the empty rose-colored chair and out the door. The sun had set, and the perfection of the night stabbed at him. From a radio somewhere on the block Eddie Fisher sang "Lady of Spain."

He looked down at his father's teeth in his hands. The undertaker would need them for the wake. They shone in the starry night, accusers. He walked into the alley beside the building, kicking away the litter. He looked up at the sky and saw his father, suitcase in hand, walking towards the train station.

"I love you," he said.

His father did not turn around.

Journal: Donald A. Johnson

I am the only Negro in the creative writing class. It's a situation that seems strange to me now, since I've been working in the South with so many black people around me. I have to be careful again. Everybody will be looking at me to see if I belong.

But I'm tired of being careful. I'm not going to write what white folks want to hear, but I'm not going to hide things from them either. My father is always worried about how colored people behave when white people are looking. It's like we can be ourselves, with all our faults, only among our own. It seems we go to two extremes. Either we try to be perfect imitation whites, or we do the *Big, Black and Bad* number, shoving it right up whitey's ass. Either way, we're dancing to white people's tunes, reacting to *them.* I want to write honestly about who I am, where I come from and what I've seen.

Our professor has published three books of short stories. I've read some of them, and I think they are very good, very honest. I think I can learn a lot from her. I talked with her the other day, and she said she liked my writing samples a lot. She suggested I think about writing a book about my life. I was sort of stunned, and I said, "I'm only twenty-four years old, isn't that sort of presumptuous?" But she said I had a wonderful story about growing up Negro in America and taking part in the civil rights movement, something that will be a huge part of our history. That it's not only the leaders or the elected officials who are history, but people like me, ordinary people, who get swept up into its flow. Our lives are history too.

Our first assignment is about childhood, and I started to think about Growing Up Colored — which is Grandma Johnson's word, my father doesn't like it. He thinks *Negro* sounds more dignified, that *colored* makes people think of tenant farmers and black folks shufflin' and jivin'. It's funny, white people think we are all alike, but we get tied up in knots about what we ought to call ourselves, and we're incredibly conscious of skin color, all the subtle variants of it. There's a rhyme that used to go around our neighborhood: "If you're white, all right; if you're brown, stick around; if you're black, step back." The closer you got to white, the more pale you were, the more your features seemed like white people's — thin noses and "good" hair — the more status you had. I'm sort of medium brown, and I have good hair — which is curly but not kinky, I don't have to put straighteners on it. Grandma Johnson always used to brag about my good hair, but to me, even that wasn't good enough, not after I saw *The Yearling.*

That was my very favorite movie of all time, maybe because it was about a life that I could only imagine, in rural white America. Claude Jarman, Jr. was a boy who had a pet deer, and he also had the brightest, most golden hair I ever saw, so pale it was nearly pure white. For many months after I saw that movie I was Claude Jarman Jr. in my imagination. I even made our dog, Thunder, be my deer. I would drag him out in the backyard, and I would talk to him in my Claude Jarman, Jr., voice and pretend he was the yearling, looking up at me with big, beautiful deer eyes. Mainly Thunder just looked at me with stupidity, because in dog IQ, Thunder was somewhere between imbecile and moron. Sometimes he looked up at me and snarled, because he was not only stupid, but mean tempered as well. He always made me wonder if colored people couldn't even have brave and loyal dogs like white people had, at least in the movies. I think maybe Thunder didn't like colored folks, that was it, and if he had belonged to a nice family in Silver

Spring he would have been Lassie. But he got stuck in Northwest with a bunch of coloreds, and that made him cross.

Everybody I adopted from the movies to be in my imagination was white: Billy the Kid and John Wayne from *Flying Leathernecks* and Lash LaRue. I especially liked Lash and his way of dealing with bad guys. I cut a big piece off my mother's clothesline and went around lashing everything, including my sister, Darlene, who went crying to my mother, and Lash LaRue got grounded for three days. After that I only did it to Thunder, who snarled and ran under the porch. I got so into being these heroes that sometimes, when I'd look in the mirror, I was amazed to find this dark face staring back at me, with hair that might have been "good" but would never be Claude Jarman, Jr.'s. I remember one day I hopped on my bike and pedaled furiously, and when I got to the top of the street I looked up and said, "God, how come you didn't make me white? I'm so smart I deserve to be white."

There was a lot of talk about "passing" in my neighborhood, and it was hard to figure out what the consensus was. People who passed were sort of looked down on, because they were cheating, but anybody who could pass and didn't was thought to be a sucker. The girl in our neighborhood who was, everybody agreed, the most beautiful, could have passed in a minute. She looked a lot like the movie star Jeanne Crain. Jeanne was in a movie that everybody in the neighborhood saw and talked about for weeks, called *Pinky.* I guess it was very daring at the time, because Jeanne Crain played a schoolteacher who was colored but who could pass. She falls in love with a white man, and he wants to take her north to marry him, and no one would ever know she was colored. In the end, she decides not to pass and go north, but to stay at the colored school where she is a teacher.

My sister, Darlene, was outraged. "I think she was stupid. She could go north and have a nice boyfriend and wear lots of nice clothes and be rich and she stayed in *school*? That's really dumb." Darlene missed the racial angle completely, but the idea that anyone would choose school over almost any alternative except lynching was incomprehensible.

But Billy Williams, who was nearly sixteen, much older and more sophisticated than the rest of us, had a reasonable theory about why Jeanne Crain begged off. He said that for white people, passing was the worst crime black people could do besides raping white women and that they had a special jail where colored people who tried to pass were taken. In that jail there was a big courtyard where the "passers" were burned at the stake. We all believed it. Since you hardly ever saw any colored people in the movies, or on television — my dad had the first set on the block with a seven-inch screen — it was clear that it was very important for white people not to have colored people among them who weren't maids or railroad porters. So white people probably would support such a jail; even the nice, polite ones, like Officer Raymond, who came to our school to explain that policemen were our friends, or Miss Greer, who helped out at the school infirmary, or Mr. Carlson, the mailman who always said hello when he passed by. I thought of them all standing around in the courtyard where Jeanne Crain was tied to a post with straw piled up around her legs, the way Ingrid Bergman was in *Joan of Arc.* Miss Greer was saying, "It really is a shame, she's very good looking."

And Officer Raymond said, "Yes, and a good teacher too, but she tried to pass. Rules are rules." Mr. Carlson would light the fire and say, crossly, "This is the third one this week, and it's making me late with the mail," and they'd toast Jeanne like a marshmallow.

It was no surprise that people wanted to pass into the white world. As far as I knew — and this was true with most people in my neighborhood — the white world was a place where everything was perfect, where nobody ever had a hair out of place, where there were no dust balls (those were cleaned up instantly by the colored maid) and the main problems people had were whether Beaver would pass his test or Lucy would get a job in show business. And all white families were always wonderful, like Ozzie and Harriet. Harriet never got crabby like my mother did sometimes and nagged me to clean up my room and Ozzie never gave Ricky or David a whack, the way my father did now and then with his belt (but only when I really deserved it). And they never argued about money, the way my mother and father sometimes did; my mother wanted to save every dime and my father loved to eat out and go to a show from time to time. Sometimes he'd bark at my mother, in exasperation, "God's sake, Evie, the Depression is over, we're not living in a shantytown!" When I was really pissed at him, I imagined walking back into the house looking exactly like Ricky Nelson. They certainly would be surprised, and they'd treat me nicer. My dad would never take his belt to Ricky's white ass, of that I was sure.

It's funny, I always thought I'd grown up so insulated from what other black people had to put up with, because my neighborhood was an enclave of privileged colored people. I had thought to myself that I grew up almost white. But as I look back, I see how obsessed we were with color, how important it was to us to be *almost* white. Even though we lived in a colored neighborhood, and until I went to Gonzaga for high school I hardly ever saw a white face, we were obsessed by the white world and its culture, its standards, its prejudices. It seems that hardly a day went by that the white world didn't intrude on my life — whether I was pretending to be Claude Jarman, Jr., or being proud of my good hair or wishing I could be Ricky Nelson so I could see the look on my parents' faces when I walked in the door. *(Oh, my God, Evie, look who Donald has turned into! We'd better be nice to him!)* My father never called me Donnie, like everybody else, because he thought Donnie sounded like a colored name, but Donald had class. Even my name had to be almost white.

I wonder if I will ever get away from that. Even if we win the struggle in the South, even if we succeed in integrating the schools and getting rid of colored drinking fountains and all-white lunch counters, will I ever know exactly who I am, or will a part of me always be those images created by the white world that I can never weed out of my soul? All my life, no matter how old I get, no matter how much I accomplish, deep down, will I believe it would all have been better if I really *was* Ricky Nelson?

That is something I am going to have to think about.

SHE WAS an old pro at this White House stuff by now, having been there six times. She casually flashed the White House press card to the guard at the gate and strolled up to the West Wing entrance without her stomach muscles cramping or her hands shaking so badly she was sure everyone would notice. Sometimes she just sat and stared at her card, with her picture in color and the words *White House Press* on it. She put it on top of all the other cards in her wallet and flashed it, trying not to be too obvious, at the checkout counter when she bought the groceries. It was silly, but she did it anyway. And since the editor, Charlie Layhmer, had gotten lots of compliments on the spreads she and Jay had been doing about the famous and near famous who came to the White House, he even let them go into Washington on company time now and then. She was for real, a member of the White House Press Corps. The sense of adventure she had known as a child came flooding back. She had been a tomboy whose knees were always skinned and whose face was often begrimed with dirt. She loved climbing trees higher, faster than anyone else. Her father had gone away to the war when she was five, and for four years all she knew of him was a photograph of a tall, thin, dark-haired man in a uniform. The photograph became more real than her memories. Then suddenly he was back, and at first it was strange; her mother, who had talked so long about his return, seemed edgy and out of sorts, but that soon passed and they were a family again. Until the night a year later when her father's car skidded off an icy pavement when he was coming home from an AMVETS meeting. Four years in combat in Europe and he didn't get a scratch, but he was killed instantly when his car slammed into a tree. He went back to being only the figure in the photograph, and she and her mother to the tight little family unit they had been before.

Her father had been the owner of a small drugstore in Belvedere, so her mother sold half ownership to the man who had been running the store and went to work. Mary was in school by then, and she stayed with her aunt after school until her mother returned home. Now and then her mother had dates with men; she went out for a time with a salesman Mary didn't like much, because his fingers were stained brown from nicotine and he was fat, not at all like the slender young man in the photograph. One night she heard her mother and the salesman arguing, his voice rising in an angry rasp. "That goddamn kid, that's all you think about!" and she never saw him again. She was glad.

In school, she was dutiful and got A's, but what she liked best was after school, when she could run and climb trees. Puberty hit like a bombshell. All sorts of strange and unsavory things were happening to the sturdy little body that had served her so well. Worse, at school, girls who used to be full of interesting talk about movies and games and trading cards now only talked about boys. She thought about boys, too, but they never seemed to think about her. She didn't know how to do the stuff the other girls just seemed to inherit along with their periods — flirting and teasing and inviting.

She was bewildered by this turn of events — she would gladly have packed puberty in, who wanted periods? — but she was also mystified by the new feelings and urges she was starting to experience. She picked out the popular girls to study, but of course there was the hand-eye problem with Barbara and the allergies with Mary Jane and Becky she could only admire from afar. She looked horrible in black, and besides, dying before thirty didn't seem like much fun, especially since she expected she wouldn't get to do a lot of living before then, at the rate she was going.

By her senior year she was just coasting along, having no idea at all about what she might do with her life. The guidance counselor, Mr. Sweeney, suggested dental hygiene. He suggested that to all the girls, along with nursing school, but Mary did not find the prospect of sticking her fingers into people's mouths and getting them covered with saliva especially appealing. Mr. Sweeney didn't talk to her about college, despite her A average, because in Belvedere, only rich girls went to college, and she had no interest in nursing school.

Harry Springer came into her life as suddenly as fairy godmothers appeared in the tales her mother read to her when she was a child, and no apparition with a magic wand could have surprised her more than Harry. She had, in her usual fashion, mooned over him from afar, as did nearly every girl in the school. He was the captain and the star of the baseball team, and everyone agreed that he was "very cute."

On her dresser was the picture of him as he had been that spring, wearing a baseball uniform with the word *Belvedere* lettered in red across his chest, holding his bat high and his rump thrust out, the way Bobby Doerr used to stand. His hair was as golden as the hair of the Little Prince, in her favorite storybook. The face had not changed, essentially. The man had outgrown it. Some faces seem made for a certain age, oddly out of place at others. Harry Springer's face, round and open, was made for eighteen. On the torso that had thickened from too much beer and too little exercise, it looked misplaced. It might come into focus again at forty-five, with lines in the right places.

Harry was going steady with Sally Quigley, the first girl in the class to bleach her hair, and she'd had knockers since seventh grade. Mary agreed to go out with Pudgie Bird, who managed the baseball team, and was well liked by all the boys, because he had mastered the art of sychophancy at a tender age. She dated him only because he hung around with Harry. It was certainly not a coup to be seen with him, but at least it did not put one beyond the pale, such as dating Clifford Maylin, who had terrible acne, or George Bruno, who was a thug.

The actual dates were all right because Mary now and then got to dance with Harry and joke and talk with him. Parking afterwards was an exercise in masochism, listening to Harry and Sally sighing and moaning in the front seat while trying to keep Pudgie's fat, fast little fingers away from anything strategic.

When Sally's family moved to Detroit, Harry was heartbroken for an afternoon, and then he started to date another popular girl, and Mary and Pudgie stayed in the backseat, maneuvering.

The more impossible it seemed that Mary could ever get Harry Springer, the more desperately she wanted him. When he went off to the state All-Star game — major league scouts would be there, it was said — she reconciled herself to the inevitable. If he signed with a major league team, they would ship him off for seasoning to the minors someplace, where he would find other girls willing to share the front seat with him. The way the men in town talked, he might be the first local boy to play with the Washington Senators, and as a big league player, he would be as far out of her reach as the moon.

But Harry came back to Belvedere after the game somehow different. The talk about the Senators continued, but he no longer wanted to hear it. He asked her out, no longer immune to her adoration, which she did not even try to hide. Now she was in the front seat, and stopped maneuvering. On the fifth date he lay on top of her and unzipped his fly, and he thrust himself into her. She braced for the terrible pain of defloweration, legend in the girls' locker room. Mary Frances Conlan had actually fainted at one story of a girl who had bled to death screwing, although the worst story — believed by one and all — was of the virgin who was given Spanish fly by her boyfriend and was so overcome that she grabbed the nearest thing she could find to plunge into her lust-bedeviled body; it turned out to be a screwdriver. She died horribly, of course.

There wasn't much pain as Harry bucked up and down, but not much fun either. When he said, "How was that, babe!" she sighed, *"Wonderful,"* while she wondered, Could that be it? What they wrote all the poems about, what Romeo and Juliet died for? In the locker room, it was practically Scripture that some girls were frigid, and that they could never enjoy sex unless they went to a doctor and maybe had some kind of mysterious operation — which was not as good as Spanish fly but at least cured you of being frigid. She guessed she must be frigid but hoped she would get over it, because she was as much in love with Harry as ever.

After that, Harry dumped her. She heard stories that he had been seen at a roadhouse where the really wild kids hung out, the ones who Would Never Amount to Anything, and drank themselves senseless. Harry had been seen with an actual whore — which Mary pronounced "war" because she had seen it written but never heard it said.

As graduation neared, she was in a panic. She was a slut now, and she was in love with a man who didn't want her. No other man would want her either, because all men wanted virgins to marry, that was sacred writ in the locker room too. They felt cheated if they didn't get a virgin, and sometimes, even after many years of marriage, would throw it up in a girl's face in an argument, "You were a slut and I married you anyhow."

How could she get a man, now? Becky Bellingrath, who had a store of arcane information, said that there were people you could go to who would insert a little sac full of pigeon blood into your vagina, and on your wedding night you would bleed convincingly. But one girl had unwittingly been given blood from a sick pigeon, and when the sac burst, all the pigeon germs seeped into her body and she died a horrible death, her face contorted and screaming in pain. Or you could buy a horse. Girls were known to break their hymens in vigorous riding, so if you owned Trigger, you could say it was his fault you weren't a virgin.

Neither pigeon blood nor horses seemed a solution to Mary's problem. She was not sure how to get the former, and the latter was not practical on her street of neat little ranch houses. She was still going to her pediatrician, Dr. Adderly, and he gave her lollipops after each visit. She could not imagine herself saying to him, "Forget the lollipops, Doc, can you get some pigeon blood for my vagina?" As for Trigger, he'd hardly fit in the garage between her mother's car and the wall, and her bike was there anyhow.

She was, she realized later, a bit mad at the time. She took to waiting outside Harry's house, behind a line of trees, to see him as he came in and out. She called him on the phone, and when she heard his voice, hung up. She lived as if she were moving underwater — everything was slow and out of sync, and pain was everywhere. It hurt even to breathe.

One night, as she waited in front of his house, a car pulled up, full of boys, and Harry climbed out, laughing. As he walked not too steadily to the door, Mary ran out and grabbed his hand. She couldn't believe what she was doing; some part of her seemed to be watching from someplace else. She grabbed his hand and said, "Harry, help me. Help me!"

"Mary? What's the matter?"

"I'm pregnant. You made me pregnant, Harry. Oh, God, what am I going to do?"

His eyes glittered, bright with drink.

"Help me, Harry."

He put his arms around her. She began to weep hysterically.

"It's all right. It's all right, Mary."

He held her and wiped away her tears. She was amazed at his gentleness. She thought he would curse her or hit her.

"Don't cry. It's all right."

"What are we going to do?"

"We'll get married. We'll get married right away."

He held her and kissed away the tears. "It's all right. We'll get married."

It all happened so fast that nothing seemed real. They walked down the aisle together in First Presbyterian Church and then went to Ocean City for three days. On the wedding night she wore an absurd-looking negligee that she had gotten at her shower, which was green with ribbons on it. This time it was really sort of OK when he touched her, but very quickly he was inside her again, and once again, there was no pleasure. That was it, she was frigid for sure. But she had something worse to worry about. It was all a lie, everything was a lie, she wasn't pregnant, and he never would have married her if she weren't. What was she going to do? What the hell was the new Mrs. Harry Springer going to do?

Journal: Donald A. Johnson

Our next assignment is writing about a place we grew up in, and the impact it had on us. For me, that's easy. Growing up in Washington, D.C., does something strange to you. Maybe it's some weird kind of ray that all the marble gives off. It hits your skin, and *zap!* You're American. Branded, eternally.

I try to explain that to my friend Rafe. He's named for the angel Raphael, who wrestled with Jacob. A prophetic name. Rafe will spend his life wrestling with men and angels — and with intolerance. He will not go gentle into that good night.

Rafe is alienated from America in a way I am certain I could never be. He looks, instead, to Africa. Sometimes he even wears an African robe (I call it his bathrobe; that pisses him off), and he is studying African history. He says he may even change his name to an African one, to unburden himself of the slave name he bears in white America.

I understand what he is doing, but it's not my way. I try to think of Africa as something other than a strange, exotic place under a tropical sun, but I have trouble with that. I tell Rafe I'll never really feel at home anyplace but in the U.S., despite all the crap that floats around. (Note to me. Find another word for *crap.* It is not elegant; James Baldwin would not settle for *crap.*)

My feeling has a lot to do with my growing up where I did, and maybe being stuck with an excessively romantic temperament as well. I am a sucker for Great Dreams, and Washington is stuffed full of them, all cast in bronze and marble and stone, giving off that damn Kryptonite stuff, as powerful as the substance that makes Superman wilt.

Rafe would laugh and say they are white men's dreams, they have nothing to do with me. But I can't believe that because I grew up here, next to the monuments. I always assumed they were mine; they spoke directly to me.

I still find it hard to stand inside the great dome of the Jefferson Memorial and not be stirred to the very core by the words carved on the frieze: "I have sworn upon the altar of God, eternal hostility against every form of tyranny over the mind of man."

Because none of it — no country, no constitution — existed when Jefferson was my age. He only dreamed it, and then helped to make it happen. Where do men come from, that dream so? And if they could, so can we. That's what I try to say to Rafe, that dreams are what this country is about. And *we* can be the dreamers. We already are.

Jefferson, he said, had slaves. And even though he knew the issue of slavery would haunt the corridors of the Republic for generations to come, he let its cancer be calcified into law.

"Jefferson," he said, with that ironic grin of his, "wasn't talking to you, nigger."

But he was, even if he never meant to. I believed all the great words were meant for me, and because I thought so, they were. I read them all. "Give me liberty or give me death. Life, liberty and the pursuit of happiness." I saw them everywhere, carved, printed, etched, written. No one can tell me they're not for me and make me believe it.

Rafe answered with his Realpolitik rap — about who controls what and how the white power structure keeps us down, and it's all true. I can't argue with his analysis. It's right. It's just . . . incomplete. There's no way it can account for what I feel as I stand in the Jefferson, certain that the place is mine. Certain that there are tracks to be made in history, and that I can be a part of making them. *Entitled* to make them, because this man said what he said.

I used to ride my bike around under all that marble when I had a messenger job junior year, and I guess I got a good dose of the Kryptonite. I'm baked.

Rafe shook his head. To him, Washington is merely a city of other people's history. But it's my neighborhood. My graffiti comes from the Constitution and the Archives and the Declaration of Independence — which maybe does give you delusions of grandeur. Other people's walls read, "Marsha is a whore" or "Jersey City sucks"; mine say, "That government of the people, by the people, for the people, shall not perish from the earth." Maybe that makes you terminally patriotic.

"Just words," Rafe said. "What do they mean to me?"

I said that these words are the ultimate refutation of the white power structure he hates so much. I tell him that you can't say these words to people and not expect them to believe them. Words are more powerful than guns because they can create alternate realities. What people can imagine, they can create.

Rafe laughed and called me hopeless. but I stayed with it. "It's what we do with nonviolence," I said. "We create a different idea of who we are. We're not victims. We're not Toms. But we choose not to be violent. We resist, and a new idea is born. That we deserve the rights we are fighting for."

"We always did," Rafe said. "Whether white people believed it or not isn't important."

"Yes it is," I said, "because we didn't have the power to claim them. Now we do. We created the *idea* of ourselves as equal. And it can't be stopped."

"Maybe," Rafe said.

"It's either that, or all power comes from the barrel of a gun. And where does that get you?

Rafe grinned. "To the fucking palace, my man."

"No," I said, "then power just becomes one self-interested group killing off another."

"You've just summed up history." Rafe laughed.

I refused to argue any more. When Rafe gets into his Marxist rap he's impossible. But no one in SNCC has worked harder to make things happen. Next to Rafe, I'm a slacker. He throws himself into things, never lets up for a minute. I sort of slide in and out, emotionally. Rafe tells me I have a bourgeois soul, and he's right. It's odd, the way I grew up. It was like being inside the circle of the wagons, with the Indians out there taking potshots and whooping like crazy, but under the wagon Grandma was giving me chicken with rice soup, so I was safe. (Rafe would say there's a racist whitey image for you, all those whooping redskins.) Maybe I would have been better off growing up the way Rafe did, in the projects in Detroit, with all of it right out there raw — the poverty, the self-hate, the despair. Sometimes I wish I knew it the way Rafe does, the knife blade against the throat, the anger always glowing. I'm too middle class, I knew too much comfort. Can I ever be a writer after growing up like that?

But there's something else. I'm trying to sort all this out, and it's complicated. Rafe is much braver than I am. I've seen him look death in the eye. Not simply the idea of death, but the real thing — your brains being splattered across the sidewalk by the club that's two inches from your head. And he never flinched. He made me brave. I was more scared of Rafe thinking I was a coward than I was of the 230-pound trooper with the billy club and the roll of fat around his collar.

But there was this one day, in Alabama, when we were going to meet with some officials from the Justice Department. I went to the house where Rafe was staying, to pick him up. He was his usual jaunty self, but as he buttoned his shirt, I saw that his hands were trembling.

It hit me like I'd run into a brick wall. Rafe was *scared.* Not of some redneck who had a shotgun leveled at his crotch — that happened once and Rafe didn't blink. He was scared of some white guys from the Justice Department. Bureaucrats. GS 15's.

I'd never been much of a leader in the group. Mostly I let Rafe or the others do the talking. But that day I talked a lot. I mean, talking to middle-class white people was easy for me. Hell, I'd been doing it for years. The fathers of my friends at school were like these guys. And when I was talking to those Justice guys, as they perspired into the collars of their white shirts, I remembered the argument my mother and father had about where I would go to college.

My father wanted me to go to Howard University, his alma mater. He said I'd get a good education there, and I'd be comfortable in an all-Negro school.

My mother had gone to a Quaker college, where most of her classmates were white. She wanted me to go to George Washington University. She came to my room one day and closed the door, and she said, in that quiet way of hers, "I don't want to contradict your father. His ideas are not wrong. But, Donnie, one thing you must understand. White people are not smarter than you are."

"I know that, Momma," I said.

She sighed and was quiet for a minute. "If you do well in a world where there are white people," she said, "you will never doubt it. If you stay among your own. . . ." She was quiet again and seemed to be lost in her thoughts. Then she spoke.

"Things are going to be different for you, I believe. Your father and I, we did what we could. But doors will open for you that never opened for us. You have to be ready to walk through them, and not look back. So you see, you must know that white people have no secret. They are just like us." Then she spoke very slowly, each word sliced off and distinct: *"They have no magic."*

It was when I saw Rafe's hand tremble that I understood for the first time what my mother had said. And it was then that I felt rage, a searing, gut-piercing rage that I hadn't been able to feel even at the worst of them — the bullies, the rednicks, the stupid rabble. I wanted to grab Rafe, to shake him until his teeth rattled, screaming at him, *"They have no magic!"*

Rafe was the best of us, the smartest, the bravest, the angriest, the most compassionate. But somewhere, deep in his soul, Rafe had ingested a lethal part of the myth, the one my mother so feared. He believed that these ordinary white men, these guys mopping their brows in the heat and wanting to get the hell back to their homes in Bethesda or Silver Spring, had powers beyond his ken, that he had to be afraid. (Though I could have torn out his fingernails one by one and he'd never admit it.)

My God, I thought, as I tried not to look at Rafe's hands, this is the worst of it. The worst that white people do. It's not the dogs or the fire hoses, the layer of fear that frosts the lives of so many of the brothers and sisters. It is that white thoughts pass through the layer of our skin like gas, through our pores, our nostrils, our eyes. *They are inside our heads, where they make themselves giants.*

We did OK that day. We gained some allies at Justice, made them understand that we weren't just going to melt away, that they would have to deal with our movement. But beside the satisfaction I felt about my own performance, there was a cold lump inside me. Was it *ourselves* we had to fight most of all? Could an army of people with giants inside their heads ever make the walls come tumbling down?

I'm a sound sleeper; I was always able to drop right off, even with the tear gas still clinging to my body. Rafe says I'd sleep through Judgment Day. But that night I couldn't sleep. I walked around and around my little room, worrying about those giants. I had been so sure no one could turn us back. But now —

And then I thought of Rosa Parks. One ordinary Negro woman who said no. *No, I won't move to the back of the bus.* Not an activist, not a philosopher, just one ordinary person who said, No, no to your whole system. *No, I won't move to the back of the bus.*

How was she able to do that? From what well of strength did it come? This ordinary, middle-aged woman, and she started the whole thing, the Montgomery bus boycott, with one word. *No.* From what well of strength did that word come?

I never figured it out. But I could sleep, after that, because it was there. It was there. It was strong enough to kill the giants inside our heads. And they had to die — they *had* to — if we were ever going to be whole. If I'm a writer, can I kill them even faster than I could if I stay on the course of action? I'm good at organizing, I know that. I have the skills, I know how to talk to white people. But as a writer, can I reach much further, reach all the way across the world?

If I can, then I know the course I must follow. But what sort of talent do I really have? I read James Baldwin, and he makes me want to pack my pens and tiptoe away. He is so eloquent, he has so much anger. Mine is a different voice, thinner, smaller. But maybe I can grow. I'm only twenty-four. I hope so. Because I have promises to keep.

And miles to go before I sleep.

MARY SAT IN the third row of the State Department auditorium, waiting for John F. Kennedy to appear. She was no longer a stranger; several reporters nodded to her as she entered. She had been around long enough to be recognized, and she had been in the Oval Office. Reporters traipsed in for photo ops with heads of state or delegations from labor or the arts or boys' clubs, hoping to get a newsworthy quote from the president. They rarely did. Kennedy was too savvy to let juicy nuggets out unless he wanted them out. But now and then they'd get a quip to use in a political roundup column, or to repeat at a dinner party, thus letting their hosts marvel at their intimacy with the President of the United States. Jay was standing with the photographers, adding to his by now considerable portfolio on JFK. Charlie Layhmer liked running the pictures, because *Blade* readers were as fascinated as everyone else with the stylish young president, whether they agreed with him or not.

A door opened, and John Kennedy walked in, with his usual briskness and grace. There was something so *American* about him, Mary thought, a jaunty confidence that was somehow right for the country that had won the Second World War and now stood astride the earth like a colossus, everywhere triumphant. It was right that such a country have a president like Kennedy.

When she had gotten over simply being struck with awe at seeing the president in the flesh, she could look at him analytically. He was at his best in the press conferences, because he was so good at thinking on his feet. He had an amazing command of facts, and he was as quick with an ad-lib as many a stand-up comedian. When you read the transcript of one of his conferences, it did not seem so remarkable; you had to be there. It was the personality and the presence that made it seem so.

The New York Times asked about the possibility of pulling American advisers out of Vietnam. Kennedy said he hoped to start doing so by the end of the year, but he would have to wait and see how things went over the next few months. Reuters asked about the trade talks in Geneva, and the *LA Times* about the lease on Guantanamo Bay in Cuba. Then, with at least a dozen other reporters, Mary raised her hand and called out, "Mr. President!" not expecting to be heard. He saw her and nodded in her direction.

"Mr. President, are you going to ask Congress for new civil rights legislation, in view of recent developments in the South?"

God, she'd gotten it out, and it even sounded coherent.

He said that he was considering several new proposals, which would be decided on in a few days. Mary scribbled furiously.

"I would hope that we would be able to develop, ah, some formulas so that those who feel themselves, or who are as a matter of fact, denied legal rights, would have a remedy. As it is today, in many cases they do not have a remedy, and therefore they take to the streets and we have the kind of incident they have in Birmingham."

The next questioner said that some students in California were upset because a $1,000-a-plate dinner he was going to was displacing their prom. Kennedy grinned and said if satisfactory arrangements could not be made for the prom, he'd go to California another time.

As she and Jay walked out to the car, Mary said, "Would it be really bush to say that President Kennedy told the *Blade* he was thinking of sending new legislation on civil rights?"

"Why would it be?"

"The *Times* doesn't do it."

"We're not the *Times.* Charlie would piss in his pants to have everybody know the president answered one of his reporters' questions."

"You're sure?"

"Absolutely."

He turned out to be right. Charlie told her to write a little sidebar about asking the question, which would run with a picture of her that Jay had snapped. Several reporters even congratulated her as they gathered for the social staff meeting the editor had called.

They met, as usual, in the storage room, and its lone window had a panoramic view of the neon sign on the building next door that flashed SAHARA ROOM. The young staff members were fond of the bar's owner, Jules Galliano, because he served cheap, watered-down beer and stayed open after hours for their union organizing meetings, which went nowhere. The manner in which Jules had acquired the Sahara Room was sacred writ around the paper. It was said that he had been walking down Main Street one day when the awning on Dudley's Hardware came crashing down, striking Jules on the shoulder. Jules knew manna from heaven when he saw it, and he fell to the ground, moaning piteously. The store settled out of court, giving Jules a stake to bribe somebody to get a liquor license. It was said that he was not averse to writing a number now and then, but he never took money from *Blade* employees. Jules's dog, an irascible mongrel, had bitten Charlie Layhmer one night in a fit of pique, and Charlie had never forgiven Jules. So Jules was careful.

"Does Jules ever turn that sign off?" Sam asked Mary.

"Good Friday between twelve and three."

"Serious?"

"One year Father Carmody from St. Theresa's made a big deal that Jules had his sign on during the time of the crucifixion. Jules said that if Mr. Jesus Christ ever came to Belvedere, he'd be more at home drinking with the honest people in the Sahara Room than hanging out with some hypocritical clergymen. But he turned it off."

"The Second Coming in the Sahara Room?" Jay said. "If Christ hung around till Jules put up his dinner menu, he'd really know what they meant by 'The Last Supper.'"

Sam and Jay began to trade Jules stories, and Mary sat back in her chair and watched Jay, as she had been for the past few days, furtively. She was a woman in a man's job, and she still had to be very careful. At first she had been too eager for help, and one reporter had tutored her, but it was not long before she realized he just wanted someone to sit at his feet. When she got too good too fast, he began to criticize her and make disparaging remarks to others about her stories. After that she had asked for no help at all and tried to learn by watching, by trial and error. But Jay had sensed her uncertainty on the way to the crash and had told her what she had to know — *"This is easy. The cops or the firemen have all the information you need,"* and it turned out to be true. So maybe there were ways of taking help without admitting weakness; giving it without making a claim. Men did it. There were so many unwritten rules, rules that men knew because they were men. For her, it was like walking in a minefield.

Most of the staff had assembled, which meant Charlie Layhmer would be coming in soon. He had a fondness for entrances.

Mary looked at Jay again. He was absentmindedly doodling on a piece of paper, spirals and curlicues. She was fascinated by his hands. They were long and graceful, the hands of an artist. Suddenly she thought about those lovely, graceful, masculine hands moving to the buttons of her sweater, undoing them, sliding to the flesh beneath.

She flushed, feeling the heat rising to her face, and she stared down at her hands and hoped no one was watching her. She had to stop doing this. She found herself staring, in the car, at those long, graceful hands on the wheel, and the other day, when he had pulled off his tie and unbuttoned his collar, she'd stared transfixed at the patch of dark hair that was visible just above his undershirt. The sight had unexpectedly brought a flush of desire, and she'd looked away quickly, horrified that he might suspect. And if he didn't, Charlie Layhmer — due any minute now — surely would. Charlie was so smart, she thought, that he could read anybody's mind.

"All right everybody, listen up. Oh for heaven's sakes!" (He would stare right at her.)

"What is it? What's wrong?"

"Ah, we are having a staff meeting here, and I just wish you would stop undressing one of your fellow Blade *staff members and concentrate on the business at hand."*

"No, I'm not doing that."

"You are thinking about the penis of one of our valuable staff members. You are wondering what he would look like naked."

"Oh no, I'm not, I swear!"

"In fact, you are thinking about him wearing a black jersey and jeans, and he is taking off the jersey and you are thinking how very much you like the hair on his chest, it's just thick enough, not all over like a gorilla but not too skimpy either. Now he is taking off the jeans, and he is wearing black Jockey briefs and you are staring at the bulge he makes in his shorts."

"Oh, my God, how do you know?"

"I know everything. Now can we please get on with the meeting?"

"Oh yes, I won't think about penises anymore, I promise."

"Well, I should hope not!"

Then Charles Layhmer walked into the room. He was a small, round man with a receding hairline and a face the shape of the full moon. He looked, Mary thought, impossibly benign. It was a camouflage that enticed adversaries to recklessness. If they looked closely, they might notice a slight dilation of the nostrils, a glitter in the eye, that meant he was about to strike. Charles Layhmer approached an enemy with the sense of anticipation some men reserve for lovemaking. He cherished moronic politicians, timid bureaucrats, book-banning mothers and stupid cops. He had worked for several large papers, but they did not appreciate his talent. The big papers preferred a more tranquil breed of man.

"All right, boys and girls, we have a big one," he said. "The city council has come up with its urban renewal plan. They're going to rehab the shopping district, and that's fine. But the whole area between Maryland Avenue and Manchester Street is slated for the bulldozer, to make way for stores and garden apartments."

"But that area is where all the Negroes live," Mary said.

"By some strange coincidence, it is."

"Charlie, a lot of those places down there need to be knocked down. The houses are in terrible shape," Milt Beerman volunteered.

"That's right. But where does the city council plan to put the people who live there? In those garden apartments that start at a hundred and eighty a month?"

"They say that they can relocate everybody in existing housing," Sam said.

"That's bullshit. There's very little low-cost housing outside that area, and few people who are willing to rent to Negroes anyhow. What the council wants to do is shove Negroes out of the city and dump them on the county. This is how we do Jim Crow in the North, get people out of sight and out of mind. Reverend Johnson, down at AME Zion, says he wants to stop the whole plan unless it includes affordable housing for people who live there now."

"Don't the feds have dough for that?" Milt asked.

"Sure, but the city has to ask. And the council wants no part of it."

"That sucks," Sam said.

"I hear Joe Tarbell on the council is part owner of one of the construction firms that will make a killing. If it's true, hang him. I want everybody on this," Charlie ordered.

He handed out assignments and told Mary that he wanted her to interview people in the area slated for destruction. "Ask them if they want to move, where they'd go, how much they could afford. Take Jay with you. I want pix on that. All right, everybody out. And I don't want a big pile of overtime slips. I've got too many of those already!"

They walked together out of the building, and Jay said to her, "You know, we're all going to bust our humps, and he's going to turn down the overtime slips. He's going to take that stupid stamp of his that says DISAPPROVED, and he's going to stomp all over us."

"I know," she said. "He always does. But we do the work, don't we?"

She walked next to him, and his arm brushed against hers, sending a jolt of electricity through her. He did not appear to notice. But he seemed in no hurry, walking more slowly than usual. The spring sunshine was warm on her face, and she had a sudden thought she hadn't had for a long time, how good it was to be alive. If she could just keep on walking, her arm touching his, for a very long time, how lovely that would be. If things were different, if she were not a married woman with a child — no, that was a foolish thing to even consider. Enjoy the moment. There was no harm in that.

It was a short drive to the section of town that was called, unofficially, Niggertown. It was no different from a thousand others like it in small cities across the nation. The abandoned mower factory peered dolefully down on a street of sagging houses. The postwar prosperity that had produced a nation of split-level ranches bearing the names of colonial patriots, of shopping centers awash in an ocean of parking lots, the world of Disposalls and dryers and inlaid vinyl flooring, had not taken root in Niggertown. The warm spring air carried a curious blend of smells — new grass, smoke, the acrid scent of burning rubber. Three young children, wearing only cotton shirts and underpants, played on a plank that had been laid across an uneven puddle of muddy water. Mary walked along the street beside Jay, feeling as alien as if she had just dropped from Mars.

White children from good families in Belvedere stayed away from Niggertown as they would have stayed away from a plague ship. It was rumored that you could get anything in Niggertown, from dope to illicit sex and illegal abortions. Nice white girls who walked into Niggertown might not emerge; it was a well-known fact that black men lusted after nothing more than white women, and that Negroes in general would go to any length to slake their animalistic desires. They were, after all, much closer to the jungle than white people. In Belvedere High there was a story, believed by one and all, that a respectable white teenage girl had taken a wrong turn while driving her parents' car to the store and had been abducted by a gang of black men, taken into a house and given all sorts of drugs, after which she became mad with unnatural lust and engaged in an orgy with all the men present, for days on end. When she awakened alone and ravaged several days later in the bedroom of a deserted house, she went quite mad with the enormity of what she had done. After all, going out to the market to get some Cheetos and winding up a participant in an interracial orgy of drugs and lust could certainly dent the equanimity of the average teenager.

She was sent to an institution, where, according to legend, she repeatedly tried to kill herself by plunging anything she could find — thermometers, mop handles, the daily paper, the items varied with the imagination of the storyteller in the girls' locker room — into her vagina. (There were no end of stories of girls coming to grief as a result of peculiar things entering their sexual apertures; the Freudian symbolism was perhaps not appreciated by the eager listeners.)

The children of Niggertown had their own elementary schools, and a few of them went to Belvedere High, where they kept mainly to themselves and did not become cheerleaders or go to the prom. Though she had lived in Belvedere all her life, Mary had never walked the streets of this section of town and had driven through it only since she'd joined the newspaper staff.

They strolled along the street, and Jay paused in front of one of the houses. "How about here?"

"Fine."

They climbed the porch of the lopsided wooden house. Part of the stairs had rotted away, and Mary snagged the heel of her shoe on a loose board. The front door was open, and she rapped on the frame with her fist.

A figure materialized; a faded pink housecoat, a narrow black face dominated by a flare of nostrils. The face was lined; the dark hair was steel wool streaked with gray.

"Hello," Mary said. "We're from the *Blade.*" Her voice sounded strained and tinny to her ear. She was starting to get the hang of talking to people she didn't know who were unlike herself. "We're doing a story about urban renewal. Can we talk to you?"

"Yeah, come on in."

They walked into the dim light of the living room, and Mary looked around, cataloging the details for later use: a wrinkled green rug on a stained linoleum floor; the hole in the couch that was barely covered by a flowered throw; the metal floor lamp with no shade and, immobile as the furniture, the old man who sat on the bed by the window. He was barefoot, his large, dark feet resting on the floor. He wore trousers, a white undershirt and suspenders. She hadn't seen suspenders in years. She remembered, dimly, that her father used to wear them. The whole scene was as exotic to her as a Persian marketplace might have been.

"I'm his niece," the woman said. "I don't live here, I live in D.C., but I come up to stay with him. He don't get around so good anymore."

"Do you think the city needs public housing?"

"You move the people out of here and don't build nothing and where are they going to go? Where's he going to go? I have a houseful of family where I live, there's no room."

The change in her was startling. No longer was she placid; anger rippled through her words and seemed to crackle even in the ends of her hair. "This here's an old house. You try everything, but you can't get the bugs out. When I sleep here, I put cotton in my ears so the roaches don't get in them. But it's *his* house. They got no right to take it and give him nothing."

At the house next door, a woman sat on a drooping porch. She shoved a half-empty bottle of Jack Daniel's behind the leg of a chair as Jay and Mary approached. She was young, possessed of a fleshy prettiness that was collapsing into fat. By the side of the house a young girl with fresh, darting eyes played in an abandoned tire. The woman listened to Mary's questions, but her eyes were focused someplace else, as if she were looking at a landscape no one else could see.

"I doan want to live in no project."

"Where would you live if this house were torn down?"

"I doan know. Maybe in the country someplace. I don't want to live in no project."

Mary looked at her, quizzically. She was a board tossed on the sea; she would float wherever the current took her. Very un-Protestant. You were supposed to struggle against the elements. As you sow, so also shall you reap. But were there places where it didn't matter what you did? Where floating was survival? Could that be possible?

In another house they found a woman with broad shoulders and a laugh that rumbled like summer thunder. She was in her fifties; the house she lived in bore a fresh coat of paint and the porch was studded with new slats of wood.

"I worked in the Navy Yard in Philadelphia, and I learned a lot about carpentry," she said. She now worked in a factory thirty miles away to support herself and her two teenage daughters. Her husband was dead. He had been wounded in the invasion of Tarawa, and in the fifteen years he had lived after the war he'd had seven operations and had most of his stomach removed. Once, while he was in the hospital, she slipped carrying a tubful of laundry and was left with a permanent limp.

"I'll be glad to see the bulldozer push this old place down," she said. "I already got a new house, up on Searle Street. It cost fifteen thousand dollars. When I get it fixed up, it'll look real nice. All the houses down here are falling down. You fix' em up, and they just fall down again."

Now there was a Protestant. What was it that gave one person the will for combat while another chose to drift? Was it something you gulped with your first breath? Could it be lost, or torn out piece by bloody piece?

She asked Jay about it. "There's got to be a reason, doesn't there? What makes the difference? That woman, she should have given up long ago, with all she's been through. But she didn't. Why?"

He looked at her and shook his head. "You ask the damndest questions."

"But if we knew the answer to that, we'd know a lot, wouldn't we? I don't want to know what people do, I want to know why they do it."

"There are some questions that don't have any answers."

"No, I don't believe that. There are always answers. You just have to find them."

"Is it so important to have answers?"

"To me it is. Maybe it's because there's so much to know and I'm so far behind. I wish I could swallow an encyclopedia and know everything."

"I don't think I'd want to know everything," he said. "A lot of it I wouldn't like."

She shook her head, firmly. "It's better knowing than not knowing."

There were more houses, more brown people. In a three-story house where even the boards seemed weary, an old woman sat in a wheelchair and talked as if they were neighbors come to chat.

"That's my son," she said, pointing at a heavy, silent man frying strips of bacon on the stove. The man did not turn around. A bulb hung from the ceiling, pouring light onto walls decorated with vivid pictures of Christ, all reds and purples, a Christ with soft girl-skin and melting eyes. The woman in the wheelchair said she was seventy-one years old and she received twenty-three dollars a month from the Welfare Department for her medicine. Her son had a good job, and she had a beautiful grandchild, a baby girl. She had family, a place to live; she was blessed. She thanked the Good Lord for her good fortune. Even the seams in her skin folded into a smile. Mary was awed by her. Was she a saint, or a fool?

"My grandson has never been out of work, never. He's worked for the Sanitation Department for seven years."

Mary looked at the dark half-moon of the man's face against the light wall. His lips were dark and full. The rigid set of his shoulders was as eloquent as his silence. He had no wish for these white people to be in his house. She looked at the broad hands gripping the handle of the fork and imagined those hands gripping garbage sacks, pulling them along the ground while the flies and the sickly sweet smell of garbage circled. That smell was always associated in her mind with grown Negro men. The only Negro men she ever saw in her childhood were the garbagemen, strange creatures who even spoke in a language that was peculiar, softer, hard to hear, the ends of the words lost in a purr of sound. The Negro boys in high school rarely spoke in class, and they kept to themselves; now and then the sound of raucous laughter would erupt from the corner of the cafeteria where the Negro kids sat, but around whites they were quiet and solemn.

She suddenly felt incredibly young and ignorant. How many worlds were there, and how unknowable were they? She looked at the dark man, sensing the chasm that stretched between herself and him.

It was close to sundown by the time they finished the interviews. They drove back to the paper, and Mary typed up her notes. She took more notes than most reporters. The thickness of the pages was a security blanket. Her male colleagues simply assumed the right to put their stamp on reality, but she examined her judgments like a monk hunting down sin. As a result, she saw life as a surging mass of complexity. At first, she had been terrified of decisions, but she had come to understand that to put words down on paper was to bend time and space. Her stories were rarely brilliant, never flashy, but they were complete, and they left room for nuance, even irony.

The notes were going to take a long time. She decided not to go home for dinner but to work straight through. She had been at it for hours when something landed on her desk.

"What do you think?" Jay asked.

It was a print of the photograph he had taken earlier of the old woman in the wheelchair. The face on the glossy paper seemed so real she expected to feel the ripples when she ran her finger across it.

"Oh that's good, Jay. Really good."

"It would be hard to take a bad picture of her."

"How can she be as happy as she seems? She's old and she's poor and she can't get out of that damned wheelchair."

"She's got her family."

"Yeah, but her son picks up garbage. Nothing's going to change for them. They're going to be right there at the bottom, picking up other people's shit."

"Blessed are the poor in spirit, for they shall inherit the earth. Or was it the meek who inherit the earth? I forget which batch of losers gets it."

"You *are* a cynic."

"Yeah, from way back. Hey, if we're going to get philosophical, we might as well be drinking. Let's see what rotgut Jules is pouring tonight."

They walked across the street to the Sahara Room, where they slid into a booth and Jay ordered two Scotch-and-waters.

"We won't be able to get to the White House tomorrow, 'cause we have to go back to that slum. Jesus, that place is depressing."

"I kept half-expecting those people to grow fangs and foam at the mouth. Why did it surprise me that they're people, just like us?"

He took a swig of his drink. "People are scared of things they don't get close to. I grew up with colored kids in D.C. You didn't say *nigger* in my neighborhood, unless you said it real quiet. The people who were really uptight were the ones in Silver Spring and Bethesda. They thought people were getting mugged in front of the Library of Congress every day. People don't want to know too much. They want high walls with barbed wire on the top."

"Not me. I want to know it all."

"You're really big on that, aren't you? I never saw anybody who wanted to learn the way you do. Know what? You're horny for knowledge."

She laughed. "I guess I am, because I started so far back. When I first started, on the women's page, I was scared to talk to you guys. I was sure I'd say something stupid."

"I thought you were stuck up."

"No, terrified. I didn't go to college or anything. I was treasurer of the Class of 'fifty-six, Belvedere High School, that was it. All I'd ever done. I still think some Secret Service man is going to drag me out of the White House because I'm not a real reporter, just the treasurer of the Class of 'fifty-six."

"They'd get me too. Sergeant at arms, St. Anthony's High, Class of 'fifty-four. I only got elected because nobody could stand Barney Gretz because he had awful B.O. I was the only other candidate."

"But you were in the Army."

"Quartermaster Corps. We ordered toilet paper for Second Army."

"To me, even that sounds impressive. All I ever did was throw diapers in water and borax."

He smiled. "From borax to JFK is quite a jump."

"He really is a sexy man, isn't he? After Eisenhower, my God. I wonder if those stories about his sex life are true."

"He'd be dead if they were *all* true."

"But Catholics aren't supposed to do that stuff, are they?"

"No. That's what makes it fun."

"You don't hear those kinds of stories about Nixon."

"Right," he said. "That's because Nixon never takes his suit off. He takes baths in his suit. He fucks in his suit."

She laughed, delightedly. *"Oh, Dick, couldn't we do it just this once without our clothes on?"*

"Shut up, Pat. Keep your gloves on and don't drool on my tie."

"Take your shoes off, Dick. It hurts when you kick me in the shin when you have your, your — you know."

"Orgasm, Pat. The word's orgasm. *I can't have one without my shoes on. I'm a Republican."*

They both giggled, and she sat back in the booth as he ordered two more Scotches. The liquid and his presence across the table from her were creating a warm glow that seemed to fill the room.

"Why is JFK so sexy?" he asked her. "Every woman I know would jump in the sack with him in a minute."

"It's the eyes. They seem to look right through you. And power, of course. They say that's an aphrodisiac."

"There goes the fucking ball game. That's something I'll never have."

"Not true," she told him. "There are all kinds of power. You — shape things. Like the photo essay you did on the dump."

He looked at her blankly.

"I'd been by it a million times, and all I ever saw was a pile of trash. But in your pictures it was so sad — all those lonely and discarded things. They seemed — alive. See the power that gives you?"

He shook his head.

"You *created* that dump. It's your image that will stay in people's heads. Not what they saw, but what you made them see. You have the power to change things."

"I never exactly thought about it as power."

"But it is. You know, I used to think life just happened. Then one night I was covering the board of education, and they were going to screw up getting federal money for a program for handicapped kids because the paperwork wasn't done. I put the screwup in the lead, and it got to be a big deal, and the program got funded."

"Good for you."

She shook her head. "No. I'm not trying to say how great I was. For the first time I realized that things *are* what somebody says they are. And that night, *I* was that somebody. There are two kinds of people in the world, those that tell and those that get told."

"That's for damn sure."

"But I never knew that. I was always one of the people that got told. I think women are, a lot." She laughed, realizing that she was talking too much, made expansive by the liquor — they were on their third Scotch — and his attention. It was new to her, having someone listen. "Do I sound like I'm making a speech? But there were so many things I was supposed to think, and be, and I never asked, Who made the rules? And why? And when you start to ask, oh, that's when it gets scary!"

He nodded. "Like when you say, 'That thin guy, in the dress and the beanie, he's infallible? You got to be shitting me. And if he isn't, who is?'"

"It changes everything, once you start to ask, because then you have to make your own rules. I don't want to be one of the people who gets told anymore."

He grinned, a crooked grin that she found utterly charming. "You certainly aren't."

"Do I sound like a pompous ass? It sounds brave, but I'm scared a lot of the time. Who am I? What the hell do I know? Besides, people don't like you if you go around saying the emperor has no clothes."

"*I* like you," he said.

"Even if I am a little crazy?"

"You're not boring."

They sat in silence for a minute, enjoying the buzz of the drink and the intimacy. Then suddenly, Jay said, "Oh shit!"

"What's the matter?"

"The puppy. I was supposed to print the pictures of the fucking Puppy of the Week."

"Do you have to do it tonight?"

"I promised Milt I'd leave it for him before I left. I swear, I may go berserk one day and strangle every fucking puppy from here to Hyattsville."

They finished their drinks and walked out into the street. The lights were on in the *Blade* building and they could hear the presses humming in the bowels of the building. The night lights from the empty stores dropped pools of light onto the sidewalk, and the air was cool against their faces. They walked across the street to the parking lot. Jay stopped, suddenly, and looked up at the sky. He was tall and lanky, ungainly almost, and an unruly piece of light brown hair fell across his forehead.

"A ring around the moon," he said. "I think it's going to rain tomorrow."

"I wonder if it's an old wives' tale, about the rain?"

"No, I believe all those old turkeys. Red sky at morning, sailors take warning. It's better than the weathermen with their fucking charts." He started to walk, and then he stopped again, inhaling a gulp of the night. Then he threw back his head and laughed, a clear, warm sound that split the night around him. Mary felt her lips stretching out, the laughter bubbling up. The night air and the liquor made his elation contagious.

"Oh shit, I'm drunk," he said, and she thought that was hilarious. She had an inspiration. "Last one to the car is a rotten egg!"

He started off at a zigzag run across the lot. She ran after him, awkward in her high-heeled shoes. He was giggling drunkenly, and she passed him three feet from the car and slammed into it.

"You're a rotten egg," she gasped, and then collapsed, laughing, against the fender.

"Oh shit," he said again. He started to laugh uncontrollably and sat down on the pavement. Their laughter rolled and ebbed and burst out again. Mary's ribs ached so that she thought they might crack. When it was finally spent, they grinned at each other, stupidly. "God, we ought to know better than to slurp down the good stuff after a steady diet of Jules's beer," he said. "Too rich for the blood." He got up, slowly. "Fuck the puppy. If Milt screams, fuck Milt."

"Fuck the world," she said.

"That's right. Fuck the world!" He smiled again, the crooked smile that was so irresistible tonight.

She was still grinning as she went into the *Blade* building to get her car keys. When she came out, his car was gone. She stood for a minute, looking up at the luminous circle around the moon. The night was charged with a sense of the future, as magical and dazzling as the ring in the sky. The intensity of yearning was such that she did not know if it was pleasure or pain. She only knew she thought she would die if it went away. She stood staring at the sky for a long time, and then walked over to her car, got in it and drove away.

He leaned back in the chair at his desk and smiled. It had been one of his better performances: Cuba, the space program, disarmament — only one question, thank God, about race — and a little joke at a question by Mae Craig that brought the expected laugh. He could always get a laugh, not from scripted jokes but from a remark that came, often, from his own oblique angle of vision.

He understood irony in a way his father never had, used it as a weapon, which was very un-Irish of him. But then, he was American in a way that his father never was, in the sense that there was nothing in him of the old, dark hates and fears, the burning need to belong. Boston, with its narrow streets and its narrow minds, had never really been his home. His father, bred in those streets, had found many doors closed to him. He simply put his head down and charged, but even when he succeeded past his wildest dreams, some of those doors did not open. When the Cohasset Country Club refused him entrance, he said, "Those bigoted sons of bitches barred me because I was Irish Catholic and the son of a barkeep." He moved his family out of Boston, to places like New York and Palm Beach, and his second son grew up surrounded by contradictions.

His mother said, "Be careful. Listen to the priests, accept the limits," but his father's whole life sent the message that nothing, even religion, must interfere with ambition. Family *was a sacred word, and yet he grew up lonely, his father devoted to business and his older son, his mother to the problems of the rest of her brood. War was supposed to be glorious, but he found it veered from tedium to tragedy. He dreamed of heroes, but he became one by accident. He let the saga of his PT boat be used to get him elected, but he never thought himself a hero. He had been in love, passionately, several times, but he had seen his parents' marriage, and happily ever after seemed a sham. He had the ability to charm, but he had worked at it; a sickly child and a second son had to earn attention. Under the charm was the certainty that things were not always what they seemed and that life was not fair. After all, his brother had been golden and kissed by the gods, but death took him in an instant. His sister Kathleen, to whom he had been especially close — admiring her spirit, her independence — had seemed destined to be the most glamorous of them all. He heard of her death in a plane crash while he was listening, with a friend, to the song "How Are Things in Glocca Morra?" and he turned his head away from his friend and wept, suddenly the only one left of the three siblings some people called "the golden trio." Once, asked what he wanted, his father had blurted out, "Everything." The son knew, at an early age, that everything was not possible.*

Perhaps it was this understanding that gave him a sense of himself that his father, even at the height of his power, never had. Most people who met him marveled at it. Standing next to him, Martin Luther King envied him that presence, and of course the good looks. King, for all his magnetism, worried about his looks, his rough skin. He would have been astounded to know that the president sometimes looked in the mirror and, seeing how the steroids he took for his Addison's disease puffed out his face, was taken aback. "I don't recognize it," he said to friends. "It's not my face at all."

Lyndon Johnson was puzzled by him, tried to figure out how "this young whippersnapper, malaria ridden and yellah, sickly sickly, who never said a word of importance in the Senate and never did a thing," had moved so far in front of him. He concluded, much later, that people must have seen a dignity in John Kennedy that they liked; otherwise his ascendancy made no sense at all.

The irony, and the sense of being able to stand aside and to see himself and others at a distance, came partly from a close acquaintance with pain. To the world he presented the image of health and vigor, but like so much about him, this was invented with difficulty. In his childhood, he often escaped into that world of reading and wondering with which his family had little patience. He sometimes thought he was an alien, from some distant planet, dropped by accident into the bosom of this robust, combative band of earthlings. He learned to play and fight and run like the others, and when he could not, he learned to handle the pain with a joke, to hide his deepest fears with a quip. Some called it detachment, but only a few who knew him best understood it was his way of keeping the pain at bay. Once, hospitalized with what was thought to be leukemia, he wrote to a friend, "They are mentally measuring me for a coffin. Eat, drink and make love, as tomorrow or next week we attend my funeral."

He remembered that Ernest Hemingway had once written that life breaks people, and that some of them are stronger in the broken places, once they have healed. Perhaps it was so with him. He was a rich man's son, but that had not protected him from pain and death. Nobody in this life was protected.

Still, he was the President of the United States, and he had beaten Big Steel and had stared down Khrushchev, and there was much of the nation he had bent to his will. He trusted his own intellect and his instincts, but he knew enough not to think that the wind would always blow his way, that he would always be the master. Shakespeare said it best, he thought, in the exchange between Glendower and Hotspur in Henry IV:

Glendower: I can call spirits from the vasty deep.
Hotspur Why, so can I, or so can any man;
But will they come when you do call for them?

THE TRUCK was parked in front of the house: GUTWALD CLEANING AND DRYING: WHEN APPEARANCE COUNTS. Mary pulled her car behind it, frowning. His timing had always been terrible.

She got out of the car, and the door of the house opened and a familiar shape was framed in the lighted doorway. She would know that shape anyplace. In a world of shadows she would recognize his way of moving, shoulders down as if he were walking against the wind. She walked towards him across the lawn.

"Hi, Harry," she said.

"Hi," he said. "I was passing this way, so I dropped off your mother's coat. Thought it would save you a trip."

"Thanks. I was going to pick it up in the morning. It is a help. How are things going?"

"Good. Really good. I was telling your mother, Mr. Gutwald is planning a new branch in Frederick. He's talked to me about managing it. If it comes off. It's not definite, but it looks good."

"Harry, that's great. Just great."

"We're looking for a building. I've been spending a lot of time in Frederick. I've got a lot of ideas for the place. I've learned a lot about the business in five months. A lot."

His face was animated. Enthusiasm had always made him seem young and vulnerable. She felt her innards soften. Was it Harry, the liquor, or something else?

"The coin-op places are starting to cut in on our business. So I told Mr. Gutwald, why not beat them at their own game? Put in some machines for people who want them. That way we don't lose customers. The clothes never come out of the coin-op looking as good as they do when they're pressed. But people have to try them. Anything new."

"Sounds good. This Frederick thing, how definite is it?"

"Well, not one hundred percent. But he's sold on the idea. It was my idea, actually. We ought to be able to find a spot."

"Harry, you won't be too disappointed if it doesn't go through. I mean, you know how business is. Things don't always work out."

The enthusiasm drained from his face. She saw annoyance flicker. He erased it, with an effort. That was new.

"I know all about things that don't work out, Mare." It was his nickname for her. She said it was silly for anyone with a short name like Mary to have it shortened, but he said everyone was entitled to a nickname. "I said it wasn't a hundred percent. It looks good, that's all I said. Listen to me, Mare."

She knew their old roles. He, the balloon, floating off into some blue ether where everything would be wonderful, she the ballast, straining against the fantasies. Too many battles had unsettled her. She pounced at shadows. She would have to draw back, trust him.

"I'm sorry, Harry. That was a dumb thing to say. It sounds good; it really does."

"You were always doing that, you know. Not that I blame you. But it's not like it was. I'm not like I was."

There was something new that had crept into his voice during the past five months. She had never known strength had a sound. It came and went, and their future hung on it.

"I know. I'm sorry."

They stood facing each other on the steps.

"Well," he said, "I'd better go."

He reached out to touch her shoulder, and the touch traveled through her. In the old days, she might have reached out and touched *his* shoulder; but she leaned over and kissed him on the cheek, chastely, keeping her lips close together so the scent of the

Scotch would not drift out. She smiled at him, hoping he would read regret in her smile.

He nodded. There was no trace of anger.

"Good night, Mare."

She walked into the house and saw her mother, a woman with a round face and curly brown hair, a woman strikingly unlike her daughter. It was said around town that the widow Anderson was quite a handsome woman. In looks, Mary was her father's daughter.

"Hard day, dear?"

"Not too bad. Long."

"He's working awfully hard, isn't he?"

"Yes, he is."

"He told me he hasn't had a drink in five months. I believe him."

"So do I. It takes guts to cut it off the way he did. I never thought he could do it."

Her mother sighed. "He's complaining about his parents. But I don't want to mix in. This is between the two of you."

"Oh, God, his parents. They circle and peck, peck, peck. They drive him crazy."

"He wants to move back in."

"I know. But we agreed on a year. We'd better wait. I think I'm the problem now. I keep doing the things I used to do. Jumping on him."

"It's only natural. The laundry thing seems good. But the coaching job was a sure thing too, remember? So was the sales job. They were only sure things in his head."

"No, this is different. I get on him, his parents get on him. I just have to stop."

"You've been very patient, dear. You put up with a lot."

"Mom, you don't have to take my side all the time. I appreciate it, I really do, but I have to make some changes too. It can't all be him."

"Hi, Mommy. Can I have a glass of water?"

Mary turned around. Her daughter, her brown hair tumbling down into her eyes, the bottom half of her Doctor Dentons dangling precariously, stood in the hallway.

"Young lady, what are you doing up? It's late."

"The elephant is in my room again."

"He is? Well, we'll just have to tell that naughty old elephant to go away and let you sleep."

"He wants to sleep in my bed. He said so."

"Do you want him to"

"No. It's my bed."

"Shall I tell him that?"

"Yes, Mommy."

She picked the little girl up and carried her back to the bedroom. "Now, elephant," she said to the air, "you go home to your own bed, and let Karen sleep. No, no back talk. You go right home. That's a good elephant."

"He went home."

"Of course he did. Mommy is very good with elephants."

The little girl smiled and closed her eyes. Mary watched her, marveling at the sweet curve of her cheek against the pillow. *We did one thing right, Harry. It's a good start.* She sat and watched her daughter sleep, as always awed by the tininess, the perfection of her. "Nobody will tell you what to do or be," she said. "You can be anything you want. I promise you that." Then she kissed the child and went back into the living room. Her mother was sitting on the couch reading a book, and Mary picked up a copy of *Newsweek*. But she found herself watching her mother instead. She remembered the sound of the voices drifting up the stairs, many years ago.

"All I'm asking is for us to be alone for a weekend. A lousy weekend. I'm tired of locking doors and being so damn quiet."

"Don't you raise your voice. She'll hear you."

"Let her hear me. You hover over her like she was some kind of invalid. Let the kid out of your sight, for Chrissake."

"Don't raise your voice."

Her mother looked up and saw Mary watching her.

"Mom, what was the name of that salesman? The one who used to be around?"

"Fred? Fred Indressano?"

"Why didn't you ever marry him?"

"You needed me. I had to be mother and father to you, after Bill died."

"Did you love him?"

Her mother looked quizzical, as if she were trying to remember something vague and far away.

"I thought I did, I guess. But it wouldn't have been good for you. You didn't like him."

"I would have gotten used to him. You know how kids are."

"Well, maybe. If there had been a man who would have been good for you . . ." She shrugged and let the sentence drift off.

"But what about you?"

"I have a lovely daughter. I'm very proud of her."

Mary smiled. "You always were my best cheerleader."

"It's what women are for, Mary," she said. "Taking care of things."

"Oh, Mom, you sound like the *Ladies' Home Journal.*"

"It's true, Mary. We make it possible for the world to go on. Men could never do the things they do without us."

"But it's you who really keeps the store going. Your partner Lloyd's OK, but you're the one who really has the head for business."

"I didn't have a choice, Mary. If your father had been alive, I wouldn't have done it."

"But you're good at it. Why should women stand aside and let men do stuff they're good at?"

Her mother smiled, tolerantly. They had been through this before. "You're so much like your father. He was always impatient, wanting to get things done. You've turned into such a lovely young woman. He'd be so proud of you."

"I hope so."

Her mother laughed, remembered. "You were such a gawky teenager. You tripped over your own feet."

"You thought I'd never get a date."

"Oh no, I knew somebody would see how special you are."

Mary leaned back in her chair. "Am I special? I wonder. Am I good?"

"Mary, look at all you've accomplished. How can you say that?"

"Oh, I'm good here, in Belvedere. But out there, in the big world, would I be good enough?"

Mary saw the look of alarm in her mother's eyes, the same one she used to see when she climbed to the top of the tallest tree in the yard.

"You won that award last year, from the press association, from the whole state."

"But we weren't competing with the Washington papers. The *Post* or the *Star.*"

"You've done so much. More than any girl in your class. Why do you want more?"

"I don't know. I just do. I really feel, in here"— she put her hand on her heart —"that I'm really, really good. As good as any of them."

Her mother looked down and pursed her lips. "There are times, my dear, that I wish you weren't so smart. It's hard for a smart woman to be happy."

"Oh, Mom, that's garbage. That's just garbage. Where do you get this stuff?"

"I have lived a few years, young lady. You are book smart, but I have been around. Believe me, I know. Men can't take it when a woman is smarter than they are."

"Tough shit. They're going to have to learn."

"Mary!"

"Sorry, Mom. My language is getting awful. Hanging around the city room too much."

Upstairs, in her bedroom, the one she had shared with Harry until eight months ago, Mary sat down wearily on the edge of the bed. The Ghost of Harry Past greeted her, staring out from the gold-framed picture on the dresser. He cocked his head at her and grinned. *I'm something aren't I? I've got the whole world by the balls, and this is how it's going to be forever and ever.*

Unexpectedly, Jay materialized in her mind, standing in the parking lot with his head thrown back, laughing. She was aware of the exact locus of organs buried inside her. "The pounding of my ovaries," some French woman writer had called it — she read that in *Time.* That was biologically inexact, ovaries did not throb like kettledrums. She thought about sitting next to him as he drove, his long, slender hands on the wheel. She wondered what he would have done if she had leaned over and kissed his mouth, his warm, lovely mouth. He probably would have been so astonished he'd have run right off the road and into a tree, and they'd both have been in traction for months.

What did men like, anyhow? She had no idea. The only clues she had were the movies, and she'd tried being movie stars when she was in high school. Once, she pinned up her hair in a chignon and practiced being Grace Kelly. Grace liked ball gowns, so she wrapped the bedspread around her breasts, and she sucked in her lips in icy hauteur — which concealed, of course, a flaming passion. She stared at herself. With her lips sucked in, she looked like a flounder, not an ice princess. The bedspread was not exactly a ball gown. Pierre Balmain did not work in flowered chintz.

Marilyn Monroe was even harder. She put on a peasant blouse and hoop earrings, bent way over to show cleavage, and half-closed her eyes in a sultry come-hither look. The only person who would have come hither was a neurologist, certain she was suffering from some mysterious, wasting muscular disease.

Maybe Ava Gardner. She did, after all, look a tiny bit like Ava Gardner. Ava had a throaty, contemptuous laugh; she'd toss her head and do the Laugh, and men would fall instantly in love with her. Mary practiced her throaty, contemptuous laugh — *"Ha ha!"* — in the mirror. It wasn't half bad. She tried it out on Pudgie Bird, her perennial date, hoping it wasn't perfect, because having Pudgie in love with her would be a drag. It was bad enough when he was only interested in feeling her up. Pudgie in love would be a whirling dervish, his hands moving faster than the eye. But Pudgie had no imagination. He only asked her if she had a cough.

Ava Gardner liked bullfighters, and she imagined Ava and her lover — he dressed in his suit of lights — as he prepared to go off to the ring.

I go now to fight the bull, cara mia.

Ha-ha.

For you, my love, I will be brave.

Ha-ha.

I will cut the ears from the bull and lay them at your feet.

Ha-ha.

She wondered, when she and Jay were driving back from the White House, if she tried her Ava Gardner laugh and head toss on him, if he'd fall madly in love with her, or if he'd think she had a cough.

What if she were not a married woman, hypothetically, what would she do to attract him? She had noticed that he looked, discreetly, at her breasts now and then. She liked her breasts. They were full and gently sloping, larger than one would expect on such a slender frame. But she had never learned to use them the way Barbara Brownlee used hers, always putting them out there, so to speak. She was terrible at being obvious, worse at being subtle.

She was most comfortable with being direct, so hypothetically, maybe the best thing to do was just be direct. They'd be riding along, and she'd take them out and point them at him and say, "Well, here they are; they aren't huge knockers, but they are kind of nice. So, do you like them or not?"

She sighed. This was all very peculiar for a woman who had long ago decided she was frigid.

It was no wonder, of course, that her honeymoon had been a disaster, since she was so terrified of not being knocked up, like she was supposed to be. But even afterwards, there was some pleasure in what went before doing it, but the main event was always unsatisfying. She went to the library one day and snuck some books off the shelves — she would have been mortified to walk up to the librarian with *Sexuality in Females* in her hand. What she read was very instructive. There were good kinds of orgasms and bad ones, and that surprised her. Except for the gossip about sluts and the horror stories in the locker room, girls at Belvedere High did not talk about the details of sex. Movies were not much help either. Cary Grant and Grace Kelly might get as far as an openmouthed kiss, but after that you got fireworks or two raindrops trickling down a window or a blazing hearth. In fact, the most specific conversation about sex she could recall was when she was eight; it had been with Evelyn Morell, who lived next door, who was eleven and very advanced.

Evelyn said to her one day, "When people get married, the man sticks his *thing* into the lady."

"He does not!" Mary protested.

"Does too. That's how babies come."

"Babies come," Mary said haughtily, "from seeds. The man grows seeds, and the mommy eats them, and that's how babies get in her stomach."

That was her version of what her mother had told her. It made sense. Men had gardens — like the victory gardens people planted to help the war effort — but instead of sprouting peas and lettuce, the men's gardens grew plants with little seeds on them shaped like tiny boys and girls. When the mommy and daddy decided to have a baby, they went out and picked the right seed. She had imagined a tiny version of herself, hanging from a leaf, waiting patiently to get ingested.

But Evelyn was adamant. "No, he puts his thing in her and the baby is very, very, very little, and he crawls out of the man's thing into the mommy's tummy."

"He doesn't. What if the man pees? Then the baby would drown."

A cloud passed over Evelyn's face. She had not considered this snag in her theory. Then her face brightened again.

"Maybe the little, little babies, know how to swim," she said.

Poring over the library book, reading about vaginal versus clitoral orgasms — the latter were "immature" the book said — Mary thought she would be happy with either one. Now and then, in bed with Harry, she'd think she was on the verge of something wonderful, but it never quite happened. She looked up *frigidity* in the library book, which said it had something to do with Oedipus, which was strange, because she remembered from Classics I that Oedipus was blind and married his mother. She was not blind and certainly had never considered marrying her mother.

She decided that frigidity was something that affected a certain percentage of the population, like color blindness, and she would have to live with it as her deep, dark secret. But she kept on reading the library book, and was more than a bit shocked at what it said, very clinically, that some people liked to do. There was bondage, rubber undies, and diapers, which had not been mentioned in the girls' locker room. It was too bad, she thought with a tinge of regret, that she hadn't read this book when she was in high school and come armed with this knowledge to the locker room. Mary Francis Conlan would not just have fainted, she would have died on the spot at the mention of rubber didies.

Bondage, however, sounded intriguing. For some reason, she thought of her old neighbors, Mr. and Mrs. Pritchard, as the type who would be attracted to bondage. She pictured Mrs. Pritchard, still wearing her round wire glasses, tied naked to a post in the Pritchards' garage, next to the place where Mr. Pritchard kept the hoses and fertilizer, her considerable bulk obscuring most of the post. Mr. Pritchard, pale and skinny, would also be naked, and he'd be tickling Mrs. Pritchard with the whisk broom he kept in the glove compartment of his Plymouth. They seemed to be having a wonderful time.

But of course she'd never have the nerve to ask Harry to tie her up. Harry was very exact about what was proper and what was not. Once, when she had moved her lips down his body — the library book also said something about that — his voice had been cold and hard. "Don't do that! That's what whores do!" And she had been terribly ashamed and never tried anything unusual again. Most times she just lay quietly under him until the bucking stopped, and she'd give out a long, deep sigh of pseudocontentment. If he knew it was counterfeit, he never let on, and she assumed this was how it was with men and women — except for whores, of course, but they didn't count.

But now, unbidden, Jay Broderick was there, calling forth newly familiar sensations. A voice in her head said, again, No, this is wrong, but what could be wrong with thoughts? No one would ever know; Charlie couldn't really read minds. How could it hurt?

She climbed into bed, having decided to let her thoughts wander where they would, and there he was, in the black jersey and jeans.

She undressed him, gently; the things she had never seen were graphic in her imaginations — the taut line of his belly, the mat of hair on his chest, his genitals. She was the aggressor. He watched as she kissed, rubbed, touched and delighted him. His maleness surrounded her, intoxicated her. A male body had never gripped her this way before, and she surrendered to the image. The memory of Jay was bright, and fresh and real; she felt his weight pressing down on her, flowing into her until he filled every part of her, and once again she seemed on the edge of something very wonderful, and she was trembling all over. This *had* to be wrong.

The room suddenly seemed unbearably warm, and she threw the covers off. She was tired but energized, and knew she would not sleep. She got out of bed, walked to the dresser and picked up Harry Past in the metal frame.

Somehow, she'd managed to get through the wedding and the honeymoon, and she and Harry had moved into a small house — this one — they had bought using the money his parents had given them as a down payment. Through his father, Harry got a job in Greenway's Shoe Emporium. The pay was good, but he hated the work, squatting down and pulling off people's shoes. Meanwhile Mary, living in a state of rising panic, gulped down Phillips' milk of magnesia to calm her churning stomach. She read that tension could prevent conception, and that only made her more agitated. He kept asking if she shouldn't be going to the doctor.

"No, it's too early. I'll go later."

"Is it OK for us to be doing it? Now that you're pregnant?"

"Oh yes, it's fine."

At the end of the month her period had not come. She went to the doctor, and he did a test, and a day later he called to give her congratulations. She hung up the phone, laughing and crying until she was near hysteria. Two months later, she miscarried.

Harry embraced her tenderly in the hospital and said, "Don't cry; we'll have another baby. I'll give you another baby, I promise." But her womb lay empty and cold as a glacier. Perfidy had killed her baby; a lie lived at the heart of her life. She fell into a deep depression and looked at the doctor dully when he said, "This is normal in cases like this. It will pass." She wanted to laugh. It was God's judgment, and did that ever pass? She took the tranquilizers. She wanted to confess to Harry but didn't dare. The lie sat in her innards like a great mass of tumor, malignant and growing. There was nothing to do but live with it.

The more Harry worked at the shoe store, the more he hated it. The job was not the golden life he had believed would be his. He could not scream at his customers, so he screamed at his wife, and he started going out with his old drinking buddies. But despite Mary's certainty that God was punishing her, she got pregnant again. That, she thought, was very strange. Could God have missed her? As He did His savage arithmetic on punishing sinners, could He have misplaced the page with her name on it? *Where did that go? I know it was around here someplace. Goddamn it!*

A daughter, Karen Amy, was born the following year. Harry was marvelous with Karen. He loved to pick her up, swing her around and hold her against his chest in wonderment. "Look at what we made, Mary! God, can you believe it? We did this!"

For a time life was good, and Mary was content. This was what life as a woman was about: a loving husband, a baby she adored. But even fatherhood could not extinguish the growing rage in Harry about his lost glory. When Greenway's folded, a victim of a national recession that hit small cities especially hard, Harry was promised a coaching job at the high school, which seemed a lot more fun than the shoe store. But the funds were cut and the job never materialized. When nothing in town opened up, he prowled the retail stores in Silver Spring and Bethesda, but a bumper crop of high school students had been there before him. The federal government had jobs for janitors and secretaries, but he wouldn't do the former and couldn't do the latter. He took the civil service exam and failed it because his grammar and math were atrocious. No one had worried when he got C's and D's in high school, when he was the captain of the baseball team.

By the time he had been out of work for five months, things were terrible between them. He spent too much time out with his friends drinking, and she didn't know what to do but nag, and after a while, she stopped caring about how she looked or how the house looked. She started taking the pills again.

"This place is a pigpen. You don't do anything all day, you could at least keep the place neat."

"So you're up. It's only noon. I suppose you want breakfast."

"I'll go out and eat. Who wants to stay in this mess?"

"You could help out. You haven't got anything to do but lie around."

"For your information, I have an interview today. A sporting goods store. Right up my alley."

"You still smell of booze. Who's going to hire somebody who stinks?"

Even when they tried to be nice to each other, it ended up in a fight.

"I am trying, Mary, I really am."

"I know, Harry, maybe — maybe we ought to move. To D.C., maybe it would be better."

"We've got the house here, we can't afford to move."

"What about the coaching job?"

"Nothing's moving there."

"You have to follow up on these things. You'll never get anything if you don't follow up."

"What do you know? Have you ever tried to make a damn nickel in your life? It's hard out there."

"I know if I'd been out of work for five months I wouldn't be drinking myself into a stupor every night and sleeping till noon."

Their sex life dissolved into nothingness, between his booze and her pills and, once again, her growing panic.

"You're not always asleep when I come in. You just pretend to be."

"Yes, I pretend. You go with whores, you smell of booze. So I pretend."

"Who told you that?"

"You think you're invisible, Harry? People love to gossip. They love to come up and tell me you're sleeping with some pig!"

"Shut your mouth!"

"It's true, isn't it?"

"It's true. You don't want me. So I buy it. You think I'm a goddamn monk?"

"That's not fair!"

"There's a goddamn judge inside you, Mary, always waiting to see when I'll screw up again. You watch me with those goddamn eyes of yours. I know what they say. I don't measure up. I'm not a man. Well, I was man enough to marry you when you got knocked up. You might remember that!"

"Harry, please, let's not fight . . ."

"Jesus, let me out of here. I feel like I'm choking in this damn house. And you can go to hell!"

One day, when she was talking with another woman at the supermarket, Mary heard there were openings for typists at the new newspaper in town. Her mother said that she could arrange her hours so she could take care of Karen while Mary worked. Harry was not enthusiastic, but finally he agreed.

"What am I, some bum who has to let his wife support him?"

"Plenty of wives work these days. I can make seventy-five dollars a week. At least we can keep up with the mortgage, until you get a job."

"Hell, go take the job if you want to, I don't care. I'll have a job pretty soon. And it won't be for any crummy seventy-five bucks a week, either."

The job at the *Blade,* tedious as it was, burned off the torpor that Mary had fallen into at home. She no longer took the pills or complained of headaches. Suddenly she had lots of energy, and when one of the proofreaders was taken ill, Mary filled in for her. English had been her best subject, and she had a firm command of grammar and spelling. She was given the job permanently, with a raise in pay. Reporters started checking in with her not only on spelling but with local geography and history, and she often caught errors that had slipped by editors in the city room.

In high school, she had held a minor position on the school paper and had thought idly about being a journalist, but that had seemed impossible for a girl from Belvedere. When she first came to work as a typist, she'd looked at the reporters with awe. They seemed giants, possessed of some magical conduit between their brains and the tips of their fingers, through which words flowed onto the paper. When she began to correct their spelling and grammar, they shrank to mortal size. Soon she was reading their copy critically and rewriting their stories in her head. She checked out every book on journalism she could find in the library and read them avidly.

As she read, something very peculiar happened; the boundaries of the world began to expand; she was pushing them outward, the way she moved the metal slats on her typewriter to get more words on a line. A sudden hunger for life came upon her, so urgent that it sometimes seemed to make even the bones of her hands vibrate. Where on earth did it come from? Everybody said that a woman's creativity was purged with the creation of a child, that any woman who wasn't satisfied with that was not a real woman at all. Maybe that was her problem. God, first she was frigid and now she was ambitious. What was wrong with her? Sigmund Freud would be appalled.

A classic case, students, of Oedipal fixation and penis envy. Her inability to have vaginal orgasms —

Dr. Freud, sir, I can't have orgasms of any kind.

— to have orgasms of any kind is due to a misplaced and abnormal fixation on her father —

Dr. Freud, my father died when I was six.

— to an unnatural fixation on the memory of her father, from whom she never separated adequately.

Sir, I separated pretty good. He's fucking dead.

Watch your language!

Sorry.

— from the idea of her father, and his loss has created a psychic wound that will never heal, and she has been unable to transfer to her husband her sexual yearnings.

Sir, I try. I really do, but maybe some of it's his fault?

She is unable to sublimate herself to her husband, seeking instead gratification through naturally male activities, such as employment.

We couldn't pay the mortgage. We were going to lose the house.

— a clear example of penis envy and how if it is not dealt with by psychiatry, it will make her an unhappy, unfulfilled, neurotic, woman.

OK, so she was a freak, a mismade woman. It didn't matter. Ambition claimed her; there was nothing she could do about it.

One day she got a notice in the mail that her favorite English teacher in high school had been teaching for thirty years, and there was going to be a party for her. Mary had loved her Shakespeare class. The teacher had turned the strange, old-sounding words on the page into passion and poetry. Billy Sampson might have been snapping Barbara Brownlee's bra, and Joey Motherwell been carving rude words into his desk with a paper clip, but Mary sat transfixed, lost utterly in a Danish castle where a tormented son saw the ghost of his father.

On her night off, after she had fed Karen and put her to bed, she drove over to the teacher's house, and they talked for three hours, about teaching and Shakespeare and literature in America. Mary took careful notes; then she drove home and worked at the kitchen table until dawn, writing in longhand. Then she typed three drafts on the old Remington her mother had bought her for typing class. She was too exhausted to do more. It seemed a poor, threadbare story. There were patches she liked, where the woman came alive, but they seemed so few. Despair gnawed at her. She was a fool; she had imposed on a friend for nothing.

You see, students, that penis envy is not a substitute for talent.

She started towards Charlie Layhmer's office three times, and three times she backed away. She was trembling when she walked through the door on the fourth try.

"I don't care if I get paid or anything, Mr. Layhmer. If you think it's good enough to stick in someplace, fine, but if it's no good, say so, don't be polite."

He read the story while she waited; now her legs were shaking. She was light-headed with her own daring, awaiting sentence with a mixture of fear and dread.

My dear, these are things that men do, you should go and just find some man you can subordinate yourself to . . . Why did Charlie Layhmer look exactly like Sigmund Freud?

Charlie Layhmer looked up at her in surprise, appraisal in his eyes. He liked surprises. They made the days bearable.

"I'm going to run this as the lead in the women's section tomorrow. You've got a nice touch."

He gave her five dollars for the story and said she should write others. She walked out of his office and went directly out the door, to the small park behind the *Blade* building. She wanted to scream, to whoop, but she was too inhibited for that. So she ran around and around in a little circle laughing, then fell to the ground laughing some more and lay flat on her back. A woman passing by stared in disapproval, assuming she was drunk. Finally, she allowed herself a very small whoop. Then she picked herself up and walked back into the building, knowing that her life had suddenly veered off in an unexpected direction.

The story appeared the next day, with her name, and under it the words *Contributing Journalist.* She stared at it, ran her hands over it, transfixed. Had there ever been words so glorious in the history of the world? Never. There it was in glorious black and white, nothing could undo it, nothing.

Of course, students, I could be wrong about this penis envy thing.

At long last, she knew who she was. Mary Springer.

Journalist.

Journal: Donald A. Johnson

We are supposed to write about the fears or prejudices of our childhood. My essay, I'm sure, will be different from the others in the class, because they are white. They are going to write about how they encountered a member of a despised group, perhaps how they came to the understanding that the people they were taught to hate were not so bad after all. But I am not a member of the dominant group, so I have a somewhat skewed take on the issue. Those white kids will never imagine a world that floats in space above them, one which they will never be privileged to enter, and one which must be so wonderful that it makes your own life seem tawdry and dull beside it. I expect they cannot imagine such a thing. But I can. Oh, yes, I can.

The red convertible is seared into my brain cells, its color as fiery and tantalizing as the day I first saw it. It was old and dented, and the muffler must have been peppered with holes, because the roar sounded like an airplane engine. But it was as red as fire engines, as blood, and it was going sixty or better.

"Damned fools," my father muttered, as the convertible sailed by us. Inside were six Negro men — I saw them as men, but I guess they were barely out of their teens — wearing bright-colored Hawaiian shirts and men's hats scrunched far down on their heads so as not to be ripped away by the wind. A car radio blared a raucous rhythm-and-blues song, and beer cans were held aloft like banners.

My father frowned, but I — oh, I was enchanted. *That* was freedom — a red convertible going sixty, beer, music, wild shirts and men's hats. Oh, how I wanted to grow up!

My father's frown was echoed, I knew, in the other cars on the one-lane highway that wound through the Maryland countryside, loaded with kids and inner tubes and picnic baskets. White fathers would certainly mutter, "Damned crazy niggers!" and their offspring would peer through the open windows of backseats at the disappearing convertible as they might at the elephants at the National Zoo, to see exotic and mysterious creatures pass by.

I, meanwhile, was gripped by a mysterious schizophrenia. While I desperately wanted to be in that red convertible, I was also seized, even at my young age, with a responsibility for my race. I instinctively knew that such behavior, exhilarating though it might be for the individual, was bad for us as a whole. What one Negro did reflected on all of us. White kids could skylark around in convertibles and there would be no consequences to Caucasianhood proper. But in my family, at least, we knew the rules. One must be *A Credit to Our Race.* I always thought of it that way; and I was sure red convertibles were not a part of it. We could be *A Credit to Our Race* by knocking out hulking German fighters or sliding hard into second base, but those were about the only fun ways to do it, and how many of us could be Joe Louis or Jackie Robinson? Mainly, we had to be boring and polite and get good grades.

But such thoughts did not occupy me for long. We were on our way to Sparrows Beach, and soon I would be floating in my inner tube in the warm, brackish water, keeping a wary eye out for any U-boats that might venture past, happy with the world and my place in it.

Sparrows was *our* beach. The other cars, with the whites in them, would turn off on the roads to Scientists Cliffs or Mayo Beach or Beverly Beach. They were for whites only. Sparrows Beach was for Negroes, and every Saturday on hot summer days we were on the road before eight for the thirty-mile ride to Chesapeake Bay, a trek we shared with at least a third of the residents of Washington, D.C., or so it seemed on the jammed and winding road.

My mother packed the lunch — ham-and-cheese sandwiches on white bread lathered with mayonnaise or chicken salad creamy with mayo that crunched with little bits of celery. My parents were second-generation Washingtonians and proud of it, and we ate what most middle-class Americans ate. (I mean, it was really very strange; we were exactly like the white people in the cars that were all around us, but they didn't know that.)

My mother, of course, was in charge of making sure we didn't starve on the trek to the beach. She knew that spoilt mayonnaise could kill; but without it the sandwiches tasted like cardboard, so it was a necessary evil. My mother kept a sharp eye on the hamper, putting it in the shade and checking it every so often as anxiously as she would a sick child. She watched me and Darlene as we ate our sandwiches, a flicker of fear in her dark brown eyes. Despite the ice, and the wax paper, had lethal bacteria stolen between the two pieces of Wonder bread?

The result of this was that I was probably the only kid in America who had mayonnaise nightmares. It was mortifying. What a stupid thing to be afraid of. Snakes or demons or witches were respectable terrors, but how could I tell my parents I had mayonnaise nightmares? In them, I inadvertently ingested rancid Hellmann's, and I fell to the ground, mortally wounded by mayonnaise. My eyes bulged from my sockets, my tongue grew black and swelled to fill my throat, my stomach burst like a balloon at a birthday party. My mother sobbed, and the other adults stood sadly by and watched my death throes.

"Should have been more careful with the mayonnaise," said our neighbor, Mr. Williams, as I groaned and thrashed and croaked; with my tongue the size of a sneaker, that was the only sound I could make. It was at that point that I would wake, soaked with sweat.

Occasionally the nightmares would have an added feature, jellyfish. At Sparrows Beach, there were nets to keep out the millions of jellyfish that spawned and bloomed in the bay, especially in August. Sometimes I would float right up to the edge of the nets in my inner tube, to mock them, packed in quivering masses on the other side.

"Die, you suckers," I would snarl at them. In their fury, they would hurl themselves at the nets, which always held, as a shiver of danger curled up my spine. But they could not get to the tender brown flesh that swam in the safety of the enclosed areas. Now and then, one or two would sneak by, and they could give a nasty sting with their tentacles. Then a parent would fish the offending creature out of the water with a stick, leaving it gasping on the beach.

But some nights the jellyfish would take their revenge on the child who taunted them. They would surge past the nets in a great, gooey mass to the shore, to rise up on millions of little gelatinous legs they had miraculously sprouted, and come marching straight towards me. They would hurl their yucky, slimy bodies on top of me and begin to ingest my flesh. They would eat it, inch by inch, smacking their gooey lips with each tender brown morsel as I shrieked and shrieked.

Mr. Williams would look on sadly and say, "You just got to be careful around jellyfish."

But nightmares aside, there were no happier times of my childhood than those I spent at Sparrows Beach. Sometimes I would paddle my inner tube out as far as I could and peer curiously at the shoreline on a far curve of the bay where Beverly Beach was. I strained my eyes, but all I ever saw was the line of trees near the edge of the shore. So I imagined the details: sand as white as a swan's throat, azure water like the pools Esther Williams swam through at Saturday matinees. Heaven, I used to imagine, was acres and acres of those pools — whose waters could instantly turn to violet or green or red and sprout mermaids in gold lamé — filled with colored people, backstroking. Never mind that, as far as I could tell, no black bodies were ever allowed to frolic with Esther. But they did let Ricardo Montalban in the water, and at last he was swarthy, which was close.

There had to be something wonderful about those white beaches, since white people were so careful to guard them from us. Why would they bother to put up signs and posts with chains across them simply to protect the same brown sand and brackish water and jellyfish that *we* had? How they kept the jellyfish away I was not certain. Maybe it was a death ray, or mind control, or something mysterious. White people could probably do death rays, if they put their minds to it. Ah, what places they must be! Beverly Beach was more exotic to me than Xanadu could have been.

But then I grew up, and mostly forgot about all that. When I learned to drive, my friends in high school — and later in college — and I would head for the ocean beaches on the Eastern Shore. There were some cottages glad to have us, and there was too much ocean to be fenced off, and the water was blue and bracing, not tepid and greenish brown.

So I was surprised, one day during my junior year in college, when I found myself driving that winding road that led to the Chesapeake shore. It was a bleak November day, I'd had it with studying, and I just got in my car and headed off down the road, aimlessly, I thought. I kept going down that familiar road, passing landmarks long forgotten, and then, suddenly, I saw it. At first I thought there must be some mistake. When I was a kid, the ride had seemed to take forever. How could I be here so soon? But there it was, the sign I had passed so many times: Beverly Beach.

I turned down the road, feeling a strange throbbing in a corner of my neck and a dryness in my throat. There was no one around, but the feel of danger once again curled up my spine. I soon reached the parking lot. There was no one in the wooden ticket booth, and no chain barred the way. I parked the car and walked the few yards to the place where the straggly grass disappeared and the sand began. Then I walked across that sandy strip and looked at the water. It was brown.

I squatted down by the edge of the water and stuck my hand in it. It was greenish brown and cool — but not yet chill — to the touch. A dead beetle floated by, and I looked out at the water. The posts that held the jellyfish nets stood faithfully on guard, awaiting another August.

To my amazement, all I felt was sad. And more than a bit cheated. All that fantasy. All that white energy spent on keeping us out, and this was *it*? Just another brown spit of sand on the bay, no different than Sparrows Beach? Esther Williams wouldn't have stuck a pink toe in this water. No white sand. No death rays.

It should have been better. It should have been *wonderful.* All that time I'd wasted, imagining.

I drove back to school, knowing that a piece of my childhood had vanished as surely as the jellyfish from the bay in October. I had the sense that I should have been constructing great notions in my head, about the banality of prejudice and the illusion of power, but I just felt — sad. I wanted my money back. I wanted the magic, even though it wasn't time.

At long last, I had come to face to face with my Xanadu: Beverly Beach. And it was not at all what I had imagined.

HARRY SPRINGER gripped the wheel, his mood swaying between righteous anger and self-abasement. Was it so much he asked? She was his wife, dammit! What was he asking? To touch her, to hold her, get rid of the emptiness inside that seemed to stretch across a distance greater than the Argentine pampas. Not that he knew a hell of a lot about the pampas, but it was the one thing he remembered from geography; ever since the fifth grade it was the image he had used for *vast.* Who was she, the goddamn Supreme Court? He thought, abruptly, of how good it would be to drive out to Barneys, see some of the guys, have a beer. One beer, what the hell could it do?

I am an alcoholic. I will always be an alcoholic.

How many times had he said that in the AA meetings? He fought against the words, at first. No, he wasn't really a drunk, not really. Just a young guy who got mixed up, lost his job. Only one beer.

I am an alcoholic.

One beer would mean two, and he'd be on the floor by midnight. It had been "one beer" the night he'd gotten so tanked up that he ended in the city lockup and lost even the crummy job in the grocery store bagging produce. One more episode like that and it was finis, all she wrote, babe. All that agony, the hard slogging of the past eight months, just to wind up on the floor at Barneys? Fuck that.

She was right, he hadn't proved himself yet. Anybody could climb on the wagon for a few months. Four more months — it stretched ahead of him, like the pampas. No, think of it one day at a time, that way it wouldn't seem so long.

He laughed ruefully to himself. He was waiting. Hot damn, that was something new. He had always wanted everything right away, thought he deserved it. Marge, the old broad in the AA group, called his drinking one little boy's massive temper tantrum. Foul-mouthed old broad, but she had something.

Jesus, growing up was hard, especially at twenty-five. Why didn't anyone ever tell him how hard it was? It was one of those secrets they kept from you, like sex. You had to learn it by doing, so of course you got it wrong.

But he was doing it. He would show her he could do it. Her approval was a beam of light ahead, towards which he was moving. Sometimes he thought it was the only thing that kept him going, a fucking star in the East. Why was it so important? He didn't know. He only knew it was, and that was it.

I am an alcoholic.

He thought about Klein, the skinny hebe pitcher. He wondered what ever happened to Klein. He never made it to the bigs. Had he ever tried? Did Klein know what it was like to be crawling in his own vomit on the floor of a drunk tank? He thought about Klein a lot, the kid who had one hell of a curveball and threw it right through Harry Springer's life.

Harry had gone off to the All-State game in his senior year certain that the big league scouts in the stands would be looking for him. That was what all the smart guys in town were saying, nobody like him in the league for twenty years. Harry Springer, bonus baby — it sounded good to the ears. He'd have to fight the broads off.

The first time he came to bat in the game, Klein threw him a curveball he couldn't even see, much less hit. He missed the ball by two inches. He'd never seen a curveball like that. How could that skinny hebe throw so good? And even *he* wasn't good enough for the big leagues. With each pitch, the bigs grew dimmer and dimmer. In the small regional league the Belvedere Blades played in, Harry Springer was a standout. But he'd never seen kids who could play like this.

"You wanted to be DiMaggio," Marge, the old broad said. "I wanted to be Jean Harlow. We ain't none of us stars, kids, we're drunks. Maybe because we wanted things we couldn't have. You got to take it one day at a time, and get the fucking stars out of your eyes."

"They're gone, Marge." The last one went out the night he hit bottom, crawling around on the cement floor, crying and heaving while an old drunk kept hitting him on the back. They all thought he was finished when that happened, even his parents. They wrote him off: boy drunk. They were wrong. He wasn't ready to pack it in yet. Fuck it, he'd show them all.

He turned the wheel in the direction of his parents' house.

Mary walked into the city room and saw Jay at the desk cropping a set of pictures. She walked over, sat on the edge of his desk and clutched her raincoat close to her body.

"Dick, guess what I have on under my good Republican cloth coat."

He looked up. *"What, Pat?"*

"Black panties and a peekaboo bra."

"For Chrissake, Pat, you want people to think we're Democrats or something?"

"Look, Dick, I'm so horny I'm gong to do it with Checkers."

"Checkers is dead."

"He's in the freezer. And he's a hell of a lot livelier than you."

They both cracked up. Dick and Pat had become their own private little joke. Sam Bernstein looked at them and shook his head.

"Too bad Nixon didn't win. You could have taken that act on the road."

"Yeah," Jay said. "Too bad. Dick Nixon is one guy we'll never hear from again."

"That's a shame," Sam said. "I liked the way Herblock did his five o'clock shadow. 'Would you buy a used car from this man?'"

"Anybody thirsty?" Jay asked. "How about we hit the Sahara Room?"

"I got to finish an overnight," Sam said. "You guys go on. I'll catch you later."

Jay and Mary walked across the street and slid into a booth.

"We're getting a hell of a reaction on the urban renewal story," Jay told her. "Charlie's been on the phone all day."

I wonder if Charlie knows what he's stirred up."

"What do you mean?"

"Things are coming out of the woodwork. My mother is getting it from a lot of people because they saw my byline."

"What kind of things?"

"How come your daughter is helping that Jew bring a lot more Niggers into town?"

"That Jew? Charlie? He's a Unitarian."

"I know, but people see bylines like Bernstein, Speigel, Rosenberg, and they get ideas. Some people say the *Blade* is a *Jewspaper.*"

"What's the local viewpoint on Irish Catholics?"

"You didn't see this place go for Kennedy. Irish Catholics are drunks who want to sell the country to the Vatican."

"Jeez, this is a bigoted place."

"Like most, I guess. But I think that we've really picked up a rock and a lot of things are going to crawl out. Especially if the Negroes organize to fight the plan like they're talking about doing."

"Do you think they have a prayer?"

"With the paper against the plan? Maybe. But there's going to be a fight."

"I wouldn't mind a little action. You know, if I thought I could keep body and soul together, I'd go down South and get some shots of the civil rights marchers."

"Could you make it, freelancing?"

"It's hard. Especially when you haven't got a name. This is my first real job as a photographer, not counting the Army. I think I've got to get more experience before I go out on my own. Or maybe I'm just chicken."

"What's your dream job?"

"That's easy. *Life.* I want to be another Capa. Mydans, Eisenstaedt. I want to be really, really good. But I'll be thirty in a couple of years, and those guys were already famous by then. In this job, you have to make it young, you have to hustle. I got started late. I may never catch up."

"I know that feeling."

"I don't want to end up like Pete Franklin, hanging around a small paper, shooting crap, doing weddings on the side. I think most people end up never getting to do what they want. Who was the guy who said that most men lead lives of quiet desperation? Boy, was that sucker right."

"Do you think that's really true?"

"You bet your ass I do. In my family, we had a fucking monopoly on quiet desperation. My father drove a cab and died at forty-eight from bad kidneys. He was a smart man too; he said if he'd gone to college maybe he could have been a professor, or a lawyer. He just lived and died and nothing ever happened to him."

"But you're so good, Jay. Everybody says so."

"You think life's like Sunday school? You're good and you get a gold star on your forehead? There's a thousand photographers who are good, and they all have a head start on me."

"So you think life's a jungle?"

"You bet it is. Don't let anybody tell you different."

"To me it's like fourth grade. I keep thinking I have to put my hand up and ask for things. This job, it's like a present that I think somebody's going to come and take back. I don't feel like I'm . . . entitled to it. Some days, anyway. Other days, I feel like I'm hot shit."

He laughed. "Keep thinking that. Have it tattooed on your chest: 'I Am Hot Shit.'"

"You know what, we ought to have a secret club, like we used to do when we were kids. The Hot Shit Society. And we'll keep on telling each other how great we are."

"Good idea. Give me your hand."

She extended her hand, palm up.

"I should spit on it. That's what we used to do to seal a bargain."

"Yuck. Isn't there some other way?"

"Yeah." He raised her palm to his lips and kissed it. "You are now a Hot Shit, for the rest of your life."

She picked up his hand, turned it over and kissed his palm. "I dub thee Hot Shit."

"Hey Pat, if you do it in the freezer with Checkers, can I watch?"

"You're sick, Dick. Sick, sick, sick."

"You're screwing a dead cocker spaniel, and I'm the one who's sick?"

"OK, you can watch, but only if you don't wear your suit."

"You're a hard woman, Pat."

"Take it or leave it."

"OK, OK, but I'm keeping my shoes on."

The group of students had traipsed in to give him a plaque; he had forgotten what for, he got so many of the damn things. He usually forgot them five minutes after they had left, but in this group there had been a girl — he nearly gasped audibly when she walked in, her honey-colored hair swinging gently with the motion of her body.

Kathleen.

The resemblance was so eerie that he was still thinking about her hours later. It figured, with only a few basic elements to work with, that a number of human beings who were totally unrelated would end up looking exactly like each other. Still, it was unnerving.

She had died a long time ago, but she lived on in his mind, radiant as ever. She had been the only rebel in a family overpowered by a father's iron dream. Her older brother became the perfect surrogate, groomed, like a fine racehorse, to carry the family colors. But Kathleen rebelled, against her church, her mother and the requirements of a dynasty in the making. She had said it would be a relief not to be a Kennedy anymore when she married, because there were enough of those as it was.

She had seemed to carry sunlight with her; all of his friends fell in love with her. The man who was her first innocent love spoke for all of them when he wrote her obituary: "Bright, pretty, quick, vivid, filled with ever bubbling enthusiasm, eager, eager to learn everything. . . . Kathleen. Little Kathleen. Where have you gone?"

If his brother was a shield, deflecting his father's ambitions, his sister was a guide to finding an independent path. She married a member of the British aristocracy despite her mother's objections. When he died in battle, she fell in love with a married man who was divorcing his wife, and when her mother said she would declare her dead and no more a member of the family, she decided she would marry him anyway, and not go to talk to a bishop about it. "Really, it's my life," she said. She was with him when a small plane crashed against a mountainside in a storm, killing them both instantly.

Her brother could see her face, still, with its heart shape and the Fitzgerald jaw, and the honey-colored hair glinting in the sunlight of a British country lane. When he had visited her that last summer in England, she had confided in him that she had found her Rhett Butler, a man who could carry her away, make her laugh and cry, the sort of passion she had never expected to find. And the hidden romantic in him had envied her. She could lose herself in love, risk everything for it, in a way he never could.

And when she died, something in him, too, was stripped away. He had lost his best friend, the one person to whom he could talk of his doubts about God, and even about his father. When they were teenagers, after parties she would come into his bedroom, wrapped in her bathrobe, and they would talk and gossip and giggle for hours. A friend who saw them together thought them so much alike they should have been twins; they acted like twins, together.

After she died, for a time he had almost longed for death; he seemed to promise Kathleen and Joe that soon he would be dead too. He was unable to concentrate. Sitting at a congressional hearing, he would find himself suddenly back in time, laughing, dancing, walking down a country road, with Kathleen. He found it was better when he took some girl he hardly knew to his bed, because he could imagine that she was a friend of Kathleen's, and in the morning they would all be together, laughing, joking, Kathleen with a beau and he with a girl, the way it always had been. Finally, he decided he had to live, and if he did, he would burn brightly, fiercely, live as if each day were his last. If death could come at any time, to anyone, then you had to take what you could.

He wondered, sometimes, what his life would have been if his brother and sister had not died. He would not, assuredly, be president, and he liked being president very much. But what of that other life, the one he would have chosen for himself, that was not to be?

Perhaps there would be time for that later. He would be a young man, barely into his fifties, at the end of a second term. Perhaps he would buy a newspaper, or write a syndicated column. He suspected that he would have been a journalist if fate had not intervened. How odd it would be if it turned out that he could have all of it, his father's dream and his own independent life.

Was God so capricious that he gave Joe and Kathleen everything — beauty, charm, health, love — and then took it all away, while he gave their brother sickness and loneliness, and then showered him with all that should have been theirs? Was God a jester? A sadist? Or merely an observer. His mother firmly believed that God was just and fair.

He was not so sure.

THE TELEPHONE on her desk jangled, and Mary picked it up.

"Mary Springer, please," said a crisp male voice.

"Speaking."

"This is the White House Press Office. If you can come by this afternoon, we can do your picture with the president."

"Sure," she said, trying to sound offhand. "What time do you want me?"

"At four. The Oval Office."

She put the phone down and made a strange sound, something like a squeak. She was, after all, a member of the White House Press Corps. A shriek would not be professional. She got up, her heart pounding. She was going to meet with the president, in the Oval Office! She went home and changed her clothes four times before deciding on the right outfit: the silk blouse and the tailored skirt with the beige shoes, not too severe, speaking of a crisp — but not unattractive — competence.

She drove into Washington, singing off-key all the way in. She could hardly believe it. She, Mary Anderson Springer, was on her way to a rendezvous with destiny. (Wrong president, but the right thought.) She wanted to leap out of the car when she stopped at red lights, and pound on the windows of adjacent automobiles and tell them she was on the way to the White House to chat with John F. Kennedy. They would doubtless regard her as daft. But Jay was off on assignment, Milt was out sick and Charlie was at the Rotary lunch, so she hadn't even been able to crow a bit.

When she walked into the West Wing, Mac Kilduff, the assistant press secretary, greeted her and ushered her into the Oval Office. Kennedy was seated at his desk, and he rose and walked over to her. She wondered if it was proper for the president to get up for a civilian. She felt the proper protocol might be for her to fall facedown on the rug, but after all, he wasn't Allah, just the president.

He extended his hand, a grin on his face. "Always a pleasure to see the *Belvedere Blade,*" he said. The mischief was there, in his eyes. He was teasing her, but she didn't mind. The *Belvedere Blade* was hardly a shining light of the media elite. But John Kennedy — and his press people — knew that there were hundreds of small papers, and taken together they had millions of readers. The Press Office had set up a program whereby their Washington representatives could come in and get their pictures taken with the president by a White House photographer. Each picture would appear — usually quite large — in the hometown paper and would generate no end of goodwill on the part of the newspaper and its reporter. The *Times* and the *Post* men might sneer at such obvious press agentry, but the reporters who toiled in relative obscurity for papers in Terre Haute and Salt Lake City and Belvedere, Maryland, who never got to be on *Meet the Press* or *Face the Nation*, were delighted with the whole idea.

"The photographer will be here in a minute," the president said. "Want a cup of tea? It's a fresh pot."

"Yes, thank you," she said, barely believing that she was going to be sitting in the Oval Office, having a cup of tea with John F. Kennedy. If he had said, "Want a cup of camel piss?" she would have said, "Yes, thank you."

He motioned for her to sit in a chair next to his rocker, where he settled as a maid brought in two cups of tea. She sat down and, without thinking, crossed her legs. After she did it, she wondered if it were the proper thing to do. (She rather liked her legs. They were long and slim, and with the short skirt in fashion these days, and the high heels, they could draw a man's eye. They did. He looked. She thought, Oh, my God, the leader of the Free World is staring at my legs!

"You're young to be covering the White House," he said. "Did you study journalism in college?"

"No," she said. "I never went to college. I worked my way up from typist."

He looked at her, appraisingly. "That's very good. How did you manage that?"

"I sort of brazened it out. I wrote a story and took it to the editor, and he liked it. So I got hired."

He laughed. "Once I wrote a story and took it to my father and it got printed. He was the ambassador to England. Your way was harder."

She grinned at him. He had a way of poking fun at himself without losing his sense of dignity. "I guess it was," she said.

"So, how am I doing in Belvedere?"

"Everybody loves reading about you. And your family. When we run pictures of Caroline and John, the papers always sell out right away. It's always the best-read page in the paper."

"Umm. How about my civil rights bill?"

"Well," she said, "that's another story." She told him, briefly, about the housing battle. He listened intently, taking it all in. When he focused his attention on you, it was as if nothing else in the world existed for him, and you felt you were saying the most important words that could be said. She could not help thinking, as she talked, how handsome he was. It was not so much the perfection of his features, which were even but unremarkable, but somehow, when he listened there was a seriousness so intense it was compelling, and when he smiled, or looked at you with those remarkable blue eyes, there was an aura that set him apart from ordinary people. Of course, she realized, part of it was the setting. The Oval Office and the flags and the naval painting gave out the crisp clean scent of power. But it was more as well. The ease with which he seemed to inhabit his own skin was infectious. Even now, despite the setting, she felt perfectly relaxed and at ease chatting with him. It was his doing, not hers. And, she observed, he had a lovely mouth, playful lips, quick to stretch into a smile.

The photographer came in and snapped several pictures of them as they were intent on their conversation. Then the president rose, and she got up too, and he walked with her towards the door.

"Do me a favor, *Belvedere Blade,*" he said.

"What?" she asked, surprised that he would ask for something from her.

"Talk to me from time to time. Tell me what they're thinking in Belvedere. I'm cooped up in this place, and sometimes I need somebody to tell me the truth. Only that. Not what I want to hear. The truth."

She nodded. "I'll do that."

Driving home, she thought about that request. It had never occurred to her that the president might need someone to give him correct information. At his command were all the powers of land and sea, a mighty navy, an army that made the legions of Rome seem puny, a network of global communications that stretched from seas to mountaintops and broad plains. Tons of information, oceans of it, poured from across the planet into the tiny end point of the Oval Office.

But she knew, too, that people had a motive to shape that information into a form pleasing to the ear of the man who sat in the office. People liked to tell powerful men what they wanted to hear. Careers hung on that fact. She saw it even in the microcosm of the *Blade,* where reporters rushed to Charlie with good news, but when the news was bad, they either kept it to themselves or tried to shape it in a way that would at least keep the teller in a good light. Yes, it was easy to see why a president would need people — even unimportant people like herself — to tell him the plain, unvarnished truth.

She had noticed, of course, that he had looked at her legs several times. It was a practiced male glance — not a leer or a furtive peek, not something calculated to make her uncomfortable. It was just — there. She wondered, idly, what it would be like to kiss that lovely, playful mouth. Quite nice, she thought. The president would not be one to stick his tongue right in a person's mouth without so much as a by-your-leave. He might get around to it eventually, but he had manners and would work up to it, she thought.

What if she were not a respectable married woman, and had wished — like so many other women undoubtedly did — to arouse the libido of the president? What would she have done? Would she have put down the cup of tea, unbuttoned her new silk blouse, and used the same phrase she'd imagined for Jan: "Well, here they are; they aren't huge knockers, but they are kind of nice. So, do you like them or not?"

What would he have done? Would he have been horrified? or simply have gotten up from his rocker and jumped on her, right in the Oval Office. And what would that have been like?

As she pulled up to the turn at the corner of Thirteenth and Piney Branch Road, she realized, with sudden horror, what she had been thinking about. Good God, her slide into degradation had been rapid! The Reverend Mr. Swiggins had been right; even a few evil thoughts could drag one down into the pit of unspeakable depravity. A few days ago she was undressing Jay Broderick, fantasizing about his penis, and now, great heavens, she was thinking about kissing the mouth that had said, "Ask not what your country can do for you," and flashing her tits in the Oval Office. Charlie Layhmer would be *truly* horrified this time.

"Oh, my God, you've gone from undressing a staff member of the *Blade* to the President of the United States, the commander in chief! This is probably treason."

"No, it was me who was undressing, he was just sitting there."

"Humping on the rug in the Oval Office is just sitting there?"

"Do you really think it's treason?"

"Let's ask J. Edgar Hoover."

So there she'd be, again, in the White House basement, with J. Edgar wielding the rubber hose. The president would walk by, and he'd say, "Edgar, what did she do this time?"

"Sir, she had a sexual fantasy about the President of the United States. Clearly a felony."

"About me? What was it?"

"It was only a short one, sir," she would say apologetically.

"She flashed her tits in your office, Mr. President. With the flag in full view."

"They are very nice ones, Edgar. Do you want to do it again, Belvedere Blade?"

"Yes sir, if you'd like.

"Mr. President, remember the dignity of the office! Hail to the Chief! God Bless America! The bombs bursting in air!"

"Oh, Edgar, you're such a spoilsport," the president would say. And he would sigh, regretfully.

"Sorry, kid, I tried. I like tits, but I guess Edgar's right. We just can't have them flashing about willy-nilly, can we?"

When the pictures arrived a few days later, in a plain brown manila envelope with the words WHITE HOUSE printed in the upper-left-hand corner, she ripped it open eagerly. There were two eight-by-ten glossies. In one, she had her mouth open like a guppy, disgusting, but in the other she was speaking with a properly serious look on her face, and he was listening intently. She took it into Charlie Layhmer's office, but not before deliberately wiping from her mind any images of boobs or penises, presidential or otherwise.

He looked at the pictures, and his whole face brightened. He knew, of course, that it was all set up by the Press Office, but it would be a conversation piece at the next Rotary lunch. He would let it slip, casually, of course, that the *Blade* had a special relationship with the White House, and JFK chatted with its reporters on a regular basis (and, if they were to infer with its editor as well, he would not disabuse them of the notion. The next time he pissed one of them off, they might remember that they were talking to a man with powerful connections and not threaten to pull their ads).

"We'll run this three columns, front page," he said. "Write a story on what you talked about."

She went back to her desk and tried to write the story without making it too self-inflating. As she struggled, one of the pictures whooshed away from under her nose. She looked up. Jay was examining it closely.

"Hey, impressive, you and the president." He looked closer. "There's a speck of dust on the print. Mine never have those."

"You can get a picture of yourself with JFK, too," she said. "Sign up in the Press Office."

"I'm not a reporter. Just a photographer."

"I don't think that matters."

"Yeah, I think I'd like one of those. I'll send a copy to Father Hannigan. Inscribed. 'You thought I'd never amount to anything, you old fart. Up yours. Affectionately, your former student.'"

When the picture ran, Charlie had copies of it laminated so he could hand it out to everybody who stopped by the paper. He mailed copies of it to the advertisers, and he ran it in a full-page house ad for the newspaper which suggested that, along with the *Post,* and *Times* and the *Herald Tribune,* JFK ingested the *Belvedere Blade* over his morning coffee. She began to realize that she needn't have worried about Charlie being a mind reader. If he'd had an actual picture of herself and JFK humping on the Oval Office rug, he wouldn't have been horrified at all. He'd have run it *four* columns with the caption "Belvedere Blade has close ties with President Kennedy." Milt would have made them airbrush out her tits, of course. It was a family newspaper.

She did look at the picture more often than was seemly. She kept a copy of the house ad in her bottom drawer, so she could pull it out and look down at it without anyone else in the city room knowing what she was doing. She could still hardly believe it; there she was talking to the most important man in the world, and he was listening.

But she did remember what he had asked her. "Talk to me from time to time. Tell me the truth."

She looked at the picture, and she made him a promise. That was the least she could do after committing treason.

"I will," she said. "I'll tell you the truth."

THE JUKEBOX in the Sahara Room played "Ebb Tide"; it usually did on Saturday nights, since that was one of three songs you could dance to. Saturday nights the kids from the junior college invaded, pushing the regulars to the bar or to booths in the corner.

Sam Bernstein sipped his Scotch and looked at Jay. "Not a bad crowd tonight. The college girls are starting to look good."

"Keep thinking statutory rape."

"Right now I think twenty years in Sing Sing might be worth it."

Jay sipped his beer. "So how come you aren't in D.C. this weekend?"

"I got a lot of stuff to do on the urban renewal coverage. Things are really popping."

"Yeah, I'm going to shoot the meeting at AME Zion tomorrow night."

"Hey, Jay, see that one over there? The blond? She looks like she might be at least nineteen."

Jay looked. "Seventeen, not a day more."

"She's cute."

"Cute? Yeah, they're all cute. But they're so goddamn young. They don't even remember Tom Dewey, for Chrissake."

"This is your criterion for an acceptable woman?" Sam asked. "That she remember Tom Dewey?"

"Or Alger Hiss. I'm not picky."

"Great pickup line. 'Hey, babe, come to my place and we'll talk about Alger Hiss.'"

"My only other one is 'Wanna fuck?' Alger Hiss is classier."

"So how did you stand on Joe McCarthy?"

"I prayed for him a lot."

"You did what?"

"He was practically a saint at St. Anthony's High. Every morning after the Our Father we said 'And God bless Senator McCarthy.'"

"You were praying for Tail-Gunner Joe?"

"What did I know? They told us he was going to get the Commies. Commies torture Catholics and make them renounce their faith."

"Joe Stalin had a purge in Northwest Washington?"

"They had me believing it."

Sam got up, and Jay watched the young girls and boys, dancing with their cheeks pressed together. The sight depressed him. He traced the swirling pattern of the Formica table with his forefinger, wishing he had a dollar for every night he had spent like this, drinking in a bar and thinking maybe he'd pick up some girl. He thought, inexplicably, about Debra Paget, with whom he had been in love for about five years — before his taste got refined and he started thinking about Jacqueline and her white gloves. He had seen every forgettable movie Debra Paget had ever made, epics in which she wore a sarong or a toga and spoke her lines with the sincerity of a realtor selling underwater lots in Florida. He fell in love with her bee-stung lips, but even more with her shoulders, which were small and round and achingly vulnerable. It was dumb to fall in love with shoulders — everybody else lusted after boobs. Debra Paget's boobs were very nice — the parts that hung out of the togas, at any rate — but it was the shoulders that got to him. Debra Paget, where was she now? Probably married to a Texas oilman, a great, vulgar hulk of a man who bought her pearls and humped her on satin sheets, the small shoulders pinned under a chest curved like a barrel, sprouting coarse hair the color of sand. Sweet Debra. Life was cruel.

He smiled to himself, thinking of the agony of loving Debra Paget.

He'd had the most amazing fantasy life from early on, and Debra had been a big part of it. She was a near occasion of sin for him, no doubt about that. He had thought himself the world's biggest lecher. Walking to confession, he left a visible trail of filth behind him like the contrail of a jet. Of course he always guessed wrong and got the booth with Father Hannigan.

"Bless me, Father, for I have sinned. My last confession was two weeks ago. I, ah, I cheated on my math test. I disobeyed my mother two times. I, ah, had impure thoughts seventeen times."

"What kind of thoughts?"

Cough. "About — girls."

"And were these thoughts followed by impure actions?"

Swallow. "Yes, Father."

"Alone or with others."

"Alone."

"You touched yourself in an impure manner?"

Cough. "Yes, Father."

"Causing your seed to be spilled on the ground?"

"Not on the ground, exactly."

"The sin of Onan. God gave you a temple, your body, and you defiled it. Hands, the same hands that make the sign of the cross, touching your sexual organs and defiling the temple."

"I'm sorry, Father."

"You drive another thorn into the flesh of Christ with your impurity. And if you cannot think of the agony you are causing Christ, think of the men who have been driven insane by such acts. They sit, in hospital wards, never to see the light of day again. Do you wish that to happen to you?"

"No, Father."

"Make an act of contrition."

"Oh, my God, I am heartily sorry, for having offended thee . . ."

He was chained to a wall, in the insane asylum, next to an ax murderer and a paranoid schizophrenic. The hair growing on his palms was even longer than Rita Hayworth's flowing locks. The doctor and the nurse came by on rounds. They stopped in front of the ax murderer.

"He's looking pretty good, Nurse."

"Yes, we've rehabilitated him. In a few days he's going home. We don't think he'll do it again, but just in case, we took the carving knives out of the drawer."

They moved on to the schizo.

"He's doing well, too, Doctor. He had a hundred and thirty-seven personalities, and now it's down to three. They can go home, too."

"And this one? The self-abuser?"

"Oh, I'm afraid he's a lifer. Sad, isn't it? He was an altar boy once. Masturbation is such a tragedy."

"No, I promise," he screamed. "I'll never do it again, never!"

"He says that all the time"— the nurse sighed —"but of course, it's incurable. He'd do it with anything: bedsheets, the morning paper, even once with a holy card."

"No!" the doctor said.

"It was disgusting. Semen all over St. Christopher, on his halo, and even a few drops on the Christ child's little white dress."

"No, that was a mistake. I was doing it in bed and the holy card — it was in my Latin book, and it slipped out —"

"Oh, he was quite insatiable. He would go into the boys' room and do it, and he'd keep his mouth closed tight so he wouldn't make any nose, and he'd do it in the shower, and once he did it in a bus, under his raincoat, and at the Sylvan Theater, during Pagan Love Song *while Esther Williams was swimming. He once did it while listening to* The Rosary Hour *on the radio."*

"My God, what a monster."

"Yes, and when he finally went berserk, it was in the middle of trigonometry class, when he looked at his hands and saw the hair sprouting on his palms. He started to scream and scream, and Brother Benedict said to the class, "You see, boys, what happens when you play with yourself the way Satan wants you to? Now finish the trig problem on page twenty-three while we take him to the insane asylum."

There was no time that he could remember, no one moment, when he stopped believing it. He just knew, now, that he could not believe that God would send people to hell for eating meat on Friday or using a rubber or masturbating — even during *The Rosary Hour.* But Catholicism had left a residue, thin and sticky as varnish, of guilt.

"I love you."

But his father never heard, never knew.

Not loving enough isn't a sin.

Yes, it is. It's the worst one.

He was, he thought, like Lot's wife, turned to a pillar of salt. Something in him had been crippled, calcified. The power to love had been forbidden to him. Sometimes he sensed the capacity for it inside, a subterranean river he had never been able to reach. He would always turn aside, run away, from anyone who asked him to love. He always had.

"I love you, Jay. Please give me a chance. I can make you happy. I know I can."

He could still see her, standing on the dance floor in the enlisted men's club, wearing the wide felt skirt, a good style for girls with hips, pleading with him. And all he could hear was a voice inside himself saying, I don't want to love her.

Her name was Marilyn Krebbs; she had chunky thighs but a pretty face and nice eyes. He had met her at a mixer at the club, and she took him home to meet her parents, who fed him and were kind to him, treating him like a son. Marilyn yielded, button by button, in the backseat of a borrowed car, and finally went all the way in her parents' parlor one night when they'd been at an American Legion social. This went on for three years, until Marilyn told him that her parents had saved up a thousand dollars for a wedding present. He looked at her and thought of waking up next to her every morning for the rest of his life, seeing the round face and the plump shoulders that were not at all like Debra Paget's, and he stopped calling her and wouldn't return her phone calls. He made the mistake of going to the club again one night, and she was there. She came up to him on the dance floor, her eyes bright with pain and shame, and begged him not to leave her. He tried to get away.

"Don't do this, Marilyn."

"Give me a chance, Jay, please!"

"You'll meet somebody. Better than me."

"I don't want anybody else. I love you."

"No, you don't. You don't love me."

"I do. I do love you!"

She took his hands and put them on her breasts, and he yanked them away and said, "For God's sakes, Marilyn!"

"I'll always love you!"

He walked away from her, because he couldn't think of anything else to do. To blot out the memory of her eyes, he went on a fucking spree, coupling with women who lived on the periphery of the base — waitresses, bar girls, even the wife of a captain who was bored and lonely. It seemed absurd, after a while.

"Jay, there's somebody who wants to meet you."

He looked up. Sam had a pretty young girl, with a cascade of chestnut hair, in tow.

"Ann Smithton. She's a fan of yours."

"I've seen your pictures. It must be exciting, your job."

"Sometimes it is."

She slid into the booth beside him. "What do you take pictures of, mostly?"

"Murders. Birds. Worthy Matrons of the Eastern Star."

"Did you ever take pictures of anyone famous? Like the president?"

"Yeah."

"Oh, how exciting. Where?"

"At the White House."

He could see she wanted to talk to him, but his laconic answers discouraged her. A young man came up to the booth and motioned towards the dance floor, and she looked at Jay. He stared at his drink. She got up to dance with the young man.

Jay traced the swirling pattern of the table with his finger again.

You are now a Hot Shit, for the rest of your life.

Her palm had felt cool and soft beneath his lips. The gesture had been, to him, shockingly intimate, not what he had intended. It seemed more erotic, somehow, than the image of her naked on the bed. Once again, the thought of her eased him, filled him with quiet. He sat, staring at the table, letting her fill his thoughts.

Sam slid into the booth. "You muffed it, Jay. That click really had the hots for you. Cute, too."

Jay shrugged. "Didn't know Alger Hiss. Too bad."

"I'm going to order another round."

"Not for me, I got to get up early and print some stuff."

"You and Mary have really been churning it out. You like working with her?"

"Yeah, I do. Jeez, she's bright. She's got one of those kinds of minds, closes in on the target, like a laser."

"Knows Tom Dewey isn't an expressway."

Jay looked at Sam. "No, it's not like that, I just . . . like working with her."

"She's separated from her husband, you know."

He felt, for an instant, the breath catch in his throat. "Some months now, I understand. He drinks."

"Oh," Jay said,

"You guys from the *Blade*?"

Jay looked up. A middle-aged man, beer in hand, was standing by the edge of the booth.

"Yeah," Sam said.

"Nigger-loving bastards."

"You got a beef," Sam told him, "write a letter to the editor."

"Nigger-loving cocksuckers."

"You have to admit," Jay said to Sam, "his vocabulary is impressive." He said to the man, "Look, pal, we're not bothering you. Why don't you go back and sit down?"

"Nigger-loving Jew bastards."

Jay saw Sam's fists clench. He reached over and put his hand on Sam's. "Come on, he's just a drunk. Don't pay any attention to him."

"Jewboy."

"You want to step outside and say that?" Sam had half-risen in his seat.

"Oh shit!" Jay said. He pulled out a bill and tossed it down on the table. "We're leaving," he said to Sam. "Now."

"Dirty Jews," the man said again. Sam grabbed the man's arm, but Jay pulled him away.

"That's what we don't need," he said. "You on page one for assault and battery." He bragged Sam across the floor to the door.

Outside, Sam took a deep breath and said, "You should have let me clobber him."

"This is just starting. You're not going to be able to punch out every guy that makes a crack."

"Doesn't take long for the Jew stuff to pop out, does it?"

"Right after the nigger stuff. Come on, we're going home."

"What a night. I'm still horny and I didn't get to put out the lights of a guy who said 'Dirty Jew.'"

"Nigger-loving Jew bastard, to be exact."

"Maybe I'll hit you."

"You can hit me, but you're going to have to stay horny. That good a friend I'm not."

"Just as well," Sam said. "My mother would kill me for fucking an Irish Catholic."

It was oppressively hot in the laundry, as usual. The dryers generated so much heat it was impossible to keep the place cool, especially on a warm night. Harry walked to the machine that had been repaired, checked the circuits. It looked OK. He had gotten good with these machines; it wouldn't be long before he could repair them himself. He closed the back panel. The smell of detergent curled into his nose — God, he hated that smell.

The scent lingered in his nostrils, tickling the small hairs and making him want to sneeze. He tried to sneeze but couldn't, nearly gagged. The sensation triggered a panic inside him. Was this where he would spend his life? In this hot, damp room, with the fluorescent light bouncing off the garish yellow of the machines, smelling the stink of bleach and Tide? Had it all shrunk down to this?

They used to do a special cheer for him, each girl with a red and a white pom-pom, spelling out his name a letter at a time, waving the red pom-poms, the people in the stands picking up the cry until it seemed to fill the air itself; other towns went mad for football, but in Belvedere baseball was the game, and he was the best in twenty years. They told him that.

They promised him specialness; he *was* special, then. He had felt it, and carried with him a certain pity for ordinary boys. Everyone had conspired to make him feel that way — the girls with the pompoms, the sports columnists who wrote about him as if he were Ty Cobb, not only a high school athlete, the men who clapped him on the shoulder to relive a double play, touching him as if the feel of his flesh could peel back the years and bring them face to face with their own lost youth. They lied. They all lied. He was never special. He just thought so.

He tried to tell the other members of the AA group what it had been like to feel special. None of them could understand, because none of them had experienced it. It was so real, he said, he had this specialness inside and he knew it would never go away. It was like a part of him, an arm or a leg. And Marge, the old broad, had said, "High school ain't life, kid."

But nobody had ever told him that. If he hadn't felt so special, if he couldn't remember exactly what it felt like, his life now wouldn't be so bad. It was the loss that was unbearable.

Suddenly he hated them all, for lying to him. He hated them with a fury he didn't know he owned; hated his father, who had puffed up like some tropical fish when everyone loved his son but backed off when he stumbled. Even his father couldn't forgive him for not being special anymore.

There was a basket filled with bras and panties on top of one of the machines, and he grabbed the basket and began to hurl its contents piece by piece around the room, cursing them for not telling the truth.

"Damn you! Damn you to hell! Damn your fucking souls to hell!"

When the basket was empty, he threw that, too, and it hit one of the machines and skidded across the floor. He looked at the room; the bras lay scattered across the floor and the tops of the machines, looking like small, dead birds that had fallen from the sky. He stood and looked at them, the tears rolling silently down his cheeks.

He went and picked up the basket, and wiped his face with his forearm. He stooped and picked up the bras and panties one by one and put them back in the basket, neatly folded. He put the basket where it had been, on top of the machine. Then he turned out the light, opened the door, locked it and walked, slowly, out to his car.

ST. JOHN'S AME Zion Church was a white wooden structure, built in the manner of small-town Protestant churches everywhere, except that it ended abruptly where the steeple should have been. Unhappily, the building fund had run dry in midconstruction. The absence of the steeple gave the church an aborted look. There was no railing beside the cement steps and no handsome, glass-encased sign to let the faithful know of the events and the sermon topic of the week. St. John's was the church of the Belvedere Negroes, and it was here that many of them had been baptized and married and would receive a last blessing over their coffins.

Jay walked into the church and looked around. The pews were carved up and chipped from years of use, and exposed metal pipes hung below the ceiling; a strip of flypaper curled down from one of the pipes, festooned with the soft black corpses of flies. A small table stood in the foyer, with a box that held cardboard fans. Jay picked up a fan that had a picture of Niagara Falls on it. His grandmother used to have a fan just like it. She had flypaper, too, on the porch in the old house on U Street, and he remembered the delicious revulsion of risking a horrible, germy death by poking the bodies of the flies with his finger. He had not seen cardboard fans and flypaper in years; they had disappeared from the white world of air conditioners and aerosol sprays. Here, in the old church, time seemed, suspended.

"Mr. Broderick, good evening. I hope you haven't been waiting long."

The Rev. Raymond Johnson, pastor, was a small man with a broad and amiable face. "Things may be a little slow getting started. Sunday night, people have family dinners."

Jay and the minister were not strangers; he had been in the Johnson home many times to photograph church socials. Charlie delighted in publishing three-column pictures of the potluck suppers at St. John's while giving fancier dinners at white churches only two columns. The white ministers were annoyed, but how could they complain without displaying a noticeable lack of Christian charity? Their discomfiture could make Charlie smile for an entire morning.

"Excuse the condition of this place," the minister apologized. The building fund's been suspended because of the urban renewal plan."

"I like this church," Jay said. "It doesn't look like a fucking bank. Uh, I mean —"

The minister was used to Jay's frequent lapses into the vernacular. "No, it does not look like a bank."

The door opened, and Mary walked in, wearing her khaki raincoat, her hair ruffled from the night breeze. She smiled at Jay, an artless, unconcealed smile. It warmed him. When a smile split the seriousness of her face, it made her seem very young, and playful.

She introduced herself to the minister, sticking out her hand energetically, like a man would. There was no coyness about her. She went straight at things.

"Reverend, I understand that some members of the Student Nonviolent Coordinating Committee will be coming tonight."

"Yes, my nephew, Donald Johnson, is coming from D.C. and bringing a couple of people with him."

"And he's been active in the civil rights movement?"

"Yes, he was on several of the early Freedom Rides, and he's been working on voter registration in the South."

"That takes guts."

"Yes, especially in the early days. Not much support, no white reporters around. Just a few people going it alone."

"How many people will be here?"

The minister shrugged. "Hard to say. It's tough to get the people here organized. It takes all their energy just to survive. But I hope we'll get some."

Jay and Mary took seats in one of the pews in the rear as people began to straggle in. Jay's eye was drawn to the face of one old man, which was seamed like welded metal and held a pride the years had not erased. He had the face of a tribal chief, Jay thought. He scanned the room. There were quite a few middle-aged women wearing print dresses, a few children, but not many young people. One man walked in, and Jay tried to remember why the face — full lips, strong features — was so familiar. Then he remembered, he was the son of the woman in the wheelchair he had photographed, who worked for the Sanitation Department.

Thirty minutes after the meeting was scheduled to start, a large woman strolled in, wearing what appeared to be a floor-length white toga. She wore, also, a white headdress that reminded Jay of the garb of a desert sheikh, and a pair of glittering eyes peered out through gold-rimmed glasses. He had seen her before, too. Her title and garments were of her own choosing, and she was accepted as a person of stature in the community despite her vague theological credentials. She examined Jay and Mary closely and then, apparently satisfied, said, "I'm Sister Eulah Hill. God bless you, children."

In a few minutes the minister's nephew arrived, accompanied by three other men and a young woman. The young men were dressed in dark suits and wore ties, but the woman was more casual, wearing a sweater and skirt. Jay stared at her as she walked past the pew. God, she was magnificent! Coffee skin and a body that was perfect in its proportions. Her long, black hair was swept up and pulled back tightly, accenting the perfection of her face. It should have been the face, he thought, of some Ashanti princess, ruling over a biblical kingdom of long ago. He had never seen a woman more beautiful.

The minister opened the meeting with a prayer and introduced his nephew. The young man was tall and slim, with a finely molded head and erect carriage. There was something in the way he held himself that set him apart from the other men, even though one of them was much older. He was clearly the leader of the group.

"One of the lessons we learned in the South," he said, "is that nothing changes unless we make it change. No one would have given the bus boycott in Montgomery a chance. A lot of people said, 'Don't waste your time. It won't change anything.' But it did. The Freedom Rides did. In his speech last week President Kennedy said, 'Those who do nothing are inviting shame as well as violence. Those who act boldly are recognizing right as well as reality.' Belvedere invites shame if we do nothing. In the South, they keep us out with laws. In the North, they do it with urban renewal plans, with architects' drawings and double-talk. It's all the same. They are going to run you out. That's what they'll do, unless you stop them."

The people in the church listened and nodded politely when he finished. Annoyance flickered across his face. The smiles of the people in the church were a wall, Jay thought. He wanted anger, and he was getting smiles. The young man might break his heart against that wall. Would it ever move for him? Did things change? Did they only seem to move, but not really change at all?

He shook his head. He was getting like Mary, asking questions that had no answers.

Donald Johnson introduced the young woman who had come with him, and she spoke of the first wave of Freedom Rides in the South.

"Were we frightened? Yes, we were, all the time. We got threats that we were going to be dragged out of the buses and lynched, or that there were going to be bombs on the bus. But the best part for me was the people who helped us anyway. Teachers, housewives, ministers, farmers — sometimes sharecroppers who had nothing but a tar-paper roof over their heads. We were just passing through, but they had to stay and face whatever happened. Their courage made us know we were right, that we weren't going to be stopped."

Jay slipped out of the pew and began to photograph her as she spoke, transfixed by her beauty, the way she moved her hands with a fluid grace. Her perfection intoxicated him; he lost himself in it through his lens. When she stopped speaking, he slid back into the pew again. As he rewound his film, he felt a prickly sensation: someone watching him. He turned around in time to see Mary's eyes dart away. Did it show that much? Probably. What was she thinking about the way he had looked at the beautiful brown woman? Did she care? Something in her eyes told him that she did.

He looked at her out of the corner of his eyes. She had taken off her raincoat. She was wearing a brown shirtdress, a terrible color, too much like a uniform. It occurred to him that she had little style or flair in the way she dressed. Next to the Ashanti princess, she looked small and plain. He wondered if she had small, round Debra Paget shoulders.

He stopped thinking about it. He didn't want Mary with her small face and shirtwaist dresses. He didn't want Debra Paget with her bee-stung lips, or the Ashanti princess, or beautiful Jacqueline. Somewhere in the world there was a woman who moved with grace and beauty, created only for him. He would find her, someday.

There was a lively murmur of approval as the young woman finished speaking and stepped back to her seat. The minister rose, but before he could speak, Sister Eulah Hill lifted herself out of the pew.

"Sister Hill, would you like to speak?"

The woman did not reply, but she moved out into the aisle and walked to the front of the church, rocking from side to side; she reminded Jay of a large goose. She turned to face the group.

"I been livin' here since nineteen thirty-seven. Back then, we didn't have no electricity and no running water. We had to burn our own trash because the city wouldn't come out and pick it up."

A few heads nodded in the audience.

"I been here a long time, and I know one thing, you got to believe in the Lord."

"Amen!" Several voices, with feeling.

"The Lord, he don't fix no broken windows or pick up no trash. But the Lord Jesus is Salvation."

Her voice deepened; the words were almost melody. It was the meter of the gospel service, and the people in the church understood it.

"Fancy homes and fancy cars don't do no good if you forget about the Lord."

"That's right."

"Amen!"

"Amen!"

"Jesus!"

Heads bobbed and nodded. The whole church seemed alive now, charged with emotion and melody. Jay felt his own body flow into the sound and the cadence. He sat back luxuriating in it, wishing it would not end. But he looked at the minister's nephew and saw that he was frowning. Their eyes met, and the young man looked away. Jay wondered if he were embarrassed that white people should see this. Did it have too much of the Happy Darkie for him? He understood, and yet . . . There was a depth of feeling, a joy in this old church that had vanished from the fancier churches all over town. When all these people got middle class, when they had dishwashers and Oldsmobiles and prayed like Episcopalians, would that be better? Was change always for the better?

Shit, he was doing it again. All this thinking was making him tired.

When Sister Eulah Hill finished, the son of the woman in the wheelchair stood up. He had been silent through the chanting.

"I'm James Washington. And I think Mr. Johnson is right about what's being done here. We're being shoved out. I don't think we ought to sit back and take it."

There were a few sounds of approval from the crowd.

"If anybody wants to get a group together to try and fight this thing, we can use my house anytime. If we don't do something, we're going to find ourselves pushed right out of our city, before we even know it!"

Several other people in the church, three women and two men, volunteered to form the committee and to meet in a few nights. The Reverend Johnson suggested that they end the meeting by having everyone rise and sing "We Shall Overcome."

Feet shuffled, people moved, and a haphazard circle formed. With their arms crossed, gripping other hands, the people stood and swayed, singing:

> Deep in my heart I do believe,
> We shall overcome someday.

Sister Eulah Hill was standing next to the Ashanti princess, and Jay moved to photograph them, liking the juxtaposition of their shapes, the one solid and round but surprisingly graceful, the other lithe and limber. They were both survivors, he knew instinctively, because they could bend with the wind, but they would not break.

When the song ended, the people began to drift away; Jay saw Mary, talking intently to the minister's nephew, and she was nodding and taking notes.

She walked with Jay out of the church as the visitors climbed in a car to go back to D.C., and they both stood by the curb and watched it go.

"They're making history, you know. They *are* history. It's going to be the big event of our generation, Jay, the civil rights movement. And we're seeing a part of it."

Her face was animated, and she was charged with excitement; he thought he could hear it crackling on her skin.

"You do like the action, don't you?" he said.

"Oh, yeah, I do. But he's right. Nothing changes unless you make it change."

"Sometimes."

"No, all the time. President Kennedy said it. 'A journey of a thousand miles begins with a single step.' That's what I want to do, Jay, make things happen."

"You think you can?"

"Tonight I do. After hearing them. Don't you?"

"I don't know. Maybe it's all written down somewhere, what's going to happen."

She laughed. "You sound like some kind of mystic. I didn't think Catholics believed in predestination."

"They don't. I don't. Not all the time. But sometimes."

"Maybe when you're born and when you die. But in between, you can make something of life, not let it float away." She smiled. "Oh shit, that's so Protestant. I sound like Cotton Mather."

"Cotton, baby, can I give you a lift to the paper?"

"I'm going back to Reverend Johnson's house. I want to talk to him some more. My house is pretty near here, so I walked over. I'll walk back. I need the exercise."

"You're going to be physically fit, like the prez says."

"I'm trying."

"You did beat me in a race, as I remember. In high heels."

"And drunk."

"Jesus, I'd challenge you to a rematch, but I'd probably get beat again."

"Do I look all that athletic?"

"You do look a little bit like Wonder Woman, now that you mention it."

"Hey, don't knock Wonder Woman. She was my favorite. I used to pretend I could stop bullets with my bracelets too."

"I liked the tight blue short-shorts. Do you have those?"

"No, but I have these steel bracelets."

"Pat, for God's sakes, why are you walking around the living room with just your panties and steel bracelets on?"

"Living out my fantasies, Dick. Don't you have fantasies?"

"Yeah, I have this fantasy that I shaved before the debates and I used Man Tan."

"Oh well, I guess it's back to the freezer."

They both laughed, and the minister came out, and she got into the car with him. Much later, as he was lying in bed, tired but unable to sleep, he thought about her standing on the curb saying, "That's what I want to do, make things happen."

He was afraid for her. You didn't say things like that out loud. You whispered them and you might escape the notice of the gods. His mother had never mentioned good fortune without invoking a litany of saints. He himself had decided he was going to die in the most colorful and romantic way possible, maybe taking a bullet in some exotic war in the high valleys of the Hindu Kush, before the kidneys got him. His grandfather had died of complications of kidney disease, and then his father. He pictured his own kidneys as a pair of lamb chops (biology was not his strong suit) tucked away inside him, ready at any minute to swoon and spread poison inside him. You could live, with bad kidneys, if you spent half your life plugged into some fucking machine, but what was the point of that? He pictured his funeral, if he never made it to the Hindu Kush, if it was kidneys after all. His uncles would be there, and Father Hannigan and the old ladies in the parish who liked to come to wakes, and he'd be stretched out in the coffin, his face pale and pasty as wax.

"My, doesn't he look lovely, Agnes."

"Oh yes, Hanlon's does a beautiful job."

"Such a fine looking man. What a pity."

"Very nice suit. Too bad it's going to be put in the ground to rot."

"Oh, it'll probably last longer than he does. In a couple of weeks, he'll be crumbling to pieces."

"And he never made it to Life, *Agnes. He just stayed in Belvedere, Maryland."*

"You couldn't tell, from looking at him now, Brigit, that he drank."

"Did he now? His complexion is so nice."

"They are very good at Hanlon's. Mr. O'Malley, last week, shot himself in the head, but you'd never have guessed."

"Did he start drinking when he got fired from that newspaper?"

"Yes. And then tried shooting weddings, but one day he passed out right in the wedding cake. They had to scrape the frosting off the negatives."

"Oh my."

"And then he couldn't afford the rent, and he started living in his car with the police radio, taking pictures of car wrecks and trying to sell them to the tabloids. That's how he died; his kidneys burst on the Baltimore-Washington Expressway, near Glen Burnie, just after a drunk plowed into a family of five."

He reached over, lit a cigarette and inhaled, but he knew he was going to throw it away before he smoked half of it. The night terrors were coming on him again. It was what he called the black and hopeless mood that ambushed him sometimes, late at night, when the busyness of the day was not there to screen it out. The night terrors had begun after his father died, and they came without warning like a sea squall. They brought with them a nameless dread, a sense that the universe was hollow at the center, that no God existed beyond the stars to hear his prayers, that safety was an illusion and meaning a sham. There was nothing to be done about the night terrors. Drink didn't drive them away, or pills, or getting in his car and driving. Once he had called Norma at 2:00 A.M., and she was willing, but he felt more alone than ever with her arms around him. She stared at him as if he were mad when he tried to talk about it. Night terrors were not in Norma's vocabulary. The night terrors simply had to be ridden out, and so he rode them, alone and frightened, a sailor on an unknown sea. He knew, when they were on him, why people killed themselves.

He thought again of Mary, throwing her brave words against the gathering night. She fairly shone in his mind; he saw her eyes, the shaft of her nose, the curve of her breasts. And then a peculiar thing happened. The terrors were gone. Glinda, the good witch, had simply waved her wand and ordered them away.

He laughed and said to the image of her in his head, "The Munchkins thank you."

Suddenly, he wanted her desperately. Not just carnally, though that was part of it. He wanted to devour her, meld with her, own her luminescence. He had the absurd notion that, with her, he could not die. It was crazy, *he* was crazy. She was only a girl in a raincoat, why should she gleam like an archangel? The future was sealed, he could not change it.

Or could he?

"I felt happy today," he said. "Not special, not magic, but happy. It sort of snuck up on me. I think that's a good sign."

The people sitting near him on the metal chairs nodded. There was Jim, the postman, who used to carry more than just the U.S.

mail in his bag; Old Marge; Sherri, the young housewife who used to hide it in the maple syrup bottle and Mark, who had been a successful lawyer until he drank it all away — house, wife, kids — and ended up getting gang-raped and nearly beaten to death in an alley.

At first he had resented them, bitterly. Who were they? A bunch of drunks, losers. He sat, sullen, on the chair, listening to them, thinking, I don't belong here. But then Sherri had looked at him and said, "You don't want to be here with us, a bunch of alkies, right? That's how I felt too. 'I'm not like *them.*'" Then she had laughed. "But I was, Harry. And so are you."

And to his shame, he had suddenly begun to cry. But they weren't shocked or surprised.

"We've all cried here, Harry. Comes with the territory."

He looked at them now, astounded by how much a part of his life they had become. He had told them things he had never told anyone, not his mother or father. They were the only ones who knew how hard it was, and they were smiling at him.

"It feels good, doesn't it?" Sherrie asked. "To feel happy. Not the kind that comes from a bottle."

"I think," he said, "I think maybe I can be happy, even if I'm not special. If I'm just like everybody else. I think I could be good at business. I'm organized. I can keep three or four balls in the air at once. I never knew that."

"You're no dummy, kid," Marge said. "We knew that right off the bat."

"I think maybe I am smart," he said. "I didn't think so because my wife — she's so smart it used to intimidate me. But I'm smart in a different way. I see how things fit together. Putting this deal together, for the new laundry. I just *knew* how to do it. So the owner's been letting me carry the ball."

"You're on your way, Harry," said Jim.

Harry leaned back in his chair. "I only thank God I didn't wreck it all. I could have lost my wife and my daughter, if I hadn't come here . . ." He let the sentence drift off into the air.

"It's easy to lose everything," Mark said, quietly. He was forty and looked sixty. His wife had remarried, moved out of state with the children. "People can only take so much. They see you killing yourself, and they can't make you stop."

"My wife never gave up on me," he said. "We had screaming fights, and finally she threw me out, but the door's open. The night I hit bottom, she came with my father to bail me out. He yelled at me and called me a stinking drunk. She looked at me and gave it to me straight. 'Harry, you're doing this to yourself. You can stop it if you want to.'"

"Smart girl," Jim said.

"Yeah, like I said, she's real smart. She's real pretty, too. My daughter looks just like her. She had to put up with a lot of crap from me, but she's never given up on me. I think she's been — a saint."

"Nobody's a saint, kid," Marge said.

"I know, but she comes close. I always felt she was . . . judging me, all the time. But she was right, and it was me that was wrong. I was terrible. I went with"— he looked around — "I don't know if I should say this in mixed company —"

"Whores," Sherri said.

Harry reddened and nodded.

"Harry, I used to sleep with men I didn't even know, just so they'd give me booze," Sherri said. "There's nothing you can't say to us. We've heard it all."

"I always felt dirty when I'd been with them. The things they did, the way they talked. And they weren't even ashamed. Sometimes I feel like going back to them just for . . . relief, because my wife and I, we're not together. But I don't want to do that ever again. I want to wait for my wife. I can't make it without her."

"You're doing it on your own, Harry," Sherri said. "Don't give anybody else the credit."

"But she's who I'm making it for," he said, "she and my daughter. I didn't know how much"— his mouth was dry, he found it hard to say the words — "how much I loved her until I didn't have her anymore. See, I have to earn the right to have her love me. And that's what I've been doing, these last few months."

"Love isn't something you earn," Jim said.

"Yes it is. I used to think it was something you got for free. *I* got for free, anyhow. But it isn't. I have to earn it." He paused. "I want to be a person worth loving."

"You are," Sherri said. "You already are."

He shook his head. "No, not yet." He looked around at the group. "But I will be."

The word came back from Birmingham; King was going full speed ahead with the campaign. The administration had asked him not to press now, with Police Commissioner Bull Connor still in office, but King had protested that the movement had a momentum of its own, it could not be stopped.

He put down the phone and sighed. "That damn preacher is going to fuck me out of a second term," he said, to the air.

There was no rancor in the words that was not totally personal. For the son of a rich man, he had grown up peculiarly free from the casual bigotry of the upper classes. He had moved through Riverdale and Palm Beach and Hyannis Port without picking up any of the nasty, small burrs of prejudice that clung to most such people. Perhaps it was the curiosity he had inherited from his mother, for he had traveled more than most young Americans and met all sorts of people, high and low, and as long as they didn't bore him, he did not judge them. The war was part of it; all sorts of men were thrown together by chance, and you might owe your life to someone with a very different pedigree.

However it happened, he had come to an ease with people that was genuine. At his inauguration, as he waltzed gracefully and naturally with the wives of Negro officials, the word spread through the Negro community like an electric current. Eisenhower, though he had sent the troops to Little Rock, had kept a distance from people of a darker shade. Adlai Stevenson, the great liberal, had asked a friend to telephone Coretta Scott King when Martin was in jail, but he did not speak to her, on the excuse that they had not been formally introduced. (A young white civil rights worker named Harris Wofford was convinced that it was really Stevenson's discomfort with Negroes, which he had observed on more than one occasion. He switched his allegiance to Kennedy.)

His instincts, when he acted too fast to be tempered by caution — came from a basic decency and sense of fair play. During the campaign, his staff bickered loud and long over whether the candidate should telephone Mrs. King when her husband was jailed on a trumped-up charge in Georgia. How would it play in the South? But when his brother-in-law Sargent Shriver walked into his hotel room and said he ought to make a call, the candidate, weary from a long day's campaigning, said, "What the hell, that's the decent thing to do." The phone call may have won him the election.

His brother Bobby, whose emotions lay much closer to the surface, blew his stack and screamed that Shriver and his allies could have wrecked the whole campaign. But then, a few days later, when Bobby learned that King was going to get five months on a chain gain for driving with an out-of-state license, and was denied bail, he ignored good form and legal ethics to call the judge personally and ream his ass, saying that any decent American judge would have King out on bail by sundown. He was.

The man in the Oval Office sat back in his chair and thought about race, something he did not like to do. What the hell more did King want, anyhow? He had used his Justice Department as a battering ram to force open Ole Miss, to protect the Freedom Riders, to enforce voting rights. Didn't that man understand he had a whole world to contend with? An entire legislative package — education, housing, highways, defense — to get through Congress? A network of southern senators and congressmen could be coiled into an iron mesh that would keep anything from getting through. If you moved slowly enough, carefully enough, stroked and flattered and favored, you could get past them. But King was not going to let him do it.

Damn.

He'd had no background and no particular interest in matters of race when he came to public life. Harry Belafonte had briefed him, during the campaign, and found him untutored and unemotional on the matter, but willing to learn. Belafonte had told him it was King, not Jackie Robinson or any of the other Negro celebrities, who was the key to the hearts of the colored people; Belafonte said that civil rights would become to them a sacred crusade, and it was Martin who was at its center.

The preacher's father — after the phone call — came out for Kennedy, "despite his Catholicism." The candidate learned of the statement as he was walking towards the campaign plane, carrying three-year-old Caroline in his arms.

"That was a hell of a bigoted statement, wasn't it?" he mused. "Imagine Martin Luther King having a bigot for a father." Then he grinned. "Well, we all have fathers, don't we?"

When he had met with Belafonte, he knew Martin Luther King only as a preacher who had led a bus boycott in Montgomery, a minor figure on the political scene. How odd, he thought, that two men from such different places and such different temperaments should have been cast in leading roles in the ever-fascinating theater of politics.

The two had met, on occasion, but they were always somewhat ill at ease with one another. Perhaps it was because each man saw in the other something missing in himself. For Martin Luther King, conscience called him to huge and noble deeds, into the lions' den. Yet there was a side of him that loved the celebrity status those deeds brought with them. He railed against the "Cadillac preachers" who neglected the needs of their people, but he also loved riding in Rockefeller's private plane and dining with the literati on Martha's Vineyard and being called personally by Lawrence Spivak of Meet the Press. *He envied the ease with which John Kennedy moved in that glittering world, envied his seeming freedom from the tortured conscience that would let the preacher accept the amenities but have difficulty enjoying them. Beyond that glittering world lay a dark path to Golgotha, and he would go down the path if that was to be his destiny.*

The man in the Oval Office wanted no truck with Golgotha, and had no intentions of going there. He found the preacher's talk of noble suffering pretentious cant; he'd had a taste of suffering and wanted no more. King's intensity, his focus on the moral dimensions of every situation, struck him as narrow and stifling. He guessed that Martin couldn't take a piss without pondering its meaning. He certainly couldn't have escaped agonizing about the girls in the motel rooms.

The Irish played politics with zest; it was, after all, a sport. There was little of the gamesman in the tortured preacher, he thought. And yet. Yet . . . He had a sense that the preacher brought out the best in him, arranging the choices in such stark terms of good and evil that he was forced to throw caution to the wind and side with the good. He did well when backed into corners. But he wanted to reach for the stars, and King was always making him stare at the ugliness at his feet. There was something in Martin Luther King that he lacked; he did not understand it, exactly, but he knew it without giving voice to it. Bobby had it. His father had it, too, in a very different way. He thought that if the preacher had not been so schooled in the ways of God, he would have made a great Irish pol.

He got up, walked to the window and looked out. It was dusk, his favorite time, and the ghosts were beginning to stir. He had the strange sensation that he and the preacher would be a part of those stirrings one day, that the two of them were locked together in some strange dance that would probably last as long as they lived. Where it would lead, he had no idea. He only knew the music would not stop.

SHE HAD BEEN sent out to interview Donald Johnson, the minister's nephew, who was helping to organize the protest against the urban renewal plan. He had agreed to talk to her, because the paper had come out editorially against the current plan, and its influence, while not thought to be decisive, could certainly help.

She could see right away that this wasn't going to be easy. He stretched out his hand to shake hers, but there was no give in his body. He stood stiffly, his eyes opaque, giving nothing away. She would have thought, Arrogant, and then perhaps, Arrogant black man, if everything about his body language were not so familiar. It was her own in places where she thought people felt she didn't belong — in police headquarters and her first city council meeting. She could see it in their eyes. What's a broad doing here? You kept your back straight and your eyes blank, made a fortress of your body and they couldn't get at you, if you did everything just right.

"I'm glad to meet you," she said, and he nodded, his body still stiff and his eyes wary. She couldn't figure it out, at first, why he would be this way with her. She was hardly intimidating. Then she realized that, to him, she was not simply a pleasant looking young woman, she was *the press.* The *white* press. She had power. Often, she forgot this and was startled to see people react to her in a peculiar way. Sometimes she enjoyed it; at other times, like now, it made her edgy because it seemed so absurd. As a reporter you were supposed to be objective, you weren't supposed to have feelings or to take any sides. Sometimes that didn't work, because people didn't trust robots. Sometimes you had to be human to get anything coming back at you.

"I think what you're doing is very brave," she said. "And necessary."

She saw something stir in those opaque eyes. He was checking, to see if she was conning him or mocking him. Another familiar reaction. He apparently decided she was not, and his body relaxed, almost imperceptibly, but she caught it. She suggested they go to Art's Diner for a cup of coffee, a less formal setting than the city room. They slid into a booth, and she asked him about his experiences. He told her of riding in the second of two buses into Alabama; they got word that the first bus had been stopped and burned by Klan members, and some of the riders hospitalized. When they pulled into the terminal, they intended to walk into the "whites only" lunch counter, because the Supreme Court had banned segregation at facilities serving people crossing state lines. A group of men bearing bricks and clubs refused to let them get off the bus and demanded that the Negroes riding in front go to the back of the bus. The whites stormed onto the bus and knocked one man unconscious, forced the Negroes to the back and stayed in the middle of the aisle, blocking the way, as the bus pulled out onto the highway again, heading for Birmingham. One Negro reporter for *Jet* magazine, trying to distract the whites on the bus to keep them from getting any more violent, gave them preview copies of the magazine's next issue, with a cover story on the Freedom Rides.

"So there you were, riding on the bus with this bunch of thugs through Alabama, and they were reading about the rides all the while?"

He smiled, faintly. "Instant media."

When the bus pulled into Birmingham and everybody stumbled off, there was a melee that involved Klansmen, cops, press and innocent bystanders. One white man emerged from the men's room with a startled look on his face and was set upon by three Klansmen. A white photographer from a Birmingham paper was clubbed with an iron pipe, and a mob dragged a white radio reporter out of his car and smashed all the windows. Don was knocked into a pile of trash boxes and managed to get out to the street, where he was able to catch a cab to the home of one of the movement leaders.

As he talked, he turned, in her mind, from a Hero of the Civil Rights Movement to a man her own age, whose smile was easy and natural when he relaxed.

"Weren't you terrified?" she asked.

He seemed to hesitate a minute, and then he said, "Yeah, I was scared *shitless.*" He laughed. "I saw some news photos of myself getting off the bus, and I looked so brave and resolute. Inside I was thinking, What in the hell am I doing here?"

"Like you were in a bad movie?"

He laughed again.

"Yeah, exactly. I kept thinking, When was the cavalry going to come charging in?"

"Except they'd be on the wrong side."

"You got it. *We* were the Indians."

"Some of those guys would have killed you."

"Oh yeah. Once, people were beating on the sides of the bus with their fists, with boards, anything. If the driver hadn't gunned the motor and driven out, they probably would have killed us."

"I don't understand that kind of crazy hatred."

"I don't either. But I'm learning. I grew up pretty sheltered, middle class, in D.C."

"Are your parents pissed at you?"

"You bet. I guess I can't blame them. They worked so hard to keep me safe, then I haul my butt down to Alabama."

"I understand the way they feel. They wanted you to have it easier."

"Yeah, but who's going to do this? Some sharecropper, who can hardly keep body and soul together? We're the ones who have to do it, the lucky ones. If we let Jim Crow live, then the Constitution is a farce, the Bill of Rights is a joke. Equal justice means equal, period."

"Did it surprise you? The level of the violence?"

"Oh, we were warned. But nobody can really tell you what it's like. I saw the faces, full of hate, and it's funny, at first I sort of looked around to see who they were mad at. I mean, what could they have against me, Mrs. Johnson's good little boy? I was a Boy Scout and I won the spelling bee." He laughed again. "For a minute I had this crazy idea that I could get out of the bus and say, 'Excuse me, but I have my Forest Safety badge and I won the spelling bee by getting the word *extraterrestrial.*' And they would step back and drop their lead pipes and say, 'Oh, we didn't know it was *you.* It's those other people we don't like. The *Niggers.*"

"But it didn't matter whether you could spell *extraterrestrial.* You were still a Nigger."

"I could walk on water and I'd still be a Nigger."

"They they'd really be pissed," she said. "The first guy who did it was a Jew."

He threw back his head and laughed, heartily. She was curious about something, so she asked.

"Do you ever feel," she said, "that you see things that other people — white people — don't see?"

He looked at her, curiously.

"I mean," she continued, "it's like there's something there, and it's huge, like a big rock, and you see it and the people around you just walk by it, and they don't see it. And you think it's you who must be crazy."

"You feel like that?" he asked her.

She nodded.

"I never thought any white people did."

"I don't think men do. *I* do. It happens all the time." She thought it odd that now they were sitting and talking so easily, almost as friend to friend. She had never asked anyone about *the rock* as she thought of it, but she thought he might know.

"I think," he said, "that when you're not in the group, when you're an outsider, that gives you a third eye. You haven't been taught all the same things, you don't always react the same way or feel the same way, so you see things the group can't see."

"But that's good, isn't it? It gives you something extra."

"But you pay a price for that something extra. A lot of times, people don't want to see what you see."

"And if you tell them, they get pissed."

"To put it mildly," he said.

"Belvedere's role in the space program, do you believe this?" Sam was sitting at his desk, staring at a blank piece of paper.

Jay looked up "Charlie's big on space. Every time NASA has a press conference, he lets me go."

"Yeah, we don't cover Frederick because it's five miles outside our circulation area," Mary said. "but if *Mercury II* passes 500 miles overhead, that's a local story."

"What the fuck are you going to write about Belvedere and the space program?" Jay asked.

"Well, there's Alf G. Guttenheim, from Miller Avenue. He was a pastry chef on the USS *Kearsarge.* He made a big cake that said A-OK GORDO on it when Cooper came back."

"Yuri Gagarin, eat your heart out." Mary laughed.

"And then we have Harvey Millerburton. He works in the cafeteria at Cape Canaveral. Puts mashed potatoes on plates with ice cream scoops. Can man reach for the moon without mashed potatoes?"

Harvey Millerburton and Wernher von Braun," Mary said. "Riders to the stars."

"Yeah, but Harvey didn't try to wipe out London on the way."

"I guess Alf G. Guttenheim is my lead. How many fucking paragraphs can I get out of a vanilla cake with jelly filling and 'A-OK' out of spun sugar?" He sighed. "Maybe I'll do it as an epic poem. 'I sing of Alf G. Guttenheim and his spray can of whipped cream, who first from Belvedere's streets did sail the wine dark sea.'"

"No astronauts even drove through Belvedere?"

"I'll try Happy Hours Motel. Maybe one of them brought a floozie out there." Sam picked up the phone. "Yeah, John Glenn. Tall fella, wears a white suit with a helmet. There's twenty-five bucks in it for you." He put the phone down. "A Good Humor man, that's as close as they get."

The upper half of Charlie's body appeared, leaning Pisa-like from the door of his office.

"Mary. Sam. Jay."

The summons was issued in the half note above normal tone that meant Charlie was excited about something. The three of them went into his office.

"Any of you hear about possible trouble at Reverend Johnson's house?"

"I haven't," Mary said. "His nephew didn't mention it."

"Nothing, Charlie," Sam said. Jay shook his head.

"He's had a couple of crank calls this week," Mary told the editor. "'Nigger, stop making trouble,' that sort of thing. He didn't take them too seriously."

"I just had a call from a guy who said there might be trouble over there tonight. Wouldn't give his name. He sounded like he was calling from a bar."

"Maybe it's another crank," Jay said.

Maybe. But I've notified the police, and they're going to send a car by at regular intervals." He looked at Mary. "You're going to be there tonight?"

"Yes, there's a meeting tonight. Jay's going with me."

"I'll go too," Sam chimed in. Charlie looked at him sternly. "Have you finished the story on Belvedere and the space program?"

"Not yet."

"Well, keep on it. I want that story for tomorrow."

"Charlie, you wouldn't send me to Birmingham. Now we might have a real story, right here in Belvedere, and you want me to keep writing about fucking Alf G. Fucking Guttenheim."

"*Blade* staffers do not use that kind of language, young man —"

"Charlie —" Sam pleaded.

"Oh, all right, you can go. But I want that space story. Our readers like space.

"I promise. You'll have it tomorrow."

"I've been working since noon," Jay said. "Do I get overtime?"

"No overtime. But you can come in late tomorrow. Just think of all the experience you're getting."

"Experience," Jay grumbled as they walked out to Sam's car. "I make *eighty-three fifty* a week, and I work night and day. What am I, crazy?"

"You're three-fifty a week ahead of me," Mary said.

"You're crazier than I am."

When they reached the minister's house, they found that twenty-five people were already there; the minister ushered them into the living room. James Washington was there, as well as Don, the young woman who had been with him at the church, and several students from Howard University. The minister's nephew opened the meeting by outlining the details of the petition that would be delivered to the city council demanding rejection of the urban renewal plan, and its replacement with another plan that would involve the input of a citizens' committee of Negro residents.

"We've put out feelers to the county commissioners, and they don't want to get involved," he said, "so we have to plan to go all the way with this."

"What do you mean, all the way?" asked one of the women.

"Civil disobedience, if it comes to that. We have to be prepared to sit down on the street in front of City Hall, if need be."

"Do you think it will come to that?" the minister asked. "I'm not sure the people here are prepared for that."

"We can bring quite a few people up," the young woman told him.

"Then they'll say it's outside agitators," said a man who was sitting on the couch.

Don laughed. "Sure they will. That's what they always say. 'Our Nigras were happy until those agitators came in.'"

"This isn't the South," objected the man on the couch. "There's no police dogs up here."

"No," said the young woman, "but you have papers in triplicate that do the same thing. Nice and polite and legal. Up here, they sic lawyers with briefcases on you."

"And the bite they take out of your behind can make a German shepherd look like a pussycat," Don added.

"Civil disobedience, I don't know, . . ." one of the women said.

"It may not come to that. But if it did, we'd get good coverage.

The national media would be here, like they were in Cambridge, over on the Eastern Shore. We've got to get the media for this to work. We haven't got the votes on the council and not a prayer of getting them unless we really put the pressure on."

James Washington raised his hand. "I think we ought to do everything we have to do," he said. "What can we lose? I've lived here all my life. I own a house here. I have as much right to live in this city as any white people do."

"They're not saying we can't live in the city," one of the women told him.

"Yes, they are. Who's going to sell you a house? Or me? A decent one, anyway. Maybe they'll sell us a dump at twice the rate we ought to pay."

"Most of the white neighborhoods have real estate covenants that won't let people sell to Negroes," Don said. "Some of them won't let Jews in either."

"But there could be trouble," one older man objected. "People could get hurt."

"We're not saying we'll have to use civil disobedience," Don told him, "just to let everybody know we're willing to. If that's what it takes."

Mary was sitting in a chair by the window, taking notes. The window, on the street side of the house, was open, and despite her concentration, she gradually became aware that something was not quite right. What was it? Cars. There had been too many cars moving up and down the quiet side street. They slowed as they passed, then sped up again.

"See anything?" Jay asked, in a low voice.

"Not right now. But have you heard the cars?"

Jay nodded. He walked out the front door and stood on the porch. The street was quiet. He went back into the house again.

"Maybe we're just jumpy," he said.

At that moment a car drove down the street, slowed in front of the house, then sped up again.

"That's what they've been doing. I think I've seen that car before."

A car turned at the corner from the main road, and this time it slowed down, then stopped in front of the house. A minute later, another car pulled up behind it.

"Trouble," Mary said.

"Looks like it."

Sam moved up behind them. "Charlie's tip was on the level."

"Unless that's the welcome wagon," Jay said.

"Reverend Johnson, I think you'd better put the lights out," Mary told the minister. There were gasps and cries from the people in the room.

"Everybody keep calm," Don said, quietly. "Sit on the floor away from the windows. The police are being called. They're just trying to scare us."

The minister flicked the light switch, and the room went dark. Looking out the window, Mary could see men getting out of the cars. There was a tinkling sound, and the street light went out, leaving the front lawn in darkness. A dozen shapes drifted out of the shadows near the cars and formed an irregular knot on the lawn. The darkness hid their features, but Mary could tell by the shapes and the way they moved that they were young men.

"Hey, niggers!" one of the shapes yelled.

"Hey, niggers." Another voice. "You in there?" There was a giggle from the lawn.

James moved towards the window. One of the older women was crying. "Little punks. I'd like to beat their faces in."

"That's just what they want," Don said. "Just stay calm."

"Listen, niggers, this is white man's land. You better haul your ass off white man's land."

"Whhheeeee-haw!" came a voice.

Don laughed. "Nothing worse than a northern white man trying a rebel yell. Sounds like somebody goosed him."

"Nigger, go home!"

Mary's eyes had grown accustomed to the dark, and she could see, now, that the kid doing most of the yelling seemed to be the leader of the group. They were barely more than teenagers. There was laughter from the lawn, and the little knot of men moved across it. The lights in the houses on either side went out.

"Did you see a squad car go by, at all?" Jay asked Mary.

"No."

"Hey, niggers, you hear me?"

"I bet the fucking cops are having coffee down at Art's," Jay said.

The boy on the lawn started to chant: "Niggers suck, kill Niggers. Niggers suck."

Mary turned to Don. "Do you think they'll try to get in?"

"No. When white people want to kill black people, they come fast and they come quiet. This is just scum, having a little fun."

Mary looked out the window again. One of the dark shapes bent over, then straightened up, and she could see a throwing motion, which was followed by the trill of breaking glass. One of the windows facing the street had been shattered.

"God *dammit,* where are the cops!" Sam muttered.

Mary could feel her heart pounding; she was scared, but she was also, she realized, thrilled. This was real life. And she was right in the middle of it.

Jay was standing close to the wall, checking his electronic flash unit. "Can I get through the side door?" he asked the minister.

"Yes."

"I'm gong to shoot a couple fast ones and then get the hell back in here."

"I'll go with you," Sam said.

"No, they won't spot me if I go alone."

"Jay, be careful," Mary whispered. "Those guys sound tanked up."

"You want to see the four-minute mile, watch me."

Jay ducked out the side door and crawled behind the bushes that grew in front of the house. He crouched low and moved quickly along the front wall until he was only about ten feet from where the leader of the group was moving drunkenly about in a parody of a tap dance and singing, "Way down upon the Swanee River."

From the window, Mary could see Jay moving behind the bushes. "He's too close, Sam."

From his vantage point behind the bushes, Jay could see the face of the boy who was doing the bizarre shuffle. It was an adolescent face, pocked with craters from recent acne, the lips twisted in a rubbery sneer. Jay straightened up, stepped out of the bushes and aimed.

"Work, you mother," he said to the flash unit. He pressed the shutter, and a flash of light rolled across the lawn and then vanished. Jay took two more shots in rapid succession before the bewilderment on the boy's face turned into comprehension.

From the window, Mary saw two of the young men move in Jay's direction. He lowered his camera and pivoted for the sprint back to the door. He slithered past them, but another young man had moved up close to his right side.

"Jay! Look out! On your right," Mary yelled. He heard her, saw the blurred motion of an arm coming towards him, and tried to duck. But he was too late, and there was a peculiar explosion in the side of his face. Then he felt the damp grass against his face and hands and wondered how the hell the grass got there.

When she saw Jay go down, Mary grabbed for the nearest thing she could find — the lamp on the table by the window. She yanked the cord out of the socket and, clutching the lamp like a club, ran out the front door to the lawn. Jay was curled up, fetuslike, and one of the young men was kicking him viciously in the ribs. She raised the lamp and brought it down on the man's head and he fell like a dead weight. She raised the lamp again and hissed, "OK, you fuckers, who's next?" Then there was the wail of a siren, and a boyish voice yelled, "Jeez, the cops!" and in a mass of confusion the boys ran for the cars. Two of them grabbed their stunned companion and half-dragged him across the lawn. Sam had bolted out the door behind Mary and tackled one of the boys, and he was pounding the kid's head into the lawn when a cop came and pulled him off.

Mary knelt down beside Jay, who had struggled to a sitting position.

"Jay, oh my God!"

Don knelt beside her. "Hey, man, are you all right?"

Jay reached for his camera and ran his finger around the lens. There was no break in the glass.

"I'm OK," he said. He looked up at Mary. "Did you hit one of those guys with something?"

"Yeah. A lamp. I broke it too. It was the Reverend's lamp."

"What the hell did that little fuck hit me with?"

"A rock, I think," Don said.

Mary pulled a handkerchief out of her pocket and held it up to his face. "Hold still, you're bleeding."

At that instant a flash of light washed over them, and Jay looked up to see the grinning face of Bill McChesney, the other staff photographer, peering down at them over his Rolleiflex.

"Don't look at me, Jay, look at Mary. How about a little more pain in the expression?"

"Oh, for Chrissake."

"Come on, Jay, I'd do it for you."

He did his best John Wayne-shot-by-a-Nazi expression.

"That's great! Great!"

"Want me to bleed harder?"

"No, that's OK. Jeez, you are sort of a bloody mess, though."

"How the fuck did you get here so fast?"

"I was working a story on the cops on night patrol. Best stuff since the double murder in Niggertown." He looked at Don. "Uh, sorry."

"Bill, I got pictures of those motherfuckers." Jay handed his Nikon to McChesney. "Print them for me. Hold it down a little, they may be light."

"Will do."

Jay climbed to his feet, helped by Don and Mary. "Is everybody OK in there?"

"Yes, one of the women was hysterical, but my uncle's calming her down. We'll see that everybody gets an escort home."

A wave of nausea rolled through Jay, and he wobbled slightly. Don grabbed his arm.

"You'd better get him to a doctor," Don said to Mary. She nodded.

"I'm all right."

"No, come on, Sam will drop you off. We've got to write," Mary said.

The doctor, the husband of the art editor, examined the gash on Jay's cheek and cleaned and bandaged it. "That's a nasty cut. You're lucky. A few inches higher, you could have lost an eye. You're going to have a hell of a shiner as it is."

He gave Jay some liquid and a packet of pills. "Wash it out with the antiseptic three or four times for the next couple of days. Now go home and go to bed."

"Doc, I got to get back to the paper."

"I'll call a cab. I don't want you driving tonight."

When Jay walked into the city room, Roger came up and looked at the bandage on his eye.

"Shit, you lived. We had a state funeral all planned. Mayor Swarman would give the eulogy, songs by the Rainbow Girls and burial under the birdbath in the park. The birds would piss on you for eternity."

"Fuck you, Roger."

Mary walked out of the back shop and waved to Jay. He followed her to the light table. "Page one," she said. "Clear as a bell."

Jay looked at the picture. The pock-faced boy stood, jaw agape, staring at the camera. The faces of two of the other men were clearly visible.

"Hey, look at the motherfucker. Not bad!"

"They've already picked him up. He has a record for drunk and disorderly. Look at this one."

Jay saw himself sitting on the ground with his John Wayne grimace. Bill walked over. "I had to push it to get the blood."

"Yeah, I got photogenic blood. Jesus, my mother is really going to shit when she sees this. I never should have given her a subscription."

Charlie walked into the back shop and looked at Jay.

"You look like hell."

"Do I get overtime?"

"Yeah, yeah, you get overtime. But for Christ's sake be more careful, will you? Good job, though."

Jay leaned over the light table to look at Mary's story.

"Did you put in the part about where you hit the guy with the lamp?"

"What?" Charlie said.

"She cold-cocked one of those suckers. Hit him with a lamp, and he went down like a ton a bricks.

Charlie looked at her. "What the hell did you think you were doing?"

"He was kicking Jay. So I hit him with the lamp."

"You should have seen her. She was waving the goddamn lamp around, yelling, 'OK, you fuckers, who's next?'"

"Sam was pounding one of their heads into the ground," Mary said.

"Oh, my God, I send you people out to cover a story, and you act like it's D day. Listen, this may get real mean. I want you people covering the news, not making it. Is that clear?"

"Right, Charlie."

"OK, Charlie."

Jay suddenly swayed on his feet, and Mary and Charlie steadied him.

"Mary, drive him home and make him go to bed."

"I'm not an invalid," Jay protested, but Charlie shook his head.

"I don't want you smashing into something with your car. We'd have to pay for it."

"You're all heart, Charlie," Jay muttered, and he got his jacket and walked with Mary out to the parking lot. She drove him home and followed him into the apartment.

"How do you feel?"

"My head's pounding, but I'll live."

"Lie down on the couch. I'll get you a drink. You better take off that shirt, it's all bloody."

She vanished into the kitchen, and Jay unbuttoned the shirt. "New one, too, dammit. Six ninety-five."

He lay down on the couch and put his head against the pillow. She came in with a glass of Scotch, and he took it.

"You really are a tiger, you know. 'OK, you fuckers, who's next?'"

She shook her head in wonderment. "I don't have any idea why I did it. All of a sudden, I was just there, waving the stupid lamp around. But you know, it felt *so* goddamn good to him him."

"Remind me never to get you pissed off."

"Oh, look, your T-shirt is all bloody too. Don't take it off, you'll pull the bandage off."

She went into the kitchen and came back with a large carving knife.

"Holy shit."

"I'm not going to stab you. I couldn't find scissors. I'm going to cut that shirt down the front."

She sat on the couch beside him, pulled out the neck of the T-shirt and slid the knife under it.

"Jesus, be careful with that thing."

"You wish to talk, Amelican soldier? We have ways of making you talk."

"Name, rank and serial number — 123456 — that's all you get, you dirty Nip."

"You will talk, Amelican swine."

"Never. I'm fighting for Betty Grable and Mom and apple pie. I'll never talk."

"We lock you in room with 500 Worthy Matrons of the Eastern Star."

"The invasion is Monday night, at 7:00 P.M., and let me draw you this map of the beach."

They laughed, and she took the split fibers of the shirt and ripped it down the front. Jay rolled it into a ball and tossed it onto a chair. They were quiet for a moment.

"Hey," she said, "I was really scared tonight. I thought they were going to kill you."

"Who'd miss me?" It was supposed to be flip. It wasn't.

"I would."

Somehow, she could not remember the mechanics of it, his lips were against hers, and they were soft and cool and she was lying against his chest and she felt his tongue, a warm invader, welcome. She felt her mouth open, to let more of him in. She wanted him everywhere, in every corner of her. She felt as if she were going to melt, as if bone and tissue and fiber had turned molten. They clung together, hungry, exploring, until they heard the sound of the key turning in the lock, and the front door opened. They jerked apart, blinking at each other in surprise.

Sam and Roger walked into the room. Mary sat up straight on the couch, hoping she looked relaxed and casual. She felt her heart pounding inside her. Sam and Roger walked to the couch and peered down at Jay.

"He was a comer, too. That's how it goes in the fight game," Sam said.

"I couddah been a contendah! Charlie, you was my brudder!"

"You suck as Brando."

"Everybody's a critic."

He was kidding with Sam and Roger, not looking at her. It meant nothing to him. Why should it?

"Well," she said, "I'd better get home. Jay, don't forget to take those painkillers the doctor gave you."

"OK, Florence Nightingale."

His eyes were opaque, guarded. She felt something sink inside her. He was drawing away, shutting her out.

"We were supposed to do a story on the new wing of the hospital tomorrow at two. Why don't I call and postpone it?"

"No, let's see how I'm doing."

"There's no rush. We can do it later."

"Sure."

She started to leave, and he reached out and held her hand. He raised it to his lips and kissed her palm.

"Hot Shit," he said.

Driving home, she could still feel the throbbing in her temples. Harry had once said there was a judge inside her, but she thought of it as an accountant. Shit, why couldn't she be one of those women who could blot out the world with love? Elizabeth Taylor. Did she have a CPA behind those violet eyes?

The scent of Jay, the feel of him, surrounded her. She wanted to lose herself in the swirl of feeling inside her. Why was it she saw Harry's face, tender in the darkness, the night she had gone to him on the lawn?

"I'm pregnant. You made me pregnant, Harry."

She willed him away. She thought of Jay and shivered, thought of lying against his bare chest and kissing him, a kiss that had invaded her the way Harry's body never had. She had never imagined wanting to be possessed; she had thought that inside she was safe, inviolate. No more. She thought of the things she would do for him, if he asked, and she knew there was nothing she would not do. She felt she would die if she could not have him.

But the accountant was still there, relentless. It would be there, adding and subtracting, forever. Mary Anderson Springer always knew what she was doing.

But she was twenty-five years old, and awakened to passion. There was a current running, and she was bound to follow it. God-damn the costs. *God-fucking-damn the costs.*

Journal: Donald A. Johnson

My parents decided I would go to Gonzaga High School, a Jesuit school in the shadow of the Capitol. I wanted to go to public high school with most of my friends, but my parents thought that the public schools in Washington, by now predominantly Negro, were being allowed to decay. Gonzaga it would be. I reluctantly agreed.

Before I set off to my new school, my father had me in for a talk. Whenever we had a talk, he would get on his serious face, and he would speak slowly and with great dignity. De Lawd again.

"You are from a cultured, educated family," he said to me. "You must never let white people forget that."

"Sho 'nuff," I said. (Why he didn't kill me I don't know. I was a terrible wiseass.)

"Don't be impertinent. You have not been in the white world, and I have, and I have learned a few things. All eyes will be on you. I expect you to behave in a way that will make your mother and me proud."

"Of course I will, Daddy. You know I will."

"It will be hard, I understand that. But a lot is expected of you. You have opportunities that many of our people have not had."

He droned on, and I sort of tuned out as usual. I had heard it all before. But then I perked up my ears. He came to a subject that was utterly new. White women.

"You will now be around white girls and women. At dances. At parties. You must be very careful. When you are introduced to a white woman, do not shake her hand unless she offers it."

"What, so the black won't rub off?"

"I know this sounds strange to you, but in the white world, things are — different. Especially when it comes to Negro men and white women. I don't want you dating white girls. Some Negroes do it, but it isn't right. Besides, you will find that the kinds of white women who go out with Negro men are not the kinds of decent women you want to associate with."

I reminded him that I was only starting high school and I hadn't been out with any women at all, much less indecent ones. I didn't tell him that I would have loved to find some indecent women, of any color. Real sluts, who would do all the things Frank Yerby wrote about and then some.

Colored women, according to the lore of the white world, were earthy and sensual, abandoned. They obviously didn't know about middle-class colored girls. They were about as far from abandoned as anyone could be. I once snapped Loretta Washington's bra strap and she decked me. I mean really decked me; I went smashing into the lockers.

I'd heard stories, though, of how lower-class Negroes didn't share our lifestyle; they drank and they danced real dirty and they had sex all the time. We were supposed to look down with pity on them and to keep our distance, because none of us wanted to end up as no-account niggers. I certainly didn't. I was ashamed of them and found their very existence humiliating, at least when white people were around. Once I was walking along North Capitol Street with some of my white friends from Gonzaga when a very drunk Negro man walked by, singing at the top of his lungs. I cringed and hurried past, hoping nobody would notice. I never wondered why white people didn't get upset by "white trash" the way we did about lower-class Negroes. They never looked at some poor hillbilly up from West Virginia and thought he might befoul the whole white race.

But even as I tried to avoid the lower social orders as if they had the plague, there was a part of me that wondered what it would be like to be no-account. Just for a little while, to be a real jive-ass, hard-drinking, gambling man, with women falling all over me — indecent, no-account women who wore loud, tight dresses and wiggled when they walked. I imagined Loretta Washington, down on her luck, as one of these women. Loretta, through a hazy sequence of events, had decided not to go to college and major in English so she could be a professor at Howard, but had taken to drink and gambling and other lascivious pursuits. Instead of the modest blouses with the Peter Pan collars she wore to eighth grade, when I encountered her she was clad in a lemon yellow dress slit way up the side, and cut so far down in the front that half of her marvelous coffee-colored breasts were exposed. And she said to me, "Oh, lover man, come on and make me feel real good!" which was how I imagined lower-class, no-account, sultry women talked. Sometimes, though, in my fantasies, Loretta slipped into Frank Yerby dialogue and said things like "Plunge into me with your Saracen blade, my master, and I will give you more pleasure than the gardens of Allah." I don't think people talked like that a lot down at 7th and U Streets, just as the characters in Frank Yerby didn't say, 'Roll with me, lover man,' as they traipsed around in the fourteenth century.

But of course white women were something else again — the most desirable and the most dangerous of all. In the South, a Negro man could be lynched for even looking at a white woman. In some bizarre way, it did not seem strange that white men would be so protective of their women, because all the standards of beauty we knew about were white. When I went to the movies, I saw Lana Turner and Rita Hayworth and Marilyn Monroe. And even when a leading character was supposed to be a light-skinned colored woman, the actress who played her was white — Jeanne Crain or, in *Show Boat,* Ava Gardner. When I was attracted to girls, it was to those with light skin and slender noses, like Loretta's. I looked at really black girls and deemed them not worthy of my attention. I felt sorry for them.

Even though Gonzaga was a boys' school, I was around white

girls a lot, at dances and at parties, especially in my senior year. I hung around with a crowd of white kids, both boys and girls. The girls were from Catholic schools in the area, Immaculata, Notre Dame, Holy Names. They were pink and scrubbed and pretty, and they smelled so good, of talcum powder and shampoo and dainty sweat. We were all friends, and if my arm once in a while brushed one of theirs, it was like an electric current going right through my whole body, but of course I couldn't let it show. In fact, if a white girl had shown any sexual interest in me, I would probably have run like the blazes, since I utterly believed what my father had said about the depravity of any white woman who lusted after a Negro man.

As I had when I was a young kid, I wondered why God hadn't made me white, so those pink, nice-smelling girls would laugh and tease and smooch with me the way they did with my friends. Sometimes I'd bring a date along, but she never fit in with the group in a comfortable way — even though the white kids did try to be polite.

In college, I dated a lot of Negro women — most of them lovely, smart and savvy. But there was something missing. I guess I had a white goddess in my head, a mixture of Rita and Lana and all those girls who smelled so good and seemed so unattainable. In so many ways, the white world sets standards for us that are so absurd and so impossible. Dark skin has shades and shadows and textures that fair skin never can attain. Why aren't white people jealous of us, for our marvelous skin tones? Maybe they would be, if we made the movies and produced the TV programs and created the advertisements. Maybe then white people would be buying skin darkeners and getting injections in their lips to make them fuller. Maybe they'd cringe on the street when somebody looked at them with revulsion and said, "My God, he's so *white.*"

When I went on my first Freedom Ride, I met Marianne, who was from the University of Wisconsin. She was about as white as white people went — her parents were Norwegian. What bothered a lot of people about the Freedom Rides was that, with all those black and white young men and women, their hormones raging, all in the same bus, wasn't some kind of hanky-panky going on?

Sure it was. Not on the bus, of course. When people are smashing on the sides of your Greyhound with boards and yelling they plan to have a weenie roast with you as the weenies, you are not thinking much about sex. But we were all conscious of breaking society's great taboo, and there was something very erotic about that. Marianne and I slept together in a house in Georgia, not quite believing how adventurous we were. I'd sneak glances at her pubic hair, which was so pale it seemed hardly to be there at all. I caught her staring at me too. A brown penis was a novelty, I'm sure, after Thor and Sven or whoever. (I hoped that Sven and Thor did not live up to Viking legend, that they were small and shriveled, and pale.)

It was OK, but I think we were both disappointed. She was just a nice, sweet-smelling white girl, not a pale goddess who could transport me to some rarefied palace of pleasure to which I had never been. I was just a young guy trying to get it right, not a black brute who'd give her sex like she'd never imagined. We were just friends after that, not lovers. And I got over my yearning for white women.

Not that a gorgeous women of any color can't get my motor running, but it's not metaphysical anymore, it's just lust. I have more appreciation for the sisters, now, of any shade. I admire them for their strength, their humor, their courage. When I marry, I think she will be Negro, but I won't think I'm being shortchanged. I don't dream about goddesses anymore.

Lately, in fact, I've been dating Loretta Washington, who's getting her master's in literature at Howard. She doesn't deck me when I unsnap her bra; she still could, I suspect. Loretta is a lot of woman. I've never asked her to wear a lemon-colored dress and say, "Lover man, come on and make me feel good." She would if I asked her. I won't ask her to do the Frank Yerby dialogue about the Saracen blade, though. She's teaching Chaucer. She'd never get through it with a straight face.

"WANT TO GO to the game, Harry?"

His father stood in the hall, looking at him expectantly.

"No, Pop, I don't think so."

"The new kid is supposed to be very good. Everybody says he reminds them of you."

"I wasn't that great, Pop."

"Of course you were. The best in twenty years."

"Right."

"Say, I was talking to Coach McDonough the other night. About the assistant coaching job."

"There's new requirements. Now you have to have a phys ed degree. I'm not qualified."

"But Coach McDonough was saying how good you were."

"It's a state law. You have to have a college degree. You can't change the law."

"The job you have now, Harry, it's OK for now. There's big things ahead for you, Harry. I always knew that."

"Pop, I wish you wouldn't say that."

"You got off the track for a little while, a lot of young kids do, but —"

"Off the track! Pop, I was a drunk. I drank myself blind every night. I got arrested. You called me that yourself, remember? You said, 'Get up off the floor, you stinking drunk!'"

He saw the flicker of pain in his father's face. He regretted his words. But his father had a way of blotting out anything unpleasant.

"I didn't mean it. I was just angry at you."

"I know. I know you didn't mean it."

"You have friends in this town, Harry, people who remember."

He laughed, bitterly. "Where were those people when I was broke and unemployed? Did any of them give me a chance?"

"They still talk about you. At the games, people come up to me. They still talk about the Frederick game, remember that one? Two out, last of the ninth. I was never so nervous in my life." His father's face was animated with the memory.

He wanted to say, "Don't do this to me, Pop," but he nodded and said, "Yeah, that was quite a day."

"A coach's pay is pretty good, isn't it?"

"Will you stop talking about it! I can't get the job. I'm doing OK at the job I have. I know you don't think it's much, but I'm doing good at it."

"I didn't say it wasn't good. I just think you can do better. A lot better."

"Too bad I didn't fucking drop dead the day I hit the home run against Frederick. Then you'd have a dead hero to be proud of, not an ex-drunk who works for a laundry."

"Don't you use that kind of language in this house. This is my house, and you're still under my roof."

"You keep reminding me of that, don't you?"

His father's anger died. "Oh, Harry, why do you get so angry when I talk about the old days? I was so proud of you. What's wrong with that? Do you want me to forget it all?"

"No. But that was easy, that home run. Don't you know that? He gave me a gopher ball. I could have hit it to China."

His father chuckled. "You damn near did."

"What wasn't so easy was getting up off the floor of that drunk tank. Do you know how hard that was? I wanted to die. But I didn't. I was a drunk eight months ago, but now I'm sober and I have a job."

"You weren't really a drunk, just a kid who —"

"No, damn it, I was a drunk. *Am* a drunk. Face it, Pop, I wasn't a kid who got himself tanked a couple of times. I am an alcoholic. If I ever take another drink, I could slide all the way back to that floor, crawling in my own vomit. Give me credit, Pop, it was so goddamn hard."

His father looked at him, then dropped his eyes. He went to the closet, got out his brown London Fog jacket and put it on.

"We'd have a good time at the game, Harry. Just the two of us, like the old days. Like it used to be."

"Thanks, Pop, but I've got some work to catch up on today."

"Some other time, maybe, Harry?"

"Sure, Pop. Some other time."

"I could rent myself out to haunt houses," Jay groaned, looking into the bathroom mirror. He was wearing a blue shirt and a dark blue tie that was a match to the blotch that circled his eye and extended down his cheek.

"Stop moaning about how you look and let me use the mirror," Sam said, "I got to shave."

Jay moved back to let Sam get to the sink, but he kept on examining his face.

"You got a date?" he asked Sam.

"Yeah. New talent. Works for the Pentagon. Lives in Rockville, though, that's not too bad. You bringing Norma?"

"Oh Christ, no."

"What's wrong with Norma? She seems — earthy."

"Yeah. She's earthy. What's the reason for this party? Who's leaving?"

"Nobody. Milt just wanted to give a party."

"I'm giving Mary a ride."

"Purely a humanitarian gesture?"

"Yeah."

"What were you two doing on the couch the other night, anyhow? Talking about cutlines?"

Jay frowned.

Sam looked at him. "I think this is serious."

Jay shook his head. "I don't know what it is. *If* it is."

Sam lathered his face and started to shave. "Word of warning, old buddy. I think she's pretty vulnerable right now."

"I know."

"And you're a bleeder."

"A what?"

"Jews and Irish Catholics. Very big on internal bleeding. Figures you people are the lost tribe."

Jay laughed. "Not so internal. When I was in the fifth grade I cut crosses on my palms. The stigmata."

"You mean the wounds of Christ?"

"You got it. Sister Immaculata said good Catholics wanted to share the suffering of Christ. She prayed for the stigmata, but she wasn't worthy enough."

"You don't mean you actually cut yourself."

"Oh yeah. I figured, why pray for the stigmata when I had my Cub Scout knife. I bled all over the floor in the boys' bathroom."

"Did they send you to a shrink?"

"Are you kidding? I was a big hero. The only kid in school with the stigmata. Sister Immaculata was green with envy. I said I'd lend her my knife."

"God, it's a wonder you're not in the loony bin."

"Me? I'm fine. Now could you get out of here so I can flagellate myself before the party?"

Jay put on his jacket and walked out to the car, whistling. He had mowed the grass that morning in a burst of energy and the fresh smell surrounded him. He inhaled it with the cool night air, then stood still and shivered with delight; he had the sense that the world was magic; the passage from boy to man destroyed it in most, but it still came to him, at times. He could not imagine being alive without it. Tonight held a sense of promise that he didn't want to examine too closely. A strange thing had been happening lately with his Jacqueline fantasies. There she'd be, in some *House Beautiful* bedroom with satin sheets and great art on the walls, and when she elegantly peeled off her Oleg Cassini dress–ball gown–Chanel suit–riding costume–Yves St. Laurent lounging pajamas, her face would change and she would turn into Mary, standing naked in front of him, smiling, with the white gloves and the freckles on her pale shoulders. What a wardrobe she would have, he thought wryly, if she could just pick up the stuff Jackie dropped. All she'd have to do was say, "excuse me," hop out of bed and scoop it all into a bag. She would get not only a great fuck (he was always fantastic; they were his fantasies, after all) but a closetful of designer clothes as well.

He doubted that she'd ever worn a pair of forty-five-dollar silk panties, not on a *Blade* salary. But she was not the type for purple no-crotchies either. Tailored, no-nonsense cotton panties, perhaps with little flowers on them. He saw her in them, naked except for the panties, her graceful breasts bare, looking more seductive than anything Frederick's of Hollywood could offer. The image aroused him. He groaned.

No, this would not do. He banished her, and she went, regretfully. He replaced her with the Lady in Black, lovely in her black velvet gown, the Chrysler Building twinkling across her shoulder. That was better. Soothing. He kissed her red-lipsticked mouth, and she too turned into Mary, lying against his bare chest, and he was kissing her desperately, and she was kissing him back. It was odd; he had kissed plenty of women in his day, but nothing had been as searing as that kiss, on the lumpy sofa with the stuffing coming out, under a window that looked out on an alley. What was it about her that seemed to make everything so magical — even without the Chrysler Building or the satin sheets? And what was he going to do about it?

He pulled up in front of her house, and she ran out and bounced into the front seat, the way a little girl would. The movement, totally graceless, charmed him. She was wearing a black sheath dress with a round neckline that was designed for sophistication, but her ebullient mood gave it the opposite effect.

At the door, Milt Beerman greeted Jay with "Well, Primo Carnera, glad you got here," and Jay grumbled, "Another face joke. Just what I need."

Jay and Mary joined a group in the corner of the room, where a heated discussion about the urban renewal plan was taking place.

Jay complained that all they ever talked about was work, and then they started speculating about JFK's girlfriends, but in a few minutes it was back to urban renewal. The room grew warm and the laughter louder and the glasses filled and emptied. Sam came in with his date, and as soon as someone put "Tenderly" on the stereo, Joe Rosenberg, who covered the cops, asked her to dance.

Sam groused to Jay. "One of these times that son-of-a-bitch is going to bring his own date."

Sam asked Mary to dance when Bill Haley blared "Shake, Rattle, and Roll," and Joe showed no sign of releasing Sam's date. Jay sat on the couch and watched them all. Mary's face was flushed, and she was laughing as she moved her body in the dance that was innocent and erotic all at once. He wondered how she could change so quickly; one minute she could seem small and plain, and the next instant radiant, almost beautiful. When the music stopped she dropped, laughing and breathing hard, onto the sofa beside him.

"Sam, I'm getting old. Medicare is around the corner!"

She threw her head back against the couch, and Jay studied her throat. It was a lovely throat, soft and white. She saw him studying her and she said, "Did I make a complete ass of myself?"

He shook his head. "You've having fun, aren't you?"

"Oh, I am. I haven't had this much fun in a long time."

There was an awkward silence. The phonograph started with an Eddie Fisher ballad, and she said, "This is more my speed." She turned to him; he was unaccountably nervous.

"I'm terrible. I'll step on your feet."

"I'll probably step on yours first."

At first he concentrated on avoiding her toes, but her body was warm and he could smell her perfume and he pulled her close against him. After a while he realized that they were not really dancing, just holding each other the way lovers embraced. He looked around to see if anyone was watching them, but no one seemed to care. A sweet lassitude came over him, and he wished it would just go on and on, the music and her body against his. He felt again the sense of calm flowing through him.

Finally, the party started to wind down and people began to

leave. Regretfully, he released her. She got her coat, and they walked together towards the car.

"How about one for the road? Sam has a new bottle of Courvoisier we can steal."

"That sounds good."

He drove to the apartment, and when they walked in he turned on the lamp by the sofa instead of the overhead light. He got out the brandy and found two old shrimp cocktail containers that looked vaguely like liqueur glasses.

"Watch out," he said, handing one to her. "When you're used to Jules's swill, this stuff can pack a wallop."

She took a tentative sip. "Oh, that's good. I've never had brandy before."

They sat silently, sipping the drinks, aware of each other. He was not a calculator; elaborate schemes of seduction were foreign to him. The situation was not clear. She was still wearing her wedding band.

"That was a good party," he said.

"Yes, it was."

"After everybody got over the bad jokes about how I look." He touched his face, gingerly.

"You don't really look like Primo Carnera."

"I bet you don't know who he is."

"He was this big, hulking figure, but he had a glass jaw."

"That incredible. You must be the only girl in America who know about Primo Carnera."

"I read everything. The sports pages, I read cereal boxes." She was silent for a minute. "Your face does look awfully sore. Does it hurt much?"

"Only when I laugh."

She reached up and touched his face. Things were no longer unclear. He pulled her to him and touched her hair and started to kiss her mouth; it opened under his, and he explored the softness of her lips and tongue. It was strange how things with her were so astonishingly intimate; a touch, a kiss. When kissing her was no longer enough, he moved his hands across her body. He slid his hand down the neck of her dress and discovered she was not wearing a bra; he found that deliciously wanton; it excited him. He pulled the top of the dress off her shoulders. She did have freckles, tiny ones, on her pale shoulders. He felt himself sliding out of control, not just physically but as if his whole being were being pulled under by a wave. A voice inside his head said, loud and clear, I don't want to love her.

Then she shuddered and moved in his arms, and the voice was still.

"I want you," he said. "I want you so much."

"Yes," she said, very low, into his shoulder. Then she said, quietly, not looking at him, "Do you have something?"

He nodded and took her hand and led her into the bedroom. He closed the door and touched her face and said, "Only if you want to," and she nodded.

He undressed her, fumbling with zippers and hooks. The only light in the room spilled in from the streetlights outside, and where it touched her, it made her skin seem translucent. Her breasts were as he had imagined them, full and sloping and gently curved. How was it he knew so much about her?

"You're beautiful," he said. He reached for the buttons of his shirt to undress hastily, but she surprised him by taking his hand away and undoing the buttons herself. He stood still while she undressed him, and when she slid to her knees to remove his underpants, he was startled again at how intimate, how tender and erotic the gesture was, all at once. He thought he had never felt so naked before, not like this.

They walked together to the bed, and he touched her, explored her. She didn't close her eyes but watched him, her eyes on his face, and that excited him too. Then she said, "Let me touch you," and he lay back on the pillow. At first she touched his face, running her hands across its plains and valleys. Then she moved her hands and her lips to his chest, his belly, and tentatively, her hands slid between his legs.

He gasped at the touch, and she said, "Do you like this?" and he said, "Yes. Don't stop. Please."

He was astonished at her delight as she touched him, as if his body were some beautiful object. He had never imagined he had the capacity to draw this from a woman. He had never thought of himself as particularly handsome or desirable. A wave of gratitude washed over him. He understood that no one had really made love to him before.

He reached up and drew her body down on top of his, feeling her weight on him, a lovely burden. They moved together until he could stand it no longer, and he said, "I need you now," and he reached over for the condom, his nimble fingers suddenly clumsy. She slid underneath him, and her legs parted, and he drove into her, seeming to float, layer by layer, into the deeps of her. He began the shuddering dance that would, at its height, obliterate the world, and he heard her call his name, just once. He knew it was a sound that would echo through the rest of his life.

When it was done she huddled against him, and he stretched his arms around her, kissing her hair, wanting to give to her as much as she had given to him.

"Was it — OK for you?" he asked.

She touched his face and kissed him on the lips and smiled at him. He got up and went to the bathroom to get rid of the rubber. He felt an absurd throb of regret for the cloudy liquid as it rolled around the toilet bowl and vanished. *Seed* no longer seemed a peculiar word for it. He saw her belly swelling, felt his hands on it. Then he realized what he was thinking, and he said, "Jesus H. Christ."

He went back and lay down beside her. He felt that she was inside him, everywhere inside his body, and he felt a joy so fierce he thought it would tear his chest apart. It frightened him. Who could live with this?

"This isn't all I wanted," he said. "This too, but it's you, the way you talk, the things you say, Christ, that sounds dumb —"

She put her fingers to his lips. "Jay, you don't have to tell me. I wanted you to, I was afraid you'd guess and think I was — a tramp or something."

"Don't think that. Don't ever think that."

"I was — all right, wasn't I?" She was looking into his shoulder, not his eyes. "It's supposed to be like this, isn't it?"

"You were wonderful," he said.

"I want to be what you want. I always thought I could, you know, respond. You read a lot about men liking that, but what you read isn't always true."

He had a sense, then, of what her marriage must have been like, and he felt a stab of pity for her.

"If you want a biased opinion," he said, "you are the sexiest broad in the entire Golden Area region, which is what our beloved employer calls this depressed and godforsaken neck of the woods."

She giggled. "The Golden Area is not big on sex ed. I used to think Fred Astaire and Ginger Rogers were doing it. Because we had this film in school that showed little dancing sperm and eggs."

"In seventh grade Father Hannigan took the boys in one room to talk about the marriage act. I thought it was something the Founding Fathers signed, like the Stamp Act. I asked the kid ahead of me what the Marriage Act was, and he said, 'screwing, you dummy.'"

"Miss Hansen said that sex and comic books were rotting the moral fiber of America."

"I lived on comic books. Remember Captain Marvel? I liked him."

"Sure. He said *Shazam* and an old guy with a white beard threw a thunderbolt. He lived at the Rock of Eternity."

"Remember who Captain Marvel was when he wasn't Captain Marvel?"

"Billy Batson, boy broadcaster from station WHIZ," she said.

"OK, but how about Captain Marvel, Jr.?"

"Freddie the crippled newsboy."

"You're good. You're really good."

"There was a bad guy who always said, 'Heh-heh-heh.'"

"Dr. Savannah. And he had a daughter named Georgiana Savannah who also went, 'heh-heh-heh.'"

She giggled and pulled the covers up to her chin. "Jay, I don't believe this conversation. In John O'Hara, people don't talk about Billy Batson, boy broadcaster, after they have sex."

"In John O'Hara, they talk about Plastic Man."

"Plastic Man! Oh, my God, I forgot all about him. He stretched his arms and his legs out and he was so yucky."

He laughed and pulled her close. She lay against him, her head on his chest, and the eerie sense of calm descended on him again. He felt — he wasn't sure how he felt. Strong, male.

Mated.

That was it. He had the sense that this was where he belonged, that some missing piece of him had been restored. She stirred in his arms and sighed, and was quiet. He thought how good it was, just being quiet with her. It was odd that at his age there were so many things about being with a woman he didn't know.

He had the feeling he was going to learn.

He combed his hair and peered into the bathroom mirror; he was more than somewhat vain. He liked to keep a tan, and his face looked bronzed and healthy. Early on, it had been to hide the faintly brownish tones that Addison's disease, an adrenal malfunction, caused in the skin. That was under control, but he liked the tan anyway. It certainly hadn't hurt in the debate with Nixon. Helluva thing, to think he might have won the presidency thanks to a tube of Coppertone.

He ran his finger down the side of his cheek, frowning a bit at the way the lines in the neck stood out under this light, and at the slight puffiness around the jaw. It was important to him to think of himself as young, and he tended that image carefully. He swam to keep his weight down, his suits were impeccably tailored to emphasize his leanness, and he was careful about the photographs that were taken of him. He never let anyone photograph him while he was eating; he had seen a photo of Nixon wearing a lei around his neck and trying to eat poi with his fingers; the vice president had looked like an asshole. He never put on cowboy hats or Indian headdresses or kissed babies or did anything else that would make him look undignified. Sometimes, when he was traveling on the campaign, he would hunch in the backseat of a car to wolf down a hamburger out of sight of the photographers. His critics, especially the liberals, carped about his attention to style. Probably because none of those fucking guys would know style if it hit them in the balls. They all worshipped Adlai Stevenson, who could never make up his mind, even about whether he wanted ham or pastrami on rye. The fucking liberals, they always had some cause or other that they carried with them like Marley's ghost dragging his chains, moaning all the while. And they dressed like shit.

He smiled, and the image in the mirror smiled back, winningly. It was not manly to speak of charm, that was for women, but he knew it had its uses. So often hospitalized in his youth, he had no power to demand that attention be paid, but charm could bring that extra bit of care from the nurses. Unable to compete with his bigger, healthier brother Joe in athletics, he used his charm to draw a circle of other boys around him in school. He could turn it on and off at will. Once, he told a young woman he was squiring to a party that he was going to play Mr. Big Shot and bowl all the adults over; he did.

His father had a kind of charm, he knew, but it was of a rougher, more blustery sort, and it repelled nearly as many people as it attracted. But the old man was savvy. He liked to say that the New Deal had destroyed the last of the social hierarchies that had been traditional in the nation, and that Hollywood would provide the new aristocracy. On his own trips to California as a young man, he had been endlessly fascinated with the creation of illusion, the way sex appeal — rather than sex itself — could be sold like soap flakes. That was, in fact, exactly the term his father had used once in describing how his son could be sold to a willing electorate: soap flakes. He told an interviewer, "Jack is the greatest attraction in the country," and he boasted that his son's appearance at a fund-raising dinner would draw more people than Gary Cooper or Cary Grant.

He cupped his hands and splashed cold water onto his face, peered again into the mirror as he wiped his face. His best feature, he knew, were his eyes — blue, alert, intelligent, that could turn to frozen chips of ice when he was angry or could seem to fill with light when his quick, warm smile could engulf a room. He could use it with calculation; more often it simply appeared. Reporters could tell when a good line was cooking in his brain. As a questioner droned on (especially if he were particularly pompous), they could see the barest hint of movement at the corners of his mouth and the mischief creeping into his eyes. He would look like a cat, about to pounce. The wit was as often turned against himself. He could be bawdy and outrageous, but rarely was he savage. Humor was more a shield than a weapon. He was smart enough to know that he could neutralize some issue — his father, his religion, his war record — by laughing about it himself before anyone else could speak. It made critics seem churlish.

He turned his head slightly to the side, liking what he saw. He especially liked profile shots when his head was tilted upwards, so the new fullness about the jawline did not show. Privately, he would have admitted his vanity, but he raged at a Time *reporter who claimed that he had once posed for* Gentlemen's Quarterly. *He blistered the hapless man's ear for several minutes — he'd been a sailor and could swear like one — because the last thing he wanted to be thought was a dandy.*

He understood, better than most, the power of image. He had been astonished, when meeting Dwight Eisenhower as the old president prepared to turn over the reins of power, that the heroic general seemed unmindful of his place in history. He had even remarked that he thought the Allies prevailed at Normandy because they had the best meteorologists.

He ran his hands through his thick, reddish brown hair. He had a scalp massage every week, and when his aides tweaked him about it, he reminded them of who still had the best hair. He never liked to hide it under hats of any kind.

If he managed his image with all the aplomb of a Hollywood matinee idol, it was not simply to stroke his vanity. He was intrigued by the historian Richard Neustadt's idea of the president as a great actor, able to exercise power by persuading the people to follow where he led. He was stung by those who said he had shown a lot of profile but not much courage in his political life, who saw him as a callow young man whose father had bought his way into politics. He was fond of Stephen Spender's poem

I think continually of those who were truly great . . .
The names of those who in their lives fought for life,
Who wore at their hearts the fire's centre.
Born of the sun they traveled a short while towards the sun.
And left the vivid air signed with their honour.

Not born of the sun was he: that might have been said of his brother Joe. But men who invented themselves could also sign the vivid air. If there was much of the calculator in his use of noble words, there was also something of the carpenter. If you could build a structure that was grand and great, perhaps you could also grow to fill it.

The times could call forth greatness in a man. If 1860 had been a placid, peaceful year, would Lincoln be a forgotten president from Illinois? And without World War II, what was Churchill? A failed, overweight politician. He lived, after all, in interesting times, and he knew, now, he had the mettle to meet them. All he needed was time. And after all, he was young. The mirror told him that, even with the jowls.

Challenge could call forth greatness in a man.

ONLY AFTER she had decided she was frigid did she realize that a supermarket of sex surrounded her. Women practically fell out of their gowns in ads for movies, foreign films actually showed frontal nudity, lascivious paperbacks about bad, bad women littered the newsstands, and *Playboy* magazine was getting ever bolder in what its well-paid photographers were allowed to publish. Now and then she would stick a copy of *Playboy* from the magazine rack in her purse when she was doing the grocery shopping. She would have been too mortified to plunk it down on the counter in front of the clerk. She didn't think of it as stealing, exactly, but getting a look into a world she knew she could never enter.

But now, of course, it was all different. She probably could have stood it, being the shopper with the empty basket, if she had never understood what it could be like. She sat in front of the mirror on her vanity table, whacking at her hair with the brush. *Glamour* said a hundred strokes a day would make her hair lustrous, and she had gotten into the habit. She thought it just might fall out one day, every strand of it, beaten to death.

She was talking with Sigmund Freud. He had taken to dropping in at odd times, lecturing.

You know, of course, that men go to bed with women all the time, and it means nothing.

No, this is different.

Your brain is quite inoperative, my dear. You are thinking with your hormones. Right now all you want is to get into the sack with him again.

That's not true.

She tried to banish from her mind the image of him, naked on the bed, the feel of him, the smell of him; it was so real it refused to leave.

Shall I be specific? Just a minute ago you were thinking of rolling around with him in the surf, licking the salt water from his naked body, like they did in From Here to Eternity.

They weren't naked in From Here to Eternity.

Beside the point. You were also thinking about taking a bath with him, rubbing soap bubbles all over his erect phallus — and while it is in reality more than adequate, in your imagination it is humongous — and getting on top of him and thrashing about and moaning a lot. What is this fascination you have with water? Perhaps a memory of the fetal state —

Oh, for heaven's sake!

I especially like the one where you are wearing scanty clothing and twirling a baton, and he rips your clothes off and you do the most interesting things with the baton — and must I tell you what the baton represents?

Oh, my God, I thought I'd outgrown that one.

And, of course, just like a woman, one night in bed and you're smelling orange blossoms.

That's ridiculous.

There was the matter of her byline. She had thought "By Mary Springer Broderick" might seem clumsy. "M. S. Broderick" was classy, like one of the bylines in the *Times*.

He's going to leave, you know. He's going to have sex with you and you're going to break your heart over him and wreck your marriage as well, and then where will you be?

I don't know. I don't care. I love him.

You loved Harry too.

Mary threw the brush down on the table. How nice it must be, she thought, to be a man. Men looked at things so differently. Life was like one of those connect-the-dots puzzles in a child's book. Men just saw the numbers, floating in space, so they were free to move as they wished. Women saw all those connecting lines that men didn't see. The lines gave women a sense of what held the world together, kept their lives from being the empty corridors some men's lives became. But they could be fetters, too, holding them back. Mary and Harry and Karen had those lines between them. Could she just rip them out?

I'm pregnant, Harry. I'm pregnant.

She was so different now from the girl who had stood on the lawn of Harry's house and sobbed out the lie that would change their lives. He was different, too. Who was he? What were they to each other? She had read that the Chinese believed that if you saved a person's life, you altered fate, and you were responsible for that person from then on. What if you determined the course of a life? Had the lie put that responsibility on her? Had she tied them navel to navel, with a cord of words. *I'm pregnant.*

She tried to think of Harry, but he kept turning into Jay, in bed beside her. She had never imagined she would trust a man the way she trusted him. She had blurted out her discoveries, and he had not patronized her; she had a mortal fear of inconsequence. If she was paranoid at all, it was when she thought people might be laughing at her. It was easy for men to think they counted for something, because they were men and could not be disregarded. It was their birthright. A woman had to drag consequence out of the world, inch by bloody inch. With Jay, she would not be trivial. He could take her, command her, make her want to get down on her knees for the pleasure he gave her, but he would never ask her to be a mirror in which he saw only himself, magnified.

She shook her head, as if to dislodge the weight of her thoughts. She went to the closet to get dressed for work. Usually she grabbed the first thing she put her hands on. Today, she changed clothes three times. The shirtdress spoke of indifference, it was too bland. The black sheath, too obvious. The blue sweater and skirt, too dressy with the heels, but with the low-heeled pumps, it would pass. She put on mascara and rouge, and wondered if people would notice.

She went into the living room, where Karen was waiting with the storybook. It was their daily ritual, one she never missed if she could help it. The little girl was busily drawing on a piece of paper.

"What are you drawing, sweetie?"

"Bugs Bunny, see."

"That's good. What are those little round things?"

"Farts."

"What?"

"Farts, Mommy."

"That's very . . . interesting. I never saw a picture of a fart before."

"That's how Danny makes 'em. He showed me."

She laughed, delighted by the idea that her daughter had mastered the subtleties of drawing farts. She loved the way her daughter's mind worked, making wild, inventive leaps from one place to another.

She remembered herself as a child, at the top of the tallest tree. How had that little person become the girl so frightened of life that she had to trap a man into marrying her with a lie?

She ran her finger across her daughter's soft cheek. They'd try to put fetters on that wild, lovely imagination someday. People would try to make her conventional, into a nice little girl who would be seen but not heard. No way. No fucking way. Whatever else she did, she would see to that.

"Read me Piglet," Karen demanded.

"Piglet, again? Don't you want another one?"

"I like Piglet."

"I like him, too. He's silly."

Karen giggled. "That's why I like him. He's silly. Pooh Bear is very serious."

When the station wagon sounded its horn outside, Mary walked Karen out to see her off to nursery school. Then she went back inside to make herself a cup of coffee. Her mother was reading the paper.

"You're dressed up today."

"This? It's a million years old."

"Isn't that sweater a little tight?"

"Mom, I'm not Jayne Mansfield."

"You don't want to send off . . . signals."

"Oh, no, not the lecture again."

"When a woman is separated from her husband, men see her as fair game. It's true, believe me. When you don't have a husband, they are . . . forward."

Mary looked at her mother. "Are you talking from experience?"

"Let's say I know what it's like."

"I can take care of myself."

"I didn't say you couldn't. It's just that . . . it's so easy to make mistakes, on your own."

"Don't worry, I won't."

"I worry about you. You seem to think that none of the rules apply to you. You think you can just go out and act like a man and nothing will happen to you."

"Maybe I can. Fuck the rules."

Her mother frowned. "You never listen to me. You'll just do what you're going to do."

"Bye, Mom. I'll see you later."

She got in the car and drove to the *Blade.* Sigmund Freud was sitting beside her.

You should listen to your mother.

Oh, shut up.

There are rules, you know, even if you don't want to know about them.

Fuck the rules.

Must you?

Sorry. In your century, people don't say that.

Let us propose a scenario. Everyone was drinking, a man was horny, a woman was available.

Horny?

We don't say that in my century, but we should. What if, when he sees her in the daylight, he thinks that she is not beautiful, that he must have made a mistake?

I . . . didn't think of that.

Perhaps you should have.

* * *

She pulled into the parking lot. His car was there. Everything looked so — ordinary, as it always did. Had last night happened at all?

By the time she had reached the front door, she had decided it was a one-night stand for him, that was all, how could she have been such a fool, writing "By M. S. Broderick" in her notebook? She was an absolute ass.

OK, so what if it was a one-night stand? Two could play at that game. The double standard was old hat, not for modern women. She tossed her head defiantly and became — Jeanne Moreau. Jeanne Moreau, woman of the world, who used men and then threw them away.

Jeanne Moreau walked into the *Blade* building and went right to the bathroom. She choked through half a cigarette, and kept it in her fingers as she walked into the city room with elaborate coolness. He was sitting on the edge of Sam's desk, in animated conversation. He didn't see her come in, and she put her purse down on the desk and began to flip through the paper. She felt her heart thumping; it was as loud as the one in the Edgar Allan Poe story, echoing off the walls, the ceiling. She didn't look at him, but she knew he had seen her and turned around. Finally she did look up, trying to keep her heart out of her eyes.

"Hi," he said. He was smiling his crooked smile.

"Hi."

"It's a nice day."

"Really nice. I'm glad it's summer."

"Me too."

"Hasn't rained much."

"No, it's been dry."

Sam looked at them. "That's what I love about this job. The pay sucks, but the conversation is so witty."

Jay laughed and said to Mary, "Come take a look at the pictures I did at the hospital. I want your opinion."

They went downstairs to the darkroom, and she said, "Where are they?" and he grinned. "There aren't any. I just wanted to say hello."

He put his arms around her and kissed her, hungrily, and she kissed him back.

"Don't ever say I don't take you classy places."

"Oh, Dick, it's such fun necking in the war room."

"Look at all those buttons, Pat. Red ones, blue ones. Oh, God, I'm getting my first hard on since they stoned my car in Venezuela."

"Dick, don't waste it. Take me, right here on the instrument panel!"

"Ohhh! Ohhhh! The buttons hurt so good."

"Dick, I'm coming. I'm coming in the war room. Oh, Dick, that was fantastic!"

"Yeah, Pat, that was just swell. I got hard, you came, and, by the way, we wiped out Sverdlovsk."

They laughed, and he said, "I missed you this morning. I wanted to find you there when I woke up."

"I missed you, too."

"I'm going to look for a place of my own. Someplace where I can be with you without anyone else around."

"I want to be with you, Jay."

"Listen, I've got some time off. Let's go to D.C. To a nice hotel. We'll live like swells for the weekend."

They kissed again, and she leaned against him, feeling nearly faint with desire for him. She wondered what would happen if they were doing it, right there, in the darkroom, while people all around them were going about their jobs. The idea was thrilling, but if Bill McChesney walked in it could be mortifying. McChesney was very focused; he'd probably say, "Hi, guys," and stick his prints in the developer as they humped next to the enlarger. Finally, reluctantly, they pulled apart and went back upstairs to the city room. Sam looked at Jay.

"Did you get the pictures done?"

"Yeah, we picked 'em out."

"Nice shade of lipstick you're wearing. What do they call it, Photographic Pink?"

Jay wiped the lipstick off, sheepishly, just as Milt Beerman walked over to them.

"What are you guys hearing?"

"Weird things," Mary said. "My mother told me that people are saying there's going to be a ten-story housing project and they're going to bus Negroes in from Washington."

"Where did they get that?"

"I don't know, but it's all over."

"A guy yelled at me in Art's Diner this morning," Sam said. "He said something about 'busing in the niggers.' I didn't know what he was talking about."

"People seemed scared," Mary told him. "I've never heard so much talk about nigger this and nigger that. You used to hear talk like that every once in a while, but now it's all over the place."

"Do you think there could be trouble at the council meeting tonight?" Milt asked.

"The Negro group isn't about to back down," Sam said. "Reverend Johnson said this is the first time in years he's seen the people really pulling together on something."

"We could have a 'situation' on our hands."

"I'm talking to Don Johnson at two," Mary said. "And after that I'm interviewing James Washington. He's going to be the spokesman for the group."

"Are they worried?"

Sam shook his head. "They're prepared for trouble, if it comes. Don Johnson's been giving people lessons in nonviolent resistance."

"This isn't Birmingham," Mary said. "These are people I've known all my life. I think it's going to be OK."

"I hope you're right," the city editor said.

She was sitting in the minister's living room, drinking a cup of coffee that Don had brewed, talking about nonviolence. He leaned back on the sofa and tried to explain.

"The good people *have* to confront what they support when it's right in front of their noses. They think, 'That's not us,' when people talk about bigots, 'That's the guys with the red necks who wear sheets and burn crosses.' But they're the ones whose silence makes Jim Crow possible. When they have to see the police dogs and the fire hoses, they can't avoid what the system does. Or maybe they just think that chaos is bad for business. Either way, nonviolence works, because it weeds the ugliness out of hiding, brings it out into the light."

"Is it much different in the North?"

"Here, there's no system of segregation that's built into law. People can hate just as hard, but they use economic power to push us around. Bureaucrats, not police dogs. The end result is a lot the same."

"It's strange," she said, taking a sip of the coffee, "but all the time I was growing up I didn't think much about all the Negroes living in the same place. It just seemed to be — how things were."

"That's one of the great forces we have to overcome. The status quo. Whatever is, is right."

"But it's hard to think you have the right to change things. I wrote to *Newsweek* because they have men younger than me, and with no experience, starting as reporters. But the editor told me they have a rule, no women can be reporters. They can be researchers, looking things up in the library, not reporters."

"That's not fair. If you're good enough, you should get the job."

"Well, part of me thinks that, but there's another part that says maybe they're right, they know more than I do. Part of me thinks I don't have a right even to try for that job. But I know I can do it. I *am* doing it. I've covered Kennedy. I have great clips, but that doesn't matter. Nobody but me thinks it's not fair. So maybe I'm the one who's out of line."

He looked at her, surprised. "You're the first white person I've ever heard say that."

"What?"

"That you don't think you have a right to go anywhere or do anything."

"There's somebody or something inside my head, telling me I don't. It's just — *them.*"

"I have *them* too. But I know who they are. White people. They say, 'you can't you can't you can't,' and it's hard to tune them out. Who's your *them?*"

She stared down at her coffee. "I don't know. I never thought about exactly who they are, but they're there. Even my mother. She loves me, but it's like she'd be afraid that if I step over some invisible line, bad things will happen."

"My father's like that. He worked so hard to create this little circle for all of us, and we're safe inside it, but if we go outside, we have to be afraid. We have to act this certain way, or — or I don't know what will happen. But something bad. And I don't mean down south. I mean in my hometown, Washington, D.C. It's like white people are always there, like God, watching and disapproving."

"But you don't care. You've been so brave."

He shook his head. "I can't tune *them* out sometimes. They use my father's voice. He says I can't be a writer, because Negro men can't make a living that way. I hear his voice when I'm sitting in my class at Georgetown. I'm the best writer there, I know that, but the others, they don't hear voices."

"What does your father want you to do?"

"He wanted me to go to med school, take over his practice. Now he wants me to be a teacher, at a Negro college. But my professor, she wants to introduce me to her literary agent. She thinks there's a book in the things I'm writing."

"That's great!"

He frowned. "But I can't really believe it could happen, I guess because my father thinks it can't. What if I spend all my time on it, and it's no good? What if he's really right?"

"It doesn't matter, you have to try."

"Yeah, but that means I can't go back to the South. And that's where I should be." He looked up at her and shook his head. "I can't believe I'm telling you this." He took another sip of coffee. "I have this weird feeling that if I go south again, I won't come back. That I'll die there. I never thought that when I was there. Even in the worst moments, the ones when it was really possible that I could get killed, I still had this feeling that I was immortal. But not anymore. So I wonder, am I using the book idea to chicken out, not do what I should do?"

"You're organizing people here. That's important."

"Yeah, but this will be settled soon, one way or another."

"What do you really want to do?"
"I want to try to write the book."
"Then that's what you should do."
"You really think so?"
"I know so. And so do you."
"I guess," he said. "I just needed to hear it."
She smiled at him. "You just have."

Journal: Donald A. Johnson

Growing up black and Catholic meant that church was different for me than for most Negroes. It was only when I went south that I really experienced what it was like for us to have a church of our own. I'd been to my uncle's church a few times, but it always seemed strange to me, all that singing and calling out, all that energy. I got used to it in the South, began to realize what a source of strength it could be. Still, it's not the gospel rhythms that have the deepest hold on my soul; it's the Salve Regina. The Jesuits say "Give us a boy until he is seven and he is ours for life," and I guess that is true. It was my father who converted to Catholicism because of a priest he met as a young man, and my mother converted, too, after they were married.

I don't remember thinking much about color as far as church was concerned until I was in second grade and I got a holy card with a picture of a guardian angel on it. It showed two little white children crossing a bridge over a rushing river, and there was a slat missing on the bridge. The angel had its wings wrapped about the children, and you just knew they were in no danger.

I really liked the idea of a guardian angel, but I instantly had my doubts about the one on the card, who was pale white, with hair even fairer than that of Claude Jarman, Jr., and silvery wings. I needed a guardian angel because a bunch of tough white kids had taken to roaming the fringes of our neighborhood, beating up little Negro kids who made the mistake of walking down the wrong alleys. I didn't think the guardian angel on the holy card would be much help, because these kids were tough. They'd make mincemeat out of him; they'd pull his long hair and tie back his silver wings and sucker punch him in the gut. No, I needed a more rugged breed of angel. I decided my guardian angel looked just like one of the "bad niggers" from Seventh and U, his face as dark as coal with a six-inch scar running down it, his hair slicked back with oil, his dark wings glistening like a bat's, and a cold, hard smile. Just let those white toughs confront me as I took a shortcut through an alley; they'd get the surprise of their lives. He'd materialize right out of the air, and he'd look at the kids and say, "Come on, white trash, I'll kick your butts all the way back to Rhode Island Avenue."

And the eyes of the white kids would widen and their mouths would open in surprise and their leader would say, "Oh fuck, they let guardian angels be Negro?"

And my angel would smile that cold, hard smile and say, "Go and sin no more, my man."

It only gradually dawned on me, as I went three days a week to my after-school catechism classes, that all the saints were white, and that the Last Supper was as segregated as the lunch counters in Birmingham. I played saints like I played movie heroes, and once again, I had to be white. My favorite was not a saint, exactly — so many of them seemed to come to violent ends, getting beheaded and crucified and such, but on the wall of our classroom there was a picture of Sir Galahad, whose strength was as the strength of ten because his heart was pure. My kind of guy. He also wore armor and carried a lance, and if any infidel tried to behead him, he'd put a three-inch hole in the guy's navel — after a little prayer, of course.

I loved being Sir Galahad. The top to the trash can was my shield and a curtain rod my lance. I'm sure my neighbor Mr. Williams would look out his window and say to his wife, "What is that Johnson child doing now?"

What I was doing, of course, was searching for the Holy Grail. Thunder was my loyal steed. I couldn't ride him, of course — he'd bite my ass — but I dragged him through our neighborhood, searching. I mean, who knew where the Grail might have ended up. After the Last Supper, it could have fallen into the hands of one of those hawkers of celebrity paraphernalia, the guys who sell stuff like the ruby slippers from *The Wizard of Oz* or Gene Autry's hat. Jesus was a big deal back in the old days, and stuff associated with Him probably sold for mucho shekels. I pictured this Arab trader, his camel pack loaded with collectibles — crumbs from the loaves of loaves-and-fishes fame, fragments of the true cross, parchment copies of the Sermon on the Mount, suitable for framing, and the Holy Grail. Who's to say he didn't do a little business with an African traveling man who was the great-great-great-great-great-great-great-great-grandfather of somebody who took it with him on a slave ship, and passed it from generation to generation. So it could have wound up in the trash can of a family in Washington, D.C., who did not recognize its value and who happened to live on my street.

With Thunder by my side, I quested. I found a broken vase with Chinese people on it, surely a treasure worth much; a picture of a clown in a broken frame, a baseball card of Bucky Harris, and a fragment of something gold colored, which I was certain was a piece of the Holy Grail. I kept them all in my room. I was the only kid on the block with a piece of the Holy Grail.

I had a few problems with God in catechism class that year. There was a picture of him in our book — he was an old white guy with a beard, who looked exactly like a wino who always hung around North Capitol Street. It didn't surprise me that God was white — that figured — but what was he doing hanging around our neighborhood dressed so crappy? Maybe keeping track of Negro sinners? If he saw every sparrow that fell, maybe he would check out the kids on my block, too. I was always very good when he was around. Thunder always slunk away from him, with what I presumed to be stark terror on his stupid face. Thunder had not lived a good life, being bad tempered and grouchy most of the time, and I expect he feared the wrath of Jehovah for not being Lassie. I told Thunder that it was OK, helping search for the Holy Grail would get him a lot of years off in dog purgatory.

Adam and Eve were something of a problem, too. She was very white, with long, blond hair, and he was blond also. I'd have thought they were Swedes, but the Garden of Eden couldn't have been in Sweden — we'd just studied that in Geography, and they'd have frozen their butts off, wearing only a few strategically placed leaves. If these two were the parents of us all, then where did black folks come from? Even with a tan, Eve would not have looked like my mother.

Billy Williams, the sophisticated one, said that it was the mark of Cain. When Cain killed his brother, Abel, God put a mark on him so all the world would know that he was a killer. All his children would carry that mark, and people would shun them.

"He made Cain colored?" I asked.

Billy Williams nodded solemnly.

I pictured Cain, who had been blond like Adam, suddenly turning dark and getting kinky hair and looking around in astonishment, saying, "Holy Moley, I'm a Negro!"

I thought about that, long and hard. The idea of being a killer had some cachet. The white toughs might back away from the mark of Cain, even if the guardian angel was off that day.

"I have it, white trash! The mark of Cain!"

"Run, quick, he's a killer for sure!"

But if we had the mark, then it was all right for everyone to shun us. In fact, they were *supposed* to shun us. Even . . . Jackie Robinson. When Dixie Walker came sliding into second with his spikes up, he'd be saying, "This one's for Abel, sucker!"

I asked Sister Mary Imelda about this, and she said nobody knew what the mark of Cain was, and it certainly had nothing to do with skin color, which came from what sort of climate your ancestors lived in. Still, I worried. I don't suppose little white kids ever lost a moment's sleep over the mark of Cain, because they knew they didn't have it. God was white, he would never make white skin a curse.

The funny thing is, I never even considered the possibility that God was colored and Adam and Eve were, too, and Cain, God turned him white, and he watched with horror as his skin faded out and he cried, "Oh, no. I hate this stuff. It gets sunburned and it wrinkles and I look like I have TB."

But I couldn't even imagine it. I could imagine *me* white, but not *them* black. It's what happens when somebody who doesn't look like you controls all the images that you see. Even if they're not lynching you and keeping you out of their schools and their restaurants for being the wrong color, even if they're not telling you you're inferior, you get the message anyway. If you pray to a white God, how can you think yourself equal? Later on, of course, I realized that God is a spirit, he has no color, but that image of the old white guy with the beard stays with me. I guess what Rafe is trying to do, with his African garb, is to change all those images, to put new ones in their place. It's a good idea, but for me it's too late. I could wear robes and speak Swahili, but the Catholic Church got me before I was seven, and I am still Sir Galahad. But I am seeking a new grail, a better one than a piece of an old drinking cup. It's equal rights, and as an American and a Catholic I have learned that there will be no justice in America if we do not find them. God is not white, but He is just, and He loves all his children. (I suspect He even loves grouchy, mean-tempered dogs, and that Thunder's spirit is by His side, no smarter than ever but happy at last.) I am going to dedicate my life to those rights, whether it's by organizing and maybe going into politics, as some people have urged me to do, or by writing. My heart is not exactly pure (I told Loretta about being Sir Galahad, and she has found interesting uses for my lance), but I hope my strength will be as the strength of ten. There is a new day dawning in America; I can feel it, I can see it. President Kennedy has finally come to full support of civil rights and we will bury Jim Crow and then all the words on all the marble buildings will finally be true. One day we will be proud to have lived in the era of King and Kennedy, we will think of ourselves as "We happy few, we band of brothers." We will have changed the world.

He drove along, scowling, clutching the wheel and feeling edgy. He had wanted something wonderful to happen, and it had. Now he was not sure he could handle it.

He'd always been in control, where women were concerned. Always knew he could walk anyway, anytime he wanted, and it would be OK. *He* would be OK. Not that he ever wanted to be a bastard with women, he liked them, but it was very good, being in control. You didn't have anything to lose. Photography was his passion, women had been on the back burner, so to speak. His fantasy women could be summoned or banished at will; they didn't impinge on his life at all. The real ones even less so. Mary Springer was different. He couldn't stop thinking about her, and a lot of the time he worried about her. It had not occurred to him before that there were so many lethal things around — an oil slick on the road, a stray virus that could kill before you knew it was there, crazy men with guns.

When he tried to simply will her out of his mind, she wouldn't go, and he didn't know what to do about that. Sometimes he wanted to lay his heart at her feet, slay dragons for her. When he thought of her in the pink dress with the mud-caked shoes he wanted to throw his arms around her and keep all the ugly things of the world away from her. Sometimes he wanted to be her best friend, telling her all the secrets of his soul. Sometimes he wanted to gently kiss the freckles on her shoulders and run his tongue across her lips. Sometimes he wanted to throw her on the ground and fuck her brains out. Whatever the hell it was he felt, he could not control it. The ache in his chest — however it was he thought about her — would not go away.

"Damn!" he said to the image of her in his head. "Oh damn, just go away. Please." But she wouldn't. How could he live with this?

I don't want to love her.

No, I don't, he thought. I don't want to love anyone. I want to be back in control. I want it to be like it used to be.

He tried to think of how it used to be, a very short time ago, when he thought he was going to die young, taking a bullet in the Hindu Kush, and it had a melancholy poetry to it. Now he couldn't stand the thought of dying at all, because of her. *Damn.*

He looked up and discovered that he was driving through Norma's neighborhood. He felt a sudden, warm flush of feeling for Norma. Such a nice woman. So easy to screw and forget.

He remembered that he still had a print in the car, one of his photographs of Kennedy, that he had promised to give her and never had. He pulled up in front of her apartment. The light was on.

He climbed the stairs and knocked on the door, and she answered wearing a robe, with a towel over her shoulder.

"Jeez, look what the cat dragged in. I thought you'd fallen down a hole someplace."

He hadn't bothered to call her. She just went off his screen, a disappearing blip, like a crashing airplane.

"I brought you this," he said, handing her the photograph. She looked at it, and her face brightened. One of the few things that impressed her was that he hung around Kennedy from time to time. "Oh wow!" she said when she saw it. He was forgiven.

"Grab a beer," she said. "I'm going to take a shower." He wandered into the kitchen and poured himself a beer. Then he went into the living room and pushed away a pile of clothes on the sofa so he could sit down. Norma was not tidy; it used to bother him. Now, it seemed a badge of casualness that was appealing. Hadn't he always liked that about Norma?

As he pushed the clothes away, he noticed, on the arm of the sofa, a pair of the crotchless panties, green lace. Norma must have ordered them by the gross. He started at it; was it his imagination, or was it staring back, a malevolent glance? It looked like a small, evil bird with feathers made of lace. He had the sudden sense that there were legions of them, great winged hordes, like the bats that lived in caves he had read about in *National Geographic.* He had the bizarre thought that if they turned ugly — like the birds in the Hitchcock movie — they would attack him in a huge green, purple and blue storm, gouging out his eyes and leaving his flesh laid in ribbons next to the pedal pushers on the couch.

He took another sip of the beer and listened to the water from the shower and thought about Norma naked, the water rolling gently down her skin. It was a lovely thought, sheer lust, uncomplicated by anything else. He locked onto it. When she came into the room, it was obvious she was naked under the bathrobe and in a pliable mood. In a few minutes he was naked too, and they were rolling around on her bed, kicking items of clothing hither and yon. He noticed that there were no freckles on her shoulders and that her breasts, while full and pretty, seemed wrong, somehow. Making love to Norma, he felt like he was wearing another man's clothes.

He pushed that idea out of his head, deliberately, and simply filled the world with fucking. He did try to do things she liked, not just bang away, that was the least he could do after not even having called her for so long. His release was sharp, and he rolled away from her and she said, "Stay with me" — the first time she had ever asked him that. He put his arms around her, and she gave a deep sigh of satisfaction, and in a few minutes she was asleep.

He pushed the pillow against the headboard, sat up in bed, looked at her and wondered what he felt. He didn't feel anything. How nice that was. He tried to imagine what he would feel if anything happened to Norma. If she got eaten by sharks. If she were run over by a truck. He saw her as roadkill, *splat,* flattened on a highway, the blond hair with the dark roots splayed out in the tar.

A faint melancholy, that was all he would feel. How easy it would all be, married to Norma or someone like her. Comfortable, crotchless-panty sex whenever he wanted it, and he could just concentrate on making sure there was no dust on his negatives. He was in control. God, it felt good.

Of course, it was rather silly imagining Norma dead, because of the two of them, he would undoubtedly go first. Norma had the constitution of an ox. When he expired on the Baltimore-Washington Parkway (the kidneys), she would be quite admiring of the job done on him by Hanlon's, along with the old ladies. He saw them peering at him in the box (the lowest grade pine with the knotholes in it, he always knew Norma was a cheap bitch) along with their two children who looked exactly like her, with blond hair and dark roots. They did not seem especially sad.

His face is such a lovely shade, Agnes, sort of pinkish yellow. He was blue when they brought him in.

Mr. Hanlon is an artist. The rosary in his hands is a lovely touch. He'll rot away, but the nice blue rosary will stay like that till Judgment Day.

He had such a nice wife and children.

Of course she played around, you know.

No!

Oh yes. The milkman left more than the cream. The gas man came twice a week to check the meter. And they had oil heat.

The poor man.

Well, he drank so much he probably couldn't do much in that department anyhow.

Norma would get his worldly goods. His Nikon and his car and the apartment, and — *oh, my God* — his prints.

The thought of Norma owning his prints gave him a sudden throb of panic. Why hadn't he had the presence of mind to will them to his mother? She could at least have given them to the branch library. He imagined Norma going through them, the prints that he had so lovingly mounted and that he dusted all the time to keep pristine. She was tossing them in a green garbage bag — the shot of the little boy at the circus that had won the state competition, the abstract blur of the racing cars, the Ansel Adams–like shots of the Grand Canyon he took on his last vacation. She kept the Kennedy stuff and the celebrities. She hung them over the couch so that when she was fucking with her new boyfriend, JFK and Jackie could peer smilingly down on them.

He sighed, flattened out his pillows and pulled the covers up over him. He was more tired than he thought, because in a minute he was asleep, and in his dreams he found himself in a strange landscape, sometimes a bleak and empty city street, sometimes a dark forest where moonlight filtered through the trees in eerie patterns. He was looking for something very important, something he had to have, but he could not remember what it was. On the street he opened doors, and there were people behind him. He pulled one door ajar, and there was the Lady in Black, her zit-free skin gleaming, and that was nice, but it wasn't what he was looking for. Jacqueline was behind another one in a shimmering white gown, but she wasn't it either. He had a terrible, empty feeling in the pit of his stomach. What was it? If he didn't find what he was looking for, would he wander forever in this dark, dead landscape?

The dream shifted and he was in a dozen other settings, one after the other, taking photographs. For a time it would seem that everything was all right and ordinary, and then he would realize that something was wrong, he had to find something and he didn't know if he could. Then he was back to the strange forest, and he saw, through dead branches, far up ahead of him, a figure in a pink dress, wearing a raincoat. He started to run towards her, but as he ran she seemed to keep getting farther and farther away. Finally, just as he was about to fall to the ground, exhausted, suddenly she was there, and she turned towards him and smiled. He said, "Oh, thank God," and he kissed her mouth, and in his chest was a joy so fierce he thought it would tear his ribs apart.

He woke up then, and he turned over in bed, ready to put his arms around her, but she wasn't there. It was Norma, curled up in the fetal position under the blanket.

He sat up and looked around him, at Norma's room. What was he doing here? What the hell was he doing here?

He got up and dressed quickly. Norma stirred, turned over and burrowed deeper into the covers. She really was a nice woman.

"I'm sorry," he said to her sleeping figure. "I'm really sorry."

He went out to his car. He thought he had been asleep only a few minutes, but the dawn was beginning to streak the sky. He got in the car and drove past Mary's house. It was dark, and her car was parked outside. She was in there. She was in there, and she was safe.

There wasn't any free ride, that was it. If you wanted to stay in control, if you chose a woman who could be turned into roadkill and it would hardly make a dent in your day, then you had to spend your life dreaming of something wonderful that you would never have. You would wander in your dreams through empty streets, looking for it. But if you loved someone, you have to live your life on the edge of a terrible cliff.

That was the deal. That was it. Take it or leave it.

He thought of her standing naked in his room that night, the streetlights turning her skin the color of some lovely silver fish, her breasts full and gently sloping. He remembered running after her through his dreamscape, desolate because he thought he could not find her.

That was the deal. Take it or leave it.

He'd take it.

At least for now.

"NIGGERS SUCK!" came a male voice, very distinct, from the back of the room. Jay looked into the crowd to see where the voice had come from, but there were dozens of people standing at the rear of the hall, crowded close together, and he couldn't see who yelled.

"How many are in here, anyhow?" he asked Mary. She was sitting in the front row of the council chambers, and he stood up in front of her. The council members had not yet taken their places on the dais, but the hall was already hot from the press of bodies.

"Must be nearly a thousand," she said. "There's hardly room to move."

"Have you ever seen a crowd like this here before?"

"If they get fifty people, it's a big deal."

"Niggers suck!" a different voice cried out. But again, the identity of the caller was lost in the crowd. Jay looked at the front row. James Washington, formally dressed in a suit and tie, was clenching and unclenching his fists. Don Johnson, sitting next to him, reached out and touched his hand. "Don't let them get to you," he said. "That's what they want. Don't pay any attention." He grinned. "Makes them shitfaced."

At that, James smiled, too, and relaxed in his seat. His large, well-muscled body looked out of place in the suit, Jay thought; it confined him.

Jay looked around. There were quite a few dark faces, grouped together in the front, but at least three-quarters of the crowd was white. The room was noisy and the mood unfriendly. Though there had been only a few shouted epithets, the hostility seemed to crackle along the rows of seats. There were more men then women in the crowd.

Jay squatted down beside Mary. "Not a lot of happy campers."

"I've never seen people in this town so upset," she said. "Not a good sign. This crowd is going to intimidate the council."

"It's not exactly *Profiles in Courage* up there."

She laughed. "Joe Tarbell makes Chicken Little look like a tower of strength."

"Here they come now," Jay said, watching as the seven council members filed in and took their seats. "The Seven Dwarfs."

"That's exactly how they're going to vote."

They looked at each other and said it in unison: "Snow White."

The council members, their faces pale and grim, looked out at the crowd. Joe Tarbell banged the gavel and called the meeting to order.

"Fucking niggers!" called a voice from the back.

"Anybody who is out of order will be removed!" Tarbell barked. Two city policemen stood on the side of the hall monitoring the crowd. A chorus of boos emerged from the audience.

"This is a special meeting on the urban renewal plan," Tarbell said, "and we will move immediately to the printed agenda. The first speaker will be James Washington."

"Niggers suck!"

Tarbell banged the gavel, and James Washington walked to the podium, to a microphone set up for the speakers. His hands were shaking as he stood before the microphone, Jay thought, but when he began to speak, his voice was strong and clear. Gutsy, Jay thought. A crowd like this could intimidate even the most experienced speaker.

"My name is James Washington, and I live at Thirty-three Grant Avenue and I work for the city. I was born in Belvedere, as my father was. This is my city, and I speak tonight for the Negro community. What we ask is not special treatment but simple justice. We also ask for compliance with federal law. These are the points that the Negro community insists [there had been much debate over that word] be incorporated into the urban renewal plan."

"Shut up, nigger!"

The epithet was greeted with a mixed wail of sounds: cheers, boos, calls of *shh!*

"First, the inclusion of seven hundred and fifty units of low to moderate housing, with additional units of elderly housing in the construction plans. Second, the appointment of a relocation officer, from the Negro community, to coordinate relocation efforts during construction and to assure that those people moved out of the area have first call on new housing. Third, application for federal relocation funds to help those families uprooted by urban renewal. And last, the passage of a fair housing act to ensure that no city residents will be discriminated against."

"No!" came a voice from the crowd.

"If these points are accepted by the council," James said, "Belvedere will have an urban renewal package that is in compliance with federal regulations and will ensure justice for all residents, Negro and white."

"What about the busing?" a heavyset man yelled.

James looked up from the paper he had been reading. "There's no busing planned. These units will be for residents of Belvedere."

"No," the man yelled. "They're going to build a project and bus in colored people from D.C. Drug addicts, criminals. That's what they're going to do."

"That's not true," James said. "That's a wild rumor that is not true at all."

"It's true!" A cry from another part of the room. It set off a chorus of similar calls.

"Liar."

"We heard it. It's true!"

"Tell the truth."

Joe Tarbell stood up. "I promise you, there are no plans to bus anybody."

"Shut up, balls-fuck!" screamed a man from the back.

"Remove that man," Tarbell sputtered, his face reddening.

But the two policemen were not sure who had called out.

"Remove him!" Tarbell croaked, nearly apoplectic.

The two policemen moved to the center aisle and pulled at the shoulders of a man in a blue windbreaker.

"What the hell is this?" the man shouted. "I'm a citizen, you can't do this to me!"

Jay elbowed his way close to the policeman and shot several pictures as the two officers struggled with the man in the jacket, who was screaming at the top of his lungs. Sweating and struggling, the policemen managed to drag the man out of his seat and propelled him up the aisle and out of the building. The noise had risen to a din.

"We have presented to the council a petition containing twelve hundred signatures," James said, raising his voice so it could be heard clearly over the noise.

"Fucking nigger!"

"Remove that man!"

The two policemen hustled a teenager in a motorcycle jacket out of the hall.

"The failure to heed the voices of these people, many who have lived in our city for generations, will be met with firm and decisive action," James continued, his voice clear and strong. "We will not be pushed out of our homes."

A man in his forties, wearing a red bowling jacket, rose from his seat and said, "Are we going to let this jungle bunny tell us what to do?"

"Hell no!"

"Shut up, you creep!"

"Yee-haw!"

"They're going to bus convicts in."

"Remove that man!"

The policemen, hot and sweaty, moved in again, and the middle-aged man started swinging wildly as they grabbed him. Another man tried to grab the arm of the policeman, but he was shaken off. A third man grabbed one of the officers by the shirt and was elbowed roughly in the mouth. Jay, shooting at close range, realized that in another minute the melee might spread throughout the hall. Then Tarbell began to bang his gavel.

"Executive session! Executive session!" The noise in the hall had become deafening.

Don jumped to his feet and yelled at Tarbell, "You can't go into executive session! You haven't finished the public agenda!"

But the panic was clear on Tarbell's face, and he and the other councilors hurried off. The policemen got the man who had screamed out of the hall, and the disappearance of the councilors quieted the crowd to an angry buzz.

Jay went back to the front of the hall, where Mary was talking to Don.

"Do you think they're going to try to ram the plan through, as it is?"

He nodded. "Tarbell was panicked. He was about to go in his pants. Did you see his face?"

"He was terrified," Mary said.

"Will they vote in the closet?" Jay asked.

"They can't vote in executive session, it's against the law. They have to take the vote in public," Mary said.

"But just wait until you see how fast they do it," Don told Jay.

"What's next if it passes?" Mary asked.

"We meet tomorrow morning. We'll go for an injunction, and probably a public protest."

Jay walked with Mary to the edge of the stage. There was still an angry murmur rolling through the crowd.

"Who needs Birmingham?" Jay said.

Mary shook her head. "I thought I knew these people. I knew there were some people who were full of hate, but I didn't expect this. Jay, I know a lot of these people. They go to church on Sunday and love their kids and have weekend barbecues. That last man they dragged out has a Boy Scout troop."

"I always knew the fucking Boy Scouts were fascists."

"Did you see those faces? They were irrational. Those nice people, and all of a sudden they're ugly and mean."

"It surprises you?"

"I used to think my hometown wasn't like that."

"On this one, Mary, everybody's hometown is like that."

The door of the small room at the rear of the stage opened, and the councilors filed out and quickly went back to their seats. Joe Tarbell, still looking pale, tapped the gavel.

"After a discussion in executive session, the council has decided to call for an immediate vote."

James stood up. "You haven't heard the speakers," he said, but he was drowned out by a wail of boos from the floor. Tarbell ignored him.

"Mr. Sapier."

"I move that the city's urban renewal plan be adopted, with no further amendments."

"Second," said John Donovan.

"This is illegal!" James called out. Again, a wave of noise made his words inaudible.

"Mr. Donovan."

"Aye."

"Mr. Sapier."

"Aye."

"Mr. Tweksbury."

"Aye."

"Mr. Hendren."

"No!"

"Mr. Atkinson."

"Yes."

"Mr. Roccolini."

"No."

"My vote is aye. The motion carries. This meeting is adjourned."

James Washington stood up again. "The public hearing was not held. This meeting is illegal."

"Shut up, nigger!"

"Go home!"

"Shut your mouth!"

Tarbell was already walking from the podium, and he and the other council members vanished through a rear door. Jay looked around at the crowd. The mood was still volatile. He could sense the repressed violence that seemed to hang in the air with the haze of smoke. But he saw that two more uniformed policemen had entered the hall. Their presence, along with the disappearance of the councilors and the outcome of the vote, seemed to be taking the edge off the situation. The angry buzz began to quiet, and people started to drift out into the street. Don and his uncle, James and several others from the coordinating committee walked out together, engrossed in conversation. A few people cast angry looks at them, but no one approached or called out. Jay and Mary stood in front of the hall, watching as the people filed out.

"Round one to the Great White Hope," Jay said.

"Round two starts tomorrow."

He looked at his watch. "Do you have to write?"

"Yes. Then I'm going to meet James Washington at his house for a profile I'm doing."

"Want pictures?"

"Yes. That's a good idea."

"He was good tonight. He could be one hell of a speaker, with his size, that deep voice. Funny, isn't it, how this kind of a thing can bring out talents in people they never knew they had."

"If a bus driver hadn't refused a seat to Rosa Parks, Martin Luther King might just be another small-time minister."

"I wonder if he ever wishes that's all he was," Jay said.

"Do you think so?"

"The time is out of joint; O cursed spite, That ever I was born to set it right!"

"Hamlet?"

He nodded. "We had to memorize the whole fucking soliloquy junior year." He laughed. "I identified with Hamlet like crazy. He had a dead father, couldn't get it on with girls and he sulked a lot. They called him a Dane, but I knew he was an Irish Catholic."

"The melancholy mick? It loses something."

"No, I like it."

He drove back to the paper and went into the darkroom to print his pictures. He hummed, tunelessly, as he went about his work.

He printed the pictures from the meeting and then went to work on a roll he had taken at the community center, when the famous violinist Nathan Rubenstein had given a concert the week before. He had thought he would be bored with the assignment, but once the violinist began to play, Jay was transfixed by him. He was a big, awkward man with truck driver's hands, and the instrument seemed dwarfed by them. Jay had moved in on the hands with his telephoto lens, capturing the texture of them — the veins knotted and standing high, a contrast to the smooth and burnished wood. He did this sort of story well. Nobody on *Life,* he thought, did it better. He saw Hedley Donovan, in his office in the Time-Life Building, picking up the phone. "There's this young guy, I saw his stuff on Rubenstein at a paper in Maryland. Get him. I want him."

He had that daydream at least three times a week. He'd sent his stuff to *Life,* along with probably every other photographer in the United States. He sighed and pulled one of the prints out of the developer. He thought, as he often did, about what would have happened to him if he hadn't been so desperately bored one day in the Army that he signed up for a photography course. It was the accident that changed his life.

Ever since he was a small child, he would look at things and see that they were beautiful — the curve of a leaf against the earth, an old rocking chair against a wall, a sunset. They stirred an emotion in him that lay somewhere between pain and pleasure, and left him edgy. Sometimes he would see something he thought was beautiful, and his eyes would fill with tears. But it was a secret he kept well hidden, especially as he grew older. A man, crying over something because it was beautiful? It made no sense.

His first assignment in the photography course was to shoot a roll of pictures at random. He wandered around, photographing things he liked: an aged, gnarled oak, a black cat against a white wall, the face of a drunk, the headlights of a sports car, a child, covered with mud and laughing. When the instructor taught them how to print and enlarge from their negatives, he stood and watched as the white sheet of paper floated in the pan of developer. The image formed, as if called by black magic from another world, and he trembled with an excitement he could not have named. He was no longer mute. He had found the language he was born to speak. But he had come so close to missing it, and he shivered when he thought how barren his life would be without it. His near miss only heightened his sense of how precarious life could be.

He finished the prints and went upstairs to the city room, amazed to find that two hours had passed; time seemed to stand still when he was printing. Mary had finished writing the meeting story. He picked up his Nikon, and they headed out towards the house where James lived. She explained that he had taken his truck to a friend's house to pick up a crib for his daughter that the friend was giving him, but he should have returned by the time they arrived.

As Jay drove along the darkened road, he barely saw something coming at him, very fast. He swerved violently to the right, throwing Mary against the side door. Luckily, it was locked.

The car sped past them, its lights out. It disappeared quickly into the night.

"Fucking lunatics!" he swore.

"They almost hit us head-on! Probably tanked full of booze."

Jay kept driving and in a few minutes pulled in front of James's two-story, wood-shingled house. The pickup truck was not there.

"Let's wait inside," Mary said. "I want to talk to his wife anyhow."

"As they got out of the car, Jay paused, sniffing the air. "Do you smell something?"

"Smoke. Somebody must be burning something."

The acrid scent grew more pronounced. Jay looked around to see where it was coming from; then a flicker of light caught his eye.

"Jesus, the back of the house! It's on fire!"

They both started to run towards the house, but they had taken only a few steps when an entire side of the house exploded in flames, the force of the blast spewing broken glass and pieces of wood and shingles out across the grass.

"Oh, my God!" Mary cried out. The left side of the house was aflame, but the right side had not yet ignited. The front door was on the right side, and Jay ran through it, followed a step behind by Mary. The interior was beginning to fill with smoke, and it was hard to see anything. Jay stood still for an instant, letting his smarting eyes adjust; then he heard a whimpering sound in one corner of the room.

"Over there, Jay!" Mary called out. The old woman was sitting in the wheelchair, coughing and sobbing as she tried to move her chair. Jay lifted her, and she gasped, "The baby. Nina!"

"Where?" Mary asked her.

"Upstairs. Please, upstairs!"

Jay made sure he had a firm grip on her frail body and carried her out the front door. Several of the neighbors had rushed up to the house, and he ran to a man and said, "Take her, she needs help!" and the man took the frail old woman in his arms and carried her towards a house across the street. Then Jay ran back through the door. The interior was completely filled with smoke now, and he looked for Mary. He couldn't see her, and a wave of pure panic washed over him as he screamed her name.

Then he saw her. She had taken an afghan from the living room and tossed it over her head, and she was trying to go up the stairs, but a sheet of flame was advancing towards her. She took the afghan from her head and tried to beat back the flames, coughing and choking as she did so.

He ran to her and grabbed her shoulders. "You can't go up there! You can't!"

"The baby is up there. I have to get up the stairs."

She shook him off and tried once again to go up the stairs, but he put his arms around her and dragged her back.

"Karen, if it was Karen!" she said. The stairwell had become a wall of flame, but still she struggled with him. A piece of flaming plaster fell at his feet, and he was starting to choke and gag from the lack of air. He heard the wail of sirens from outside.

"We're getting out of here!" he shouted, and he half-dragged, half-pulled her back out through the door. A crowd had gathered in front of the house, many of them screaming and sobbing. The firemen were dragging hoses across the lawn.

"A woman and a baby," Jay gasped. "Upstairs."

A fireman nodded, grimly. "We know."

Mary had dropped to her knees on the ground, inhaling huge

gulps of fresh air, and Jay ran after the fireman, raising his Nikon. He shot off two rolls of film in rapid fire. The frame house was burning fast now, and the hoses the firemen had trained on the flames seemed to have no effect at all. They had their ladders up to the second floor, but the flames were so intense that they could not get in. The hoses were also being aimed at the houses on either side, and the water sliding off the canted roofs caught the light and splintered it, giving the illusion of a moving, beaded curtain. The water streamed onto the ground, quickly turning the brown earth into mud that sucked at the firemen's boots. Jay's mind became an extension of his camera, sorting images, collecting them. For a time, nothing existed for him except the shapes that swam into view before his lens. He heard one of the firemen say that the blaze in the kitchen had ignited the gas line to the stove and that had caused the explosion.

Finally, he lowered his camera and turned around to look for Mary. Her eyes, he saw, were riveted on the upstairs window where the flames twisted and danced. He thought of what would happen to flesh and eyes and hair in that inferno. In an act of will, he forced the image from his mind. He looked at her and saw that a trickle of blood was running down her face.

"You're hurt!" he said, alarmed, and he took out his handkerchief and wiped off the blood. There was a small gash on her forehead; a piece of flying glass had cut her, but she had not even been aware of it.

"Jay," she said, seeming not to notice that he was wiping blood from her face, "the car. They set it. They set the fire."

He had forgotten all about the car with its lights off.

"My God," he said.

She kept looking at the window. "They were in the room right over the kitchen."

"Are you all right?"

"I'm all right. It's murder. Those people in the car, they killed them."

Jay felt a hand on his arm, and he turned to see Don.

"James! Where's James!"

"He's not here."

"Thank God! Nina? The baby?"

Jay said nothing. He looked at the house. He turned back to Don and saw the dawning horror in his eyes.

"Oh, God, *no*!"

"We tried. Mary tried to get up the stairs, it was all on fire. There was no chance."

"I should have been here. If I'd been here!"

"You might be dead too. It exploded. It just exploded."

Mary had been standing quiet, listening, but now she looked at Don and said, "A car almost hit us on the way. Going very fast, lights off."

Jay suddenly remembered what Don had said: "When white people want to kill black people, they come fast and they come quiet."

Don's face was slack with pain as he looked at the burning house.

"He gave his address," he said. "I didn't know he was going to do that. Why didn't I tell him?"

"Don't," Mary said.

"It was one of the things we never did in the South. Never let them know where you're staying. I got careless. If I had known he was going to do it —"

Mary reached out and touched his shoulder. "It's not your fault. Anyone could have found his address in the telephone book. It's not your fault."

"He's here, Don," said a voice, and Jay turned to see the Reverend Johnson, tugging at his nephew's arm. The two men walked quickly across the yard, and Jay followed them, his camera raised. James ran towards the house, and he would have plunged into the burning structure if two firemen had not restrained him.

Jay was very close to James, but the man neither saw nor heard him. His face hung in the orange light, eyes wide in disbelief, jaw slack. Then the face stiffened, seemed to freeze and stretch taut, the eyes turning to slits. He tried to break free from the grip of the firemen, but they held him firmly. Finally he stopped struggling and let out a howl, a sound that sliced through Jay; he felt as if someone had hit him in the stomach with a hammer.

Abruptly, James turned away from the house, ran up to the fire engine and began to beat savagely on the hood, making no sound except for a rasping in his throat. His fist thumped again and again against the metal. Then his body went limp against the hood, and the minister and his nephew stepped up, put their arms around his shoulders and led him away.

Jay lowered the camera and once again turned to look for Mary. He found her talking to the fire chief. He waited for her to finish and then said, "I've got to get back."

"I'll go. I've got what I need."

"They'll remake page one. We'll have to hurry."

Back at the *Blade,* Jay went right to the darkroom and developed and printed the pictures. He took them to Milt, and the city editor asked him to lay out a centerfold spread of pictures of the fire. He did so, happy to occupy his mind with the mechanics of shape and size and cropping. It was only when it was done that he realized his hands were shaking.

Milt came over, looked at the layout and said, "Great pictures, Jay. I'm sending them out on the AP wire. This one wraps up Photographer of the Year for you, buddy."

He realized, with a twinge of shame, that he had already thought of the state competition. Did James's wife and child have to die so that he could have a little silver plaque? What were the ethics of profiting from someone else's pain? What right did he have to invade the man's private agony, to spread it over a newspaper page so a hundred thousand people could spill their morning coffee on it? Would that horror really let people see what hatred could do? He hoped so, for he knew if he had to do it again, he would not lower his camera. Even when he was so close to the man's agony that he could feel it, he would keep on shooting.

He made a final check on the layout, and then he went into the city room, where Mary was finishing the last page of her copy. She wore a flesh-colored Band-Aid on her forehead. They walked out to the parking lot and got into his car.

"Just drive, Jay," she said. "Anywhere."

He drove along the back roads, while she rested her head against his shoulder, and then he pulled off on the side of a wooded road and took her in his arms. He wanted to blot out the images in his mind with the feel of her. He held her, not gently, and was surprised to find that her body answered his in kind. Her tongue explored him with a desperate ardor, while his hands found the warm flesh beneath her blouse. They spoke not a word but hurled their bodies at each other like gladiators. He carried her out of the car and laid her on the ground, pinning her beneath him, and she dug her nails into his back and bit his lip like a frenzied animal. The pain her teeth and nails inflicted seemed more like pleasure; the dividing line between them had vanished. He wanted to love her, hurt her, make her feel every sensation that existed in the world. He drove himself into her, battering her, feeling her answering movement, as violent as his own. He heard her cry out, and his own release was sharp and explosive. He rolled over onto his back, feeling the damp earth and leaves against his bare skin. She put her head on his bare chest, and they lay that way, not speaking, for a long time.

"We're alive," she said, finally.

"We're going to live a long, long time," he said. "I promise you. I promise." As he said it, with the feel of her against him and the smell of the damp earth, he believed it was true.

It was only later, sitting in his bed, sleepless, smoking a stale cigarette, that he was afraid. His hands were trembling again. He was not a coward. He was brave, reckless sometimes, in a physical sense. He'd broken an ankle in a parachute jump as an Army photographer, overcoming primal terror to hurl himself into the void; he'd cracked a rib photographing a stock car race from the front seat when they hit a wall. It was only with his secret, sheltered self that he was timid. That was where you could get clobbered.

He remembered how his father had looked in the months when he knew he was going to die, and he thought of the frozen horror on James's face. He was familiar enough with pain to know it was not a searing flash that came and went. It was a gnawing presence, and every way you turned, around every corner, you confronted it. If you loved someone, you extended the coastline where pain could get at you. He thought of James's face, and he groped for the words of a prayer. He had not prayed in a long time. "*Dominus vobiscum.* The Lord be with you. *Et cum spiritu tuo.* And with thy spirit."

He lit another cigarette, inhaled, thought of how he'd felt when he went back into the house and couldn't find her, for a minute. Even the memory started his hands shaking again.

I don't want to love her.

If he ran away, he wouldn't have to be afraid. If you had nothing to lose, no one could take anything away.

I don't want to love her.

There was still time to turn away. He wasn't committed, he'd made no pledge. It would be so easy, to turn away now, before things had gone too far. Pretty soon now, there would be a bridge he'd have to cross. They'd not spoken of it, but it was there. He'd have to either cross it or run like hell. He was good at running like hell. And she had a child. What did he know about raising kids? But if he wanted to cut out, he'd have to do it soon; it was getting so intense. It was wonderful — oh yes, it was still wonderful — but in the end, he'd go. He knew it. He always had.

Not loving enough isn't a sin.

Yes, it is. It's the worst one.

He took a deep drag on the cigarette. The fucking thing would give him cancer, but it helped. His hands were still shaking. He sat, smoking, staring into the darkness, at whatever it was that was out there, for a long time. Then he turned over and went to sleep.

He turned over in the bed, to a position that would be comfortable for his back. The faint smell of perfume clung to the sheets. Physically, he was sated, but something in him was unsatisfied. Women, inevitably, were a disappointment. Especially if they succumbed too easily, and, of course, now they did.

There had always been something about him that attracted women. Even when he was young and skinny and trying to bulk up with milk shakes, the charm was developing. His older brother, with the movie star looks, gave little thought to the girls who flocked around him. To prove his power, Joe once saw his younger brother in the Stork Club with a beautiful woman, moved in and ended up leaving with her. The second son studied girls, asked other girls about them: what did they like, what pleased them? From early on, the chase delighted him. One young woman described him to a friend as giving off light, not heat. Sex, she thought, was something for him to have done, accomplished; the pursuit was the exhilarating part.

He moved in a world that was totally incomprehensible to most young Irish Catholic boys. At a time when many of them were making acts of contrition after the mere thought of sex, hearing lectures by priests about the danger to their immortal souls of lust, the second son was attending prep schools with the sons of the Protestant rich. His father might send his daughters to

Catholic school to get piety, but he wanted no such clerical drag on his sons. They went to Choate and Harvard. The stringent morals of the middle class did not apply to the gilded and frisky sons and daughters of the American aristocracy. At an age when many Catholic boys were struggling with the sinfulness of soul kissing, the second son already had a nickname for his penis (J.J.) and boasted to friends of its busy schedule. He had a few semiserious romances with "marriageable" girls, but the girls moved on, married others and retained affectionate memories of their relationships with him. He was not the sort of man one went mad with grief over when it ended; light, not heat.

In his midtwenties, he fell deeply, passionately in love for the first time, with a beautiful Danish journalist who worked at the newspaper where Kathleen worked. She reminded him, in fact, of his favorite sister — she was lighthearted, bright, eager for life. But she had met Hitler when she visited Germany on assignment for a Danish paper, and the FBI was suspicious that she might be a Nazi spy, so much so that they wiretapped her assignations with him. He thought the charges ludicrous, and talked of marrying her. But his father, who approved of a fling but was appalled at the thought of a marriage, moved in forcefully to break it up. The son, who was trying to carve an independent path, nonetheless would not openly defy his family, as Kathleen later would. Or perhaps he sensed in himself something Kathleen would tell a young man who fell in love with her, "I'm like Jack, incapable of deep affection." That was not true — for Kathleen.

He would later write to the Danish woman from his command in the Pacific that she was the brightest spot in his twenty-six years of life. She had loved him, but knowing his father would never permit a marriage, had married another man she admitted she did not love. At times in his life he had wondered if things had been different, if he had married her, whether he would have found the heart's ease that seemed to have escaped him.

He did not think deeply about the pattern he had fallen into with women, in which movie stars and secretaries alike came and went from his bed; perhaps to do so would have meant facing un-

pleasant truths. Like all members of his family, he scoffed at psychologizing. Action was the answer to life's problems, not self-awareness. Those who knew him well thought there was a Jekyll and Hyde aspect to his pursuit of women. Cautious in so many other areas of his life, in this he took absurd risks that could have destroyed him politically, and at several times came close to doing so. Some of his friends thought he was competing with his father, who well into his sixties tried to seduce the women his sons brought home. (Certainly bizarre behavior: was the father trying to assert the primacy he had always known?) Others thought he found in risk a needed reminder that he was still alive. Once, the wife of a friend asked him why he was trying to behave like his father. Why was he unable to form deep attachments, courting scandal at a time when his career was beginning to blossom? He struggled with an answer and finally said — sadly, she thought — "I don't know. I guess I can't help it."

He turned again in bed, restless. His wife was away on a trip. He found himself wishing she were there.

The marriage had nearly come unglued after she'd miscarried in her first pregnancy and he had been remote and preoccupied. But there were strong bonds that held them together. Two children, of course, and a third on the way, but there was more. Both had survived lonely childhoods, she from a broken family, he from one in which his parents were often absent. Both were consummate actors, self-inventors. Her performances, even more than his, gave his administration its cachet. And she had a will as iron as his own. She held herself aloof from the wildly physical competitions of his family; she won by refusing to play on anyone's terms but her own. Unlike his mother, she would not simply pretend that infidelities didn't exist. She knew how to punish him — by a witty barb, by a sullen silence, or by extravagance. With the last, was she saying, "See, I can be as reckless as you?" *She did not bore him. He loved it when men looked at him with envy when he stood beside her. But there was no blueprint inside his head for marriage, other than that of his family. In that struggle, he identified with the winner, his father.*

But lately, he had noticed, the pursuit, as easy as it had become, so much more glittering its prizes, was beginning to pall. He had telephoned a friend who knew of his infidelities, to say that he was in a room where there were two naked girls but he was reading The Wall Street Journal. *"Does that mean I'm getting old?" he asked.*

Perhaps he was simply moving away from old demons. His father was now a crippled old man, no longer a rival. His friends thought he seemed to be starting to settle into the role of family man, enjoying his children, having a new appreciation for his wife. No longer the second son, he was now the star around whom the family orbited.

Or perhaps he was beginning to dispense with his desperate grip on youth. He had been a boy so long, the persona was hard to shed. If he had projected himself far into the future — which he was loath to do — he would have had trouble picturing himself as an aging rake, like his father, prowling the houses in Palm Beach and Hyannis, barging unannounced into the bedrooms of women who were wives of his guests or girlfriends of his sons. He had joked about it (Lock your doors, the ambassador likes to prowl) and saw his father as a Rabelaisian character, but he could not see himself aging in that way. The one thing he had an absolute horror of being was a joke. No, perhaps it was time to invent another persona — statesman, family man, sage. No young woman had yet looked at him with pity, but the time would come, even for him. Not soon, but it would come.

He turned again, the pain in his back a dull ache. He was alone in his bed, and sleep would not come. He was awake for a long time, but finally, it did.

PIERRE SALINGER, the press secretary, tapped her on the arm as she walked into the West Wing.

"Got a minute? The president would like to see you."

"Of course," she said. What else did he expect her to say: "Nah, some other time, I have to wash my hair? When the leader of the Free World called, you went.

She walked into the office, and he was standing at the window, looking out. When she walked in he turned and said, "*Belvedere Blade,* what the hell is going on in that town of yours? It's all over the *Post* and the *Times.*"

He walked back to his desk and sat down. She sat in a chair opposite the desk.

"It's pretty bad," she said. She told him about James Washington and how he was helping to lead the fight for new housing, and how his wife and child had died for it. "All he had was this crummy little house in Niggertown, and they were trying to take it away from him. And he said no, he wouldn't go. And he's still saying no."

"Jesus," he said, shaking his head. He picked up a pencil and began drumming on the desk with its eraser. She had noticed that he was never completely still; even sitting down, he tapped his feet, drummed his fingers. There was a restless energy in him that never seemed to switch off.

"People are saying crazy things," she told him. "Like they're going to bus in drug addicts. These normally sane people, they're going nuts."

"In the nineteenth century the mobs in Charlestown burned down a convent full of Irish nuns," he said. "They thought the nuns were stealing babies. It's the same. No different."

"Some people say," she suggested quietly, "that you haven't done enough on civil rights."

He looked at her, intently. She didn't drop her gaze but looked into those bright blue eyes. He'd asked her to tell the truth. Then he nodded, drumming the pencil again.

"Do you read history, *Belvedere Blade*?"

"It was my best subject."

"Well, history is full of magnificent failures. Great causes that went down the old tubes. It's easy for you people to stand out there and throw rocks because I'm not moving fast enough, but I'm in here, and it's not so easy. Timing is everything, in history. I'm going to have to kick a lot of butt, I'm probably going to have to let some idiots get appointed to judgeships. I'm going to get this goddamned bill through, and a fat lot of credit I'll get for it from you people!"

He seemed to be pouting a little; odd, she'd never imagined presidents pouted. But she thought about what he'd said. In all her history texts, presidents made great speeches and took heroic stands. You never read about them wheeling and dealing or appointing assholes, or getting pissed when they didn't get credit. But that was probably what history was really like.

He leaned back in his chair and sighed. "So what's going to happen? Is this thing going to go up like a tinderbox? Christ, I don't need that right on my doorstep."

"I don't know. It could get bad. Now, I think the Negroes won't stop. They were scared at first, a lot of them, but now — I don't think anyone wants to turn back."

"No idea who set the fire?"

"Some people are saying it was the Klan. Or some other crazy white supremacist group. White people are scared too."

He shook his head. "Stuff like this starting in the North could really screw up my bill. The race thing is a lot more complicated, up here. Listen, let me know if you sense there's going to be bad trouble. There are things we can do."

She said, "I have this friend, he's Negro, and he's helping to lead the protest. He's smart, and he's educated, and he's not going to stay in the back of the bus anymore. He's as American as I am. His father grew up being careful, watching what he said around white people, but Don's not like that. He's going to make us actually do what we say America's all about. I think there are a lot of Negroes like that. They won't wait anymore."

He glared at her.

"Do you think I don't understand about not wanting to wait? They wouldn't let my father into clubs because he was Irish. They didn't want me to be president because I was Catholic. You tell your friend that he isn't the only one that had to fight for what this country is all about. Tell him I understand."

"He'd say understanding isn't enough. That things have to change."

"Jesus Christ, I know that!" he said. "What the fuck do you think we've been doing these past few months, sitting on our asses?" Then he remembered he was talking to a woman. "Excuse me," he said.

"You told me to tell you the truth."

He looked at her. "I did, didn't I? Well, thanks, *Belvedere Blade*, you've made my day."

She walked to the door, but before she left he said, "OK, keep doing it. I did ask. It's a pain in the butt sometimes, but I asked for it."

Driving back home, she wondered if she should tell Charlie about her off-the-record conversations with Kennedy. She decided not to. The president was using her to get information, to talk to someone close to real people, not Washington insiders who tended to share the same point of view. And she was using him, to learn about power and how it worked, something she hadn't seen that much of in her young life.

She thought about what he had said about timing and history.

She was beginning to see that there were great forces at play in the world, and even a man as powerful as Kennedy could not control them all. Don Johnson was a part of those forces, in the vanguard of a people seeking long-delayed justice. He and the others were pressing Kennedy, forcing him to move faster than he might think prudent, but also creating the momentum that would make it possible for him to move. The southern sheriffs, with their fire hoses and their police dogs, were helping to propel it. But Kennedy needed the support of the North to get the bill passed, and the North had to feel its own peace and tranquillity was secure. But little Belvedere could turn out to be a big problem for Kennedy; it was no surprise he was watching it.

She felt a sudden shiver through her body as she realized that a national drama was playing itself out, and she was a part of it. A small part, but it was incredibly thrilling to be this close. This was why people plotted and lied and betrayed to get close to power, so they could feel like she felt at this moment. Nothing else — except maybe sex — was as compelling. And of course that was why the two were so often linked. She was already a bit addicted herself. OK, a lot addicted. She thought that if anybody tried to take this job away from her, to say she couldn't ever be a journalist again, she'd rip their eyes out. Never again could she go back to being what she had once been, a woman who got told, who bought all the rules that men made. Never again.

She drove home, and because she had promised Karen that she would make her a special treat for tonight, she decided to try the new cake mix she'd bought. As she dumped the mix in the blender she thought this was very bizarre, that she'd just been talking to the President of the United States and now she was in the kitchen baking a cake. Her life had certainly taken some unexpected turns.

As she was finishing the frosting on the cake, the doorbell rang and it was Harry; he always dropped by on Tuesdays to deliver the cleaning. Lately, she'd made sure she was out when he stopped by, but she opened the door and invited him in. He glanced at the cake, and she offered him a piece. She poured him a glass of milk, and he eagerly took a bite of the cake. She remembered, with a pang, how she had enjoyed cooking for him early in their marriage. He always ate with such gusto.

"This is good cake, Mary. It's really good."

"It's a new mix. I thought I'd try it."

"I like it." He took another forkful. "An awful thing, about that fire. Think they'll get the guys?"

"I hope so. We saw them. The photographer and I. But they were going fast with their lights off, so we weren't much help to the police."

"You were in that house, Mary. That was dangerous. It was on fire."

"I tried to go up the stairs, but the flames were too high. I kept thinking about Karen. What if it had been Karen up in that room? I had to try."

"What kind of animals could burn a child to death? I mean, I don't like the idea of busing in a lot of niggers and riffraff, but to do *that*?"

"Oh, Harry, that story isn't true. It's just a rumor. Nobody is getting bused."

"Everybody believes it. Everybody I talk to. They're scared of things getting like they are in Cambridge, with riots and tear gas."

"That won't happen here."

"Listen," he said, "I bought the new building in Frederick. I mean, I bought it for Mr. Gutwald. I have to hire a driver and two countermen. I'll be glad to get out of the damned truck."

"Harry, that's great."

"Well, it's going to take a lot of work, especially at first. A lot of hours to get the place going. Also, there's a hobby shop in the same shopping center, and the owner is retiring. I told Mr. Gutwald he ought to grab it. I checked it out. It makes a good profit. The markups are fantastic, and you get a lot of repeat business."

"Is he interested?"

"Maybe. He just sticks his money in the bank; he's one of these old conservative Germans. I try to tell him he ought to make his money work for him."

"Harry, you sound like a capitalist."

He laughed. "I guess I do. But there's money to be made around here, Mary. The area has been depressed, but in a few years it's going to be so built up you won't recognize it. There's going to be millions made by people who can look ahead. But the people with money around here are too conservative."

"Mr. Gutwald has the money, that's for sure."

"Yeah, but he lets it sit in the bank and collect four percent. I think I'm persuading him. He figured his son Bert would take over the business, but Burt likes it out in San Diego and doesn't want to come back. So I think, in some ways, I'm a substitute for Bert."

"Things seem to be going very well."

"Finally. You know, it's taken me a long time to grow up. I read the other day that Bob Feller and his father used to spend hours in the backyard, throwing the ball. I never bothered. I used to cut practice so often the coach threatened to throw me off the team. I wish he had. I wonder why nobody ever kicked me in the pants, made me wise up."

"Everybody liked you. You were the most popular boy in school."

"Yeah, but high school isn't life. When I went down to see the guidance counselor — remember old Haskell? — I him I was going to be a major league baseball player, and he said, 'That's nice.' You'd think he might have suggested I should think about something else, just in case, but all he said was 'that's nice.'"

Mary smiled. "He told me I was going to get married and wouldn't have to work so I ought to take Home Ec."

Harry laughed. "Is he still there? Let's go down and punch him out."

He ate another mouthful of the cake and said, "You know I never told you this, but what helped me straighten out was the way you managed things. I finally figured out, if you could do it, I could too. I mean, I'm a man. I'm supposed to be the strong one."

She picked up the carton of milk that was on the table and put it in the refrigerator. "You'll do fine, Harry."

"Well, I think so. I think I'm going to really have it together before long. Then we'll talk. You and Karen, you're my life."

She turned to look at him. "No, you can't live for us. You have to live for you. You have to find out what *you* want."

"Well," he said, "that's not so easy."

He left in the truck, and she sat at the kitchen table, staring at her hands and blinking back the tears. She had known he would be coming this morning, so she had put her wedding ring back on.

"Oh, Harry!"

If only she had a time machine, to take her back to that night she had stood on the lawn, a little crazy, to take back the words. *I'm pregnant.* But if she did that, there would be no Karen. Her daughter's sturdy, perfect little body gave her such delight, and she saw in the soft curve of the cheek and the quickness in her blue eyes the shadow of the adult she would become. She could no more imagine her child nonexistent than she could wish for her own extinction.

Her child? Not hers alone. Theirs. He was the father of her child. She had waited so long for Harry to be a man. Why did it have to happen now?

She shook her head as if the motion could dislodge her thoughts. Then she went upstairs to get dressed for work, thinking of the story she was writing on James, of how he had buried his wife and child and vowed to carry on the fight. It was different from other stories she had done. He was not a string of disembodied quotes, he was coming alive on the page as no one had done before. Her own writing, she knew, was getting bolder, surer, and it excited her. A few months ago the city room had seemed like a vast universe she had to conquer. It was shrinking fast. There was a large world beyond it, and there might be a place for her out there. Jay would never stay in Belvedere. He sucked up the essences of things with his camera, and Belvedere would soon be picked clean. And if he went, she could go with him. With Jay, there were no boundaries. With Harry, her territory was paced off and staked out. Could she live anymore in so small a space? Could she survive, alone, outside it?

She opened the drawer of her dresser, and Sigmund Freud was standing there, a smug smile on his face.

Whither thou goest, I will go? Thy people shall be my people? Yeah, something like that.

Or are you leeching onto a man, because you don't have the guts to go yourself?

That's absurd.

Is it? One part of you is thinking about him; another part is writing the lead to your story. You are supposed to be lost in love, but you just did a forty-word lead. What kind of a woman are you?

You can't just live for love. You have to work, too.

Ah, you sound just like a man.

If you even say the words "penis envy" I'll hit you.

And what about your husband? The man who you married. Who loves you.

I . . . I don't know.

He is who he is and where he is because of you. There is a debt.

He'd know. After a while he'd start to hate me. He'd know I didn't love him anymore.

You are quite strong. You could make it work.

I know.

But you don't want it to. You want to put yourself above everything.

He vanished, and she stood looking into space. She loved Jay, but she was tied to Harry. Unworthiness clutched at her. Didn't Jay deserve something better, a woman who could live and die and breathe only for him? Real women did that. And Harry, a good man whose life she had determined, how could she hurt him again? God, why couldn't she just live, and hurt no one?

There were no answers to those questions, so she put them aside and got in her car and drove to the Reverend Johnson's house. Don was waiting for her, looking tired and drawn. She guessed he had slept very little in the last few days.

"Did you see the editorial?" she asked him.

"Yes, it was very good. If we win this, the *Blade* deserves a lot of credit. *When* we win it. Now, we have to."

"You've asked for an injunction?"

"Yes. The NAACP has filed an amicus brief too. We're asking the court to stay the action of the council."

"Do you have a chance?"

"Iffy. Courts don't like to step into local battles like this one.

The federal regulations are vague enough so that it might get federal funds. The plan doesn't specify that Negroes are barred from the new apartments, but of course economics will keep most people out. The council is trying to argue that there's no intention to discriminate."

"Our story on the fire went out on AP. The *Times* had a piece. You're getting national coverage."

"That should help."

"If it doesn't?"

"We go to the streets."

"James will be there. He told me so."

"He's amazing. I sometimes wonder where our people get their courage. He's determined we're going to win this."

She walked to the window and looked out on the quiet street. "When you change the rules, is there always a price to pay? And who pays it?"

He knew what she was asking him. He shook his head.

"The question you have to ask is, Are the rules right? And if they're not, you have to change them."

"No matter what?"

"Yes. No matter what."

"You sound so sure."

He looked at her, and she saw that he was not as sure as he sounded; and he looked, all of a sudden, very young.

"I *have* to be sure," he said. If not —" He paused. "Do you think I haven't said to myself that if I never came here, they'd still be alive? Don't write this, please, but do you think I haven't asked myself what right I had to come here?"

She was surprised at how much he had come to trust her. Perhaps it was because they were both outsiders in a world where other people made the rules.

"Your uncle asked you to come."

"But why did I do it? Was it because I felt guilty that I wasn't in Birmingham, where a lot of my friends are? Because I had a nice, soft, cushy spot in a writing class? Did I do it for my own ego? T. S. Eliot once wrote that doing the right deed for the wrong reason is, in fact, the greatest treason."

"Does it matter? If what you did was right?"

"It's like the way I felt in the South, sometimes. I was going to come and go, but those people had to live there. Do I have the right to ask other people to face the consequences of what I've started?"

"You couldn't have known what was going to happen here."

"I knew something violent could happen. God knows, I've seen enough in the South to know what happens when you take the lid off. Only — I've never been responsible before. Not personally."

"Maybe the reason you do something doesn't matter, in the end."

"To me it matters."

"If it's any help, I think you were right to do this. A lot of people would have lost their homes. Why should they have to sit back and get kicked around?"

He looked at her. "Aren't you supposed to be objective?"

"Yeah, I am. But there's a time when some things are right, and that's that. You have to say so."

"That attitude," he said, "is going to get you in trouble in your business."

She looked at him and nodded. He was right about that.

But once you started to trust your own perceptions and judgments, there was no going back.

"Any detail, Mr. Broderick. Anything at all." The trooper was pressing, politely but firmly. "Run it through your mind, like a film. Anything you pick up on would be helpful."

Jay was sitting in Charlie's office, across from the state trooper.

"It was so fast," he said. "I just got a glimpse. Two men in the front seat, maybe one in back. I'm not sure about that."

"You couldn't identify anyone?"

"No. Like I said, I only got a glimpse."

"The car was a Ford?"

"I think so. A 'fifty-six, I'd say, or 'fifty-seven. I'm pretty good on cars."

"No numbers on the plates?"

"No, I couldn't see the plates. I tried after they passed me, but it was too dark."

"Any other detail? Anything at all, no matter how unimportant it seems."

Jay ran the scene through his mind, for the hundredth time. "No, nothing." He ran it again. "Wait a minute, there was something. Hanging down. In the rear window, I guess."

"What was it?"

"Gloves. I just remembered. My headlights caught them. Small boxing gloves."

"Good. That may be a help."

When the trooper left, Jay walked over to Milt in the city room. "They're going all out on it," he said.

"Charlie's done an editorial calling for the FBI to come on."

"Any chance?"

"Doubtful. No interstate angle on it. Hey, look at this."

Milt handed Jay a photo torn from the AP wire machine.

"Jesus, I wish I'd taken that one."

In the photograph, George Wallace was standing in the doorway of a University of Alabama building, and the assistant attorney general Nicholas Katzenbach, backed up by federal marshals, was asking him to stand aside. The governor was opposed to desegregating the stage's colleges.

"That's historic," Milt said. "A hundred years from now, that picture will be in the history books."

"They'll think we were nuts. Federal troops to let people go to school?"

"Speaking of school, why aren't you on your way to the science fair at St. John's?"

"Shit, I thought you forgot."

"Shoot for a spread, in case we need it. And don't talk to anybody."

"What?"

"You open your mouth, you get in trouble. I had a call from Father Carmody at St. Theresa's today. I sent you up there to shoot the new organ. How could you get in trouble shooting an organ?"

"Look, I'm minding my business, and Carmody says to me, 'How come I don't see you at Mass?'"

"How did he know you were Catholic?"

"Probably the stigmata."

"The what?"

"Never mind."

"He said you were — and I quote — blasphemous."

"Oh, hell no. I just told him I was a Druid. I said God is a Tree. A sycamore, on the Baltimore-Washington Parkway."

"I'm not going to tell Charlie. He'll be bullshit."

"Charlie's always bullshit at me. Hey, any messages for God? I'm driving by him tonight."

"Get the fuck out of here, Jay."

The science fair was one of those corny assignments that Charlie loved; he said it built loyalty to the *Blade* to have parents see the pictures of their kids' models of the solar system and volcanoes that spouted baking soda. It was a special challenge for him to take these assignments and make them sing. He did pretty well, he thought afterwards. Just the kind of light feature that played so well in *Life*. Hedley Donovan would look at it and say, "Jesus, look what this guy can do with a science fair. Get him. I want him!" He saw himself thirty-seven stories up in the Time-Life Building, chatting with Mydans and Bourke-White about exposures and f-stops. They never had to take pictures of Father Carmody and his goddamned pipe organ.

He thought about Father Carmody, and his mood soured. Carmody could have been a double for Father Hannigan, the bête noire of his martyrdom fantasies, and that fact alone pissed him off. All that innocent pleasure, down the toilet, thanks to one old Irish priest.

He was the most celebrated gladiator in all of Rome (after seeing Kirk Douglas in Spartacus*), but he had converted to Christianity and would kill no more. He had already dispatched scores of opponents, stuck them in the gut with his pitchfork-shaped sword, and they bled copiously, as Caligula gave the thumbs-down signal from his skybox. Now Caligula was really POed. He decreed that his favorite gladiator was going to be thrown into the arena with the newest warrior from the wilds of Britannia, and if he turned the other cheek, tough darts.*

He was in the locker room, dressing, his magnificent body glistening with oil, when the warrior burst in on him. It was Drusilda, the warrior queen of the Britons, captured and brought to Rome in chains for the sport of the arena. She was dressed in furs, her wild, dark hair falling across her metal breastplate. She wore a tiny piece of fur across her crotch, and the muscles of her long and shapely legs gleamed with fine beads of sweat. She smelled of rose water and musk.

"What's this shit about you not fighting?" she growled. "I never thought Romans were wimps."

"I have accepted Jesus, our Savior, and I will kill no more."

"Who's Jesus?"

"The Son of God, the Supreme Being, infinitely perfect, who created all things and keeps them in existence."

"I thought Thor did that."

"Thor is a pagan invention. Jesus is the true Lord, and he commands us to love one another."

"Thor says we should kill and loot and pillage."

"That crap is for pagans. Jesus tells us to love those who hate us, and we will have eternal glory in Heaven."

"That sounds neat," Drusilda said. "How do you get to be a Christian?"

"Believe in your heart, and you will be saved."

A sudden glow of light bathed the room, heavenly music drifted in the air, and Drusilda fell to her knees before him. Suddenly, she lifted the hem of his gladiator skirt, her round lips moist, her breasts heaving under the metal plate —

"Stop right there." Father Hannigan's voice boomed in his mind.

Oh, jeez, I'm doing it again. OK, no more gladiator.

His hands were tied to two marble pillars, a Christian hiding in the catacombs, hunted down by the evil emperor. Again and again the cruel lash bit into his back. He groaned but refused to burn incense to the pagan gods. Disgusted, his torturers untied him, and he fell, bleeding, to the floor.

"Leave the Christian scum to die with the dogs," they said.

The beautiful wife of the emperor, dressed in her silks and robes, came to the dungeon with her handmaiden. She saw him lying, naked and bleeding, on the floor.

"Such courage he has," she said to her handmaiden.

"Cute buns, too," the handmaiden said.

"Let us ease his pain. Such a brave man should not be left to die with dogs. Get me the oils and the healing herbs."

She rubbed the ointments into his bleeding back, then cradled his head in her arms, not caring that his blood stained her silks.

"I will not refuse my God, though I die," he murmured.

"Rest easy, Christian. I will help you, if I can."

She rubbed the oil across his chest and belly, gently. Of course, the torturers would be back, and they would flay him alive with their metal-tipped whips, but in the meantime . . .

"There?"

"Ah yes, that's good."

"And there?"

"You are very kind, milady."

Gently, her hands went lower, lower . . .

"This Christian is hung like a horse," the handmaiden said.

Milady's fingers touched him gently, gently, and he moaned, and she rubbed him a little bit, and he moaned some more, Ohhhhhh, Ohhhhhh. Ohhhhhh. Oh shit!

"That is enough. You have a very warped idea of martyrdom."

"This isn't a blow job. It's only a little . . . massage. Can't a martyr get a massage before he's flayed to death?"

"Not where you were getting it. And what's this 'hung like a horse' business? Do you think martyrs obsess over penis size?"

"Maybe they think about it once in a while."

There was a sudden grinding noise from the front of the car. Father Hannigan and his lecture vanished. The car started to pull to the right, and the noise got louder.

"Fuck!" He pulled the car to the side of the road, got out the flashlight and went to look at the tire. It lay hopelessly flattened against the ground.

He kicked the tire, viciously. "In the fucking boonies."

He went back to the trunk to get the spare; it was there, but the jack wasn't. He remembered he had loaned it to Roger, who hadn't bothered to return it. He started in on Roger, questioning his sexual habits and his ancestors fifteen generations back. When he tired of that, he looked up the road. The nearest house was at least a half mile away. He could probably drive on the tire, but it would be slashed to ribbons, and it was a brand-new tire.

While he was debating, he heard the hum of an engine and saw two headlights coming towards him down the road. He waved his flashlight, and a truck slowed down as it passed and pulled to the side of the road in front of him. A man got out and walked towards him.

"Hi," Jay said. "Thanks for stopping. I got a flat and no jack. Can I hitch a ride to Belvedere?"

"No jack?" Jay could see the man now in the glare of the headlights. He was young, stocky, with close-cropped hair. His manner was amiable.

"I did a real half-assed thing. I lent my jack to a guy and forgot to get it back."

"I got a jack in the trunk. You got a good spare?"

"Yeah."

"I'll give you a hand. I wouldn't leave a car out here. The damn kids go joyriding, and they like to strip cars."

"Thanks a lot."

"I drive this road a few times a week. I had a flat here myself, so I know how it is. There's nothing out here."

Jay rolled the spare to the front of the car and squatted down to pry the hubcap off the old tire. The man returned with the jack, slipping the edge of it under the Chevy's bumper.

"That's a good jack," Jay said. "The one I got, you have to be an engineer to figure it out."

"Cars are a pain in the ass," the young man said. "They make the damn things to fall apart."

"This one's falling apart on me now. I run it a lot."

"I got one of those compacts the first year they came out. A fucking lemon. It was always in the shop."

Jay put the spare on; the young man pumped the jack again and the car descended. Jay looked at the man's thick, well-muscled arms with a twinge of envy. He had sent away for a Charles Atlas kit to try to get arms like that through Dynamic Tension, but he got bored after a week. His arms were sinewy but too thin, he thought, and he was still self-conscious about them.

The man pulled the jack away and said, "You live in Belvedere?"

"Yeah. My name's Jay Broderick. I work for the *Blade.*"

He stuck his hand out, and the man took it, a firm handshake.

"Oh sure, I've seen your pictures. I'm Harry Springer. You know my wife, Mary."

Jay's mouth gaped open. He closed it, quickly, glad for the darkness.

"Oh sure. We work together a lot." The simple sentence seemed charged with innuendo. Harry didn't appear to notice. Jay struggled for a neutral sentence. "Hey, I really appreciate your help. I've got some pictures I have to get in tonight."

"Glad to help you. Mary's always got deadlines to meet, so I know it's tough. Nice to meet you, Jay."

"Thanks again."

Harry put his jack in the truck and drove off. Jay stood staring after him.

Harry Springer. Jesus H. Fucking Christ, Harry Springer.

He pulled the Chevy back on the road. Harry Springer was no longer a name without a face. He was a nice guy. That was depressing. There were so many guys whose guts he hated the minute he saw them. Why couldn't Harry have been one of those, a loudmouth or a prissy-assed jerk? He was a good-looking guy. Well built. Women liked guys with muscles like that; well hung too, probably.

He had a sudden mental picture of Mary in bed with him, those large hands touching her in the places *he* had touched. Jay was suddenly and irrationally furious with her. Oddly enough, it was Father Hannigan's voice he heard inside his head. "If you went to the Hecht Company, and you saw a nice, clean blouse in a plastic package and a dirty, wrinkled blouse, which one would you buy? You know, of course. That's why you should marry a good Catholic girl, a virgin. No man wants damaged goods."

Damaged goods? Where the fuck had that come from? In what corner of his subconscious was that kicking around? Did he want a virgin? The Lady in Black, was she one? No blood on the sheets or cries of pain — that was no fun — but she was virginal. He had invented her, so of course she surrendered only to him.

The women he had wanted, as opposed to the ones he had screwed, were they virgins too? Yes, they were. It was the all-American dream, the girl who spread her legs only for you. Why should he be immune to it? He had the sense of being cheated. *Damn.* Other men got the dream girls, hymens intact, why couldn't he?

I don't want to love her.

Why should he have to take seconds? She wasn't beautiful, really, and he had never had a virgin. Even Marilyn, for all her resistance, had admitted one night that the boy next door got there first. It was one of the reasons he couldn't love her. Why did somebody always get there first?

And then he thought of Mary kneeling on the bed beside him, touching him as no one had ever touched him before, and his whole body flamed with the need for her touch. He felt a flush of shame for what he had been thinking. It was so complicated, this business of loving someone. He suddenly hated Father Hannigan and the whole fucking universal, apostolic, holy Roman Catholic Church for making it harder.

Damaged goods? *Father Hannigan, you stupid prick, don't you know we're all damaged goods? That's what life does to you if you don't stay in a fucking church and pray all day.*

He thought about Mary and her sad, failed marriage, and about Harry, who thought a woman who enjoyed sex was a whore, about himself with his night terrors and his dreams about his father, a picnic for a shrink if ever there was one.

Damaged goods, that said it all right.

Damaged goods.

Journal: Donald A. Johnson

I am supposed to be doing another chapter on my book, but all I can see in my mind's eye is that tiny casket, so small it seems impossible it could hold even the smallest human. How can they want to kill our children? Where does such hatred come from? What sense of triumph can they get from that small coffin? There is a depth of human rage and cruelty that I cannot comprehend. I have seen its face, but I still can't put myself in the shoes of those who wear it. I simply can't imagine myself wanting to kill anyone's child — not the head of the KKK, or the white citizens' councils, or Hitler's — if he had one. Rafe tells me I have to learn how to hate, but how can you hate what you can't even understand? I could kill those men in cold blood, easily. That's revenge. But their children? What is it in those men's lives that could be satisfied by killing? It's not as if someone were invading their land or taking their homes or their wives. Is their grip on — what? identity, self-esteem? — so precarious that this is the only way they can feel like men?

Do they need people below them in the social order so they can at least feel superior to someone? I've seen the absolute rage on the faces of people who were smashing the sides of our bus, some with their bare hands. Their faces were not even human; it was as if they had been taken over by some primal urge, some law of the pack.

Since that time I've thought a lot about hatred. I think that the bus was a symbol that things were going to change, and that scared the shit out of them. None of them have any hope that change could be for the better. Before I went South, it hadn't really occurred to me that there were white people who couldn't have the American dream. Oh, maybe a few winos on North Capitol Street, but not regular white people. De Tocqueville says that Americans are more anxious than Europeans, because in Europe the class structure keeps people in their places. People know what to expect. Our freedom means that a lot of people will be losers not because of what their fathers did but because of what they didn't do. At least Negroes have something to blame if we don't get very far. If the American myth says that all people have a chance, those white people who don't make it have no one to blame but themselves. "The fault, dear Brutus, is not in our stars, but in ourselves, that we are underlings." How it must enrage them to think that the only people below them, the only people who give them a sense of being anywhere on the ladder at all — *us* — might somehow get ahead of them. So in some real sense, they have to keep us down to feel that they exist at all.

Dr. King believes that most people are good people, that if you appeal to the best in Americans, you can bring it forth. Is he right? Maybe, but you are going to bring out the worst in some of them, and how do you protect yourself against that? How do you know where that free-floating hatred will strike? It's like the wind, it's there, and it's capricious.

And what do *I* do? I can't stir the blood with a clarion call the way James Baldwin can. I can't explain how white society twists our souls, the way Richard Wright does. Mine is such a small voice. The literary agent said it was humane and wry, but I think that may mean it lacks scope, and intensity. Do I have a right to follow my own small, particular dream when Martin Luther King is leading what may be the greatest battle for human rights in history? Am I exaggerating my talent so I won't have to go back to the South?

I feel wrenched two ways as it is, being a student in my nice, safe writing class some of the time and trying to keep the Belvedere protest going the rest of the time. One thing I know: the bastards aren't going to win this one. Not when there are people like James, who will never give up now. What more has he to lose? He will die, now, rather than quit. They don't understand how they make us strong. The people who were hesitant before, now they are all together. I can't think about what might have been if I hadn't come to Belvedere. If I hadn't been in the church that night, or if James hadn't. What happened happened. I'll make myself crazy thinking anything else. Loretta says that the hatred is just a poison; it's in the country's blood, and it is bound to come out somehow or other. She says the alternative is to be silent and to let them do anything to us they want to do, and we can't do that anymore. She's right. We will not be silent anymore. The time for silence is long past.

Deep in my heart I do believe
We shall overcome someday.

I have to believe that. For James's little girl and his wife and for Medgar Evers, shot right in front of his kids, and for all those black men who have been hung up on trees and lynched, for all the deaths that stretch back and back and back through time, to the stench of the hold of the slave ships, I have to believe,

We shall overcome.

Mary leapt from her seat and called out, "Mr. President!" She was no longer afraid to compete for the president's attention in this raucous forum. John Kennedy saw the flash of her red blouse as she jumped up, and he nodded and pointed his forefinger in her direction. She suspected he enjoyed overlooking some of the important papers and calling on the younger, lesser members of the Washington press corps.

"Mr. President, your administration has done more for civil rights than any other in recent years. Do you think the upcoming March on Washington will help or hinder your efforts?"

He cocked his head slightly to one side as she asked the question, a sign he was listening attentively.

"I think that the way the Washington march is now developed, it will be a peaceful assembly calling for the redress of grievances. We want citizens to come to Washington if they feel they are not having their rights expressed."

"Some people say they're concerned about the continuing demonstrations. How do you feel?"

He paused a minute, considering his answer. I — ah — I have warned about demonstrations which could cause bloodshed. Some people, however, who keep talking about demonstrations never talk about the problem of redressing grievances. You can't just tell people, 'Don't protest,' but on the other hand, 'We are not going to let you into a store or restaurant.' It seems to me it is a two-way street."

Fifteen reporters jumped to their feet. The president smiled — he enjoyed the conferences, they gave him a chance to shine — and called on Tom Wicker of *The New York Times.* Wicker asked another question about the march, and Mary scribbled as fast as she could. Negro leaders were calling for a massive, peaceful march on the capital to demand the end of Jim Crow and to support Kennedy's civil rights bill, the most sweeping one ever sent to Congress by an American president. Key southern congressmen were opposed, so the bill faced an uphill battle.

As Jay and Mary walked back to his car, she said, "You could strip naked on Main Street the day of the march, and no one would know. Charlie's sending just about everybody."

"Speaking of naked," he said with a grin.

"Why do I think this is not about work?"

"I've got reservations for the Washington Hotel for the weekend. We're going first-class all the way."

"Do you know I've never stayed in a hotel, my whole life."

"Not anywhere?"

"No. We sometimes went to a cottage at Ocean City, but a real hotel, never."

"You're in for a treat."

"I hope I know how to behave."

"You're a big-shot reporter, you cover the president. If anybody gives you any lip, flash your press pass."

"What do we do, Jay? We're not married. Hotels won't let us stay together."

"Simple. We register as Mr. and Mrs. They don't check unless you look really suspicious."

"I shouldn't wear the black silk stockings and the green eye shadow?"

"Not till we get to the room."

That night she left work a few hours early so she could read to Karen and tuck her into bed. She was packing her suitcase when she felt someone watching her. She turned around to see her mother at the door of her bedroom. Her face was pale and tense as she watched Mary put her clothes into the bag.

"I know where you're going. I'm taking care of Karen so you can be with that man! You're going off with him, that photographer. Do you think I'm stupid?"

Mary sighed. "I'm a grown-up, Mom."

"You're a married woman. Or have you forgotten?"

"I am separated. Legally separated."

"I didn't raise you to be that kind of woman."

"I am not a whore, Mother."

Her mother blanched. "Oh, Mary, he's using you, don't you see? He's going to bed with you for — for his animal instincts. And when he's through with you, he'll throw you away."

"Oh, Mom, it's not like that. He's a wonderful man. He's sensitive, he's gentle."

"Will he want to marry you?"

Mary turned away and resumed packing. "I don't know. I don't care."

"My dear, you are acting like a fool. You think you can behave like a man? Take what you want when you want it?"

"Yes, why not?"

"Because when a man sleeps around, they say, 'Boys will be boys.' When a woman does it, she's a slut. There's a double standard; don't think there isn't."

"I know there is."

"You could wreck your marriage. If Harry finds out, you think he'll take you back?"

"How come all of a sudden *he's* taking *me* back?"

"I know your marriage was far from perfect. But he's doing so well. When he settles down, he can give you a good life."

"I don't want anyone to give me a life. I want to make my own life."

"It's terrible to be a woman alone in this world. Take it from me. I know."

Mary looked at her mother. They had never talked in any detail about her life before. Her mother had carried on with quiet strength and never complained. Now there was a mixture of fear and anger on her face.

"You did good, Mom. I know it wasn't easy, but you did it. I can too, if I have to."

Her mother shook her head. "No, you don't know, how men take advantage. The things they do, and say, that they would never do to a respectable married woman."

Mary closed the suitcase. "Whatever happens, I think my marriage is over."

"No! Mary, don't say that."

"We were kids, Mom. Stupid kids. I think it's going to be painful for Harry at first, but in the long run we'd both be better off if we got a divorce."

"Movie stars get divorced, not people like us. Do you know what a divorced woman is? She's a piece of meat. She's some man's leavings."

"This isn't the Victorian era, Mom. This is nineteen sixty-three."

"You think you're so smart, and I'm some — old fossil. You'll find out."

Mary put the suitcase on the floor. "There's no point in this discussion, Mom. We disagree."

She picked up the suitcase and started to move towards the door when she heard her mother's voice, icy cold. She had never heard that tone in her voice before.

"How dare you dismiss me like that! How dare you! I gave up everything for you, everything, and now you run around rutting with some man like a disgusting animal, leaving your daughter."

The force of the attack stunned Mary. Her mother stood glaring at her, ashen, and trembling.

"I'm a good mother!" she said. "You know I am!"

Her mother did not reply, but the pretty face twisted, in anger or pain, Mary could not tell which.

"I didn't ask you to give up everything! I never wanted you to give up everything! Why couldn't you live for yourself, not for me!"

"Because I was a whore. While your father was away, I was with a man. I did what you're doing, and God punished me, he took away my husband. Because I was a whore, your word, and that's right."

Mary stared at her mother, whose whole body was now trembling. She never imagined her mother had such a secret. She shook her head.

"No, that's not right. God doesn't punish people for having sex.

My father was away for four years, do you think he was faithful the whole time? And if he wasn't — this is crazy. God didn't punish you. Or him."

"I only know actions have consequences. You think you're doing something you'll get away with, and you don't. Nobody ever gets away free."

"Maybe not. But you know what? I don't care. I love him, and I'll take what I can have. It's better than not ever knowing. Not ever having anything."

Her mother's face seemed to crumble as warring emotions played across it; her pretty mother; for the first time, Mary thought, she looked old. How had she lived with that guilt for all those years?

"Mary, I want your life to be better than mine was. I don't want you to make the mistakes I made."

"I have to make my own mistakes. I know you love me, I know you want to protect me, Mom. But don't you see, I have to find my own way. The worst thing is if I don't try. The worst thing is just to stay where I am, and all my life I'll wonder, What could I have been? That's worse than anything God can do to me."

"I can't talk you out of this, can I?"

Mary shook her head.

"I pray you find it, whatever it is you want. But I can't stop being afraid for you. I'm your mother."

A horn sounded outside. Mary picked up the suitcase again and looked at her mother. "I love you," she said. Her mother nodded. "I love you too."

She hurried down the stairs and ran out to Jay's car and got in beside him. It was dark, but she thought, too late, that she had been stupid not to meet him someplace else. Someone might see her with the suitcase.

"Sorry I was late," he said. "Milt made me do two church social pictures tonight. McChesney said he'd do them for me, but Milt had a hair across his ass and made me do them. You got everything?"

She made a mental note: Toothpaste. Clean panties. Diaphragm. "Oh damn!"

"What's the matter?"

"I forgot to leave my time slip for the week in Charlie's box."

Irritation skittered across his face. "Damn it, Mary, that means you won't get your check. We'd better go by the paper."

"Don't bother. I'll do it on Monday."

"Last staff meeting Charlie said he wasn't going to accept any more slips on Monday."

"He always says that. He never does anything about it."

They were driving along the main road that led out of the city and onto the highway that would take them to Washington, and the car's headlights swept across the billboard that stood at the edge of town: BELVEDERE. A CITY OF PROGRESS AND PLEASANT PEOPLE.

Jay snorted. "Progress and pleasant people. That's a hot one. At least we'll be getting out of this pisshole for a little while."

"Yeah, it's good to get away."

"This place is full of WASP Babbitts with tiny minds. They want urban renewal? They ought to drop a bomb on it and start over."

"I'm a WASP."

"You're different."

"Oh, come on. I suppose the Irish are great examples of tolerance."

"I don't make any claims for the Irish. But this town is full of pricks."

"You can't write everybody off in a whole city."

"I can if I want to."

"That's dumb."

"I don't care if it's dumb or not. I don't want to argue about it. I got shit tonight at every fucking assignment."

"*You* started it."

"*I* started it? I just made a little remark, and you climbed all over my back."

"I did not. I said Belvedere wasn't the very worst place in the entire world."

"I don't want to argue. It's a stupid argument, so knock it off, for Christssake!"

She turned to stare at the dashboard, furious. Who did he think he was, Genghis Khan, ordering her around? She looked at him. He was gripping the wheel, scowling. She felt that she was seeing him for the very first time. What was so great about him? He was a very ordinary-looking man, why hadn't she noticed that before? The shirt he was wearing was a bilious green, the kind a farm boy would wear. His clothes were terrible and his manners worse. Sitting next to her in the car, Sigmund Freud shook his head, sadly.

You are committing adultery and throwing your marriage away for a man who is not good enough for you. Just like a woman.

And his clothes are terrible.

Yes, they certainly are. Have you ever read Anna Karenina*?*

You mean where the woman takes a lover and ruins her marriage and throws herself in front of a train?

That's the one, yes.

I'd never throw myself in front of a train because of him. He's a jerk.

Ah, how women become disenchanted when libido fades. An hour ago you were madly in love with him.

Well, that was an hour ago. Now I think he's an asshole.

What do women want?

They want men not to be assholes.

I never thought of that.

You should have, you're fucking Freud.

Then he reached over and touched her cheek and said, "Hey, I'm sorry. I didn't mean all that. I had a lousy day and was taking it out on you."

He looked tired, and very young and vulnerable, and she hated herself for thinking he was an asshole. She moved over beside him and rested her head on his shoulder.

"Honey," he said, "when I get like this, ignore me. I act like a jerk sometimes when I get pissed off."

The endearment warmed her; it was what her father used to call her mother. He seemed unaware that it was the first time he had used it, but she felt a rush of gratitude towards him. He was, she realized, very much like her father, tall and lean, and there was a reservoir of tenderness inside him that she sensed was like the father she remembered.

"I made reservations for us. Mr. and Mrs. Jay Michaels. That's my middle name, Michael. In case, you know, anybody tried to check."

"I'm Mrs. Michaels. Oh, I'll have to remember that. What if they ask me for some kind of identification?"

"I don't see why they would. We're just an ordinary couple, checking in for the weekend. We'll have to look like we do this all the time, so they won't know we're two hicks from Belvedere."

"You're not. You've been lots of places."

"Yeah, Fort Dix, Fort Hood. To me, a Howard Johnson's motel is putting on the Ritz."

"We have to move up in the world, Jay."

"We sure as hell do."

He pulled the car up in front of the Washington — a block from the White House — where it was driven off to be parked by a valet. A bellman took the bags, and Mary followed Jay to the counter. The lobby was lovely, all polished wood and lush carpet, and Mary could feel her heart pounding wildly inside her chest. The treasurer of the Class of '56 was not exactly a woman of the world. She wanted to take his hand but thought it might look gauche. Did they look married? The clerk looked at her, and she had the feeling she had just sprouted a huge scarlet *A* on her chest, like Hester Prynne's.

Jay said, "Mr. and Mrs. Michaels," to the clerk, and it sounded so absurd she wanted to giggle. The bellman took the bags and carried them upstairs, and Jay tipped him fifty cents. The bellman looked at his palm and slammed the door on the way out.

"Fifty cents I tipped him, the ingrate," Jay said. With the slamming of the door, her apprehension came unstuck. They were safe; she felt almost guilty. She kicked off her shoes, letting her feet sink in the pile of the carpet.

"Jay, what is this, the presidential suite or something? You can wade through this rug. How much did it cost?"

"You're not supposed to ask that."

"Come on, how much?"

"Fifty-six dollars a night."

"Fifty-six dollars. Oh, my God!"

"We big-time photojournalists travel in style. Let's see how the view is."

He walked to the window and opened the curtain. Below them, the city was blinking and tiny and perfect.

"There are people who live like this, all the time," she said, in awe.

"Comes the revolution, we'll turn it into a fucking steel mill. Come on, let's shower."

"You go first. I'll unpack."

"No, dummy, this is supposed to be a big sex weekend. I don't want to shower by myself."

"Oh."

He laughed and kissed her and said, "You really are a hick. Hurry up, I'll get the shower warm."

She got undressed, and he called out, "Hurry up, I'm turning into a prune!" She went into the bathroom and stepped naked into the shower with him, and thought how odd it was that she felt perfectly natural naked with him, and, with Harry, she had never undressed with the light on.

"I'm going to put soap all over you, I'm kinky that way," he said. "Let's see if everything's there. You have the nicest boobs. One, two — three? I don't remember three. Oh well, I like you 'cause you're different."

"Rat," she said and tickled him and he squirmed. She took the soap and said, "My turn," and started to slowly soap his body all over.

"See, Pat, isn't this more fun than getting into the shower with Checkers?"

"Yeah, he gets a little smelly sometimes when he thaws out too much."

"This is almost as thrilling as the time I nailed Alger Hiss."

"Oh, Dick, you're getting to be a sex fiend. Let me put soap all over you!"

"Oooh! Ohhh! Oh, God, this is so sexy. That's it, Pat, put a little more soap on my tie."

She laughed and kissed him, and he picked her up and carried her, soaking wet, into the bedroom, and they made love on the rug, leaving soap and big water stains all over it. Dried off, she nestled in his arms and went to sleep, and in the morning they made love again and went out to savor the delights of a whole day together. They walked along the Chesapeake and Ohio Canal and bought a little print of the canal in a shop in Georgetown. Later they went to the museum and wandered through a room where a collection of pharaohs looked sternly down on them. He stood in the middle of the room and said, "I suppose you're wondering why I called you here today," and she laughed as if it were the wittiest line ever spoken. They walked together, holding hands, and she thought she would try to memorize everything she felt and saw, so that she could remember it for the rest of her life. It was something she could fold up and pack away like some priceless object, and if she never had another like it, she could take it out from time to time and remember it.

Much later, back in the room, he was quiet, subdued almost, and she turned to him and began to touch him, loving the taste and feel of him — the salty taste of the skin near his shoulder, the softness of his nipples, the texture of the hair on his chest — he was so beautiful. But, of course, you weren't allowed to say that about men's bodies.

He stood up and led her to the chair, where he held her and kissed her breasts. She wanted to say to him, "I adore you," but instead she knelt before the chair and rested her head on his thighs, and he bent forward, his hands cradling her buttocks, his lips against her hair. He was still sitting in the chair when she rose and guided him into her.

She began to move on him, feeling she was both possessor and possessed, and she asked, "Do you like this?" and he said, "Yes. Oh yes."

She remembered as a child, at Ocean City, being tumbled in shallow water. She was not afraid but exhilarated as the wave rolled her over and dragged her onto the sand. She wanted that same feeling now, to be dragged out of control into the foam, over and over and over and over. All of her senses imploded into some molten center where the barriers between their bodies simply melted away. She called his name, an incantation, and she heard his voice someplace far away.

He held her close to him as his breathing slowed, held her tightly, as if he feared she might turn to vapor and drift away from him. "I love you," he said. "I love you so much it scares the shit out of me."

She felt he had opened a door in his chest and let her walk through it. She put her finger up against his lips, ran her finger along his cheek.

"I never thought — I never knew I could love anybody like this. I don't want to lose you, Mary."

"I'm here."

He shook his head. "I want you to leave Harry for good and marry me."

"Oh, Jay."

"We're good together, Mary. Not just in bed. God knows we're good there." He ran his fingers lightly across her breasts. "We could be a team. Your words, my pictures. There would be no stopping us."

"You make it seem possible."

"It is. Is is possible."

"I have a child, Jay."

"I think I could learn to be a good father. I don't know much about it; but I could learn."

"I'd have to get a divorce. I didn't think Catholics believed in divorce."

"I do. Why should two people bump along, tied to each other, miserable? It doesn't make any sense. It's not a big deal. People get divorced all the time."

"Not in Belvedere. I don't even know anybody who's been divorced."

"We've got bigger things ahead of us than Belvedere. Come here." He took her hand and led her to the window. Below them, the city blinked and moved, a miniature toy put together solely for their enchantment.

"We can do it," she said to him. "Oh, Jay, we can do anything!"

He laughed. "That's the spirit. We can do anything!" He laughed again, amazed at himself. "Look at what you've done. You've made me an optimist, me, the original gloom and doom Irishman."

"I'll marry you," she said. "Oh yes, I'll marry you, and we can do anything!"

He had never had a day quite like it. He had come to Berlin to see the wall for himself, and its raw ugliness sickened him. He could not imagine a life constrained by concrete and iron rods. Then he went to Rudolf Wilde Platz, where half the population of West Berlin spilled out across the square and into the surrounding streets. He stood on the platform, his words floating out over the loudspeakers up and down the square, bouncing off the buildings in an eerie echo.

> *There are some who say that communism is the wave of the future.*
> *Let them come to Berlin!*
> *And there are some who say in Europe and elsewhere we can work with communists.*
> *Let them come to Berlin!*
> *And there are even a few who say that it is true that communism is an evil system, but it permits us to make economic progress.*
> *Lass sie nach Berlin kommen! Let them come to Berlin!*

And the crowd roared with a sound that was like the howl of a huge animal. At first, he was exhilarated; a sensation of power surged through him, thrilling him to his fingertips. For one mad instant, he thought that if he asked that crowd to turn and march to the wall and tear it down with bare hands, it would obey him. But even as the adrenaline pumped through him, he was afraid of this sudden strength.

How many men had experienced such power, to know that their will flowed from them directly into the bloodstreams of the crowd, that it could control their hands and hearts? For some, the thrill would be all. But rationality was his religion, perhaps even more than Catholicism. The rule of the mob seemed to him a horror, anathema to the discipline of democracy. He believed that modern technology and communication, which pierced the veil of old secrets, moved in favor of Western democracy and against authoritarianism. But he worried, too, that the earth might not survive that long. Seeing the wall stirred up his misgivings. He was one of two men on the planet who had stood on the brink of Armageddon. Both of them knew — as no others — how it felt to have the power of hell at their fingertips. It was one thing, he realized, to know, intellectually, that the power existed, another to feel it so close that the hairs on the back of your neck stood on end and you thought, Oh shit, it could happen. I could end the world. There was unusual emotion in his voice when he said before the United Nations, "However close we sometimes seem to that dark and final abyss, let no man of peace and freedom despair. . . . Together we shall save our planet, or together we shall perish in its flames. Save it we can, and save it we must."

As a serious student of history, he knew that blunder, stupidity, ego and error were too often its horsemen. After World War I, two German officials met, and one said to the other, "How did it happen?" and the other replied, "Ah, if only one knew." He thought it intolerable that one day, two survivors of a nuclear war might stand in the debris of civilization and have the same exchange:

How did it begin?

Ah, if only one knew.

He had traveled a long way from the boy who had wondered, after his brother's death, if he were boxing with a shadow. He had carried his father's hopes, and now he realized it was, instead, the future of the earth that rested on his shoulders. He had wanted the job because that was where the power was. Now he had it, and it sobered him. One lesson he had learned was how much he could not do, how complicated the world was. But he determined that he would take the world back at least a few steps from the abyss into which he had stared. His words still bristled with the challenges of the warrior, but he knew there was a man halfway across the world who would not take that final step either. Together, they had to forge the cold and brittle peace; anything else was simply madness.

From Berlin he traveled to the place both his grandfathers had left so many years before, to try their luck in a raw, unfriendly land. In Ireland, the crowds gathered around him as if he were some long lost nephew, and old women touched his cheek as if if he were a child. For the first time he understood, with his heart, something of his roots, of why old men gathered in bars in South Boston and listened to the sad laments of a blood-soaked land whose gray skies and lush green grass had not been able to hold them. He had grown up in Palm Beach and Hyannis, more American than Irish, perhaps more English in temperament than either, but the old country stirred that hidden romantic inside him. His wife had written a poem about him early in their courting days, and she had known him better than he imagined.

> *Part he was of New England stock*
> *As stubborn close-guarded as Plymouth Rock.*
> *But part he was of an alien breed . . .*
> *The lilt of that green land danced in his blood.*
> *Tara, Killarney, a magical flood,*
> *They surged in the depth of his too-proud heart.*

He hated the idea that anyone would think him sentimental, but in Ireland the coolness thawed under the weight of poetry and the past. As he was preparing to board the plane for home, he stood facing a throng of well-wishers, and he threw to them the words of the song he had learned by heart, sounding odd in the broad, flat tones of New England:

Come back to Erin, Mavourneen, Mavourneen,
Come back around to the land of thy birth.
Come with the shamrock in the springtime, Mavourneen.

He looked out at the crowd and paused, and when he spoke it was not from a script.

"This is not the land of my birth, but it is the land for which I hold the greatest affection."

He paused again, looking out at the crowd and the green land beyond, the wind making a tangle of his hair, and he made them a promise: "I certainly will come back in the springtime."

"I'VE NEVER SEEN so many people," Mary said, looking around her as the vast space of the Washington Monument grounds filled up with humanity, spilling over its edges into the bordering streets.

Washington had not seen anything like it before. Twenty-one chartered trains had pulled into Union Station that morning, and buses poured through the Baltimore tunnel, heading south to Washington, at the rate of one hundred per hour. A young Negro man had come on roller skates all the way from Chicago, wearing a banner with the word FREEDOM on it. An eighty-two-year-old man had ridden his bicycle from Ohio to the nation's capital.

The high, clear voice of Joan Baez singing "Oh Freedom" and "We Shall Overcome" piped over the public address system as Mary looked around her in amazement. She was standing with Jay and Don; they had come with the Belvedere contingent on a charter bus an hour earlier, and how they would ever find it again in this crush remained problematic.

"I had no idea it would be so big," Don said, looking at the throngs of people, black and white, milling around on the Monument grounds.

Indeed, there had been apprehension in some quarters about the march. John Kennedy hoped it would be large enough to build a groundswell of support for his civil rights bill, on which he had now staked the prestige of his presidency. J. Edgar Hoover, the chief of the FBI, with his pathological hatred of Martin Luther King and the civil rights movement, had warned Washington notables to expect violence. (Hoover, who had files bursting with damaging material on the president's sex life, used them to extract the authority to put wiretaps on King; Kennedy had secretly warned King about the taps. It was a treacherous game with the highest of stakes.) On the Hill, the mood on the eve of the march was psychic terror, as if hordes of marauding Negroes were set to sweep through the city like Genghis Khan and his Mongols. Malcolm X denounced the march as puppetry, in which a white president was simply using Negro leaders for his own cynical political ends. Four thousand troops were stationed in the suburbs, backed up by 15,000 paratroopers on alert in North Carolina. The Washington Senators' baseball games were canceled, some stores barred their doors and the sale of liquor was banned for the first time since Prohibition.

What few people had expected was what was actually happening: an explosive outpouring of hope and good humor, Negroes and whites walking along, often hand in hand, singing and praying, in an atmosphere that was as far from terror as a county fair.

"How many people do you think are here?" Don asked Jay. Jay shook his head. "There has to be at least two hundred thousand here already. And they just keep coming."

"Man, oh, man," Don said. "Look at it. Just look at it!"

The three young people grinned at one another. Since Don had come to Belvedere that first night, a friendship had developed among them. They had been out to dinner together in Washington a number of times, often joined by Don's fiancée, Loretta. The meetings had ostensibly been to discuss the urban renewal plan, now enmeshed in a legal wrangle, but the pretext of business soon vanished. They were the same age, and they had much in common; they were part of the generation that saw itself as the vanguard of a bright new age. The prejudices and taboos of their parents, they believed, had no hold on them. The old division of race hardly mattered.

"Hey," Jay said to Don, "this would be a great place to shoot your book-jacket picture. With the monument in the background."

"OK. But how should I look? I don't want to be grinning like an idiot."

He had told them, the night before, that Doubleday, through his literary agent, had offered him a book contract, with an advance of four thousand dollars.

"Four thousand dollars!" Mary had said with a gasp. "Don, you're rich!"

"What are you going to call it?" Jay asked.

"I'm not sure. I'm trying to think of a title that doesn't sound too pretentious. It's about growing up colored in D.C."

"Something classy," Mary said, "like Baldwin. He has great titles."

"But not so grand. I mean, this is really a small, personal book; it's not in the same league as Baldwin's essays."

Mary shook her head in disagreement; he had given her several chapters to read. "It's different, but I think a lot of people will be able to relate to it. I mean, we were all kids, and we had dogs and went to movies and thought about weird things. I think your book will help a lot of white people realize that you aren't different than they are, that people are all alike, they're just people."

"That's not exactly, *The Fire Next Time,*" he said ruefully.

"That's the sequel," she said with a smile.

Now Jay had Don move so that he could take a portrait photo with the monument and the crowds behind him.

"Just relax and look right at the camera. No, too serious; you look like you have a toothache. That's it, relax. Good. I'll do a whole roll, and you can pick the one you want."

"Oh, my God!" Mary said. "Look, it's James Garner, and he's walking with Diahann Carroll."

"There's Harry Belafonte!" Jay aimed his camera in their direction. "And Charlton Heston. Oh shit, it's Brando. It's actually Brando."

"Show him a movie star, and he forgets all about great literature." Don sighed.

"My boss is going to love these," Jay said, still shooting. "Real movie stars, only forty-seven and a half miles from Belvedere."

Finally, the huge throng began to lumber off down the broad lanes of Constitution Avenue, towards the Lincoln Memorial, as

Peter, Paul and Mary sang one of Bob Dylan's new songs, telling an older generation that their sons and their daughters were no longer theirs to command.

She and Don walked along as close as they could get to the leaders of the march, as Jay darted back and forth shooting pictures. Martin Luther King and Roy Wilkins and A. Philip Randolph and other famous names in Negro America linked arms as they walked up the avenue, the sunlight filtering down through the thick mesh of trees overhead, dappling their faces and their bodies. The huge river of people moved on and on, under the arch of trees. It seemed to Mary that every spot in Washington was blanketed by a carpet of humanity, singing, smiling, calling out. It seemed to her as if a sea of love swept down the broad boulevard, wrapping Negro and white together in its embrace. She felt a lump rise in her throat.

"Oh, Don," she said, grasping his arm, "this is what America is all about! It isn't all words, this is it, it couldn't happen anywhere else. Nothing will ever be the same, not after today!"

He turned to look back down the avenue, where the crowd stretched as far as he could see, and he, too, was caught up in the emotion of it all. "I never thought I'd see anything like this. Not in my hometown. Not ever! My God, look at them all!"

By the time they arrived at the Lincoln Memorial, the crowd stretched around all four sides of the Reflecting Pool and far beyond. Roy Wilkins stepped to the microphone and announced that, halfway across the world, in Ghana, W. E. B. Du Bois had died that very morning. The father figure of the Negro intelligentsia and the NAACP had soured on America and turned to communism as the hope of the world, but Wilkins said nothing of that. "At the dawn of the twentieth century," he said, "his was the voice that was calling to you to gather here today in this cause."

Under the platform, away from the public view, heated arguments were taking place about the speeches. John Lewis of SNCC was about to give a speech harshly critical of the government, belittling the civil rights bill. Lewis and the NAACP's Roy Wilkins shook their fingers in each other's faces as they argued about the speech. A truce committee that included Dr. King, a white minister and A. Philip Randolph retired to a guard booth under Lincoln's giant knee. A compromise draft was hastily produced on a borrowed typewriter.

But to the people in the crowd, no such emotions were apparent. There were speeches and songs, stretched out to fill the hours of the long afternoon, and the good humor of the marchers did not abate, even as they mopped their brows in the August heat. The day was beginning to wane by the time Martin Luther King walked to the platform, standing before the cream-colored knees of Lincoln, where, years before, the great Negro singer Martin Anderson had sung when the Daughters of the American Revolution refused her their hall because of her race.

Mary's feet were aching. She had been standing and walking all day. She slipped off her shoes and plunged her feet into the cool water of the Reflecting Pool, and Jay saw her and snapped a photograph. Dr. King began to speak in his rolling preacher's voice. He had labored long over his text, but on that spot, in front of that huge throng, he began to soar away from the text. Behind him the gospel singer Mahalia Jackson called out, "Tell 'em about the dream, Martin!"

And he did.

"I have a dream," he said and he repeated the phrase, mingling it with "My Country 'Tis of Thee" again and again, words of hope and optimism and joy, his voice ringing out over the huge, hushed crowd. Mary sat very still, thinking that she had never before been held in such thrall by a speaker; she looked to her right and her left, and no one was moving. The words gripped the huge crowd like a giant claw; it had no will to do anything but listen. The speaker told them of a day when "*all* God's children, black men and white men, Jews and Gentiles, Protestants and Catholics, will be able to join hands and sing in the words of the old Negro spiritual, 'Free at last! Free at last! Thank God Almighty, we are free at last!' "

Later, in the Cabinet Room of the White House, John Kennedy, who knew a helluva speech when he heard one, would greet the preacher with an outstretched hand and the very same words, "I have a dream."

* * *

Mary, Jay and Don walked slowly back in search of the Belvedere bus, wading through the incredible pile of debris left by the largest crowd that had ever come to the city. They were quiet, each overwhelmed by the emotions of the day. Never before, as Mary had said, had the dream of America seemed so real. They felt they could reach out and touch it with the soft pink haze of the ending summer day. It was one of those days, they knew, that comes once in a generation, the kind you tell your grandchildren about. I was there, standing in front of Lincoln, on the day that three hundred thousand people marched and Martin Luther King called out, "I have a dream." How lucky they were, to be young, in this time, when John F. Kennedy challenged them to bear every burden and Martin Luther King led the March on Washington. It proved that everything was possible, that tomorrow glittered with hope and dreams. Other generations might find disillusionment and failure, not theirs.

It was 1963, and they owned the future.

Journal: Donald A. Johnson

One of the students wrote an essay about being in the Army, and we discussed it in class today. I said that I didn't think I would go and fight for the United States of America, not now, not today, if another "police action" like Korea broke out in the Mideast or in Vietnam, where we have some troops. They were fairly shocked by that. I said I didn't think I would spill my blood for the Stars and Stripes, even though I spent my childhood lusting to do just that.

I used to be pissed, in fact, that I missed World War II. It started when I was three, so nobody could accuse me of shirking. Three-year-olds do not make great infantrymen; changing their diapers interferes with combat readiness.

It seems that for as long as I remember, I have been going to war movies. When I was a kid, I always came home convinced that war was the greatest game of them all, better even than Lash LaRue or Finding the Holy Grail. I saw Spencer Tracy spend thirty seconds over Tokyo and John Wayne take Iwo Jima and Alan Ladd outwit the Jerries behind enemy lines in France.

Our neighborhood was an easy place to turn into a war zone. Mr. Williams's neat woodpile was a perfect B-29. I flew it regularly over Tokyo with Thunder as my bombardier. I barked orders at him, and he just looked back at me with his stupid stare. How they let him into the Army Air Corps I'll never know. Mr. Williams used to peer out the window at me, wondering what I was doing. He would say to his wife, "What on earth is that Johnson boy doing in my woodpile all the time, with that dog of his? That is the strangest colored boy I have ever seen, I swear it is."

Sometimes I was John Wayne, capturing Japs. I made Darlene be a Jap, and I tied her hands behind her and marched her up and down the alley behind our house and called her "Dirty Jap." Sometimes she thought it was fun, but when she got tired of it and I made her keep marching, she'd escape and run in the house to my mother, crying, and my mother would order me not to make Darlene a Jap anymore. So I made her a Nazi, which was, after all, following the letter of my mother's command.

(I have this terrible fear that I have warped Darlene forever, that on her wedding night she will ask her new husband to tie her up and whisper "Dirty Jap" in her ear and he will wonder how come he got the colored girl with the weirdest sexual fantasies in all of America.)

It never occurred to me that the Japs I saw in the comic strips — little yellow men with buck teeth — were the same kind of racial stereotype as the shuffling, grinning Negro. I absolutely believed that Japan was crammed with buck-toothed little yellow people who liked nothing better than to while away an afternoon by torturing American pilots. I knew I would be very brave if they tortured me. I'd laugh in the face of the little yellow Jap who tried to make me talk. Once I made Darlene tie me up and pretend to be a Jap general. When I told her she could hit me, her eyes lit up, and she gave me a real whack. Thunder growled at her, the only loyal thing he ever did. Darlene got mad at Thunder and whacked him too, and he howled and ran under the porch. Neither of us wanted to play that game again. But I made Darlene and Thunder play Bataan Death March, in which I made them tramp all over the neighborhood while I yelled at them and prodded them with the butt of my toy rifle. I yelled "American Dogs!" at them in my best Japanese accent, which was not an insult to Thunder, I guess. Darlene got bored with this pretty fast and wanted to go play with her dolls. I told her I would bayonet her *and* her dollies if she tried to get away. She ran howling to my mother, who called me into the house.

"Did you tell this child you were going to stick her with a bayonet?"

"She was on the Bataan Death March. That's what happens."

"What Death March?"

"Everybody knows about the Bataan Death March."

"You just march yourself right up to your room, Mr. Donald Abednego Johnson, and stay there until I say so." When she used my full name, I knew I was in deep shit.

Most of all, though, I used to play Dying in Combat. It was the best way to die, very dramatic. You got shot, and you gave a grunt, and you fell to the ground, and everything got very quiet and violins played in the background. Your best buddy cradled your head in his arms, and you gave a brave smile, and you said something like, "Every time you see the flag waving in the breeze, think of me. Every time there's a home run at Yankee Stadium, or a sunset, or a Fourth of July parade, I'll be there, buddy. Now go out there and give 'em hell!"

And you'd close your eyes and die, and the music would play real loud. Sometimes, at the end of the movie, they'd show the guys who died, marching off into the clouds with cocky grins thrown over their shoulders, carrying full battle gear as they headed to the Pearly Gates, clouds swirling about their ankles. Death was only a minor inconvenience before you marched off into soldier heaven with all your buddies.

I used to practice dying, a lot. I'd clutch my stomach, and I'd roll over two or three times, and I'd make my speech, looking up at the sky. Sometimes Thunder would come over and stand on my face, which ruined the dramatic effect. I'd shove him away, and he'd just stare at me. It is sort of hard to make a stirring death speech when staring into the snout of a stupid dog. Especially when he drooled on my chin, which Alan Ladd never had to put up with.

In the movies, all the American soldiers were whites, but sometimes there were newsreels of the Negro divisions that were fighting overseas. Everybody in my neighborhood was especially proud that Negroes were fighting, and shedding their blood the same as white Americans. When men fought and died for the same cause, surely they'd see that we were Americans too. After the war, when President Truman desegregated the armed forces, and then Jackie Robinson broke the color line in major league baseball, we thought everything was going to be different. But Jim Crow was as strong as ever.

I tried to explain to my white classmates why I didn't want to go and fight now, for a country that was still keeping my people at the back of the bus. Why should I want to go out and shoot people who had never lynched a Negro or killed a Negro child or passed any laws that kept Negroes as second-class human beings. I would die in Alabama or Mississippi if I had to, but not in some foreign war. I am an American, but I believe we have to fix what's wrong in our own country before we can police the world. My father says I shouldn't say such things, because white people will think we are afraid to fight. If all the graves with the little white crosses on them from World War II didn't convince them, then they will never be convinced. I'm tired of caring about what white people think. When Jim Crow is finally buried, when Kennedy's civil rights bill is passed, then I'll enlist. I'll be the first one in line. And if they shoot me in some foreign land, while I gasp out my last breath as I stare up at the sky, at least I won't have some stupid dog drooling on my chin.

"HAVE I FOUND a sweet piece of ass," Roger said. "She's coming over later. Eat your hearts out."

"There goes my night's sleep." Jay groaned.

"I hope this broad is *quiet,*" Sam said.

Sam and Jay were sitting at the kitchen table having a beer.

"You guys sure are in a crappy mood tonight. Pissed because you're not getting any."

"Sure, Rog. We're not great lovers, like you."

"I take that back. Jay's been dipping his wick lately. They say the married ones are the horniest. Can't get enough."

"You son of a bitch!" Jay knocked over his chair and spilled the beer from the can trying to get to Roger. He grabbed his roommate and slammed him against the wall. "You keep your fucking mouth shut, you fucking son of a bitch!"

Sam grabbed Jay and dragged him away. "Roger, you stupid shit, watch your mouth."

Roger slid away from Jay's grip, rattled, aware he'd violated the code. There were the girls you just slept with, and you could say anything about them. There were the ones you were serious about, and that was a different matter, entirely.

"Jesus, Jay, I didn't know. Sorry, man."

"You say another word about her and I'll mash your fucking face in."

"I'm sorry. Honest, I'm sorry. OK?"

Sam pulled Jay back to the table, and Roger scooted out of the room. "Come on, Jay, he's not worth getting pissed about."

"He's got a rotten mouth."

"This is Roger we're talking about. What did you expect, 'How do I love thee? Let me count the ways'?"

That made Jay laugh.

"I haven't told anybody," he said. "Mary and I are going to get married. She's going to get a divorce from Harry."

"Hey, that's great! Congratulations. Did this happen over the weekend?"

Jay grinned. "Yeah, it did."

Sam looked at him and laughed. "That blush makes you look like a Victorian virgin. Must have been some weekend."

"It was."

"This calls for a real celebration. Let me break out the hard stuff."

He went to the cabinet, got out the brandy and poured a glass for himself and one for Jay. "God, Jay, you're getting married. That makes me feel old."

"We're getting on, old buddy."

"Christ, yes. Three more years and we're thirty. We'll be bald and we won't get hard-ons."

"JFK's forty-six. He's got hair, and from what I hear, his prick is still active."

"I knew there was a reason I voted for a Catholic." Sam raised his glass. "Cheers."

They touched their glasses and drank.

"Funny," Jay said. "I'm breaking all my ethnic traditions. I'm happy."

"Irish Catholics aren't allowed to be happy?"

"Oh shit, no. Maybe you can be for a while, but you have to pay for it. Like Héloïse and Abelard. He had himself castrated, and she went off to a nunnery. That's a Catholic love story."

"And I thought Jewish guilt was bad. A lifetime of misery, OK, but we don't *ever* think about cutting it off. A little snip, but not the whole megillah."

"The saints smiled a lot, but only when someone was burning them alive. Martyrdom is the Irish Catholic idea of having an orgasm."

"Does Mary know what she's getting into?"

"She doesn't mind when I ask her to nail me to the bedpost. The crown of thorns is a bit too kinky for her taste, though."

"You are going to get hit by a bolt of lightning one of these days."

"Not me, I'm on good terms with God; I throw a little plant food at him every time I drive by."

"You make me wonder exactly what Kennedy *does* in the Lincoln Bedroom."

"You know that bad back of his?"

"I hesitate to ask."

"Flagellation. Sometimes he does it himself, sometimes he asks the Secret Service in to give him a few good belts. 'Oh, Agent Snedlock, it hurts so good! Ask not what your country can do for you . . ."

"Your religion is weird, Jay."

"Everybody's religion is weird. That's the nice thing about religions."

They were both silent for a minute, and then Jay said, "How the hell did Roger know?"

"Everybody knows, Jay."

"What?"

"It's all over the paper. Somebody from the back shop saw the two of you together in D.C."

"Oh fuck."

"People were bound to find out. You light up like a Christmas tree when she walks in. People were starting to put two and two together anyhow."

"It's not that I want to hide anything, but her husband has to agree to a divorce. The fewer complications, the better."

Sam nodded. "I understand."

Jay went into the living room, called Mary and asked if he could pick her up in ten minutes. He drove to a street some blocks away from her house and parked the car.

"A million people in D.C., and we get seen by two people from Belvedere," she said. "How do we do it?"

"Your luck plus my luck, that's how. I'm sorry, Mary. This was the one thing I didn't want to happen."

"It was bound to, I guess. I only hope Harry doesn't hear about it secondhand."

"You have to talk to him."

"I know. I will, Jay."

"The longer you put it off, the harder it's going to be."

"I know. Jay, maybe we ought to . . . not be together for a little while. Until I see Harry and talk to a lawyer."

"I guess that would be the best thing."

"I'll get it arranged soon. Then we won't have to go slinking around, like we're doing something wrong."

He felt a sudden surge of panic. What was he doing, sitting in a car at midnight and talking about lawyers and divorces? His life was getting so complicated.

She picked up his mood and said, "Jay, I want to be with you, it's just that people — well, they always like to think the worst. They like to gossip. We'll be old hat in a couple of weeks. They'll have something else to talk about."

For the next week they saw each other only in the city room; they were careful not to go out for a drink together, careful not to let their bodies touch when they walked by each other. When they spoke, it was formally and only about work. Mary kept busy with a series of meetings in the Negro community; the legal wrangling over the urban renewal plan was continuing, and there was hope for a settlement. She picked up the phone three times to call Harry, but each time she was swept by such feelings of guilt and panic that she put the phone down again. She cursed herself for being a coward and told herself she must do it. She did find time to talk to a lawyer, and the meeting left her depressed. Divorce was so much more complicated and messy than she had imagined.

After one night meeting, she stayed late to finish a story on federal urban renewal regulations, tortuous in their complexity. She struggled with it, trying to make the issues clear but not to oversimplify. By the time the story was done, her head was throbbing. She walked out to her car and opened the door, when suddenly, from behind, a hand gripped her shoulder. She jumped and let out a cry.

"Who were you expecting. The Wolf Man? It's only me."

"Jay, you scared me. I thought you left an hour ago."

"I've been waiting out here. What took you so long?"

"I've been fighting the renewal piece. God, it's complicated."

He stepped close to her and rubbed her shoulder.

"I hate it when a story isn't coming," she said. "I'm beat."

She could feel the tension in him through his fingers; he was like a spring coiled too tightly. When he spoke, his voice was low and urgent. "I've been going out of my skull, seeing you every day and not being able to touch you."

"I know."

"I feel like a goddamn criminal, like everybody's watching me."

"I feel it too." She looked around to see if anyone could see them where they were standing. There was no one in sight.

"Mary, come with me tonight. We could stop at one of those places on the expressway. No local people go there."

"Jay, it's late."

"I need you, Mary. I need you so bad!"

She felt his fingers tighten on her arm. The throbbing in her head was getting worse. She thought of the bed in her room, with its clean, fresh-smelling sheets and the cushiony pillows, so inviting. But there was an appeal in the grip of his fingers on her arm she could not refuse, so she nodded. "I'll call my mother and tell her I'm working on a story in D.C. and I'm staying over. She probably won't believe me."

Mary drove her car to a secluded spot outside town, parked and locked it. She climbed into Jay's car; her head was really pounding now. She found an aspirin in her purse and swallowed it without water; it left a bitter taste in her mouth. She closed her eyes and tried to sleep in the car until Jay pulled up in front of a row of squat wooden cabins advertised by a green neon sign that announced: V CAN I S — three letters were dark.

"It's not fancy, but it's safe."

She waited in the car while he registered, then she followed him into one of the cabins. He switched on the overhead light and the room greeted her. Its shoddiness appalled her; bile green peeling paint, pink and green chenille bedspreads tossed across the beds, the furniture a cheap plastic imitating wood.

"Jay, turn out that light, please. It's too damn bright."

She went into the bathroom and splashed cold water on her face. She peered at the dark patches under her eyes, and the strange yellow of her skin in the light. She dusted powder on her face, but it didn't help. She washed out her panties and hung them up on the rack to dry — at least she would have clean panties in the morning, and then took out her diaphragm and put it in. The act felt awkward, even obscene.

When she came out, he was naked in bed waiting for her. She undressed quickly and climbed into bed with him. The mattress was uneven; it sagged badly in the middle.

"God, I've missed you!"

He began to caress her, and his breath was coming fast. She tried to want his hands on her, but all she could feel was the ache in her head. She did the things she knew he liked, mechanically, but she wished he would hurry. The whole thing seemed ridiculous; *he* seemed ridiculous. She knew he was trying to hold back, to bring her with him, but finally he said, "I have to come," and she said yes, but she was still dry, and it was hard for him to enter her.

When it was through he rolled over on his back and stared at the ceiling. They lay side by side, not touching.

"It was lousy for you."

"It's all right."

"No, it's not. I feel like I've — used you."

"No you haven't."

"Yes I have. You didn't want me. You know what that makes me feel like? A goddamn rapist."

"I'm just tired. My head aches. It's not you."

"I'd rather have you tell me to get lost than to have you lie on your back and think of England."

That struck her as funny, and she said, "Actually, it was Weehawken, New Jersey."

His sense of humor, however, had vanished.

"I don't want you to fake it. It makes me feel like a charity case."

"I wasn't faking."

"Oh no?"

"Maybe a little. It seemed — impolite to lie there like a lump."

"*Impolite!* Jesus Christ!"

"It's not a big deal; so one time, it isn't great. It happens."

"It makes me feel like shit."

"You really don't want me to be honest, Jay. You want me to fake it so your male ego won't get all bent out of shape."

"That's not true."

They were silent, not touching, not looking at each other. Even though she could no longer see the peeling paint or the bile green walls, she was acutely aware of them. But she *could* see Sigmund Freud, sitting on one of the plastic chairs.

And so, tell me what you are thinking.

Fuck off.

You are wondering if this is what your life is always going to be, crummy rooms with peeling paint and chenille bedspreads.

No, I am not thinking that.

Yes you are. To be exact, you are thinking of the living room of the man you interviewed, with the Bauhaus chair and the Kerman rug and the very good early Picasso lithograph.

She had gone to the home of a young lawyer who was running for Congress; he was witty and erudite, and he'd flirted with her, mildly. She was not deceived. It was good strategy on his part. But the thought had crossed her mind. *I could live like this.*

To be precise, you are thinking that there is no law that says everything you have has to be second rate.

I don't care about that stuff.

Liar. You would love a Kerman and a Picasso.

Maybe an eeeny-weeny Picasso.

And a gigantic Kerman.

Are we talking symbols here?

No. Sometimes a rug is only a rug.

That's a relief.

And you are thinking that the man lying next to you will never be as good as you want him to be.

No, he's just — clumsy sometimes.

The man with the Picasso would never be clumsy. He would be sophisticated, and he would know how to take care of things.

No, you can't make me think bad things about him.

My dear, we are inside your *head, remember.*

Jay turned to look at her. "Mary, let's not fight. We've got to get out of Belvedere."

She could see his mouth, laced tight like a pair of shoes, his forehead furrowed. "I don't want any more of this, meeting in parking lots, sneaking off to crummy dumps. I don't want this."

"I know. I don't either."

"When are you talking to Harry?"

"This week."

"Why have you been putting it off?"

"He works a lot of hours. I've had trouble reaching him," she lied.

"You've got to do it soon."

"I will."

"Will he make waves?"

"I hope not."

"Me too. Listen, I've started looking for another job."

"Where?"

"New York, I've got some contacts there. It has to be somewhere you could find a job too. New York would be a good place."

"Don't take just anything, Jay. You'd be miserable at some place where you had to shoot routine stuff."

"Mary, I make eighty-three fifty a week. I'm twenty-seven years old, twenty-eight in a couple of months. I've got to start making some real money. The lawyer says this state is out for the divorce because the only ground is adultery, right? So we have to go to Mexico. You know how much I've got saved up? Three hundred dollars, that's it."

"I've been saving every week since I came to the *Blade.* With my mother pitching in for food and helping with the mortgage, I have a thousand dollars saved. That's enough to go to Mexico with."

"I don't want to do that. You worked hard for that money."

"But it's my money. Harry didn't have anything to do with it."

"What were you going to use it for?"

"A college fund, for Karen. But she's only five years old. That's kind of silly."

"No, it's not silly."

"Jay, I'm the one who has to get the divorce, why should you have to pay for it?"

"I'm the reason you're getting the divorce."

"But if you only have three hundred dollars saved up, that's not enough."

"Why not? We could fly down. It only takes a few hours. That's why they call them quickies, right?"

"If both parties agree, yes."

"So that's what we'll do."

"I checked on what it costs to fly to Mexico. Three hundred dollars, each way. Not counting hotel and food."

"Christ, it costs that much?"

"Flying's expensive. I could fly down myself."

"No. You're not flying to Mexico all alone. No, I don't want that. Jesus H. Christ, this fucking newspaper. If they paid me a living wage, I could have saved up. I don't spend shit. I got a beat-up old car, and all I have to my name is three hundred lousy dollars!"

She thought, without willing it, of the young lawyer, sipping his cocktail. He would never let life maneuver him into a corner where all he had was three hundred dollars and a beat-up old car.

"Look," she said, "the money's in the bank. All I have to do is take it out."

"No."

"Oh, Jay, why not?"

"We're not going to Mexico on your money! I'm not the kind of guy who bums off a woman."

"That's ridiculous. You're not bumming off me."

"Mary, my father brought home a paycheck every week of his life until he got too damn sick to work. Even when he was, with poison spilling through his guts, he brought home money. He was a man."

"I make money, too. I don't want anybody slaving away to support me."

"I'll get the money somehow."

"What are you going to do, rob a bank?"

"I'll think of something."

"That's nothing but stupid male ego, that's all it is."

She saw his back stiffen and his mouth draw up into a line again. It was so simple. Why was he making it complicated?

But he was angry, and his voice was cold and brittle. "Stupidity is one of my faults. Any others you want to mention?"

"I didn't say you were stupid. You're twisting my words around."

"I may be dumb, but I'm not deaf. I heard what you said."

"I only said —"

"Skip the explanation. I'm not one of the twelve-year-old minds you great journalists write for."

"You don't have to be snotty about it. You're behaving like a child. You want to make a big deal out of nothing."

"Faults two and three. Now I'm snotty and childish. You stick the knife in and twist it around, don't you? No wonder old Harry hit the bottle."

She sat very still. She hadn't known he had an instinct for the jugular. The sentence was a hook, and it lodged inside her.

"That's right," she said quietly, pulling the sheets up around her. "I was a lousy wife. Why don't you remind me that I'm a cheater too? I'm married to him, and I sleep with you. That's a good one to throw in my face, so I won't forget I'm a slut. Will you remind me of that too, Jay?"

She watched him as the anger transmuted into misery. He was shaking his head.

"Oh, Jesus H. Christ, I didn't mean that. I swear to God, I didn't mean that."

"Are you sure?" she said, evenly.

"No, I —" His voice choked. "Christ, that was a rotten thing to say." He got out of bed and walked up and down beside it, clenching and unclenching his fist.

"I'm such a fucking jerk, I can't get anything right. I could fuck up a free lunch. *Christ!*"

He slammed his fist into the headboard with such savagery that she was afraid he had broken his hand. She scrambled out of bed and put her hand on his shoulder.

"Don't, Jay. Please, don't!"

He sat down heavily on the bed and stared into the darkness. Her stomach tightened. He looked just like Harry had looked when the world defeated him.

"Oh, God," she whispered.

Harry's black and bitter stare had nothing to do with her. It was the world that did things to him. Or was it? She had driven him, goaded him, tried to make him what she wanted him to be. Now there was Jay, owning Harry's stare. It terrified her.

"Jay," she said. "Jay, am I a bitch?"

He looked at her in surprise. "No," he said. "Of course you're not."

"I'm twenty-five years old, and all I've done is make two men miserable. I made Harry so ashamed that all he wanted to do was drown everything out. Am I doing it to you too, Jay? What kind of a person am I?"

"It's not you, Mary. It's me. It's the things I'm — not."

"What things?"

"I — I don't cope with things very well. I should have it all under control. Some guys, they seem to be able to do everything right. I fuck things up."

She put her hand against his face. "Don't think that about yourself. You're so bright, and so talented. A lot of people would give everything to do what you can do."

He held her hand against his face; she could feel his fingers tremble.

"I did one thing right. I love you. I don't want to mess this up. You're the best thing I have in my life. But I'm scared shitless that I'm going to lose you."

"I won't let you," she said. "I promise."

He put his arms around her, and they lay quietly for a while. Then he said, "I'll take the money, but only as a loan, OK? We'll set up a special fund for Karen, and I'll pay it back, like I borrowed it from the bank. How's that?"

"Great. Why didn't we think of that before?"

"Because we're a couple of dummies, that's why."

He pulled her to him, and she lay with her face against his chest, suddenly afraid of the world and what it could do to both of them. He stroked her hair, and a memory stirred. Long ago her father, on a night the wind had frightened her, had taken her into his bed and held her. She buried her face in the tangle of hair on Jay's chest and closed her eyes, and the fear went away.

She awoke later, to find him sitting up in bed, smoking a cigarette. She reached up, took it from his mouth and put it out in an ashtray.

"Bad for you."

"I know."

She reached over and ran her finger across his chest, down his belly.

"Good for you?"

"Oh yeah. Doesn't cause cancer."

"Thank God."

He laughed, and she knew it was all right again. She moved her hands across him, exploring, and felt him harden and grow. What a marvelous invention it was; she loved its curves, its weight, its texture. Suddenly the hunger that had been absent earlier returned in a rush.

"I want to do anything, everything," she said.

He sat on the edge of the bed, and she knelt before him; her lips and tongue found him, and he gave a soft moan of pleasure. Harry thought this the province of whores, but it delighted her to be at once obedient and powerless, and powerful and commanding, in control and abandoned. Then he pulled her to her feet and began to kiss her slowly, her breasts, her lips, her belly. They lay down on the bed, and he said, "I love to do this to you." He spread her legs, and she thought he was going to enter her, but he bent to kiss her, a kiss so surprising that she began to shiver with pleasure. She had never imagined wanting anyone to do this to her, but now she thought she would die if the pleasure were to stop. The shivering seized her whole body, and she gave herself up to the whirling sensations. He did it to her again and then again, with a touch, a kiss, a bite, until she heard her own voice crying out. She had always thought that men were naturally selfish with sex, but his pleasure was so much a part of her own that it was hard to tell where one ended and the other began. When they came together, it was explosive. She wondered if the occupants of the next cabins would think people were being murdered in Number 23, with all the caterwauling going on.

Afterwards, as they lay together, she reached up and tousled his hair and said, "You're quite a stud, you know that?"

His answering smile had more than a hint of male arrogance, and that pleased her.

"You're a pretty hot ticket yourself, lady."

"After tonight, Dick, I'm putting Checkers in the trash compactor."

"Don't do that, Pat. Those rough edges can irritate your skin."

"No, Checkers is history. Next time, Dick, you'll tie me to the bedpost and we'll do it that way."

"Take off my tie? Pat, you mean really take it off?"

"Checkers can't do bondage. He hasn't got any thumbs."

"You're a hard woman, Pat."

"You can put it right back on, I promise."

They giggled, delighted with themselves, and then he put his head down on the pillow and in a few minutes he was asleep. She watched him; men always looked so vulnerable when they slept, like little boys. She touched a tendril of his hair, gently, and thought that she would wish to die rather than hurt him. She thought, unexpectedly, of having a child with him, a boy who would be a mixture of the best of both of them, the way Karen had her eyes and hair and Harry's mouth, and his way of tilting his head to look at something.

She thought of Harry standing in the kitchen: "You and Karen, you're my life." She had to tell him. But she had discovered that marriage was like a climbing plant that grew inside you; you kept ripping the sprouts of it out, but you only found more and more. Could she ever hunt them all down and destroy them? Why was it that now all she could remember were the good things?

Harry. Why wouldn't the image of him go away and leave her in peace? She had made her choice. Maybe when he knew. Maybe part of it was guilt, because she hadn't been able to tell him. He hovered even now above the bed she shared with Jay, a reproachful phantom.

Leave me, Harry, let me be.

Still he floated, so she ignored him and went to sleep.

He hung up the phone, and a smile played about his lips; talking to his brother was in some ways like talking to himself. They had been together so long that they understood, with few words, a universe of meaning. A close friend who often saw them together thought it strange to hear them converse. Neither finished a sentence. They were so much on the same wavelength that they interrupted to complete each other's thoughts.

They were so different, he mused. The words people used to describe him — cool, detached, ironic — were not the words they spoke about Bobby. The boy in the middle of the pack, always competing for the attention of his two older brothers, the boy who identified with his mother's silent suffering, Bobby threw himself into things with an intensity that at times startled even his brother. If the man in the Oval Office seemed a Catholic Brahmin, if he pulled away at times from the unruly tribe that was his family, Bobby was fiercely tribal, pure Celt. The poet Robert Lowell, meeting Bobby for the first time, murmured, "My, he is unassimilated, isn't he?"

He leaned back in his chair, his fingers tapping restlessly on the edge of the desk. He had thought, when he was younger, that his brother Joe would be the figure at the center of the tribe, that Bobby would orbit around that centrifugal force. He had seen a life for himself somewhat apart, as a journalist or a college professor.

But they had become more than brothers. Sometimes, it seemed that they were two men sharing the same life. They both knew that the bond existed, he mused, but rarely did they speak of it. Only once had he voiced his need, when his brother asked, "Well, Johnny, what about me?" as he was forming his presidential team. He wanted his brother as his attorney general, and he met the arguments against it with the one appeal his brother could not resist. "What I need is someone who's going to tell me what the best judgment is, my best interest. There's not a member of the cabinet I can trust in that way. I have nobody. There is nobody."

His brother warned him, "If you announce me as attorney general, they'll kick our balls off." And he had grinned and said, "You hold on to your balls and I'll make the announcement."

His brother amused him, sometimes, with his passions. The world he saw was one of complex shades of gray, shadows constantly shifting. For Bobby, the world was black and white, in high relief. He sometimes joked about "Bobby and his Negroes," but he knew that he relied on his brother to feel that mysterious and hidden pulse he himself could not sense so viscerally, of those who were suffering. Bobby was getting an ear for it, the way a dog hears a whistle pitched too high for humans. And he admired, grudgingly, the Puritan strain in his brother so lacking in himself.

If his brother was a prism, through which the world was refracted, so too was he a lightning rod, drawing off all sorts of fevered hatreds and resentments. The South could hate Bobby and believe the president simply misguided. That was useful.

He worried sometimes about his brother, who was perhaps less than half the life they shared. Had he sacrificed a life of his own to be part of two as one? They shared even the woman who was the most glamorous sex symbol of the day (as their father had taken as a mistress a glittering star of his time). He had first been attracted to Marilyn's freshness, the sensuality that seemed as natural as breathing. It was not a love affair for the ages. She complained to friends that his lovemaking was perfunctory, that he made love like an adolescent. Light, not heat. But the two would gossip for hours, on the phone or at Peter Lawford's beach house on the Pacific, about the rise and fall of the powerful in Hollywood, a subject that had long fascinated him. In time, her desperate need for self-esteem, her plunge into drugs and alcohol, alarmed him. It made her dangerous. He did not wish to be cruel, even when he was, but he had been unwise to send Bobby as the emissary to tell her it was done.

Like the Puritan he was, he fell desperately and guiltily in love with her. Perhaps it was her very vulnerability — the thing that alarmed the man in the Oval Office — that was such a magnet for his brother. Bobby was a sucker for strays. But he was tribal. His wife and his children were too close to his heart for him to ever think of leaving them. Her illusions were forlorn, and doomed to fail, and her rage at being used and discarded was white hot. They had hovered close to the flame of scandal. But she was gone and the tracks of their involvement hastily covered after her suicide. If the escape had tempted him to thoughts of invulnerability, there was always J. Edgar Hoover to remind him of catastrophe.

Some people even talked of another Kennedy presidency someday. Did not a dynasty have its heirs? It troubled his image of himself that he did not want to imagine Bobby as president. He had thought of himself as generous. But, to be honest, it was not that Bobby would fail but that he would succeed that was troubling. Might Bobby's reach be greater than his own? Could that moral fervor be transmuted into a greatness he himself could only wave at?

He shook his head. There was no sense worrying about the future. What would be, would be. For now, their twinship served its purpose. There would be time, later, to sort it out, to uncouple.

They were young; they had at least half a lifetime to do it.

MARTIN LUTHER KING looked distracted, Jay thought. The man whose voice had rung out so powerfully over the hundreds of thousands at the march was struggling with his answers as he stood in front of the White House. He had come from a meeting with President Kennedy, and Jay kept snapping pictures as the reporters descended on him. He was wearing a suit and tie and perspiring in the heat of the September day — a month often as hot as August in Washington.

A few days earlier, on September 15, at 10:22 A.M., a powerful bomb blasted the face of Jesus from the stained-glass window of the Sixteenth Street Baptist Church in Birmingham, Alabama. Four young girls — dressed in white from head to toe because they were about to lead the Youth Day Sunday service — were in the basement ladies' room. The bomb had been planted in the basement. There was a terrible roar, shaking the foundations of the church, and all four girls died. One could be identified by her parents only by her feet and a ring on her finger.

The horror of such savagery rippled through the nation. President Kennedy had ordered the FBI in to investigate the bombing — the worst of twenty-eight bombings in the city whose perpetrators were still at large. There was fear that racial warfare could break out in Birmingham. Kennedy had jawboned local officials, urging them to end Jim Crow, but he was loath to send in federal troops.

King had come to an edgy agreement with the president, who would send two presidential envoys to Birmingham. Other Negro leaders said this was not enough. Pierre Salinger, the press secretary, had announced that the envoys would be the former Army secretary Kenneth Royall and the former Army football coach Earl Blaik.

Mary stood on her tiptoes to see over the very tall wire service man who stood in front of her. She was hoping Kennedy would emerge to answer questions, but he was nowhere in sight. There were a number of Negro reporters in this group, not a common sight at the White House, and they were taking the lead in the questioning.

King mopped his brow and said, "This is the kind of federal concern needed," but the reporters picked up his tentative tone, and they pounced, with the Negroes being especially tough. Was sending a couple of retired Army men really an adequate response to the horrible tragedy in Birmingham? Did he know that no Negro had ever played for "Red" Blaik's Army teams?

King's replies were short and hardly displayed the eloquence for which he was famous. He darted away quickly after responding to a few questions, relieved to be out of range.

Mary and Jay walked down the winding drive to the White House gate, and she said to him, "He wanted more."

"Yeah, but if you send troops in, George Wallace would have another chance to be a martyr."

"But these two Army guys, what can they do? I think I'd be pissed if my church had been blown up and they sent an old Army football coach. What's he going to do, Sixty-three Blue up the middle?"

"It's a mess, all right. Good item for your column, though."

Mary had developed a column called "White House Watch" for the *Blade,* dealing with the comings and goings at the executive mansion. Readers seemed to like it, since she wrote it with a mixture of sass, style and solid information, and Charlie had given her more space and used her picture. Jay's photographs, of dignitaries and Kennedy relatives, often accompanied it.

But there was more on her mind than the news today. She had

finally summoned the nerve to call Harry, to tell him they needed to talk tonight. His voice on the phone had sounded cold and distant, and she thought, with a coldness in the pit of her stomach, He knows.

Back at the paper, the hours crept along. She had work to do, but every time she looked at the clock, the hands seemed not to have moved at all. Finally, as the time approached, the muscles in her stomach began to cramp. She tried not to think about it, to deliberately relax, but she could not. She gobbled Rolaids and waited. She had told Jay she would meet him in the small park behind the paper before she saw Harry. He was coming to the house.

Jay was waiting for her, pacing. He bent to light a cigarette, cupping his hands near the flame, and in its light his face seemed alien to her. He could have been a stranger. How much did she know about him, really? She was astounded at the panic that clutched at her. She sat down on a bench, and he sat down next to her, occupied by his own thoughts. She wished he would turn and look at her.

"I'd better go soon."

"You still have a few minutes. How do you think he'll take it?"

"I don't know. He sounded funny on the phone."

"Did he say anything?"

"No. Only that he'd come over."

"Are you sure you don't want me outside in the car? He won't do anything crazy, will he?"

"No, he won't. I just wish it was over. I'm a coward, I guess. I was going to write him a letter, but that wouldn't be right. I have to tell him face to face."

"Yes, you do."

She felt a stab of self-loathing. She should have handled the whole thing herself. Why was she dragging Jay through all this? Why did she need him to hold her hand?

"Jay, on the divorce, all Harry would have to do is sign his power of attorney over to a Mexican lawyer. It would be all arranged. I'd go to the courthouse in Juarez and present a paper, and we'd be divorced."

"And if Harry doesn't agree?"

"It gets complicated."

"Yeah, complicated."

He was very tense. She wondered if he wished he were free of the whole mess.

"It bothers you, doesn't it, this divorce thing."

"No, I'm worried about you, that's all."

He put his arms around her, and that was what she'd wanted him to do all along. She felt safe that way. She wished she could stay here, next to him, and forget what she had to do. But she got up from the bench and said, "I'll call you."

"I'll be at the apartment. You'll call me right away?"

"Yes."

She drove home and found her mother waiting in the hallway. Her mother's attitude had softened since she had learned Jay wanted to marry her, but still she was anxious.

"You're sure, Mary? You could be making a big mistake."

"I'm sure."

"I'll be next door, at Rita's."

Her mother left, and Mary went into the living room and sat on the couch. She thought about Harry, the way he had looked in his baseball uniform, so young and full of hope; the gentleness in his hands when he'd held Karen for the first time; his face in the kitchen: "You and Karen, you're my life."

"Forgive me," she said to the empty room. "Forgive me, please."

She heard the door open, and Harry came into the room. He was wearing a blue shirt with the sleeves rolled up high so the muscles in his arms would show; he was proud of those muscles. She didn't like the shirt rolled up that way. She thought it looked cheap, lower class. They'd had a fight once, when she told him that.

"Hello," he said. He never said "hello." He always said "Hi," with that way of tilting his head. He knew.

"Hello, Harry."

He walked in and sat in the chair opposite her. He did not lean back but sat rigid. He looked right at her, and his eyes were frozen circles. She groped for words, but they came out in uneven chunks, not the way she had rehearsed it.

"Harry, I've been thinking, well, about you and me."

Her palms were sweating, and her stomach churned, but she plowed on, feeling clumsy. "I think it would be better for both of us if we didn't get back together."

He was still looking at her with the frozen blue circles. That wasn't like him.

"We were married so young, and things didn't go right from the beginning. Maybe if we had been older. But we were kids. I wasn't any good for you, Harry."

His silence baffled her. She rushed to fill it. "I haven't made you happy. A lot of it was my fault. I didn't know how to be a wife. I wanted to, but — maybe we have to admit that we made a mistake. People do."

He looked at her, cold as stone. She had never seen him this way. When he was angry he roared with outrage, and when the anger was gone he sat and stared at the wall. She looked at his hands, resting on the arms of the chair. They were short, blunt, strong, unlike Jay's hands, which were long and tapered. Harry's hands seemed odd to her now.

"Are you asking me for a divorce?" he said.

"Yes. I think it would be best for both of us."

"I thought that was it when you called me. You haven't called in a long time."

"I've been thinking about it for a long time, but I didn't want — I didn't know how to tell you."

"You and that photographer. I heard about that. Now all of a sudden you want a divorce."

"No, I was thinking about it before —" She paused, certain he could tell she was not speaking the truth.

"Before what?" He was still looking at her calmly. She wished he would get angry and yell. She knew how to handle him then, make him feel that he was in the wrong.

"Say it. Before what?"

"Before I met Jay."

"Before he fucked you."

"Don't talk like that, Harry. Let's not be — unpleasant." That sounded absurd, a line from an English parlor drama.

"No. Let's not be unpleasant. That wouldn't be nice."

He was mocking her; she hadn't expected that. He was still sitting motionless in the chair.

"You don't like the word? It's *fuck,* babe. You don't like the word, but you like doing it."

"Please, Harry, can't we be civil?"

"My wife." He leaned forward in his chair. "The hotshot reporter. A guy who works in a laundry isn't good enough for her. She gets hot panties for a guy who carries a camera, shacks up with him like a bitch in heat."

"Harry —"

"It's OK for me to live like a goddamn hermit all these months so if I'm a good little boy I can come home to momma. I bought a load of shit from you, babe. It's all over town that I got horns; the only one who didn't know was me." He looked directly at her. "Does he have a long one, babe? Do you like it when he rams it into your cunt? Good luck to him, because you're a cold bitch. I been in bed with a lot better ass than you, babe."

He was angry now, but it was still a cold, controlled anger. She could see his hands trembling.

"Do you suck his cock? Do you let him lick your pussy? Do you do tricks for him, like a whore?"

"Stop that, Harry."

"Tell me, what does he do to you? I want to hear it."

"I'm not going to sit here and listen to this."

"I'm going to say what I like, and you're going to listen, whore."

"I was always faithful to you, Harry, when we were together. Can you say the same thing? You'd come home smelling of cheap perfume, it would stink up the room."

"You were always so holy. The big saint. You didn't waste any time the first time some guy tried to get into your pants."

"It's not that way, Harry. I love him. Can't you understand that? I love him."

That rocked him, she could see it in his eyes. But his anger congealed again, and he clenched and unclenched his fist, still resting it on the arm of the chair.

"I used to take you out in the car, and you let me feel you all over, right away. Let me grab your tits, do whatever I wanted. You were hot for it. You were trash then, and you're trash now."

She was dumbfounded. Had this been eating at him all along?

"I was a girl, a normal girl. What did you want, a block of ice?"

"You're a whore-cunt, and I made the mistake of marrying you. How many guys did you put out for, besides me?"

"What a filthy mouth you have. You drag things down to the gutter. You always have."

He got up, walked over to her and looked down. "I'm good at four-letter words." He reached down and put his hands on her breasts, hurting her. She tried to pull away, but he was too strong. "Four-letter words. Like *fuck*. Like *cunt*. Like *Mary*."

His hands held her, painfully, and she hated him for making her so powerless. She wanted to kick him, bite him, but she thought of Karen, asleep upstairs, and she remained still. He put his hand up under her skirt, between her legs, and jabbed his finger into her. "Cunt."

Then he released her, and she jumped up, gasping with outrage. She was too angry to care whether he hit her or not.

"Now go and pick on somebody your own size, you bastard! The only guts you ever had came from a bottle!"

She hated the words the moment she said them, but she could not take them back. She had always known exactly how to shame him. He stood still, vibrating with rage, his mouth working. She realized, suddenly, that he was trying not to cry. She was so shocked that the anger suddenly left her.

"I'm sorry, I didn't mean that. Harry. I didn't!"

"You want a divorce, fine, you get one. For adultery. I want to see you stand up and admit you're a whore. Try and tell the judge you're a fit mother after that. You're not a fit mother, you're a whore. Go ahead, try to get Karen after everybody sees you're a whore."

A sob rattled through him, and he turned and ran out of the house. She stood still, staring at the spot where he had been. Her anger was gone. His sob still sounded in her ears. How he must have cared. So much more than she. Guilt embraced her, for not knowing how he cared. She began to shake, and she sat down in the chair until the shaking was under control and then called Jay to come over. Her mother came back from Rita's, but Mary avoided her questions. When Jay's car pulled up, she ran out and climbed in the front seat.

"What is it? What happened?"

"Jay, drive, please. Anyplace."

They drove in silence for a while. "He said he'd divorce me for adultery. He said he'd prove I was an unfit mother."

"Oh, Jesus."

"I did a stupid thing. I got mad at him. I should have known how hurt and angry he was. But he said things —"

"What things?"

"Rotten things. About you and me."

"What? Tell me what he said, the prick."

"I don't want — Oh, God!" She began to sob, her whole body shaking, and he pulled the car off the road and held her. "What did he say?" and she heard the anger in his voice. She remembered how he had smashed the bedpost, and she was suddenly afraid of what Harry and Jay could do to each other.

"Oh, Jay, he was almost crying. I was such a fool. I thought we'd have this nice little chat. He knows it's all over town about us."

"Christ!"

"To try to take Karen away from me, I never thought he'd do that. I never, ever thought." she wept again, desperately, against his chest, her breath rasping. When she was spent, she rested against him exhausted, and he stroked her back.

"Mary, what are we going to do?" He sounded tired, drained.

"I don't know."

There was a long silence, and then he said, "I'm not going to ask you to choose between me and Karen. I can't ask you to do that."

She thought of Karen, the bright eyes and the high, clear voice, who liked to draw farts and ride her wagon at breakneck speed down the hill. She had never known she could love a child the way she loved Karen. Often she'd be at work on a story in the city room, and something that her daughter had said that morning would pop into her head, making her smile. She thought of Harry, raising their daughter. Belvedere would make her nice, docile, polite. She wouldn't let that happen. Belvedere was not going to get Karen.

"If I had a kid," he said, "I could never walk off and leave her. Not for anybody."

"I know."

"I thought, what the hell, plenty of people get divorced. But I never figured this. I should have."

She did not answer him.

"I won't ask you to choose."

They sat in silence for a long time, and then he said, "If I were smarter, maybe I could think of something. But I can't. Every way you slice it, it comes out the same way. I can't make things come out the way I want them to. I never have." He laughed, a bitter laugh with no mirth. "Maybe you're better off without me, anyhow. I got the Midas touch in reverse. Everything I touch turns to shit."

She looked at him, his face etched with misery. In a few hours, she had reduced one man to tears and another to self-loathing. The thought awed her. She had always thought of herself as a woman a man could easily do without.

He took a deep breath and said, "Well, it's been a long night. We'd better get out of here."

He turned on the ignition, and she reached over and shut it off. Then she pressed her mouth against his and kissed him, an erotic kiss. She felt his mouth open under hers, and then he jerked away.

"What the hell are you trying to do to me, Mary?"

"I know what I'm doing."

"Tell me. I don't like guessing games."

"I love you. I want you now. Tomorrow. For good."

"What about Karen?"

"I wasn't thinking: he couldn't get her. He has a police record for being drunk and disorderly. I was so wrought up I wasn't thinking straight. Now I am. A private detective could get so much on Harry in twenty-four hours he'd have no case. The whoring, the drinking. Would a judge give a child to an ex-drunk?"

"You'd get a detective on him?"

"If he forces me to it, yes."

He frowned.

"You think I'd like that?" she said. "My God, it would make me sick, but if he tried to take Karen, I would."

"Jesus, that would be a mess."

"That's right, a mess. You don't have to stay around for it, Jay."

"What do you mean by that crack?"

"Fair warning. It's going to be messy and ugly. But I'm going to get the divorce. Harry could name you corespondent in a suit, I couldn't stop that. But you're free to go, Jay. You don't owe me anything."

"Is that what you think of me? That I'd just say, 'It's been fun,' and light out?"

"No, I think you'd stick it out, even if it made you sick to your stomach. Like your father, driving his cab while he was dying. You're like him, you wouldn't quit. But I don't ever want to be a weight around a man's neck, Jay. Not again. I have too much pride for that."

"You'd never be that. Not you."

"Promise me, Jay, if there's ever a time that you don't want me, you won't stay out of pity."

"What kind of crazy talk is that?"

"Promise me."

"I promise."

"Make love to me."

"Here?"

"Here, on the ground, anywhere. If you want to."

"I want to."

"UP YOURS, CREEP," Mary said into the receiver, and then slammed it down.

At the next desk, Jay looked up and said, "The mayor is calling again?"

"One of our readers, calling us nigger lovers."

"Yeah, I've been getting it too."

Sam looked up from his typewriter. "I get nigger-loving Jew. A twofer."

"Did you hear there was a cross burning out in Howard County last night?" she said.

"The Klan, in Maryland?" Sam asked.

"They were pretty big in the state in the twenties. They haven't been around for a while."

Jay's phone rang, and he picked it up. "Yeah, this is Broderick." He paused. "Yeah? Well, same to you, pal."

"Another one?"

"Yeah. Some of the folks are pissed at me."

The *Blade* had used boxcar type for the headline. HIGH SCHOOL ATHLETES ARRESTED IN FIRE DEATHS. The story went on to say that it was a detail remembered by the *Blade* photographer Jay Broderick that had helped crack the case. The pair of boxing gloves hanging in the rear window of the car had jogged the memory of one of the state troopers. He recalled that a senior a Belvedere High

School, a member of the football team, had been picked up twice for reckless driving, and his car had a pair of gloves hanging in the rear window. Under questioning, the young man had broken down and admitted that he had been driving the car the night of the fire. He said they had only meant to set the fire as a warning, that they had no intention of killing anyone.

"Do you believe that stuff about the kids not wanting to hurt anybody?" Sam asked Mary.

"Maybe. But when you set a fire, you have to be an idiot not to know it could happen."

"Their lawyer is trying to say it was just a prank that went wrong," Jay said.

Sam shook his head. "Burning down a house is not a fucking prank. It's arson, and in this case, murder."

"It's all people are talking about," Mary told them. "I was out getting reactions. People are upset. They know the kids, they know the families. You know who they're mad at? The Negro community. For starting the whole thing in the first place. One guy blamed *us* for bringing in 'outside agitators.'"

"Sounds like George Wallace."

"Will the DA go for murder one?" Jay asked.

"I think he will," Sam said. "This is a national story. The wires are carrying our stuff; the *Times* and the *Post* are on it. How can they plea-bargain, when a woman and child were burned to death?"

Milt walked over to Jay's desk. "Great work on picking up on those gloves, Jay. Have you got the pictures for me?"

"What pictures?"

"Miss Darnestown. Didn't you shoot that Wednesday night?"

"Oh, yeah." He reached into his desk. "Miss Darnestown, nineteen sixty-three. She's sixteen, and she's got legs like Bronco Nagurski but the boobs you would not believe. I don't see how she can even stand up."

Milt peered at the picture. "Oh, my God, that's too much cleavage. This is a family newspaper."

"Milt, that's all this girl has got — head, feet and cleavage."

"Well, you're going to have to ink it in."

"How about I take the schlong I took off the puppy and paste it on Miss Darnestown's tits?"

"Real funny, Jay. The time you stuck Richard Nixon's head on Miss Hagerstown, it almost got in the paper."

"I should have done it the other way around. Nixon has better legs than Miss Hagerstown."

"I need the picture right away."

Jay sat down with the bottle of ink and a sigh. "This is a crime, desecrating a natural wonder. Milt, I am an artist, a fucking artist, I capture life with my camera. What the fuck am I doing here, splashing ink on Miss Darnestown's tits?"

"Just do it. And give me a caption."

As Jay was typing the caption the phone rang.

"City Room. Broderick. Oh, for Christ's sake, go fuck yourself, you pervert."

"Jay, what the hell —" Milt said.

"He asked me if I had sucked any black cock today."

"How many of those have you gotten?"

"At least a dozen."

When he finished with the picture, Jay beckoned to Mary, and she walked over to his desk.

"Hey, I heard from the guy I told you about, the art director at the new magazine they're starting in New York."

"Does it sound good?"

"Yeah. The guy who's backing it has lots of dough. He wants to make it a real slick city magazine, you know, arts and politics and profiles, stuff like that."

"Are they hiring any writers?"

"At first they're going to use mainly freelance. But if it flies, they'll need some staff people. I told him about you, and he said you sound perfect for them. Somebody who's done politics, and can write features."

"What are they paying?"

"If they hired me for staff, I could get maybe two hundred a week. That's pretty good money."

"New York. I've never been there. Broadway, the Great White Way — oh, Jay, it would be exciting to be there!"

"If I got the job, we could pick up and go. You have custody of Karen."

"Go? Just like that?"

"Just like that."

"But Harry —"

"He couldn't do anything about it. Maybe he wouldn't try to fight the divorce; once we were in New York, he'd know you really mean it."

"I could do that. I could. There's nothing in the separation agreement that says I can't leave the state."

"Sure you could do it."

"Do you think I could get a job? I haven't got a college degree."

"You've got great clips. You've covered the White House. Charlie would give you a good recommendation. And you could freelance for a while until something opened up on the magazine."

"We could just go. Like Gypsies. I've been so careful, all my life. It would be an adventure! New York!"

"I'll take Manhattan, the Bronx and Staten," he sang, off key.

She laughed, excitedly. "Manhattan. Even the word sounds sophisticated. Oh, Jay, I won't be a hick anymore!"

He smiled. "City slickers, that's us."

"Harry, it's been a long time, sweetie."

"Sure, Dotty, long time." His speech was slurred, even though he'd had only one Scotch. Why were his words sliding together?

"Too long. We had fun, didn't we?"

"Sure," he said. "Fun."

She ran her fingers across his lips. "You can come upstairs with me if you want. You remember the way."

He went up the stairs with her to the small room. It was familiar; he had been there before.

Dotty wasted no time. She took off her bra and cupped her breasts. "You always liked these, Harry. Love me up, sweetie."

He touched her breasts, and the desire flamed in him, as it always did. But there was something else too, that had always been there, the self-loathing that he had to buy a woman, because his own woman didn't want him. He looked at her, and she seemed lewd and dirty, standing there flaunting her body at him.

"Come on, sweetie."

He took hold of her nipple and squeezed it, hard.

"Easy, baby, you're hurting me."

"Whore," he said, and he slapped her face.

"Harry, what are you doing?"

"Dirty whore," he said. He grabbed her wrists.

"Sugar, what's the matter? Are you drunk?"

"Not drunk. That's why I see what you are."

"You were never like this, Harry. You never hurt me. That's why I liked you. Love me, baby, don't hurt me."

He put his hands on her throat. "Dirty," he said. "All women are like you. Dirty whore."

"Don't hurt me. I'll do anything you want."

"Get on your knees."

Gasping, she sank to her knees, and then she started to cry, the tears rolling silently down her cheeks. The sight of her tears sliced through the haze in his head. Why was he doing this?

He lifted her to her feet. "I'm sorry," he said. "I won't hurt you."

"Are you all right, baby?"

"Yes, I'm all right."

"Let me love you."

He let her lead him to the bed, and she undressed him and touched him expertly, in ways that aroused him. But the room seemed to be moving around. He lay still and let her touch him, and then he said, "Mary?"

"Close your eyes. I'll be Mary, if you want. I'll be anybody."

"Touch me, Mary."

"Yes, it's Mary, and I'm touching you. Close your eyes. I'm Mary."

"I'll always love you, Mary."

"And I'll love you. I always will."

He felt the tears, warm on his face. "I couldn't ask her to do anything dirty. She's my wife."

"It's all right, I'm here."

"Fuck me, Mary. Please fuck me."

"Yes, I will."

She moved her body on his, and he closed his eyes. He saw her dark hair and her beautiful, high breasts and her eyes, the color, he thought, of chocolate, and they were smiling at him. He felt himself drowning in her.

"I love you, Mary!" he cried out, and the room was whirling like a carousel, and he laughed as he went around and around and around and her dark hair was whirling too.

Then the carousel stopped, and he opened his eyes to see her better, but the woman lying on top of him had blond hair and smelled like a cheap flower and her eyes were not like chocolate. The scent of Scotch whiskey filled his mouth and nostrils, and he thought he was going to vomit.

The tears were still warm against his face.

Journal: Donald A. Johnson

Loretta told me she had a special surprise for me for my birthday, and she'd give it to me when I came to her apartment. I love surprises, so I hurried over. I was surprised, all right!

She opened the door, and there she was, in a harem costume, a silver bralike thing, cut down as far as it could go and still be technically *on,* displaying her gorgeous pomegranates, and silver panties with gauzy, see-through pantaloons attached and a silver veil. Strapped to her thigh was a golden dagger.

She smiled at me and said, "Sahib, I await you."

"Holy shit, you've been reading Frank Yerby!" I said.

Her face fell. "You don't like it?"

"Oh, God, I love it!"

"Let me take you to paradise, sahib."

She did. Or about as close as I am ever going to get. Frank was right: bodice ripping is a lot of fun; and Loretta did some interesting things with the dagger that Frank probably thought about but couldn't put in his books, he being resolutely *soft* core.

Even Frank's execrable dialogue, in Loretta's soft, throaty voice, sounded classy. She reminded me that Chaucer was the Frank Yerby of his day, as far as soft core was concerned, albeit a lot less flowery. The Wife of Bath's Tale was pretty raunchy. In those days, life was short and brutal, so you grabbed what pleasure you could, and told tales about it.

Loretta said that my birthday present could last all year, since the oeuvre of Frank Yerby was considerable and there were a number of characters we had yet to explore — Arab princesses, South Sea beauties, Viking queens. I wondered if she could manage to do Fancy (of *Goodbye, My Fancy*), a cut-rate Scarlett who made a habit of pulling her ball gowns down around her waist whenever her lover, Gaylord, came around.

"Honeychile, I can do that white trash southern slut a lot easier than you can do Gaylord." She sneered.

"I can do white," I said. "I used to be Claude Jarman, Jr."

"Who?"

I have to educate the woman. She may know Chaucer, but she has a lot to learn about movies. She doesn't even know Lash LaRue. It will be an even trade, I'll get Chaucer and Shakespeare, and she'll get Lash and Claude and Ricky Nelson.

Which brings me to the question of where, exactly, I fit on the spectrum between Frank Yerby and Shakespeare. I know there are going to be people who will be unhappy with my book: my father, for one. I write about a lot of things that middle-class colored folks all know about: our obsession with skin color, how lighter is better; our need to have white people approve of us, how even the strongest and fiercest of us, like Rafe, can't help feeling that whites have some magic that we don't have, how we are perpetually reacting to what they think and what they say. It's OK to say these things among ourselves, but to hang out the dirty laundry, as it were, where white people can see it, might well be considered treason.

I understand the reaction. We have enough trouble as it is; they have so many things to use against us, why give them more ammunition?

But I am not writing for whites — or for Negroes either. I am writing for me and, perhaps, for the future. One day, some people — maybe my own grandchildren — will want to know what it was like, being who I am, coming of age when I did. Being a writer, I have found, gives you a certain amount of power. You create a world and make people see it through your eyes. I don't want to abuse that power. There are some things I know about my family that I would not write, because it would cause them too much pain. But I must be honest in what I do write about.

Sometimes I ask if I am glorifying myself, exaggerating my own role in this life. Probably. But there is a certain arrogance in writing that is inescapable. You create — like God does. (Speaking of arrogance.) It's an act of assertion that is primal, you can't escape it. Once you pick up a pen and make a scratch on paper, you're into it.

But there are rules, and one of those is to be true to the truth. You must write of things as you see them and know them, and you must not create a self that is other than that truth. You may emerge, on the page, as a fool or a bully or a whiner or an asshole, but that's the price you pay for the power you appropriate. You may fail. You may be ridiculed. You may be attacked. Or all of the above.

I used to think writing was safe. It was, when I was the only one who saw it. Now, I'm going to throw my words out there so everyone can look at them. Can look at *me.*

I have fantasies about the worst that can happen — including having Roy Wilkins say that the whole NAACP plans to boycott the book, which is a disgrace to the entire race, and having my classmates at G. W. getting together in a bar and remembering what a total asshole I was. I can imagine their dialogue, quote for quote. It scares the living daylights out of me.

But I am going to be an author. I've just put the check for my advance in the bank. There is no turning back, now. All I can do is hang on and hope I'll survive the ride.

When she walked into the Oval Office, he was sitting on the edge of his desk, lost in thought. He looked up, saw her and asked her a question about the subject that had obviously been on his mind.

"Tell me, do the people in Belvedere think much about the bomb? Do they really believe we're all going to go up in a puff of smoke one of these days?"

"We recently had a man-in-the-street poll on that subject," she said. "It's funny, people don't think it's going to happen tomorrow, they're not all out building bomb shelters in their basements. But it's there. It's like this low hum; you don't always realize you're hearing it, but it's there."

He nodded. "What about you? You're — what, twenty-four, twenty-five?"

"Twenty-five," she said.

He shook his head again and smiled. "God, I remember being that young. Twenty-five."

Then he seemed to recall the subject at hand. "So, do you think about it?"

"I have a little girl — she's five. Sometimes I wonder if the world will even be around for her to live to an old age. I think it will, but —" She shrugged.

"Yes," he said, "I think it will too. For my daughter. My son.

But . . ." His voice trailed off; he seemed pensive. "Did you ever read much about World War I?"

"You mean how people really didn't want to go to war, but they did anyhow?"

He stood up and walked to the window, looking out at the garden. "I've been reading about it again. That's one of the places I'd want to go, if I had a time machine: Europe before the Great War."

She thought it odd that here he was, the most important man in the world, and he had daydreams like ordinary people. About having a time machine and going off to the places in the past that intrigued him.

"It was a glittering world," he said. "They waltzed to Strauss in the palaces in Vienna, and they traveled in private railway cars, and they sat in the cafés in Paris and rode in their carriages in London, and they didn't know they were doomed. They had peace and prosperity and science, and they turned it all into a desert. Even after they saw it coming, they couldn't stop it. 'The lamps are going out all over Europe; we shall not see them lit again in our lifetime.' They lost a whole generation of young men. Because of a series of stupid accidents. All by accident."

It seemed he had forgotten she was there and was musing to the air. It was not lost on her that he knew he was the man who could do it. Not far away was the officer who kept the briefcase with the codes that held the keys to the powers of hell. That briefcase could turn the whole planet into a desert.

He turned back to her again, as if he could sense what she was thinking, and said, "You know, people think a president can do anything, that he has so much power. But I've learned by being here" — he waved his hand to indicate the Oval Office — that there are many things you can't do. So much that's beyond your control."

"So many accidents?"

"Yes. But what you can do is set things up so accidents might not happen. Improve the odds."

"I used to have nightmares about the bomb," she said. "After we had to duck and cover in school."

"What were they like?" he asked. She had noticed that he was always interested in small details about people's lives, facts you'd never think a powerful man would be at all interested in. He was immensely curious; he probably stored all that information away and used it all, somehow.

"I dreamed I was standing on a hill and I saw the big cloud, and then everything was flying and tumbling around, like they did in the tornado in *The Wizard of Oz,* except everything was burning, including people. Flying through the air and burning."

He nodded, looking thoughtful again. She wondered how he was storing that image, and what he would do with it. Flying through the air, and burning.

He looked at her. "How will people take it if I propose some new limits on nuclear weapons? Are they scared enough, out in Belvedere, so they'll support it? Or will they listen to the people who say I'm getting soft on communism?"

"I think they'll support it," she said. "I think the Cuban missile crisis really sobered people up. I mean, suddenly it almost happened. It wasn't just science fiction anymore."

"Good. That's what other people are telling me. It's time. The timing is right."

"History is about timing," she said.

He looked at her, and that quick grin flashed across his face. "You're learning, *Belvedere Blade.* Nice to see that in the press. It's rare."

When she left the Oval Office she drove back to Belvedere, to the Reverend Johnson's house. The president had asked her about the status of the housing battle — he'd remembered that too — and she had told him she hoped the negotiations would succeed. But when she walked into the minister's living room, she saw Don pacing. Something, clearly, had happened.

"We're going," he said. "The negotiations have fallen apart. We hit the streets on Tuesday."

She frowned. He seemed elated. Not that he was eager for confrontation, but the enforced idleness of the past weeks had taken a toll. He had been tense, restless, because of the inaction. Now, at least, he knew what had to be done.

"What do you think you can get?" Mary asked.

"The council's deadlocked. The mayor can vote in case of a tie. We had him, but now he's got cold feet because of what's happened."

"Yeah, people don't want to believe it. Nice kids, good families."

"What if it had been the other way around? If a white woman and her baby had been burned to death by three black men. Do you think they'd be talking about a prank?"

"No. They'd go to the electric chair."

"If they weren't dragged out and strung up on a tree. We have to put enough pressure on the mayor so he can't chicken out."

"The national media will be around. We're a big story already."

"The locals may be upset because they know those kids, but people outside of Belvedere don't have any sympathy for them."

"Some of the businessmen I talked to want this to go away. They don't want Belvedere to seem like Birmingham."

"We're counting on that. The fastest way to cool things down would be to pass the new plan. Belvedere looks progressive, and we call off our troops. No more demonstrations."

"Can you get the mayor without them?"

He shook his head. "No, we just have to scare him more than the other side does."

"Mayor Swarman is not exactly Winston Churchill."

"He's not even George Wallace."

She laughed, and he poured her a cup of coffee.

She took a sip and asked him, "Don, when this is over, have you decided what you're going to do?"

He nodded. "I'm going to get my master's at Georgetown. And finish the book."

"It's going to be wonderful. You have to promise me an autographed copy."

"You'll get the first one off the presses. You've been a lot of help, you know. You were really the one who convinced me it's worthwhile. That it isn't trivial."

"I think you made the right decision. It's not like this will all be over in the next year. There's going to be plenty of time for you get involved in civil rights again. Maybe go into politics, the book will help. Look what it did for Kennedy."

"I don't think I'll get the Pulitzer Prize."

"Who knows? I'll vote for you. The *Blade* has a lot of power in these things."

He laughed. "Hey, I hope you and Jay are coming to the wedding. It's going to be a big party. With all my relatives and all Loretta's, we're going to have to have a tent."

"We wouldn't miss it. We might be in New York, on that magazine I told you about, but we'll come back for it."

They chatted for a while longer, and as she looked at him she thought that his conviction, his passion, was the same as that which impelled a handful of men to dress up as Indians and dump tea in Boston Harbor. How odd, that a country born of a revolutionary act should be so frightened of this new revolution. She wondered if, years from now, men like Martin Luther King and Don Johnson would be calcified into marble and trite, patriotic sentences in history books. She realized that all the history she had been taught was a sham. It was dehydrated, bled of passion, ego, courage, hate. She sipped her coffee and watched him as he talked. He *was* history, and so, in a small way, was she. And they were both young, a little scared, unsure of what life might hold for them, but knowing there was work to be done.

As she was leaving, he reached out and touched her cheek, a gesture of intimacy that seemed natural for two people who had become friends, who understood each other. It didn't matter that he was a man and black and she was white and a woman.

It was only later she realized that no one she had grown up with would have thought his touch anything but scandalous, and she a traitor to her race. Friendship between a black man and a white woman was inconceivable in Belvedere. To whites, Negroes were as alien as Martians would have been. It was her mother who made her remember that. When she drove back to her own house, it was still early, and her mother was finishing her morning coffee. Mary joined her, passing up the coffee but having a glass of juice. Their relationship, on the surface at least, had regained its former shape.

"You were over at the house of that Negro minister again," her mother said. She spoke the word *Negro* not with scorn but with some trepidation, as if it were frightening.

"It's part of my job, Mom. It's a big story."

"I know. But people are talking a lot about that young man. They tell me that you ought to stay away from him. They say things about him."

"What sorts of things?"

"Well" — her mother paused — "they say that when he was on one of those buses — you know, the Freedom Rides — that he was in orgies with white women."

"Oh, Mom, that's nonsense."

"I know that, but people believe it. They know you've over at the house where he's staying a lot, and somebody said . . ." Her voice trailed off.

"What?"

"At the fire, that terrible night. One of the firemen said that you were . . . touching that Negro man. I know that isn't true, but —"

"Yes, I touched him. Of course I did."

She saw the alarm in her mother's eyes, and she said, "It's not like that! Jesus Christ, he was watching two people he knew burn to death. I touched his arm, just to — because he was a person, and he was hurting. Because what happened was so awful. You would have done the same thing, if you'd been there."

Her mother nodded. "Mary, I understand, but I'm afraid. People are so angry, they're twisting things. It's so crazy. Even my friends. They talk about those high school kids as if they were the innocent ones, as if the Negroes had done something to them. They say it's all the fault of those damn niggers. And they blame the newspaper. I'm afraid someone might hurt you."

"I'm being careful, I promise. Charlie's hired a guard at the paper, because of the threats. We'll be OK."

Her mother nodded again, but her face was pale and she was twisting her wedding ring, a sure sign she was upset. She said, "Whatever you do, Mary, I'm on your side. Even when I'm scared for you. Remember that."

"Thanks, Mom. I know that. I always have."

Her mother handed her the morning copy of the *Blade* and said, "Did you see this?"

The paper was opened to the obituary page, with the headline LOCAL BUSINESSMAN DIES SUDDENLY.

"Mr. Gutwald? How did it happen?"

"It was a heart attack. He was out trimming the hedges, and he collapsed. Joan found him lying on the lawn."

"What about the business? What will happen to the business?"

"Joan won't want to run it. She was always telling her husband they ought to retire and move to Florida. Maybe Bert will take it over."

"Bert's in San Diego. Harry says he likes it out there."

"I hope Harry won't lose a job again. When he was doing so well."

"Bert knew Harry in high school. He wouldn't fire Harry."

"Well, I hope it works out for the best."

Before she went to the paper, Mary drove to Jay's apartment. He was making himself a sandwich. He gave her a broad grin when she came in.

"I got it!"

"Got what?"

"The job. In New York."

"You got it? You got it! Oh, Jay, that's fantastic!"

"I start in four weeks. We can give Charlie three weeks' notice, take our time driving up. Then we can get a place."

"Three weeks? That's such a short time. Karen has her nursery group, and I have to look for a job. I haven't even got my résumé typed up."

"Maybe Karen could stay with your mother for a couple of weeks while we got settled. Then we could drive back and get her."

"Are you saying we should get a place together? Now?"

"Why not?"

"I'm not divorced."

"In New York, who would give a damn?"

"But if we have to go to court, it would look bad."

"Right, I wasn't thinking. So we'll get separate places. Technically we won't be living together. But we can spend as much time together as we want."

"Yes, that would be better."

"Manhattan," he said. "It'll be a gas, Mary. You and me in New York."

For the rest of the week, she spent the morning hours before going to work making an inventory of her possessions. The old skirts from high school, the dresses that were out of style, they could all go into a box for Goodwill. But even as she sorted and packed, it didn't seem real. Was she really going to do it? Leave Belvedere, her marriage, the first job she'd ever had, where it was safe?

"I will," she said. "Yes, I will."

Other people did it, they just walked out and started fresh, someplace else. She had told a lie when she was eighteen years old. Did she have to pay for it the rest of her life? She picked out clothes for New York, trying to make herself believe it. It had been so fresh in her mind the first day they talked about it. It had seemed to hover in the air, like a mist, so real she could touch it. Now it was receding, and she had to bring it back. She clenched her teeth and grimly packed her wardrobe for New York.

"I'm going to make things happen" she had said to him. It seemed half a lifetime ago. The gray wool — basic, but too old? No, it was classic, and it fit well. Take the gray wool.

She spent the nights at Jay's apartment, leaving early in the morning so she could spend time with Karen. Her mother worried that people would not approve, but it did not matter anymore what people thought. They knew, to hell with them. When she was with Jay, the future seemed inevitable. The feel of him, the smell of him, kept her doubts at bay. One night, when Sam and Roger were away, they made love on the kitchen floor and in the shower and in the living room. She was insatiable; she couldn't get enough of him.

"Go easy on me, woman, I am only human."

"I am Drusilda, woman warrior, and I want to do feelthy things to you."

I knew I should never have told you about that."

"Drusilda loves the sword of Spartacus."

"If I keep this up, my balls are going to drop off from sheer exhaustion."

"Spartacus has such nice balls."

"Cut that out! Get your hands off my body. Jesus, I used to believe you were shy."

"I was. You debauched me."

"You debauched easy, you have to admit."

"Umm. Drusilda wonders what an orgy would be like. Have you even been to an orgy?"

"Me? Oh, sure. I have one every week with the Worthy Matrons. We fuck squirrels. They're fast little buggers, you have to be quick to get them, but they're nice."

"Do people really do it with sheep? I read that they do."

"This is a hell of a conversation. I personally have never fucked a sheep, but out in the boonies, where there's nothing for miles and miles, I guess they pass the time by fucking sheep."

"Jay tell me about New York."

"They fuck rats in New York. No sheep there."

She poked him. "That's disgusting."

"You think a squirrel is hard to catch, you ought to try a rat. You have to aim just right. Fucking roaches is a real challenge, though."

"Oh, ugh. That makes me sick to think about it!"

"The roaches don't like it much either."

He laughed, and she cuddled next to him, and they were quiet for a while. Then he asked, "Mary, what's happening with Harry?"

"He's trying to buy the business. I guess he needs a loan. His father could lend him a few thousand, but not enough."

"How much would it be?"

"Forty thousand."

"Could Harry raise that much?"

"Bert wants to sell it to him. It's a sound business, and Harry's been running the branch, so he knows the ropes. I think he could get a loan."

"Sounds like it. Well, we'll be out of here soon enough."

"That's right. We will be. Do they have good schools in New York?"

"Good as here, I guess."

"Karen's going to be starting first grade. I'd like to be sure she gets in a good school, not in a bad neighborhood."

"I'll ask the editor. He has a couple of kids, so he probably knows."

"That would be great."

"You and me, in a couple of years when we're both making some dough, we could have a kid, huh?"

"Yes. I want to have a baby with you, Jay. But I want to keep working, too. I couldn't stop now, just when I'm finding out what I can do."

"No sweat. If we're both making enough money, we can swing it. I want to get some money saved up. I saw what happened to my mother and father. I don't want to be on the edge like they were, not ever."

She had been thinking about having a baby with him, had wished for the heaviness in her womb that meant life was stirring. Sigmund Freud pounced on that one.

You say "anatomy is destiny" is old hat, my dear, but look what you are doing.

It was a . . . passing thought.

You were going to wrap up your diaphragm and leave it in the drawer.

No, I really wasn't. It was only an idea.

Just like a woman. Trap him with pregnancy.

I wouldn't do that

Oh no? "I'm pregnant, Harry."

I was only a kid.

You thought that if you were pregnant, you would have to leave Belvedere. You are scared you haven't got the guts to do it on your own. As I wrote in The Ego and the Id —

Oh, shut up.

You must admit, I score a point now and then.

One thing was for sure, at least she wasn't going to make the same mistake twice. If there was going to be a baby with Jay, it was going to be when they both wanted it. Her diaphragm stayed in her purse.

She tried to fill the time away from Jay with Karen and with work. She kept hearing reports about Harry. He had been meeting with different businessmen, but he had only been able to scrape up fifteen thousand dollars. Everybody liked Harry, wanted him to succeed, but they were cautious.

One afternoon she got a call from her mother's cousin, a vice president of the Belvedere bank. He was the one who had arranged for the sale of half ownership of the drugstore after her father died, and helped them keep the house. He asked her to come to his office.

"Mary, good to see you. It's been a long time."

"Hello, Jim. How's Ann?"

"She had that angina, but she's doing fine. You know, I keep thinking of you as a girl, but you're all grown up. A journalist. Your mother's very proud of you."

"She's my number-one fan."

"Mary, I want to talk about the loan to Harry, Now, I know he had some problems, but he's straightened himself out. It isn't easy to do that."

"No, and he's doing a wonderful job."

"He's asked us for a forty-thousand-dollar loan, to buy the Gutwald business. Bert wants to sell."

"It would be a great investment for the bank, Jim. And Harry would run it well."

"Yes, I think so too. But there's Harry's record."

"You mean the drinking?"

"Yes."

"But that's all over. He's been cold stone sober for nine months. He's running the Frederick branch."

"You and I know that it's behind him. But I wasn't able to convince the other officers of the bank. He has an arrest record for drunk and disorderly, and he was fired from a job for drinking. You can understand why the officers are hesitant."

"But the business is worth even more than that potentially. If anything happened the bank wouldn't lose money. The business is just going to go up in value."

"Yes, but we don't have to take the risk. There's a franchise operation with a sound credit rating that wants to buy. The bank isn't in the business of risking capital."

"What about other banks? Out of town."

"They'd run a check. The arrest record would surface."

"What about Harry's father? He's well known in town. Give the loan to him."

"He's over sixty-five and retired. We don't give loans to people that age."

She was quiet, frowning.

"But there is something."

She looked up.

"This is an unusual situation. We, the bank, that is, we like to see local businesses in local hands. We don't want outsiders running things — certain people, if you know what I mean. The franchise that wants to buy is Jewish owned. Not that we have anything against Jews, but you understand."

She looked at him, blankly.

"So I've talked to the officers, informally, of course, and persuaded them to give the loan in your name."

She stared at him in amazement.

"Now that's something we wouldn't usually do. We don't give loans to women unless they have a real good business, hairdressing or something. But we all know you, you're something of a celebrity in town. If the business were in your name as well as Harry's, the officers would agree to a loan."

"Jim —"

"You'd be a steadying influence on him, we know that. He's got a good head on his shoulders. He's going to be a good businessman. You've made a man of him."

"No, it wasn't me. It was Harry, he did it all by himself, it wasn't me at all."

"Every young man is entitled to sow some wild oats, but Harry damn near ruined himself for good. I know how difficult it was for Betty and Ralph. But to have a daughter-in-law like you, that's a blessing. I know you've been separated for a while, but when I talked to your mother a while ago, she told me you were getting back together. Did him good, the separation. Sometimes a young man needs a shock like that to straighten him out."

She had the sensation that the walls were closing in on her, that the air was escaping, and there was none left for her to breathe. She looked around, as if in panic, for a way out.

"The bank would be taking a chance on the two of you. But we know you. People say that banks are cold-blooded, all we think about is money, but that's not true."

New York hovered in the air, tantalizing. Her heart was pounding wildly. She felt as if she were about to faint.

"We'll take a chance when it seems that, in the end, we'll profit by it. We'll take a chance on people we know, like you and Harry."

She felt that she was looking at him through a long tunnel, and everything was very small, like looking through the wrong end of a telescope, but very clear and sharp. There was no chance for Harry if she turned down the loan. No one else would give him money. And if she took the loan, she was tied to him forever. She would live out her life in Belvedere, and she would never know what she might have been someplace else. New York was speeding away from her, growing tiny in the distance. She would never get out of Belvedere, never break free — she had known that all along. She would never do it, never leave; New York was a speck, speeding away.

"We're getting divorced!" She blurted it out, hearing the panic in her own voice.

Her mother's cousin leaned back in his chair. "Oh," he said. "Oh."

"We tried, but we got married too young. We —"

"I see. I talked to your mother, and she seemed to think things were going well."

"She wanted to believe that."

"Well, of course, that changes things."

"Jim, he ought to have the loan. Please, he's worked so hard, he's done so well."

"I'm glad to see there's no hostility between the two of you. That's always best."

"Jim, please, make them reconsider. The business is sound, it's been going for twenty years. You wouldn't lose anything. Harry is so good at this. Please, you can persuade them."

"Well, of course, I'll try."

"If the franchise bought it, could Harry still be the manager?"

"They have a special patented process. Most of their personnel come from the home office. It's possible, of course, that they might make an exception for Harry."

When she walked out of his office, her whole body was shaking. There were other banks, there had to be a place where Harry could get a loan. Had to be.

I'm pregnant, Harry. I'm pregnant.

The words had coiled through her life from the night she said them to this moment. She had shaped his life, bent it to her with a lie. Was he what she had made him?

It's what women are for, Mary, taking care of things.

No, it wasn't fair. She didn't owe him the rest of her life, years that would stretch out ahead of her, long and bleak and barren. It wasn't fair.

She thought about New York, tried to dredge it up from the recesses of her mind, searched for it. Found it, tried to hold on to it. A peculiar thing happened.

It looked just like Belvedere.

"I hate him!" he said. "It's not her, it's him!"

The others all looked at each other, not knowing what to say.

"He dazzled her, you know? She's like me, never been out of Belvedere. He's been around, probably went to some fancy college. Sophisticated. Has money to throw around. Took her to the Washington Hotel. Christ, the Washington! He's going to use her, and then dump her. They're all like that, those guys."

"Kid, it takes two to tango," old Marge said.

"She was crazy about me. I mean, she even — this was a nice girl, you know, a nice girl. But we had to get married, know what I mean. She was crazy about me."

"You were pretty young, Harry," Jim said.

"Yeah, we were. We made mistakes, but we were coming along. If it hadn't been for him, we'd be back together by now. A family. What right does he have to just walk in and take what's mine? What right?"

"Harry," Sherri said, "sometimes things are cracked so bad they can't be mended. Marriages."

He shook his head. "No. If it hadn't been for him, she'd still love me. I know that."

"My husband and I tried getting back together," Sherri told him. "But we'd said too much, done too much, hurt too much."

"He has no right to take my life away. And he can do it, that's what kills me. I said I wasn't going to let her get a divorce, that I'd take my daughter. But how could I get her? I'm a drunk, I don't count. How can I stop him?"

"Harry, you're young. You're smart. You're — very attractive. Let the past go. Find someone who loves you for you. 'Give me the serenity to accept the things I cannot change,' remember?"

If there was a personal appeal in Sherri's words, Harry did not hear it.

"I'm going to stop him. I don't know how, but I will!"

When he drove home to his parents' house, the lights were off and the house was empty; it was their bridge night with the Taggerts. His parents' house. He was twenty-five years old, and he was living with his parents, like a boy.

He walked into his parents' bedroom and opened the bottom drawer of the dresser. It was there, where it had been for years.

He picked up the revolver, hefted it. The clip of ammunition was beside it. He turned it over in his hand. He had fired it often enough, when he and his father used to go out in the woods and take target practice with beer cans they set up on the ground. He took the revolver and the clip and put them in his pocket.

He didn't want to ask himself why he was getting the gun. It was something he felt like doing, that was all. It felt good in his hands, heavy, authoritative. He liked the feel of it.

He went into his own bedroom, took out the revolver and the clip and put them inside a pair of work boots, as far down as he could, towards the toe. Then he got undressed quickly and got into bed. He fell asleep, and for the first time in a very long while, he slept soundly and he did not dream.

He frowned as he read the newspaper account of the ditty that was popular among American soldiers, in Saigon, sung to the tune of "Twinkle, Twinkle, Little Star":

We are winning, this we know.
General Harkins tells us so.
In the delta, things are rough.
In the mountains, mighty tough.
But we're winning, this we know.
General Harkins tells us so.
If you doubt this is true,
McNamara says so too.

He drummed his fingers on the desk, repeatedly. It was a good idea to listen to the grunts, the guys out where the fighting was going on. They knew things their commanders did not want to pass on. He knew. He'd been there. This was not a good sign.

"The fucking generals," he muttered. They always saw victory almost in their hands, even as they were getting their butts kicked. The Bay of Pigs taught him, don't trust the brass. He should have known that, from the Navy. He cursed himself, afterwards, for not following his instincts. Don't trust the brass.

He kept sending people over there. It was known now as the Saigon shuttle, people came and went so fast, and it was like the blind men and the elephant. They all got hold of a different piece of it, and when they came back they described different creatures entirely. He'd sent a general and a Foreign Service senior guy out there, and they'd held a joint briefing. The general said the war was going beautifully, and the Diem regime was beloved by the people. The Foreign Service officer said that South Vietnam was a mess and that the regime was on the verge of collapse. He had shaken his head and asked them, "Were you two gentlemen in the same country?"

His own people were kicking the shit out of each other. Governor Harriman, just off the Saigon shuttle, called one of his generals a fool, to his face. Guerrilla warfare was a tricky business, and its political side was at least as important as what happened on the battlefield. What did you do? Keep up "the long twilight struggle," like the British did in Malaysia, and hope the lights didn't go out? But how much patience would Americans have? And when did you cross over the invisible line that the French had crossed, to their sorrow, in which it became not an Asian conflict but a white man's war? That was the mistake he had to avoid at all costs. When he had come into office, there were 2,000 men in Vietnam. Now there were 16,000. Vietnam could be the key to Southeast Asia, but it could also be a bog from which he would never escape. The French had poured so much money, so many men, so much blood into that bog, and they were beaten. A white man's war couldn't be won. Where was it, that point of no return, the fatal point? MacArthur had found it by bombing the bridges across the Yalu River, bringing the Red Chinese hordes pouring into Korea. No, you couldn't trust the generals to see it. They loved the Charge of the Light Brigade, dashing madly off into disaster.

In the end, it was their war, the Vietnamese, and they had to want to win it. It was a balancing act for him, a delicate one. The main thing was to keep hanging on, but always looking for that line, the one that was so easy to miss. Careful, careful, he had to be careful.

We are winning, this we know.
General Harkins tell us so.

He drummed his fingers on the desk again.

> *Twinkle, twinkle, little star,*
> *We'll get fucked if we go too far,*

he thought. He'd guess the guys in the field would like that one. It was a good line for him to remember. But for now, hang on. Hang on.

Sometimes everything came out all right.

SAM WALKED into the city room, improvising on Tom Lehrer:

> The land of the WASP Babbitt
> Where hating black folks is a habit
> And the goyim are too dumb to make a dime . . .

Jay laughed. "Nothing like a little racial hatred and conflict to put you in a good mood."

"Conflict we got," Sam said. "Where's Charlie?"

"In his office. You think *you're* happy. He's having multiple orgasms. This is a weird business, you know. We really get off on other people's problems."

"Good news is no news. There's quite a crowd out there. I hear NBC is sending a camera crew. The wires are here already."

"Is it true that Charlie sent a telegram to Martin Luther King saying that if he'd come to Belvedere, he'd get four fire hoses, Jules's Labrador in full charge, and thirty-nine pages of coverage?"

"Yeah, but he sent a telegram back. THANKS BUT NO THANKS. PEOPLE IN BIRMINGHAM MUCH NICER."

Mary walked in, shaking her head. "Too many people out there. Not enough cops. This could get out of hand."

"How many do you think are out there?" Jay asked.

"If we had five thousand for the Veteran's Day parade, then there must be ten thousand now. People are here from all over."

"And we've got an hour until the march starts," Sam said.

Charlie came out of his office. "Are you people all set?"

They nodded.

"Sam, you and Mary will be in front of City Hall. Roger and Joe Rosenberg will be walking with the marchers. So will McChesney. Jay, you take City Hall." He looked at Mary. "You've been over at Reverend Johnson's house?"

"Yes."

"How many marchers?"

"About two hundred. A lot from the city, about thirty from the county chapter of SANE, and kids from the community college. There's Reverend Smilie from the Episcopal church, Rabbi Gwertzman and that new young priest from St. Theresa's, Father Heath. I hear Father Carmody is apeshit about his being there."

"If Christ asked Father Carmody to help carry the cross, he'd say he had to do the bingo." Jay snorted.

"What's the mood at City Hall?" Charlie asked Sam.

"Well, Mayor Swarman has locked himself in the can. They are all shitting in their pants. They don't know how to handle this."

"That's what I thought." Charlie sighed. "How about the cops? What happens if things get out of hand?"

"They got the auxiliaries out, but those guys are meatheads. All they've ever done is football games."

"No state troopers?"

"They're supposed to be on call, at least that's what Chief Grimes says. The city cops are pissed at the troopers, since it was the state police who got the line on the kids who set the fire."

"The marchers are the best organized group around," Mary told the editor. "Don says they've got forty of the students and some community people trained as marshals. Some of them have been in the South. And there's some pretty big guys."

"How about the crowd?"

"Right now it's quiet. It's hard to tell who's supporting the march, who's curious and who might make trouble. At least there are police barricades along the route. My worry is that somebody could get trampled, with that crowd out there."

"All right, keep in touch. Rosenberg will have a walkie-talkie. Get to him if you need to contact us fast."

Jay, Sam and Mary walked out of the *Blade* building and headed up Main Street towards City Hall. The building was a squat, three-story structure into which a WPA architect had incorporated a frieze cribbed from the Parthenon. The naked, sword-brandishing warriors had been a scandal when the building was new, but nobody paid them any attention now, except teenage boys who made crude remarks while the girls giggled.

Spectators were lined up eight to ten deep along the street, and the three had to elbow their way through knots of people to get to a clear spot on the sidewalk in front of City Hall. As they were standing and talking, an auxiliary policeman walked up to Jay.

"All photographers have to stay behind the barricades."

"Says who?"

"Mayor's orders."

"I've got a police press pass. I'm staying here."

"It's the mayor's orders."

"This is not Red Square. If he wants me out of here, let him arrest me. Then he can answer to my editor."

The policeman frowned and fingered the buttons on his jacket. "Wait a minute." He disappeared into the building, and in a minute he was back again. "OK, you can stay."

Jay shook his head. "Mayor Swarman could fuck up a free lunch."

Sam looked at the departing policeman. "What do you expect from a part-time druggist, Nelson Rockefeller?"

"The power of the press," Mary said.

"Yeah, power." Jay sighed. "Swarman would piss in his pants if he saw a five-year-old with a crayon."

Mary looked around at the crowd. The noise level was beginning to rise.

"A lot of men here. They must have taken off from work. I don't like that."

"Hey, now, would you look at that," Sam said. "The fucking South shall rise again."

A Confederate flag had sprouted among one knot of onlookers. It was a very small flag held by a pimpled adolescent, and it drooped forlornly against the stick. A woman standing next to him held a placard that announced in hand-lettered script, FIGHTING AMERICAN NATIONALISTS. She was heavyset with flesh stacked in rolls beneath a black jersey and a pair of slacks.

"Who the fuck are the Fighting American Nationalists?" Jay asked.

"Looks like one fat broad and three teenage punks," Sam told him. "With poetic license, I will call them a racist mob."

Mary walked over to the woman. "Excuse me, I'm from the *Blade.* Are you representing a local organization?"

The woman pointed to the sign she was holding. "Sure. We're from FAN."

"Is this a Belvedere group?"

"FAN's a national organization. We got chapters all over the country. We're from the Maryland chapter."

"How many members does the chapter have?"

The woman smiled, coyly. "Lots, but we don't reveal our membership."

I just bet you don't, Mary thought, but she said, "What's the purpose of your organization?"

"To keep the niggers from taking over. We got to stop the niggers. This country was made great by white people."

"Are you one of the officers?"

"Yeah, I'm the vice president."

"What's your name?"

The woman looked suspicious. "Why do you want to know?"

Mary smiled and said, politely, "We want to get the names of the officers of the local organizations that are here today." One thing she had learned, you had to be polite with the nuts. The nuttier they were, the more seriously you had to treat them. Courtesy and rapt attention made them spill their guts. If you got hostile, they'd clam up.

"I'm Sandra Mitchell. With two *L*'s. Will our names be in the paper?"

"Yes."

"Maybe a picture, too?"

"Possibly."

"A picture would be nice."

Mary walked over to Jay. "Make her famous. She needs the publicity."

Jay went over and took her picture, and Sandra Mitchell — two *L*'s — fluffed up her hair and smiled.

Mary scanned the faces of the crowd; one man stared back at her with a fierce glare. It occurred to her that she and the other members of the *Blade* staff could be targets if any trouble started. The newspaper's stand on the plan — and Charlie's call for vigorous prosecution of the kids who had set the fire — had angered more than a few people.

She kept looking into the crowd. Some people were obvious curiosity seekers, including housewives gripping the hands of children and kids from the high school. There was one group of young men in jeans and leather jackets who could spell trouble. With so many people, the problem was that if even a couple of troublemakers started something, it could cause a panic and people would be seriously hurt. At least some of the marshals were trained in crowd control.

In a few minutes, the sound of the approaching march could be heard, although the marchers had not yet turned the corner. The song was familiar, and intermittently melodic:

> We'll walk hand in hand, someday-ay-ay-ay-ay.
> Oh, deep in my heart I do believe,
> We shall overcome, someday.

Joe arrived at a trot in front of City Hall, carrying the walkie-talkie.

"Any trouble?" Mary asked him.

"A lot of yelling, but no real problems."

The front line of the march came around the corner. Walking side by side, arms linked, were Father Heath, looking seventeen, the Reverend Raymond Johnson, Rabbi Gwertzman, cultivating what Sam called his Haganah expression, and Sister Eulah Hill, her white tunic gleaming in the sun like crusader's armor.

Behind them came James Washington, Mrs. Wesley Darden, the president of Committee for Sane Nuclear Policy, Loretta Washington and the young woman who had spoken at the first meeting in the church, and several other clergymen. Don Johnson, wearing a green armband that said MARSHAL on it, was walking outside the line of march, his eyes darting every now and then to the crowd. Mary's eyes followed his, scanning the spectators again. She picked out a few faces: a kid in a motorcycle jacket; a sullen, unshaven man who stood quietly, watching with hooded eyes; a middle-aged man in an Army jacket, watching the march with unusual intensity.

She looked back at the marchers. The front rows of the group had arrived at City Hall, and Don held up his hand for them to stop. The song came to an end, and in the silence a cry went up from a lone voice, "Go back to Africa!"

A murmur of approval ran through the crowd, but no one else took up the cry. Mary looked to see who had yelled, but the voice had come from far back.

Don started to call out instructions to the marchers. "We're going to walk in an oval on the sidewalk, two abreast. Stay three feet apart at all times. If anyone wants to enter or leave the building, let them do it. We are not blocking the entrance."

Two other marshals started helping to ease the large group into the oval, which formed quickly, the marchers going two by two. The training had paid off. The marshals knew what they were about.

"Go home, niggers!"

"Niggers suck!"

The marchers ignored the catcalls, and the crowd did not ignite. The discipline of the marchers had infected the crowd, Mary thought. If it held, they might get away without trouble.

The marchers were moving smoothly now, in an oval in front of the building, and singing again:

> Go tell it on the mountain,
> Over the hills and everywhere;
> Go tell it on the mountain,
> Let my people go.

Don was walking outside the oval, pacing the marchers, keeping the line moving at the right speed and making sure there was a proper distance between them so that the police would not have the excuse that they were blocking the entry. He moved with a fluid grace that suggested quiet pride, competence. She looked again at the man with the hooded eyes, but they were opaque; she could read nothing in them. Mary recognized the kid in the motorcycle jacket, who had been ejected from the meeting. He concealed nothing; his features were distorted with pure hatred. The man in the Army jacket had moved closer to the front row, still staring at the march. But the one who worried Mary was the man with the hooded eyes; she sensed, rather than saw, violence there.

The marchers had come to the end of another song, and they kept walking, their voices trailing off. They had come for a reason. It was time for something to happen. The Reverend Johnson stepped out of line to talk to his nephew. Mary moved closer to hear them.

"Are you ready?" Don asked.

The minister nodded. He motioned, and Rabbi Gwertzman, James Washington, Father Heath and Reverend Smilie stepped out of the line and joined him.

"Is this the delegation?" Mary asked.

"Yes," the minister said.

"You're going to demand to see the mayor?"

"Yes, it's our right to see him."

The four men started up the steps of City Hall together, followed by reporters and the NBC crew.

"Nigger lovers!" came a shout, again, and another murmur ran through the crowd, this one, Mary thought, angrier than the last.

As the men approached the door, a policeman stepped in front of them.

"May we pass please, Officer?" Rabbi Gwertzman said.

"The mayor can't see you."

"This is a public building. Surely you do not intend to keep us out," Father Heath said.

"Wait a minute." The policeman grunted. He went into the

building and reappeared, accompanied by a corpulent, morose man in a wrinkled brown suit.

Sam, standing next to Mary, groaned. "They've sent the asshole."

Dave Fardin, administrative assistant to Mayor Swarman, used his bulk for passive aggression. He was the ideal buffer between the mayor and the citizenry. Pleas, demands, complaints and insults fell against the flesh of Dave Fardin and they were ingested, as if by some carnivorous Jell-O, and never heard from again.

"Mr. Fardin, we must see the mayor," Reverend Johnson said.

"He's in conference."

"We will wait."

"He's going to be in conference all day."

"Who's he in conference with?" Mary asked him.

"I don't know."

"If I quote you on that, you are going to look really dumb, Dave."

"I'll find out," he said.

"Didn't the mayor know these people were coming?" asked the AP reporter.

"The mayor doesn't meet with anybody unless they have an appointment."

"We have been calling his office continually to inform him we were coming," Rabbi Gwertzman said. "We were assured he had received the messages."

Fardin was silent, his most effective technique.

"We are not leaving until we have a personal meeting with the mayor, and get assurances from him about the urban renewal plan," said Reverend Johnson.

Fardin said nothing.

The four members of the delegation turned and walked back down to the sidewalk.

Sam said to Mary, "Oh, that asshole Swarman. Now the shit is going to hit the fan."

The delegation walked up to Don.

"We're not leaving," James said.

"That's right," Don said. "Are your people ready?"

James nodded, his face grim and set hard.

Don held up his hand, and six of the marchers, all students trained in nonviolent protest, walked out and sat down in the street. Six others followed them.

"Christ, the niggers are sitting in the fucking street," came a cry. The students began to sing, drowning out the cries from the crowd.

Just like a rock standing in the water, we shall not be moved.

Another line of marchers went out and sat down. Don said to the four members of the delegation, "You'll be the last, OK?"

Police Chief Grimes walked up to the Reverend Johnson.

"These people are illegally blocking a city street. If they don't get up, we'll have to arrest them."

"I understand," the minister said. "If you tell the mayor to meet with us, our people will get up."

"I can't tell the mayor what to do."

"I strongly urge you to advise him then," said Rabbi Gwertzman. "If this situation gets out of hand, he's going to be blamed."

The crowd was getting noisier. Grimes looked out at it apprehensively. All the marchers were now gathered in front of City Hall, and the crowd jammed all the side streets leading up to it. If there were a disturbance, people would undoubtedly be killed or injured.

"If those people aren't off the streets in five minutes, I will have no choice but to arrest them," Grimes said, and walked away.

There were more shouts from the crowd, vying with the singing of the marchers for dominance. People were pressing closer to get a better view, and some of the city policemen had linked arms at the edge of the sidewalk to keep people from spilling over into the street. The whole area in front of City Hall had become a caldron of sound. Jay, who had been absorbed in photographing the scene, came up to Mary and said, "If the crowd surges, get up to the front door and through it, quick. People could get trampled here."

We shall overcome, someday
Kill the niggers
Back to Africa
Oh, deep in my heart . . .

Suddenly, the wail of a siren split the air, and Mary looked around and saw that the police van was moving down the street. It pulled up in front of the building, near where the students were sitting, and a dozen uniformed officers jumped out. They walked over to one student, and two policemen put their arms under his shoulders. He did not resist but went limp in their grasp. They carried him to the wagon. There were cheers and boos from the crowd. Officers picked up each student in turn, carrying him or her off to the wagon as the din continued. When the students were all in the van, the driver turned it around slowly and drove off in the direction of the police station.

Mary looked at Don. He had been watching all this calmly, showing no emotion. She admired his coolness. Her own hands, she discovered, were shaking. The noise did not abate. The whole scene seemed something out of a madman's fantasy. People in the crowd were screaming, but at least they seemed to be getting their energy out that way. So far, things had not gotten out of control, but they were on edge, she knew. She looked at Don again; if he was worried at all, he did not show it. He was looking around, sizing up the situation. Then he lifted his hand, and another marshal nodded. Fifteen more students went out and sat on the street, arms linked together.

Sam, standing close to Mary, had to yell to make himself heard by the police chief.

"Where are you going to put them all, in the kindergarten gym?"

Grimes shook his head, gave an angry glance at the second-story window in City Hall. Then he headed off towards the front door.

"Swarman better get the fuck out here, or he's going to have a riot on his hands," Sam said.

"Maybe Grimes can talk some sense into him."

In a few minutes the siren sounded again, and the van returned, backed up by another one. The policemen moved in again. They moved to the side of a young white girl who was sitting with her arms linked to a black student. They jerked her arms away, roughly, lifted the girl and half-dragged her to the wagon.

"Oh, you're hurting me!" she yelled, and one of the SANE members screamed out, "Cossack!"

This set the crowd off again, and the noise level intensified. Once again, the wagon was filled with marchers, and the van turned away and drove off. When it had gone, Don raised his hand again, and more people walked out to sit in the street. The howl of the crowd was frenzied. The policemen were being moved, by inches, into the street. Some of the people were angry, some curious, some, now, trying unsuccessfully to get out.

Mary's eye caught Father Heath, standing on the sidewalk, swaying back and forth. Then he walked out, very deliberately, and sat down in the street.

Sam, next to Mary, half-yelled in her ear, "Gwertzman's next. He can't stand being outdone by the Catholics."

The rabbi walked out and sat next to the priest.

"He was a pompous son of a bitch before. Now he'll be impossible. A fucking hero of the civil rights movement."

"Sam, the line. It's giving!" Mary yelled.

One policeman fell to his knees as the line was breached and the wall of people poured into the street. Two young men — one of them the boy in the motorcycle jacket — charged the sitting students. He raised his fist to strike one of the Negroes, but a marshal, the size of a football tackle, stepped in front of him and absorbed the blow. Two policemen grabbed the young man and dragged him off. The policeman who had been standing by City Hall moved quickly across the street to try to force the crowd back. Mary held her breath. She thought the policemen might be simply swept away by the mass of humanity. But the line held this time, and they were able to force the crowd back a few inches. A woman fell and would have been trampled except for another woman and a man who dragged her to her feet. The noise was so intense that Mary could feel her temples throbbing.

Then the door of City Hall opened, and Chief Grimes walked out. He went up to Don, the two spoke briefly and Don nodded to him. The officer turned around and went towards the building again, and Don raised both hands in the air. The singing stopped, and the noises of the crowd quieted somewhat. All eyes were on the slender young black man with his hands in the air.

"The mayor will see us," he shouted.

A cry of triumph went up from the marchers, and another chorus of boos and catcalls and cheers from the crowd.

"And we will tell him that we will be back tomorrow and the next day and the next, until justice is done!"

The people sitting in the streets got up, and the marchers burst into a spontaneous chorus of "We Shall Overcome." There were more cries from the crowd, but Mary sensed that the flash point was past. Many people were already starting to leave, frightened by the realization of how dangerous the situation had become. The police line was holding.

Mary caught Don's eye then, and he flashed her a broad grin and the old Churchill V for victory sign. She grinned back at him and waved, and then, out of the corner of her eye, she saw a movement.

She turned. The man in the Army jacket was beside her, and as the arm flashed out from under the jacket, she saw the gun. She lunged for it but was not fast enough; the explosion rocked through the street. She felt herself pushed aside as four policemen grabbed the gun at once and wrestled the man to the ground.

She looked up and saw Don fall; the grin was still on his face as the impact of the bullet hit him, whirled him around. She never knew, afterwards, how much of the scene she remembered from actually seeing it and how much came from the photograph Jay took, freezing the moment into an image that would run on the front pages of most of the newspapers in the country the next day. He had thought he was shooting Don's victory sign, but it turned out to be something else.

A chorus of screams and cries echoed down the street.

"No, God, please, no!" she cried as she ran over to him. He was lying, face up, on the street. Loretta was kneeling next to him, sobbing, "Donnie, Donnie!" and his uncle was kneeling too, ripping open his shirt and trying to staunch the blood pouring from a gaping hole in his chest.

"Doctor, we need a doctor!" Mary called out, trying to make herself heard above the noise, and a man from the crowd elbowed his way through, knelt down and pressed his hand against Don's chest to cut off the flow of blood from the artery. Some of the students had crouched down behind cars, not sure whether more shots would be fired; others, understanding what had happened, were weeping. Policemen were pushing back a crowd of curious onlookers.

The expression on Don's face was one, still, of puzzlement. He looked around, as if he was trying to sort out what the commotion was all about. He looked right at her, then, and she saw comprehension forming in his eyes.

"Hang on," she said. "Oh, Don, hang on! The ambulance is on its way. You're going to be all right."

He shook his head slightly.

"Not," he said, "not the South."

And then his eyes rolled out of focus, and he died.

He stood, silently, in the gathering of the October day, looking at the simple headstone with only one word, KENNEDY, on it.

His second son had lived barely three days, his tiny body overwhelmed by an infection that its undeveloped lungs could not surmount. He had paced restlessly in the hospital corridor near the spot where his son fought for life in an oxygen chamber. As he paced he noticed, in one of the small cubicles, a child who had been severely burned. He borrowed a slip of paper to write a note of encouragement to the child's mother. As he wrote, he was not the head of state, just a heartsick father. A child's illness makes all parents equals.

Two hours later his son died, and he went upstairs to the room in which he had been sleeping, and he cried, alone.

The family's old friend Cardinal Cushing said the funeral mass. But when it was over, the father lingered, touching the tiny casket as if he could not bear to leave it alone. None of his friends had ever seen him so distraught. The cardinal had to tug at him to get him to leave. "Come on, Jack, let's go. God is good."

After that, he and his wife had clung together, even, sometimes, in public, something they had never been known to do.

But on this October day he stood alone by the grave of his son, murmuring, "He seems so alone here," thinking that his family had known too much of death. Of four children born to him and his wife, only two survived. His sister lay forever still under British soil, and whatever traces of his brother remained were someplace in earth or water. Nothing had been found after his plane exploded in the air. He thought of the poem his wife had memorized for him, early in their marriage, after he had told her it was his favorite:

> *I have a rendezvous with Death*
> *At some disputed barricade . . .*
> *When spring brings back blue days, and fair . . .*

But that was in the days when he was still obsessed with death. Now he had too much to live for to be enchanted by dark romanticism. He had a daughter and a son, still alive, who needed him. There should be no more children, he thought. He could not bear to lose another, and his wife was not robust. Two were alive, and that was enough. His mother had borne nine children, and then announced to her husband that he would come no more to her bed. Their marriage settled into sexless companionship, because she would not violate the church's ban on birth control. He thought such behavior odd and antiquated. He had even told a friend that he thought abortion was sometimes a rational solution to an unwanted pregnancy. The old pieties had no claim on him.

With children — unlike with adults — the detachment that so marked him vanished. He loved the way his daughter nestled into his arms, the sweet smell of her hair as he read to her from a storybook. He loved the way she giggled, on the boat, when he told her about the white whale who ate men's socks. Many a dignitary and aide had lost his socks overboard to the whale. His son, who hated to be still, delighted him when he raced about his office, poking his head into the crannies of his desk. Children touched something in him that adults never could. So long the second son, he had become the father, tending to the crippled old man and seeing his own children starting to grow tall.

He had never really thought much about middle age; he had been young so long. Only lately was he discovering that he rather liked it, now that he was there. There was an age when tousled, feckless youth was no longer becoming, but rather sad and out of place. He was even starting to like his new, mature face.

He had been self-absorbed for a long time, creating himself. He'd had to be, it was how he survived. His children took him out of that. He would watch his children learning and testing the world around them, but he would not, as his father had done, try to control their destinies.

He had worn the colors, fulfilled the dream. He did not regret it — though he wondered, sometimes, how it would have gone with him if he had not.

His children would not have its burden. They were Americans, with nothing to prove, and their lives belonged only to them.

JAY WAS PACKING his trunk when the phone rang. He went into the kitchen and picked up the receiver. It was the UPI bureau chief, congratulating him. His photograph had run in more papers than any other photo that year, except for the picture of Katzenbach and Wallace. A good candidate for the Pulitzer Prize, he said.

Jay thanked him and hung up the phone. The Pulitzer Prize. That was what Charlie had said three nights ago, and he had recoiled at the words, his heart constricting inside him. Oh no, not for *that.*

He hated the picture; he wished he never had to look at it again. It was so much like Capa's famous photo of the Spanish soldier, taken at the point of the bullet's impact, head thrown back, body reeling with the fatal blow, and on Don Johnson's face — shock, surprise, wonder — he did not yet understand what had happened to him.

"Oh, *damn,*" Jay said. He pounded his fist against the cabinet. *"Damn. Damn. Damn. Damn. Damn!"*

Did Capa know the Spanish soldier? Or was he simply an abstraction of death? Don Johnson was no abstraction. Usually when Jay printed a picture after he knew he had captured something dramatic but didn't know quite what, there was a delicious sense of anticipation. But when he had printed the picture of Don, the pain in his gut was so intense he thought he would double up with it. As the image materialized on the paper, it brought back the moment with its terrible certainty. He had known that Don was dead an instant after he pushed the shutter. He had no idea how he knew it, but he did.

It was when he walked upstairs with the print that Charlie had said, "Pulitzer Prize." The words had hit him like a blow. The revulsion must have been plain on his face, because it was the first time he had seen Charlie rattled. Charlie took a step backwards, looked at him and said, "I'm sorry, Jay."

Much later on that terrible day he had held Mary in his arms as she wept. She had written the story dry-eyed, holding her grief in check. He had cried too, unashamedly, the first time since he was a child he had let anyone see him cry. She said, over and over again, "Why? Why? Why did they have to kill him?" and he had no answer for that.

"I saw him. I saw the gun. If I had been just a second faster. A second. Oh, God, why wasn't I faster? A second faster."

"Don't," he said. "Don't do it, Mary."

"He had so much ahead of him. He was so talented, so good. That he could be snuffed out by that piece of scum, by that crazy man."

The man who shot Don was a man who lived alone, who was described by his neighbors as quiet and polite. In his house the police found material from racist groups, hate-filled ravings.

"He had so much ahead of him, Jay. It isn't fair."

"No, it isn't. But who said life was fair?"

"I keep thinking, did we help it happen? Could that sick, twisted man have read something I wrote and it stuck in his craw? Something Don said? Could I be partly to blame?"

"You know the answer to that."

She nodded. "I guess I do. It was his battle, he picked it. He knew the risks. Still —"

"He was doing what he had to do. And so were you. And he won, Mary. The council backed down. He beat them."

"Oh yes, there's going to be a couple hundred units of housing, and maybe they'll name one after him. Maybe they'll even put his name on a plaque. And in ten years, twenty years? People will see his name and wonder who he was. They won't even remember!"

"At least he died for something. How many people get killed every day for no reason? Step off a curb and get hit by a truck, that's all she wrote."

"We killed him, this stupid country of ours. Because we hate so much. We have to get rid of the hate. If we don't, we'll never be a decent country. We have to stop it."

"Well," he said, "that's not so easy."

"He said to me that if the rules were wrong, you had to change them, no matter what the cost. But the cost was too high. Oh, damn it, Jay. If only I had been a second faster, just a second—"

"No, no," he said, and he held her and they both cried until there were no more tears in them.

"We're getting out of here, Mary. Two more weeks and we'll be in New York. I want to get out of here."

"So do I. Oh, so do I," she said.

Jay got a beer out of the refrigerator, and he looked around at the familiar surroundings. It seemed like home, in a strange way, this shabby apartment. It had been his first job — his first real job; the Army didn't count. The paper had given him space, let him take chances and make mistakes, let him grow. He had grown, no question about that. He was a neophyte when he came, good but raw. But now it was time to go. He had probably stayed too long as it was, because it was so comfortable here. And after all those pictures, thousands of them, they would remember him for only one. "Broderick, isn't he the one that took that picture?" He hated the idea that they would remember him for that picture.

He heard a sound in the living room, and he said, "Sam? That you, Sambo?"

There was no answer, so he pulled out the drawer to find a church key to open the can. He made two holes in the top of the can and then turned around. When he did, he saw Harry Springer standing in the kitchen doorway, five feet away. Harry held a revolver, pointed straight at his chest.

He froze. He looked incredulously at Harry, at the gun. Harry's face held an expression he could not read. The blue eyes were glittering. Jay thought, at first, it was from drink, but he realized in an instant that it was not from liquor but from pain. Harry was standing perfectly still, and the hand that held the gun did not tremble.

Jay thought with surprising calm, I'm going to die, but still he could not move.

"You had no right," Harry said, his tone almost conversational. "No right."

Jay stared at him. His mental processes, it seemed, had slowed to a crawl. He thought he had been standing there for hours, with the gun pointed at him. He said the only thing he could think of to say: "I love her."

Something moved in Harry's face, and he raised the gun. Jay instinctively hunched his shoulders and held his hands out in front of him, crying, "No!"

There was an explosion, and Jay closed his eyes, waiting for the pain of the impact. There was a shattering sound two feet from his head. Wood splintered, dishes tumbled; a sharp pain flared near his right ear. He reached up, felt the blood. Then he pulled a splinter from the flesh of his earlobe and looked at it, dumbfounded.

He looked at the door to the kitchen. Harry Springer was gone. There was another explosion, so loud that the house seemed to rock with it. Jay stood still for an instant, not comprehending. Then he ran to the living room. Harry Springer lay crumpled on the floor. Jay walked over and knelt beside him. There was a small red hole in his temple, on the right side. Jay turned him, gently.

Then he saw it. There was a hole the size of a fist in the back of Harry's head. Part of his head had literally been blown away by a tremendous force.

He thought he heard himself give out a choked cry, but he never knew if he really made a sound when he discovered that pieces of Harry's brain were leaking into his hands.

He ran into the bathroom and stuck his hands under the water. Time had slowed down again. He watched as the small pieces of reddish gray tissue clung, then moved, finally circled the bowl and disappeared down the drain. He watched them, transfixed.

I should do something, he thought, but still he could not move. He let the water run over his hands until they turned bright red from the cold.

He heard a door slam, footsteps.

"Jay?" It was Sam's voice. Then silence. "Oh, my God! Jay, where are you?"

Jay walked to the door of the bathroom and leaned against the doorjamb. He looked at Sam, who seemed a long way off. He felt he was moving through deep water, that everything was slow and strange.

"Jay, what happened?"

"It's Harry Springer."

"Harry Springer? Mary's husband?"

Jay nodded.

"Is he dead?"

"Yes."

"You didn't, you didn't —"

"No. He shot himself."

"Did you call the police?"

Jay shook his head. He stood, looking at Harry. The ooze from Harry's head wound was staining the carpet.

Sam walked over to Jay. "Are you all right?"

"Yeah."

"What happened?"

"I was in the kitchen. He came in. He had the gun pointed at me. He said, 'You had no right.'"

"Did he shoot at you? What happened in the kitchen? It's a mess."

"Yes. No, not at me. He only — he was so close, he couldn't have missed."

"But he did."

"Then he went out to the living room. I heard the shot. I came out and found him. There."

"Jay, shouldn't you call the police right away?"

Jay, thought about that. It seemed correct. There must be an answer to Sam's question.

"I was in the bathroom." Jay looked at his hands. "His — his — oh, my God, Sam, pieces of his head fell out in my hands!"

His legs suddenly buckled under him, and he would have fallen if Sam had not grabbed him. He clutched at the side of the door, and Sam steadied him.

"Sit down, Jay. You're shaking all over."

"Mary," he said. "How am I going to tell Mary?"

"Stay there. Don't move. Don't do anything until the police get here."

Sam went to the phone and dialed. Jay sat in silence, looking at the body of Harry Springer. The crimson stain on the frayed brown rug was getting larger.

"The landlord is going to be pissed," Jay said. Then he laughed, and there was a touch of hysteria in his laugh. "The rug, Sam, the fucking rug. I'm worrying about the goddamn rug."

Sam walked over and put his hand on Jay's shoulder. "Take it easy, Jay. Let's wait for the police."

Later, a police lieutenant questioned him.

"You don't think he fired *at* you?"

"No. He must have moved his hand at the last minute. He could have killed me, easy."

"You didn't see him fire the fatal shot?"

"No, I was in the kitchen. I ran out and found him."

"What did you do then?"

"I, uh, I tried to turn him over, to see if he was still alive."

"Then what did you do?"

"I could see he was dead. I saw the hole."

"What did you do next?"

"I went in the bathroom."

"Why?"

"There was some — stuff — from his head. It got all over my hands."

To Sam he said, "That was when you came in?"

"Yes."

"You knew the deceased, Mr. Broderick?"

"Yes."

"Do you have any idea why he might want to kill you? Or himself?"

"Well, he — I know he was turned down for a bank loan."

"What does that have to do with you?"

"Nothing, exactly —"

"Then why would he want to kill you?"

"He —" Jay looked at Sam.

Sam said, "He was the husband of one of the reporters at the paper. But they had been separated for nearly a year."

"I see. Mr. Broderick, was there a relationship between you and the wife of the deceased?"

"She was getting a divorce."

"You were having sexual relations with her."

"We were going to be married. Right after the divorce."

"You were having relations with her?"

"Yes."

"Did you touch the gun?"

"Did I? No, I didn't touch it."

"Was there any kind of altercation between you and Mr. Springer?"

"No. I just saw him standing there with the gun, that's all."

"Did you say anything to him?"

"Yes. I did."

"What did you say?"

"I love her," Jay said, quietly. "I love her."

The ambulance came, and the body was lifted onto a stretcher, covered up and taken away. Jay went into the kitchen to get a drink of water, but he heard one of the medics say to the other, "Same old thing. One guy fucking another guy's wife."

The policeman said to him, "You weren't planning on being out of town in the next few days, were you, Mr. Broderick?"

"No. No, I'll be here."

Jay sat in the armchair, staring at the crimson stain on the rug.

"Come on, Jay, we've got to tell her."

"Sam, what do I say? What do I say?"

"I'll come with you."

"First Don, now this? Sam, how can I tell her this?"
"Come on, Jay."
"He's Karen's father."
"We've got to do it, Jay. It's getting late."
"You're right," he said, getting up slowly and walking towards the door. "You're right, it's getting late."

The goddamned deer, he thought as he combed his hair, patting down an errant wisp that wouldn't stay in place. This time, when Lyndon suggested that they go out and blast Bambi, he was going to say no.

His first visit to the LBJ Ranch had been eight days after the election, and he had been sensitive to Lyndon's eagerness to help, to be important. At first he had demurred when Lyndon suggested a dawn hunt, but Lyndon, who desperately wanted to be a good host, pressed him, and he reluctantly agreed.

Hunting wild animals with a high-powered rifle was not his idea of sport; it was too one-sided. Put a man with a knife alone in the woods with a lion, that might be a challenge. He simply could not understand what kind of a thrill men got from killing animals who could not fight back. It violated his sense of fair play.

He climbed into one of Lyndon's white Cadillacs — not exactly Hemingway, he thought ruefully — and they zipped off to a corner of the ranch where deer were known to feed. He hoped maybe they'd stay away that day, but no such luck. He picked up the rifle, pressed his cheek to the barrel and aimed. At that moment, the deer turned and looked directly at him, its brown eyes wide, large and lovely.

They were all watching him. If he backed down now, Lyndon would have a dandy story to tell, and the vice president was very good at stories. He squeezed the trigger, and the deer staggered and fell to the ground. He walked quickly away.

But the memory of that creature in his sights, staring directly at him, haunted him. He couldn't shake off the image. He had told his wife about it, wondering again at the sport of slaughtering a helpless animal.

That would have been bad enough, but as he looked out his window one day, there was Lyndon, loping along with that cowboy stride of his across the South Lawn, carrying the mounted head with full antlers under his arm. He took a look at the grotesque object, feigned polite interest and blanched when Lyndon suggested it be hung on the wall of the Oval Office. He imagined what his children would think. "Look, kids, Daddy shot the shit out of Bambi, and there he is, up on the wall."

He thanked the vice president and thought the matter closed, but Lyndon kept bringing up the goddamned deer until it became a sore point between them. So finally he had the damn thing hung in the Fish Room, where he wouldn't have to see it often. Lyndon was genuinely pleased.

This time, no hunting, but he told his wife he did want to ride. They had ridden together through the fields of Newport the summer they got engaged, and he had surprised her by galloping his horse at breakneck speeds across the wild, grassy fields. She was a superb horsewoman herself, and she said she thought he would look quite handsome in a Stetson, and that pleased him. An Irish cowboy? That would be a new one.

This trip to Texas was about mending fences. The state's Democrats were splitting apart because of a feud between the governor, John Connally, and Sen. Ralph Yarborough. He had to get the matter patched up, because Texas was a key part of his reelection strategy. To his surprise, Jacqueline volunteered to come with him on the trip. She had long avoided politics, but now she seemed to be moving more into the orbit of his life — which was *politics, much of it. She had been greeted in San Antonio and Houston like a movie star, with people shrieking her name. "Oh, Jack," she said, "campaigning is so easy when you're president. I can go any-*

where with you this year." And she had promised, California in two weeks.

Now, in Fort Worth, he finished dressing quickly and went downstairs, to see that a crowd outside the hotel was waiting for him. He was in a fine mood, even climbed up on a flatbed truck to do a little cheerleading off the cuff for the Democrats. A man in the crowd called out, "Where's Jackie?" and he pointed up to the eighth-floor window of the hotel. "Mrs. Kennedy is organizing herself," he said with a grin. "It takes her a little longer, but, of course, she looks better than we do when she does it."

Climbing down from the truck, he went back to the hotel for a formal breakfast meeting with Fort Worth Democrats, another crowd eager for her to appear. She made her entrance through the kitchen, and as the doors opened, she was greeted by sheer pandemonium: 2,000 Texans cheering lustily, standing on chairs to get a better view. He saw the alarm in her face, and he waved to her, smiling. Her eyes caught his, and she smiled back, and she walked towards him with her hand outstretched. He took her hand, and the crowd kept cheering. He felt a throb of admiration for her. She was not only elegant, she was a trouper. Together, he thought, they were really together now. The Chicago Sun Times *said that morning that Jacqueline Kennedy may have tipped the balance and cemented the state's electoral votes for her husband. He smiled at her again, and she smiled back, a triumphant smile.*

But back in the hotel room, his mood changed as he leafed through the pages of The Dallas Morning News. *There was a full-page ad accusing him of treason — making secret agreements with the U.S. Communist party.*

He read every word, then handed the paper to his wife. He had difficulty comprehending the people on the far right lunatic fringe. What on earth made them so batty? "Can you imagine a paper doing a thing like that?" he asked her. "Oh, you know, we're heading into nut country today."

He walked to the window; the skies were still dreary, and a fine mist filled the air. He turned and walked back to the center of the room. Thinking of the unruly crowd scene the night before, he said, "Last night would have been a hell of a night to assassinate a president. There was the rain, and the night, and we were all getting jostled. Suppose a man had a pistol in his briefcase."

He turned his right hand into a pistol, his thumb the hammer, and he jerked his thumb twice to illustrate the hammer's motion. "Then he could have dropped the gun and the briefcase" — he dropped his hand and whirled around like a gunfighter — "and melted away in the crowd."

His wife shook her head. She understood well the dramatic streak in her husband. It was his way of dealing with the ugly things that had been said in the ad. None of it was real to her. She peered out the window. It was still misting, and the cloud-draped sky was dark. There would be a forty-five minute drive in an open car, and she'd just as soon it kept raining. She looked out the window again. They'd all be looking at her, and she didn't want to be a mess. She didn't want to let down the side, after all.

"Oh," she said, looking out at the sky. "I want the bubbletop."

THEY LOWERED HARRY SPRINGER into the still-warm earth on a fall day that was fair and crisp, under a cloudless blue sky. They all came to bid him farewell — the ones who wouldn't give him a job and the ones who wouldn't give him a loan. They were there.

Jay stood on a hill opposite the cemetery and watched them. *"Dominus vobiscum. Et cum spiritu tuo,"* he said. "God grant you peace, Harry."

What had gone on in Harry's brain that night? he wondered. What impulse had traveled from synapse to synapse that made him move the gun at the last minute? When he said, "I love her," was it then Harry had known that he had really lost it all, that there was nothing left?

Questions. No answers. "May perpetual light shine upon him, and on all the souls of the faithful departed. Amen."

He looked at Karen, a small, bewildered figure clinging to her mother's hand, and his heart ached for her. What would she remember of her father? A laugh, a touch, like some half-forgotten song? Would she sit in a room, years from now, certain that the universe was hollow at the center, that no God existed beyond the stars to hear her prayers, that safety was an illusion and meaning a sham? Could he ever hope to fill the void in her life where her father should have been? At least he could understand. Or would she come to hate him one day, when she learned that her father had died at his house, at his feet?

Questions. No answers.

He wanted to be with Mary, to help her, but she was surrounded by relatives in the days that followed the funeral, and there was, of course, the scandal. The paper played down the fact that Harry Springer had killed himself in the apartment of one of its photographers, but it was easy to read between the lines. People knew. People talked. She came into the paper once, looking tired and drained, the dark circles under her eyes adding ten years to her age. She looked at him as if he were a stranger.

He went to her house late that night, after her mother and Karen were asleep. They talked, quietly, in the living room.

"You're coming with me, Mary. To New York."

She looked at him, uncomprehending.

"Once I said I was going to make things happen," she told him. "Remember that?"

He nodded.

"Well, I was right." She laughed, a bitter, mirthless sound. "I made his life happen. I made his death happen. He died hating me."

"No," he said. "I think he died loving you."

"Maybe that's worse."

"Don't do this to yourself, Mary."

"I can't lie to myself, Jay. I wish to God I could. But I can't. I killed him, as surely as if I had held the gun, pulled the trigger myself."

"That's crazy."

"No, it isn't. There are things I never told you."

She told him, then, about how she had forced Harry to marry her by telling him she was pregnant, about the miscarriage, and about the loan she didn't take that destroyed the last chance he had to raise the money to buy the laundry. He began to understand — a cold hand squeezing inside his chest — the depth of her guilt.

"It's so ironic, isn't it? He wanted to keep me, and he couldn't. I'll never be free of him now. Isn't that funny?"

"No. It's not. There's me, Mary."

She looked at him.

"He's dead. You can't do anything for him. I'm alive. I need you. It's the only way it won't all be a waste, don't you see? Otherwise, what is there? There's nothing."

"I know. Don't you think I know that? But what if every time I look at you, I see him? What will that do to you, Jay? I'm so full of guilt there isn't room for anything else."

Her face seemed to twist, its shape unfamiliar to him. He was no stranger to guilt himself. He awoke nights, sweating, feeling the soft, warm pieces of Harry's brain in his hands.

I don't want to love her.

He wanted to turn and run, to hide from the pain etched on her face. He could go now, and be safe. Nothing could hurt him, until the bullet in the high Himalayas. He could watch life go by, seeing, not feeling. Plenty of men, especially in his business, lived their lives that way, anesthetized. They did it with work or booze or just by always being on the move. He saw it in their eyes, the glaze of escaping. He could do it too. But then, he would always run, in his dreams, through a moonlit landscape, opening doors to look for something wonderful that would never be there. Either way, you paid.

"I wish I was a Catholic, Jay, and I could find someone to confess to, someone who would say, 'I forgive you.' But there's only me. And I can't say it."

All he had to do was turn away. That was all.

He shook his head. "No," he said, "it doesn't work that way. For little things, maybe, but for big things there's nobody else who can do it, you have to do it yourself."

"Can I, Jay? Can I?"

"Yes," he said, thinking, Do as I say, not as I do. "If you had stayed with him, you would have looked at him every day and thought about all you gave up for him. What would that have done? Killed him by inches, maybe."

"I could have stayed. I'm strong. I could have done it."

"Goddamn it, what do you think you're supposed to be? A saint? A martyr? Are you supposed to give up everything *you* want? Who made that rule?"

"It cost so much, what I wanted."

"You didn't do it to him. Life did. Or fate. Or whatever. Like it did to Don. And my father. And yours. Do you think you can control that?"

"No. I can't control that. But actions have consequences. I ignored them. For what I wanted."

"If you took that loan, you'd have had to stay with him. Give up any hope of working anyplace but the *Blade*. You'd have given up your life for his. Nobody owes anybody else a life, no matter what the reason! Not you, not anybody!"

He stepped close to her and pulled her to him, pressing his lips to hers. She was cold against him, unresponsive, very much like, he thought, a corpse. It's gone, it's all gone, he thought.

But then her lips opened, and he could feel her heart beating, and he kissed her desperately, savagely, as if the touch of his lips, his mouth, his tongue could be imprinted on her, could brand her so she could never forget it.

He sensed her starting to pull back, but he held her with all his strength, feeling that someone else was trying to tear her away. He felt himself rising, and he pushed against her and slid his hand under her blouse, under her bra and touched her until she sagged against him, trembling. He thrust against her, not letting her escape, and when she finally pulled away, her breath was coming in gasps. He had the sense, somehow, that he had been wrestling with a dead man for possession of her, and that he had won.

"I can't," she said. "Not here, not now."

"I know. But it's all right. It's all right."

She walked away from him, to the window, and she stared out at the street for a long time. When she came back to him, her face was different. The pain was not gone, but the haunted look in her eyes was no longer there. *She* was back in control now, he could see it. The cold hand began to release its hold on his chest.

"There's something I have to do, Jay. I have to understand it. Figure out what I did. Find the answers. If I don't do this, I'll always be in Belvedere, wherever I go."

He nodded. He thought of that probing intelligence, digging away, relentless, searching for answers. It could slice through piety, guilt, convention. It would not permit her, he thought, to throw her life away for a ghost.

"Take the time you need. All the time. I'll wait."

She nodded.

"I'm going to New York. I'll get a place. Big enough for all of us. For Karen. A big freezer, for Checkers."

"I'll keep him crisp." The merest hint of a smile was on her lips.

"In New York," he said, "when I get real horny, I'll stand in the shower and rub soap on my tie." He smiled. "But you've got to come quick, because I only have three ties."

She laughed then, and he saw a flash of her spirit, her delight at irreverence.

We can still laugh. We have a chance.

She left the next day, to spend a week in Florida with Karen and her mother, at the home of an aunt. On his last night at the paper, Jay went to Jules's for a few beers with Milt and Sam and Roger. He was seized by a sense of loss at leaving them, which he covered with cheerful profanity about what a pisshole Belvedere was. They heartily, beerily agreed.

"To New York," Sam said, lifting his watered beer.

"To *The Washington Post.*"

"Screw the *Post.* They're taking too long. I have this friend at *Newsday* —"

He drove out of town alone, with his trunk and his camera in the backseat. He looked at the bank and City Hall and at Art's Diner as they slid by. They had claimed four years of his life. Not the place he would have chosen, but there it was.

He hummed a line of the song they liked, about New York. She sang it often, off key, complaining that "Mott Street" didn't really rhyme with "what street." Would she come to him? And if she did, what kind of a chance would they have? Would he feel the slush of Harry's brain in his hands for the rest of his life? He wondered if his life was at last taking the curve he had expected, back around into darkness, the one that paralleled his father's course.

He shook his head. No more of that. "No more," he said aloud, and he let his father go. He saw his father turn and walk back into the shadows, where he did not have to follow. He had been wrong about himself. He could love, and he wasn't running away. Not anymore.

He thought of her, kneeling, her head resting on his thighs, his hands caressing her, his lips against her hair. In the end, maybe passion would be stronger than guilt, stronger than the past, stronger than anything. Time and love could heal her, as they had him. But forgiving yourself was the hardest thing of all.

He tried to say it, and, at last, he could.

Ego te absolvo.

He drove out of town and onto the broad highway that would take him north.

The sun poured down on the limousine, baking the occupants, including the governor of Texas and his wife, and, sitting beside him, his own wife. He should have told her to wear something lighter than the pink wool suit, he thought. The scudding clouds that had covered the sun earlier that morning had all been blown away.

They were heading from the airport towards the center of town, moving now at a good clip. He looked idly at the signs as they passed. One of them announced REAL SIPPIN' WHISKY, *and he grinned and thought to himself, Toto, we're not in Kansas anymore.*

Soon the crowds began to thicken; the motorcade slowed down, and the waves and cheers washed over them. They passed a Coca-Cola bottling plant, where a thermometer showed that the temperature was well into the nineties. His wife had put on her large dark glasses, because she had been squinting in the sun, and he leaned over to ask her to take them off. "They want to see you. Those glasses hide your face." She smiled and removed them, blinking in the fierce sunlight.

At the intersection of Lemmon Avenue and Lomo Alto Drive in the city, a group of small children stood, holding a sign that pleaded, MR. PRESIDENT, PLEASE STOP AND SHAKE OUR HANDS.

"Let's stop here, Bill," he called out to his driver, and he jumped out of the car and was instantly surrounded by the group of

squealing children. He smiled; children always made him smile. He tousled the light brown hair of a child about his son's age, and he solemnly shook hands with the other children. The Secret Service finally had to shoo the kids away so the motorcade could proceed.

He hopped back into the car, and they were off again. The closer they got to the center of the city, the denser the crowds became, and every time his wife lifted her white-gloved hand to wave, cries of "Jackie! Jackie!" rang out. At one point, the crowd was so close to the car that Secret Service Agent Clint Hill leapt out of the following car and trotted beside the limousine, to protect her from overeager people who wanted to reach out and touch her.

The president grinned and looked out at the crowds. He was starting to sweat from the intense heat, but the exuberance of the greeting lifted his mood. The ad in the Dallas paper was forgotten. Only a Goldwater sign held by two young men reminded him that not everybody in the throng was a political supporter. Running against Goldwater would be fun, he thought. Barry was a decent sort, even if some of his ideas were screwy. He'd love to debate Goldwater. There would be a real clash of ideas, and cultures, between them. It would be the Arizona Republican, the darling of the right wing, versus his own liberal-centrist, rational ideas. The right wing ran mainly on emotion. This Texas welcome, with people standing eight to ten deep, screaming and waving, was a good sign.

He glanced at his wife. There were tiny beads of sweat on her upper lip, and now and then she had to close her eyes because of the sun's hot glare, but she kept smiling and waving, and the crowd went wild. She was going to be dynamite in the coming campaign; he made a mental note to tell her so.

The motorcade made several sharp turns, a zig and then a zag, before it hit the straightaway again. The Trade Mart, where he was to make a speech to the pillars of the Dallas establishment —Democrats and John Birchers alike — was only minutes away, and the motorcade was only five minutes late, a good performance. He looked up ahead and saw a patch of green amid the urban landscape around them: Dealey Plaza.

Just ahead, standing near a large pine tree that grew on a grassy knoll next to the road, a Dallas businessman named Abraham Zapruder was fastening a Zoomar lens on his movie camera. He had forgotten to bring it to work with him that morning, but his secretary had cajoled him until he went home and got it. How many times, she reminded him, did you get to take home movies of a president?

Not far from him stood a young Texan who had brought his wife out to see the president pass by. He looked up to a window in the Texas Book Depository and said to her, "Do you want to see a Secret Service agent?"

"Where?" she asked him.

He pointed up to the window, where a man was clearly visible, holding a high-powered rifle with a telescopic sight.

"In that building there." She looked up to see the man standing unnaturally still, the rifle held close across his chest, a military stance.

Inside the limousine, the wife of the governor of Texas twisted around in the jump seat in which she was riding and said, "You sure can't say Dallas doesn't love you, Mr. President." He smiled at her and answered, "No, you can't."

He looked away from her and out again at the road. Not far ahead, through an underpass, was the Trade Mart. He began running his speech through in his mind, as was his custom. As he glanced to his left, something peculiar happened. The shadow was back, he saw it there, in his peripheral vision. That was very odd. He had lived so long without it.

But on the grass, standing beside his tall, young father, was a small boy, one who had to be about the age of his own son, John. The boy had lifted his hand tentatively, to wave at him. He smiled, caught the boy's eye and waved back. The boy gave a little squeal of delight and waved harder.

There was a sudden, sharp sound. The Secret Service agents in the car behind thought a firecracker had gone off. They rarely heard small arms fire out-of-doors. The Texans who were hunters knew at once it was the sound of a rifle.

There was a strange tingling sensation in his throat. He lifted his hand to the spot where he felt the sensation and looked straight ahead. The shadow was no longer on the fringes of his vision. He was staring, now, directly at it, into its cold, blank eyes.

No, he thought. Oh, no, not now. Not now!

And then he heard, and saw, nothing more.

EPILOGUE

"COULD YOU STOP here for a few minutes?" she said to the cabdriver.

"Sure," he answered. "A lot of people want to come here."

She stepped out of the cab and took her daughter's hand, and they walked slowly up the hill; the heels of her shoes sank into the newly warm earth as they walked. The leaves on the trees were the light, fresh green of early spring.

She paused and turned her head to look out at the city across the river. It was twilight, and the just-vanished sun was leaving a blue-pink haze, the shade of a lilac, hanging low across the tops of the buildings. It was a special time, she thought, mystical. The marble of the buildings still held the pink of the vanishing sun, and they were easy to identify, nestled, now, in their new wrapping of green: the Lincoln, across the river, where Martin Luther King had given his great speech; the Jefferson, with the new buds already starting to appear on the cherry trees around the Tidal Basin; the Capitol, its lighted dome signaling that Congress was still in session. No matter where she went — and she thought she would travel far in her lifetime — there could be no more beautiful spot on the planet than Washington in the spring, at twilight.

She turned back, and she and her daughter walked to the edge of a white picket fence, hardly more than knee-high, in a spot on the hill below the mansion that had once belonged to Robert E. Lee and was now a part of Arlington National Cemetery. There was no one else there at the moment, but the people who had been there before them that day had left their traces: two flags, sunk into the soft earth, and a small bouquet of spring flowers. She stood silently for a moment.

"What's the big match for, Mommy?" her daughter asked. She smiled. The little girl had a way of putting things that never failed to delight and astonish her.

"It's the eternal flame. It never goes out. It's for President Kennedy."

"Is he in heaven too?"

"Yes, I think he is."

She remembered the day she had first seen him, in the flesh, standing on the steps of the Rose Garden, in the shaft of light that made him seem so extraordinary. She had a recurring fantasy — one that first came to her on that terrible, endless weekend. She wished she could go back in time, to that afternoon, to stand once again with the heels of her pink suede shoes sinking into the earth. When he turned to look at her, she would say to him, quietly, "Mr. President, please don't go to Dallas in November. Whatever you do, don't go to Dallas." Or sitting in his office, waiting for the photographer, she would blurt it out. "Don't go to Dallas. Don't go." If only she could go back in time.

Five months ago she had stood on the White House driveway with the other reporters, as a press aide handed out small, round badges that said, TRIP OF THE PRESIDENT, on them. She had so wanted to go on one of the presidential trips — was scheduled to go on one, in fact. But not this one.

She had watched as an army of world dignitaries walked down the curving drive of the White House; never again in her lifetime, she thought, would so much rank and power be assembled together in one place; Haile Selassie, the emperor of Ethiopia, small and wizened in his khaki military uniform, walked next to the tall, gaunt, imperial Charles de Gaulle. It was a remarkable sight.

The air on that day was crisp and cold, and the notes of the funeral march rang out, sending shivers right through her body. It seemed she felt rather than heard them. In her mind she could still hear the clack of the hooves of the riderless black horse, the boots inverted in the stirrups to symbolize a fallen leader, as the horse moved down the avenue. Every sight, every sound, burned with a terrible intensity, that day.

"He made us think we could do anything," she said to her daughter. The little girl looked up at her. "Can we do anything?"

She shook her head. "I don't think so. But we have to try."

She stared into the flickering light of the flame. They would move on, they would grow older, the people who were young with him. He never would. He would walk through their minds' eyes ever young, ever laughing, always standing, the cold wind whipping his reddish brown hair and the air frosting his breath, telling them to ask not what their country could do for them, but what they could do for their country. There would be other presidents, older, wiser, who would do more than he did. Lyndon Johnson was already steering his legislative program, including the most far-reaching civil rights bill ever signed into law, easily through the shoals of Congress. But no other president would belong to them the way he did. He touched something in the young in a way few other public men ever did. No matter what happened, that would not change. The men who wrote the lyrics were right, it would always be one brief, shining moment for them; always, in their memories, burnished and gleaming as the years rolled on. No matter what the historians wrote, no matter what other, colder eyes saw about him, he was part of them when they were young, and that would never change. The way they lived their lives would be different because of him. In her own work, she thought, there would always be the belief, We can change things. We can do anything.

She looked at her daughter. Would there be someone like him for her generation? Or would there be only more gray men, who never touched them at all?

She had a sudden urge to leave something there; she didn't know why. She had brought nothing along. But she reached up for the red silk scarf that was around her neck, and she took it off and tied it around one of the white pickets. It seemed right, a bright spot against the earth.

"Good-bye," she said, and she took her daughter's hand again, and they went down the hill to where the cab waited. She looked back and could still see the scarf, fluttering lightly in the evening wind.

They got into the taxi, and the driver, a young black man, said, "It's a good place for him to be, isn't it? I mean," he added, "if he has to be dead."

She nodded. "Yes, it's a good place."

"Now it's the airport, right?"

She leaned back in the seat and put her arm around her daughter. The little girl snuggled close to her.

"Yes," she said. "To the airport."